Secrets of the Dead

Book One in the Lost Kingdom Saga

Laura Carter

Secrets of the Dead – 1st Edition

The characters and events portrayed in this book are fictious and a creation of the author. Any similarity to real persons, living or dead, or other works, is coincidental and not intended by the author.

ISBN:

978-1-7394045-0-5 (ingram edition paperback)

978-1-7394045-3-6 (amazon edition paperback)

978-1-7394045-1-2 (ebook)

978-1-7394045-2-9 (ingram edition hardcover)

978-1-7394045-4-3 (amazon edition hardcover

Edited by Eden Northover

Cover Design by Aly Scasares, owner of Sincerely Theirs Ltd

Hardcover illustration by Jesamy

Hardcover Design by Laura Carter

Map by Cartographybird Maps

Chapter Heading Emblems by Aly Scasares, owner of Sincerely Theirs Ltd

Formatting by Laura Carter via Atticus

Additional Information

Trigger Warnings:

Your mental health and experience whilst reading this book matters to me. This book contains death of parents and siblings, explicit sexual content, references to SA and cheating. If these are topics you find difficult to read, please approach with caution and at your own discretion. If you read Secret of the Dead and feel there are other trigger warnings missing, please notify me via my social channels so I can amend this page.

Due to the presence of two sexually explicit scenes, this book is classified as 18+ on websites. However, the scenes are consensual and do not depict toxic relationships. I do therefore deem it to be appropriate for 17+ or 16+ with parental permission.

Glossary and Pronunciation Guide :

If you wish to check the pronunciation of character and place names as you read them, you can find a pronunciation glossary at the end of the book.

Playlist:

I do some of my best writing after listening to music and as a result have created a very large overall series playlist. I have taken the songs relevent to certain chapters and placed them in a Secrets of the Dead Playlist. You can find the playlist linked in my socials or by searching 'Secrets of the Dead' on spotify and clicking 'playlists'. At the rear of the book, you will also find a guide for which songs relate to which chapters in the book. I recommend only listening after you have finished the book or finished the relevent chapter, otherwise the lyrics of some songs may act as a spoiler.

For anyone else that also uses writing or reading as an escape from the struggles of real life.

UNSANCTIONED ISLE
THE KINGDOM OF
NOVISIA
ELVERA
AZURIA
THE FROZEN FOREST
TISOVA
ZIVOI MOUNTAINS
MARNOVO
VOJTA
VALA
THE VELLIUS SEA
THE NEUTRAL CITY
AMORO
NERIDA
THE BAY
MERA
TROSSO
TO NOVISIAN SEA BORDER

NOTABLE SETTLEMENTS
CAPITAL CITIES
CITY STATES
MYARA
ABIS FORGE
KERES
TABHERI
THE ASHUN DESERT
NEFERE VALLEY
KHAMI
HYBROOKE FOREST
SELEY
STEDON
HYSTONE FOREST
ANTOR
DOLTAS ISLAND
GARRIDON
ALBYN
ASDALE

Contents

Prologue

The smoke rose thick and fast in the distance. Spiralling plumes gathered, a swirl of charcoal tendrils choking the bright, early afternoon sky. A blanket of darkness trailed in its wake, and all eyes that turned to it would wonder the cause, speculating what disruption had permeated the peace of the Neutral City while unaware of the chaos soon to ensue.

Those close enough would have felt the explosion and heard the rising panic as inhabitants of the city scattered. Others would have suffered, buried under the flying rubble of crumbling buildings, while those too close burned within the flames of destruction, their screams forever ingrained in the minds of their loved ones.

Word would soon spread across the realms as destruction unraveled in the city, but at least one person was prepared. They had waited their entire lives for this moment. A figure emerged from the dense and towering tree line, pulling their hood closer to their face to brace against the wind. Waves crashed against the towering island upon which they stood, yet the figure instead imagined it was the sound of the Temple collapsing on the mainland in the distance.

They closed their eyes, wishing they could smell the smoke and feel the burn. Forcing their eyes back open, they watched with excitement, and desperately wished they were there to reclaim what was rightfully theirs. *Patience*, they had been told over the years. They would need to wait until the prophecy began its course, then vengeance was theirs. A slow, dark smile curled on their face, and their golden blonde hair whipped around them in the wind.

They cracked their neck and rolled their shoulders. "And so it begins," they whispered before retreating to the tree line, ready to alert the others.

It was time for the next steps of the plan.

Chapter One

Nyzaia

Nyzaia turned the parchment in her fingers, its delicacy against her calloused skin a different sensation from what she was used to. When it had been delivered to her rooms, she sighed and wagered a bet as to who it was from. She broke the blank seal. The lavish script and exaggerated capital letters, scrawled in blood-red ink, had her rolling her eyes: a clear sign of the sender. Extravagant, even in written word. She was not surprised.

She folded the parchment and continued to flip it through her fingers, like she would a card during the many evening game nights back at the den. Perched atop one of the more expensive homes in Tabheri, she gazed over the city rooftops, overlooking the capital of Keres. The sun was beginning to set beyond the canyons and the bordering mountains of Vala, a soft glow melding into the city's eternal shade of burnt orange.

As a child, she had wondered how different the Kingdom of Novisia must look to a bird, soaring across the forests of Garridon, the waters of Nerida, the snows of Vala, and the deserts of Keres. Four realms and four ecosystems, maintained by the power of the royal families. It was one of those royal families Nyzaia now heard arriving in the hallways below. She flipped the parchment one more time as a light flame sparked from her fingertips and set it alight: a parlor trick compared to what she usually used her Keres-born fire for. The ash filtered through her fingers, carried away on the breeze beginning to cool the stifling heat of the city.

She readjusted the black fabric to hide her face, exposing her watchful amber eyes. She had spent the last four hours on the rooftop, watching and analyzing the location of the stately home provided in the note. Six guards on rotation, five servants who would now be preparing dinner in the eastern wing, and no children. The western branch had been a good choice and housed the private quarters of the merchant who owned the property, thus allowing for quiet during most of the day.

The target had surprised her. Nyzaia knew everything about everyone of note in the city, and the right-hand man of King Razik and Queen Nesrin seemed an unusual target. Kalon Hakim. The type of man she hated: lavish in all elements of life, and infatuated with money, extortion, and abuse. On too many occasions, she had witnessed her Courtesans return from his home with a black eye or split lip, yet what she hated most was he knew everything she did—every mission and every secret—leading Nyzaia to believe he had someone nearby scouting and always watching. Perhaps the merchant did it all for the King to inflate his own sense of purpose, yet that was a useless feat. After all, any secret of worth was delivered by Nyzaia to the return address on the parchment she had burned. Being in the Red Stone Assassins was one thing; being the on-call assassin for the King was another. It was a good thing they trained her to enjoy killing, regardless of who made the request.

Kalon Hakim was a mystery, a man who had appeared, unannounced, in Keres one day and began making a name for himself. Nyzaia suspected he was an escapee from Doltas Island, which didn't sit right with her. When the ancestors of Keres and the other realms fled Ithyion and founded the new land, the Kingdom of Novisia, they insisted on taking high-profile prisoners with them—people with whom they shared personal vendettas. The people were all abandoned on Doltas Island, a towering cliffside island off the coast of Garridon. Yet over the years, the rulers changed, and their vengeance dwindled, so the people on Doltas Island were left to fend for themselves. A few 'prisoners' had made their way to Keres to trade with the Red Stones, who promised to keep the secret that Doltas Island was now a surviving and thriving community. While no one knew whether Kalon hailed from the island for certain, Nyzaia suspected he did. She suspected many other secrets were kept on that island, too, but who was she to judge? Her life was far from honest.

She stretched her fingers and curled her toes, moving to the edge of the building as Kalon came into view from the corridor below. Beside him walked the King and Queen of Keres. Nyzaia schooled the fury rising within her. It was foolish for the man who requested the murder to be present for the attack. They shouldn't be there: one, because she didn't want them interfering, and two, because she had no desire to speak with them in any form but letters.

The three continued walking and faced away from Nyzaia as they paused at the fountain in the centre of the white-tiled home. The King and Queen turned to Kalon, smiling, and laughing as they jested together. The countdown began. The King's finger tapped a frustrated rhythm against his thigh, and Nyzaia glimpsed the slight change of emotion in his eyes as he tried not to glance up at her position: a vision of black against the white archways. He was impatient, clearly wondering why Nyzaia waited, prolonging the attack. The answer entered the courtyard and she lowered, crouching behind the bricks lining the rooftops. The guard on patrol bowed to the King and Queen before continuing through the courtyard and back into the building.

Nyzaia smiled, having proven her expertise. She continued counting, waiting until the merchant's guard was a safe enough distance inside that, should he turn back, she had enough time.

Rising from her position, Nyzaia placed her black gloves back on and steadied her breathing. Then she leaped. Air rushed past, but she did not feel it, shielded by the black leather molded to her body. Before the merchant could contemplate the shift in the surrounding air, she landed silently behind him, avoiding the gaze of the King and Queen who faced them both. Nyzaia did not wish to read their emotions when she killed the man before them, nor did she wish to see Kalon's pain as she pulled the dagger from her thigh and slit his throat. The King flinched as blood sprayed, painting the white tiles red and bleeding into the crimson of his sherwani. Disgusted, the Queen peered at her saree, small droplets dotting her exposed right arm. She moved to wipe it clean.

"Do not," Nyzaia ordered. The Queen listened, surprisingly, and dropped the fabric from her henna-painted hands while Nyzaia resumed her work, rolling the man onto his back. Raiding his pockets, she withdrew coins and jewels from each of his fingers, placing them in the pouch attached to her waist. She pulled at his clothes to feign a disheveled look and glanced at her surroundings. Nyzaia headed for the servant's door leading into the street and kicked it open, before returning to the fountain and the dead body beside it.

Deeming it safe, Nyzaia straightened and removed the black covering from her face, the long dark braid falling to her back: a matching shade to the woman before her. She stared into the King's amber eyes, a reflection of her own. He looked at her, assessing.

"Nyzaia," he said, his tone uninterested. Some things never changed.

"Father," she responded in the same tone.

Neither spoke, a silent waiting game to see who broke first. Nyzaia steadied her foot to avoid tapping the ground, an impatient gesture inherited from the King. She counted in her head. There was not much time.

"Where are your guards?" she asked, breaking first. He smirked. A win for him in their silent competition.

"I told them Kalon, and I had important business to discuss regarding a potential leak within the guards, which frightened them enough to not ask questions and leave us be." He picked at imaginary dirt beneath his nails. "Though it appears his own guards didn't get the message."

"Leave the blood, mother," Nyzaia said, turning to the silent

Queen. "It must not look like you had time to think about cleaning yourself."

"So smart to consider such things," the Queen said gently, yet her words seemed forced as she clasped her brown-inked hands. Nyzaia tilted her head.

"It's almost as if someone had me trained from a young age," she said, staring pointedly at her father. Grey peppered his dark hair, his skin leathery and textured; she took note of the blemish fading on his neck and scoffed. Not her mother's style. He flashed a bitter smile, one reserved for reminding her he made her who she was today. But aside from commanding it all those years ago, he had no hand in who she became. He merely set things in motion.

"Why Kalon?" Nyzaia's curiosity overcame the need to feign disinterest.

"He was becoming too powerful—he knew too much. If anything were to happen to me, it would be easier for him to overthrow your mother." The King peered down at the body with an unplaceable emotion. His straight answer surprised her. She nodded. A fair reason. "He was insistent on coming to the meeting with all the royals tomorrow. It was suspicious."

Nyzaia made a note of the information. The palace would be emptier tomorrow, with fewer guards in the city. The Red Stones would be informed.

"A pleasure, as always," Nyzaia grimaced, then headed to scale the building. She had no desire to stay and converse; her parents were dead to her the moment they handed her to the Red Stones. Stealing a glance behind her, the King appeared about to speak but closed his mouth.

"Remember to scream, mother." And with those last words, Nyzaia climbed the wall and returned to the rooftops. As she began running, a shrill scream split the silence and signaled the guards to the attack. The Queen would act flustered while her father faked concern; he would point to the open door and say, "A cloaked man ran out that way!" A robbery that has escalated the moment the thief spotted the King and Queen.

The gold clinked in Nyzaia's pockets as she leaped across rooftops, trying to shake the feeling that consumed her whenever she saw her parents. She failed to remember the last time she spoke with them, yet one would assume training to be the Princess of Keres would make her apt in conversing with those she had no interest in. Yet Nyzaia was not fooling herself; she said little because she possessed little interest in her parents or royal life unless to gain valuable information, and despite growing up faster than desired, she loved being a part of the Kingdom's Underworld. Nyzaia forced the thoughts of her parents aside, focusing instead on what to purchase with the coins jingling at her side.

As she reached the market quarter, a young woman dragged herself into the alley below. One of the Courtesans. Isha. Her short hair was disheveled and blood-streaked, matching the blood spattered across her face. She writhed.

Before Nyzaia could intervene, two other Courtesans emerged from a doorway leading into the most expensive brothel in the city: one reserved for Lords—and Kings. She had been informed of her father's attendance on two occasions in the last year. A blond, pale woman—a rarity in Keres—wrapped a cloak around Isha, engulfing her slight frame and covering the blood coating her arms. Nyzaia smiled as the woman steered Isha away.

Those in the Red Stones looked after their own: a family she was proud of.

Chapter Two

Larelle

Larelle took a deep breath, inviting the salty sea air into her lungs. She did this every morning: stealing a small moment to herself by the shore. Smiling, she swept her hand across the beach floor. Specks trickled through her thin fingers as she rose and shook her skirts, sand spilling from the dress as she approached the waters. Her soul calmed at the ocean rushing over her feet in welcome, sea spray settling on her curls.

Larelle sent a silent prayer to the Goddess to settle the pain in her heart. Another part of her morning routine.

A soft glow blanketed the horizon of the oceans bordering Nerida: the realm where Larelle was born and raised. The calm would soon be disrupted the further she journeyed into The Bay. Larelle turned from the ocean—she liked this part the least—and strode towards the stone path outside her small home. She fastened the sandals to her feet and waved at the man standing in the window as she rose. He returned the gesture and offered a smile of encouragement.

The walk from her home to The Bay was short, and soon the padding of Larelle's footfall was drowned out by the sound of bustling sailors, carrying imports from the other three realms and fresh fish from that morning. Their presence was a welcome distraction from the struggles warring in her mind, the visit she had to make that day being one of them. Another made itself known as her stomach rumbled, her mouth salivating at the scents wafting in from the market stalls.

Fish stews began to boil and froth while loaves entered the stone ovens. Larelle yearned for a full warm meal—one she did not feel guilty about finishing. Continuing down the stretch, the more lavish restaurants opposite the stalls opened, positioning tables in the street. She weaved amongst the workers and sailors, who dropped crates at stalls and rushed to prepare for the busy day ahead.

The Bay was the most popular location in Nerida, home to both the finest restaurants and taverns in the realm as well as affordable market stalls. The melding of the rich and poor always struck Larelle as odd, especially since she felt she belonged to neither.

She made a beeline for the smallest stall at the end of the market, the location of the best bread in all of Nerida. A white covering draped across it, protecting the loaves from potential rain.

"Larelle, my dear," a warm voice boomed, a familiar comfort. The man swept her up into his arms, and she inhaled the smell of fresh bread on his apron.

"Hello, Orlo," She smiled at the bear-sized man, noting the dusting of flour tinging his mustache grey.

Larelle preferred to avoid small talk. Orlo knew why she was there and why all the other frail women were, too, at this time of day. Before she awkwardly made the request, he began pulling chunks of bread from a loaf behind him and placed three small pieces in a brown paper bag. The bag looked minuscule in his hands, yet a welcome amount in her own as he passed it with a smile.

"One olive and sundried tomato focaccia, one wholemeal, and one sourdough."

She pulled two small coins from her pocket, but Orlo's rough hands stopped her.

"Please, make sure you eat these yourself." He pulled his hand away, leaving a thin dusting of white flour behind—a sharp contrast with her complexion. "And no giving it to others!" he scolded. "No matter how much she begs for the focaccia!"

"I promise," Larelle laughed, eager to feast on the palm-sized pieces as soon as she could.

"If you're around this evening, come back after sundown." Orlo turned to the stone oven and pulled an extravagantly sized loaf out on a paddle. "The leftovers will be fresher, and there are always more on weekdays." Larelle nodded and turned for the next stall; she felt too embarrassed to talk with Orlo for long.

The bright stand opposite caught her attention next, but someone beat her to it. A slight young woman with straw-like blond hair extended two small bowls to the owner while a young boy tugged eagerly at her skirts.

"You're lucky, Lillian." The owner huffed. "That's the last of the leftover spiced stew."

The little boy clapped, and his mother's relief was evident; visibly relaxing, sleeves slid from her boney shoulders as she smiled down at the boy with flushed cheeks. Larelle suspected they had run to the market to avoid missing the leftovers and smiled too, despite the growing ache as she realized only three bites of bread remained for the day. She hoped there was pasta when she returned later.

The woman was one of many in Nerida who relied on the generosity of stall owners offering leftovers to the poor rather than tossing them to the gulls like the wealthy.

Poor, she thought. The word did not faze her much now. Six years had passed, and her near-malnourished body was used to going without food.

Larelle hurried to the water's edge to head back towards the boats, avoiding the eyes of the sailors. As she pulled the first chunk of bread from the bag, she pondered whether to succumb to her hunger by immediately devouring the bread or savour the bites in case this was the last time she ate that day. It was the same debate as always, and while she wanted to trust Orlo, sales were unpredictable. All it took was one wealthy family to host a dinner party and buy up so much stock there would be no leftovers. She decided to devour the wholemeal and sourdough but savour the focaccia.

She groaned, swallowing the bread, dried from sitting out since the night prior. Usually, Larelle aimed to attend the markets at sundown but had spotted an advertisement for a private cleaning servant posted on the wall near the Fish and Dock Tavern. Yesterday, she trekked up the cliffside town and through the affluent streets merely to knock on the door and be told to return the next day. That was precisely where she was heading once she finished her bread.

"Ahh!" Larelle gasped as a shoulder barged into her, dropping the bread on the floor. She scrambled to pick it up and inspected it for dirt, but no apology followed from the perpetrator, and as she turned to address the person, a wall of tall men greeted her, each dressed in the deep blue of the Neridian sea. Silver swords were strapped to the side of each soldier, waves engraved on their pommels, with a single sapphire sitting proudly within. Soldiers, but not just any.

"Make way for the prince!" One soldier yelled. Larelle stepped to the side and peered around him as a man in his late twenties came into view, framed by dark curls and a tall stature. The waves began to heighten from behind, crashing against the walls bordering the market stalls. His hand movements controlled the water while his eyes shimmered a dark blue. Larelle breathed a sigh of relief. The King and Queen were nowhere to be seen. However, Larelle's relief was short-lived as the prince's head turned and caught her eye. The deep blue of his gaze faded back to grey, mirroring her own. She gulped. In the last six years, Larelle had encountered her brother a handful of times, and each time, it was a guessing game as to whether he would acknowledge her or not.

The stall owners glared at the unwelcome intrusion as countless soldiers escorted him through the market.

Why is he here? Larelle wondered. Her brother rarely wished to be seen anywhere near the poorer population. She retreated, avoiding his stare and the unwanted reminder that came with his presence, that she was once a royal Princess of Nerida.

"Vaughn!" The prince called, his hands swaying as the waves crashed higher.

"Yes, Prince Aalto?" said an older man, approaching his side.

"I've changed my mind. There is no need to visit the captain today." Her brother locked his eyes to Larelle's once more, though no one seemed to notice. "We head to the Neutral City at once."

"Yes, Sire," The man bowed his head. "Will you be collecting your son's request of bread for the journey?" Larelle's heart warmed at the ask; it seemed she had something in common with her nephew, despite never having met him.

"Absolutely not," he answered. "I can't bear to be around this *filth* any longer." Larelle stared unflinchingly back at him, offering no acknowledgement his response was aimed at her.

It must be the bi-annual meeting, she thought, though it was unusual for his wife, Meera, and their son, Nile, to be journeying with him. She dismissed the thought, thankful she had only crossed paths with her brother. She had not seen her father since he banished her and never wished to see him again.

Larelle stepped back as the soldiers turned and faced the prince to escort him from The Bay and back to the castle, where he would no doubt ride to the Neutral City in the most lavish of carriages. Even as a Princess, Larelle had never understood Aalto's greed or need to highlight his station. As the soldiers began marching, she perched on the low wall before the sea and twisted to face the ocean, dangling her legs.

Something tugged at Larelle then, and she turned to find her brother glancing back over his shoulder. The expression in his eyes was unreadable—perhaps a new form of hatred; after all, Larelle's presence ruined his plans for the morning.

His poor son, she thought, *to grow up with someone like him for a father*. She wished better for the boy. Aalto narrowed his eyes and flicked his hand. Boiling water exploded from the pans in the stalls, met by the owner's cries. Yet as he turned, Larelle delicately flicked her fingers and the water paused midair before lowering back into the pots. Everyone in the market searched for the wielder, but only Orlo noticed. He gave a gentle smile of thanks.

Larelle turned back to the ocean and exhaled slowly, willing the waves to calm once again. She listened to the gulls and sailors, the calls from the market stalls, and the slow footsteps of passing citizens. How different the sounds were compared to when she lived back in the castle—back when countering her brother's power was a daily occurrence. Yet while Larelle was exiled from her home and title, no one could remove her connection to water.

All royal families were direct descendants of the Gods: Nerida, Garridon, Vala, and Keres, and the realms were named after each of them. She wished everyone in Nerida could harness control over water like she could. Still, that ability was lost when her ancestors abandoned their homeland, Ithyion, and resettled on the land now known as Novisia, home to the four realms. Without a connection to the lands of their Gods, the power of those who were not direct descendants had dwindled over the years. Few citizens possessed such power, if any at all, and those who did were loosely related to the royal line.

Unlike her family, Larelle never lorded her power, and though she desperately wished to hate them, it was not in her nature. Her family was stuck in their warped, controlling ways, and nothing would change that, irrespective of the events of six years ago. Rare, happier memories occasionally emerged whenever she saw her brother, memories from before he aged and met his wife. Before he changed.

After finishing her bread, Larelle began climbing the carved steps leading to the residential areas of The Bay. It did not take long for her legs to weaken. Three bites of bread were not nearly enough to sustain such exercise. She doubted if she could do this regularly, but thinking of the coins spurred her uphill; perhaps she could purchase fresh food rather than wait for leftovers; maybe she could provide for her new family. The thought drove Larelle to finish the climb until she reached a line of expensive homes set back from the street. The home she approached was one of the smaller properties, yet ten times the size of her abode. She patted one of two chestnut horses grazing by the large paddock fence bordering the front of the house.

The woman who answered the door did not seem to recognise Larelle as Nerida's banished princess but merely another poor girl from The Bay who desperately needed work. She was likely the sort of woman in regular attendance of the castle balls as opposed to the market stalls, given the grandeur of their stately home overlooking the sea. She had likely never laid eyes on Larelle since her departure from the royal family, and even if Larelle had donned one of the nicer dresses she owned, she was unrecognizable now. Larelle twisted the beaded belt at her waist, which appeared as gold, but were simply a collection of oyster pearls gathered over the years, painted. It gave the illusion of a little more status, something the woman doubtlessly cared about.

The woman did not bother with introductions. Instead, she looked Larelle up and down, then turned to potter across the marbled hallway, beckoning Larelle to follow. The green silks of her gown flowed; her auburn hair was pinned in intricate curls above her head. Larelle wondered if she was from Garridon and married into a Neridian family, as auburn hair was more common in the neighboring realm.

"You'll find everything you need in this cupboard," the woman said, failing to hide her disdain as her eyes trailed up and down Larelle, who remained unfazed. She offered a polite smile. "You will only be paid for five hours, so you better hope you're done within that time."

The woman pushed past Larelle to return to whatever luxuriously relaxing day she had planned.

"Top to bottom!" she shouted, turning away from the parlor room. Larelle sighed but would put up with the rudeness for five silent hours of cleaning and money to take home by the end of it.

***

Five hours quickly passed. Larelle finished most of the work in four but slowed to ensure she was paid for the total time. The woman dropped a drawstring bag of gold coins in her hand before letting the door swing shut in Larelle's face. Larelle was too busy counting her coins to care, and with a satisfied sigh, she began to plan what food to take home that evening and how to budget for the coming week. Shifting to face the sea, Larelle frowned. It was darker than usual, and she peered skyward at the wisps of dark clouds coiling above.

Rain was unusual in Nerida, but long overdue, yet as the skies began to gather and darken, Larelle realized.

They were not clouds at all.

Chapter Three

Elisara

Elisara's mother once told her, 'A woman raises her voice when she is not being listened to; a man raises his voice when he is not being obeyed.' Elisara's sisters, however, raised their voices to be the centre of attention. Individually, Elisara's sisters were bearable; together, they were a nightmare—a nightmare in which the monsters did not have claws, but fingers pushing and prodding her curves; where hollow eyes were criticizing gazes, and mouths of sharpened teeth were instead mouths which never closed. But regardless of the monsters in her nightmares or waking life, Elisara was always the prey. A moment flashed from six years ago, where men were monsters with flame-tipped fingers. Elisara closed her eyes and schooled her breathing, willing the images away. The shrill laughter across the table did it for her, and she made a mental note to visit the training ring that evening. She might be seen as prey, but she could bite back.

Elisara wished to showcase that bite while sitting at the dining table but knew better than to make a stand against her sisters when they were together, who would only isolate her more, like they always had. Elisara could not pinpoint what pushed them apart.

Daeva was heir to the throne of Vala, which ensured Katerina would forever have a place in the castle. Elisara did not think it a coincidence Katerina's arranged marriage was to the future Lord of Elvera: the closest seat to the capital, Azuria, where she and her family resided. How convenient for her sisters to live so close, even when parted by marriage and duty.

While Elisara used to be bitter about their close relationship, she was now grateful. Distance from her sisters meant she was not often dragged to meetings or events; her freedom as the youngest and last immediate heir meant she lived with a relatively loose leash in her day-to-day life. While Daeva spent her days attending her father's meetings and shadowing his duties, Katerina followed closely behind and helped with dresses, hair, and, most importantly, gossip. Elisara was not expected to join. She would not rule. Instead, Elisara was to be a good wife one day to strengthen the ties between her realm and another. A smile graced her lips at the thought of *him.* A bittersweet smile, though, for reasons she was not willing to confront so early in the morning.

The shrill laughter echoed again, and Elisara stopped nudging fruit around her plate to catch Katerina's eye as she whispered in Daeva's ear. Daeva's deep brown eyes lifted to meet Elisara's, and a smirk graced her lips. Elisara schooled her features into one of indifference as she stared her sister down, yet this only spurred Katerina on. Flicking her black curls all three sisters shared, she rested her chin on her fist and prepared to direct—what Elisara assumed—would be a poorly veiled insult.

"Good morning, ladies," boomed a loud voice. A rush of cold air pushed the doors open, controlled by the speaker, who now entered the dining room. Elisara turned to meet the beaming smile of her father, Arion. The King of Vala. The smile did not quite reach his eyes—it never did these days—yet the wrinkles marking his pale blue gaze insisted it once had. His eyes glowed this morning, the only tell he was using his power. Slowly, they faded back to their darker shade as he approached the dining table.

"Morning, father," Elisara was the only one to answer as she rose and pulled out the chair at the head of the table. He squeezed her shoulder before sitting, and both sisters rolled their eyes. Elisara tossed them a sickly-sweet smile as she lifted the feather white fabric of her gown to sit. They had never spent time with their father outside of politics and were envious of the relationship they shared. While all three sisters modeled their mother's image, Elisara was her father's daughter. Katerina and Daeva both took after their mother, who rarely appeared at breakfast – or dinner.

"What are your plans today, Elisara?" her father asked. A near-by servant piled his plate with pastries—the reason for his fuller stomach in recent years.

"What she always does: sit alone at the top of the castle and refuse to speak to anyone." Katerina cut in.

"Or sitting in the kitchens with the servants as they are the only ones able to withstand her *dire* personality." Daeva added. Katerina snorted.

Power itched in Elisara's fingertips as she desperately wished to freeze their mouths shut, but as third in line to the throne, she did not possess power to the extent her sisters did, so knew better than to challenge them. A memory from the only time her power had taken over tried to surface in her mind. She blinked it away.

"Is that how one would speak to a patron of the realm, Daeva?" their father said. Those ice-blue eyes focused on Daeva as wind blew the windows open to invite in the wintery air of Vala. "Because when you are Queen, I expect you to be civil with all in your realm, especially your sister."

"It's okay, Father. I would rather be alone in the castle than shamelessly flirting with the guards at the watchtower," Elisara sat back, and Daeva glared. "Or having my sister dote on my every need."

Her father sighed, facing Elisara with a look that said, *I am trying to help you*. She concealed her laughter, and he smiled.

"Your sisters attending the watchtowers is an important job, Elisara, and not one to be ridiculed."

The atmosphere seemed to shift the moment Queen Vespera entered, all surprised by her presence. Elisara had grown up knowing not to question her mother's whereabouts; she simply liked to be alone. She supposed that was normal after being forced to marry into a realm, especially when the realm was opposite to the one you grew up in. The cold mountain airs of Vala were a stark contrast to the desert heat of Keres.

As the prince of Vala, Elisara's father married her mother to support ties with the neighbouring Keres. The alliance was merely political, and while it had never been romantic, it was one of equal respect. Elisara's mother was a woman who walked with power and commanded the attention of a room. She often wondered if her mother resented her parents for forcing their marriage, to abandon the realm she loved and trade sarees for thick-layered cloaks. Her mother had never grown accustomed to the cold, and while Elisara respected and trusted her mother, she was not the affectionate type. It was likely why Elisara was closer with her father, both craving attention from the most important woman in their lives.

"What is so important about attending the watchtowers by the Vellius sea?" Elisara asked. The Vellius sea was not a sea at all, but a large dark lake acting as the southern border between Vala and Nerida. There was little to find there.

"Yes, mother. What is so important that we should attend today?" Daeva challenged. Elisara noted the slight bite in her tone, which was not uncommon when her sister disagreed with something. Their mother looked coldly upon Daeva, unspoken words seeming to pass between them; they had likely argued about this before. It was not the first time Daeva and Katerina had shirked their duties to take a turn around the city gardens. They favoured being seen by the Lords and citizens, whereas Elisara favoured sneaking out into the city after dark.

"It is important for a Queen to be seen by all her people," her mother commented. She sipped the masala chai from her cup: one of the few things from Keres she kept in her routine. "Even when they would rather hide from their fears." Their mother took another sip before glancing between Daeva and Katerina.

"I have no fears. I just disagree with the *need*," Daeva said through gritted teeth. Elisara frowned as Katerina's fists clenched. Clearly, the two sisters had other plans for the day. Elisara glanced at her father to gauge his reaction. He seemed tired, though that was common. He always seemed to be, especially in the last few years since Elisara returned from those dark years away. It was as if he had taken on her unspoken burdens: the only one to notice the haunted look in her eyes when no one else did. He had greyed considerably in the last year; his blonde hair—a common trait in Vala—now paled, nearing the shade of white blanketing the city for most of the year.

It was almost undetectable, but Elisara noted the slight shake of her father's head as he looked to the Queen. Silence ensued, with nobody willing to break it. Elisara was done with bickering this morning and mentally prepared to return to her rooms and read. Her father seemed to think the same as he rose and brushed imaginary dust from his jacket, fixing the sigil pin to the left of his chest—an anxious tick Elisara knew well. He always did it before seeing the other rulers of Novisia.

"It's about time you made your way to the carriages, girls. If you leave now, you will be at the watchtower by late morning," her father said. No room left for argument. Daeva and Katerina shared a look.

"Now," their mother commanded. They were quick to rise upon hearing her sternness, a tone the Queen usually reserved for council meetings. Neither sister said goodbye to Elisara, but she did not care. She followed suit to bid farewell to her father, who wore that ever gentle smile reserved only for her. He adjusted his jacket and straightened the talisman around his neck, similar to the one worn by all rulers, except crafted from the stone of the highest mountain on their abandoned homeland in Ithyion after their ancestors fled the war. He grasped Elisara's hands and patted them gently, appearing to take an extra moment to analyze her face, perhaps afraid to leave his daughter alone with her thoughts.

"Remember, my star: you are in charge," he told her. She rolled her eyes.

"Yes, because I spend so much time when you are away talking with the Lords." She squeezed his hands, her fingers catching the cold metal of his rings. “I will be fine, father. It is only three days.” She reassured him. “Plus, I’ll be graced with Daeva and Katerina’s presence again later this evening.” He nodded, as if trying to reassure himself; he never worried like this with her sisters, another benefit of being the youngest. He leaned in and kissed the top of her head.

“You’re stronger than I,” he murmured into her hair. “I hate being alone.”

“You should try it sometime. Maybe you would have time to rest.”

“I’ll heed your advice, Eli.” With that, he headed for the ornate doors, covering the snowflakes intricately engraved into the handles. He trailed a light frost on them as he left. “I’ll see you soon!”

Elisara shook her head, laughing; he would not heed her advice, and she knew it.

“You’re right, you know.”

Elisara jumped, having forgotten her mother was there.

“He needs to sleep more, and if he were to listen to anyone, it would be you.” She approached Elisara, the stiff fabric of her high-necked gown trailing slowly behind.

“He’s stubborn; he will not listen to anyone.” Elisara folded her hands. She was more formal in her mother’s presence, eager to please.

“You share that trait.” Vespera's dark-painted lips tilted upwards, and Elisara bowed her head, recognizing the truth in it. When Elisara's head lifted, her mother’s signature Keresian amber eyes were analyzing. Elisara straightened. She valued the opinion of her mother, and early in life, Elisara had learned the meanings behind the looks she gave. Yet this look, she could not place.

“While we are gone, at least choose something educational to read.” She reached for the top of Elisara’s sleeve, pulling it up her pale shoulder where it had fallen loose. “Perhaps try your father’s personal libraries or something historical: brush up on your knowledge of Ithyion and how we came to be.”

"An excellent suggestion." Elisara smiled, though did not plan to take her up on it.

"Do not let them torment you," she added, unexpectedly.

She must have heard us bickering, Elisara thought, and replied with a knowing smile. Yet she could not help but flinch as her mother reached to smooth her hair, unprepared for such affection. Those amber eyes searched her own. "You are his star, which means you have his strength."

Elisara loved her father's pet name for her, the same pet name given by someone else, too, though each had different meanings. For her father, she was the star in his darkness: a reason to see joy in life, or so he told her when she was young.

"Do not venture out unless needed; you know the rules." Her mother strode around Elisara and followed the path of the King.

Of course, her final words are about rules, Elisara thought. She sighed, staring out of the window at the obstructed view of Azuria: the snowy tree line more apparent the lower you ventured into the castle. She picked up her skirts and made her way for the staircase, eager to cocoon in her rooms and bask in solitude for the coming days. A welcome oasis.

Chapter Four

Caellum

"Eight... nine ... ten... I'm coming!" Caellum called. He hid his own laughter upon hearing the muffled voices down the corridor. Light streamed in from the tall windows, and two shadows moved across the deep oak floor, before hiding behind a statue of a horse. "I wonder where Eve and Edlen are," he pondered dramatically. "They must be invisible as I cannot see them *anywhere!"*

More melodic laughter echoed against the vaulted ceilings in the Castle of Antor, the Capital of Garridon. The sound of Caellum's footsteps rebounded, too, as he continued slowly down the hallway, granting his youngest sisters some time to believe they had bested him, despite hiding in the same place they always did. They would never tire, but nor would Caellum. Spending time with his sisters brought him joy, whether that be teaching them to read or plant flowers in the garden—which often ended with dirt thrown in his face—or playing hide and seek on a Sunday afternoon.

"I suppose they will have to go hungry and miss lunch. They are lost forever." He paused, steps away from where they hid. "Or maybe,"—he jumped behind the statue—"They're here!"

The girls screamed and ran round the corner and down the next hall. The delicate white roses pinned in their dusty blonde waves fell as they scampered hand in hand, their legs fast for seven-year-olds. He laughed as Edlen struggled to pick up the skirts of her dress. Every time they played hide-and-seek, he advised her to wear something more practical, having lost count of the times this game ended with her rubbing a bruised knee from falling in the chase.

He jogged lightly behind, intent on keeping them happy with the false belief they were faster.

"You won't catch us, Caellum!" Edlen called.

"Not this time!" yelled Eve. The girls took an unexpected right-hand turn at the end of the hallway, instead of turning left. *What do they have planned?* He wondered as the girls darted, disrupting their routine of running to the dining room. As he rounded the corner, the girls collided into the dark arched doors standing high before them, using all their weight to push them open and run giggling inside.

The melody of laughter stopped abruptly, the sound of Caellum's quickening pulse replacing the silence as he slowly entered the council chambers. He straightened his tunic and combed down his hair while approaching the large circular table. Clearing his throat, he glanced at his father, brothers, and the Lords of Garridon seated in the room. Their eyes all shifted from the two young girls to him. Caellum glanced at his brothers; hopeful his older siblings would intervene for once. Kieren rolled his eyes and Dalton refrained from laughing, catching the girls' eyes as they stood sheepishly to one side. Then, there was Halston: heir to the Garridon throne, whose eyes widened in warning.

"Apologies, Lords, brothers... father." Caellum nodded to each yet bowed his head when addressing the king. Torturous seconds followed, as they often did, as his father made him wait before releasing him from the position of respect.

"Not to worry Cal, I am sure it was—" Halston stopped, and though Caellum's head remained bowed, he could imagine the look that silenced him. Out of the corner of his eye, Caellum peered at his sisters, hoping they would go unnoticed now he was the centre of attention. Eve was holding Edlen's hand tight to stop the tears from falling.

"That is no way to address another prince in the presence of our lords," the King scolded Halston, his deep voice resounding through the room. Nobody spoke. His father rose from his engraved golden chair, the metal scraping across the wood as he stalked towards Caellum, like a beast with prey, his arms clasped behind his back. Caellum was uncertain he, or any of his siblings, were breathing, having sensed the mood their father was in. This was not his overwhelming rage where he screamed or shouted, but cool indifference leaving you to guess the manner in which the sting would come.

The king's palm collided with Caellum's face. Physical sting it was then, though his words were often worse.

"Sit," he said.

Caellum tried to mask his shock. He never joined the meetings. He glanced at his sisters; Edlen was crying now, her petite body shaking as she struggled suppressing her sobs. His father exhaled, frustration painting his features.

"Auralia," His father beckoned.

Caellum met the eyes of his eldest sister as she rose from her spot by the back corner window, embroidery in hand. The overgrown ivy on the castle walls fell into the window and scattered shadows across the room; whatever light found its way through bounced off her blond locks that matched their mother's and cast a halo behind her. Caellum viewed Auralia as exactly that: his guardian angel. A gift from the Gods. The only person aside from his mother who calmed his father's anger: a welcome distraction from the rest of them. Auralia cared to pacify their father for the sake of her siblings, while Caellum had the impression their mother did it to avoid any inconvenience. Caellum credited his siblings for having raised him, not his parents.

"Take your sisters to the dining hall. We will not be here much longer." His Father instructed, scowling at the two young girls whose eyes were fixed on their delicate slippers. "They can wait until we are all there before eating as punishment for their unruly disruption."

"Yes, father." Auralia calmly agreed. She placed her embroidery on the cushioned windowsill where she had been perched and reached for Eve and Edlen's small palms, guiding them from the hall. She gave Caellum a final apologetic look and closed the doors behind her.

"I think I recall telling you to sit." His father's voice reverberated in his ear; Caellum did not realize he had stepped so close.

"Yes, father." Caellum tried to ooze strength in his voice as he headed to where Auralia had sat.

"Not there," his father called, returning to his own chair. Caellum glanced around the room, unsure of where his father meant. "If you wish to play childish games and act like a weak boy, you can sit like a child." He gestured to the fireplace set into the wall. "On the *floor*."

He said nothing else to Caellum, but continued whatever discussions were had before the interruption. Kieren no longer stifled his laughter because in that moment, he knew better; he straightened, eyes lowered, avoiding drawing any attention to himself.

Caellum knew better, too, and sat on the floor. A twenty-six-year-old man sat on the floor of a council meeting: a perfect example of how little his father thought of him. Bending his long legs, he rested his arms on his knees, and twiddled the gold ring on his index finger. An anxious habit developed from the first moment his father hit him all those years ago.

Caellum flinched as his father's palm slammed against the table. Halston shook his head, ever so slightly: a sign to not say a word, move—or hell—*breathe.*

"Would you like to repeat that, Lord Gregor?"

Caellum recognized that tone. If Lord Gregor of Albyn were the king's son, he would be on the floor by now, likely with a foot hovering above his face. Caellum watched as the youngest of the Lords gulped. While Caellum did not like any of the Lords, Gregor was the least insufferable, perhaps because they were closer in age, and both found the opinions of the older men outdated.

"The Usurper," repeated Lord Gregor, clasping his hands. "That is what was carved on the Castle boundary wall when I entered this morning."

Caellum shrank into himself as much as he could given his stature. Such slander was unheard of, and Caellum could count on one hand the number of times it was said in his father's presence. As far as Caellum was concerned, his father had terrified every citizen of Garridon into never uttering that word again.

When Caellum was twelve, a servant called his father '*the usurper,*' so he asked his father what it meant, only to be hit and banished to his room without dinner. The servant boy was never seen again. Auralia had explained it all to him: his family was not descended from the original Garridon lineage. Their grandfather, Jorah, took the throne by force from King Errard and Queen Lyra many years ago after the King became tainted with power, caring little for his people after marrying the true heir of Garridon: Lyra.

Caellum questioned why the term was rising again. His grandfather had been a noble man and created an opportunity for Garridon to be properly ruled and cared for. Yet Caellum sometimes wondered how different life might have been under the rule of a true descendant from the Gods. As they were not born of the Garridon lineage, his family had little to no connection to the earth power manifested in the royal lineage. Nevertheless, his family possessed heightened strength, though he had no idea how or where that came from; no one asked or discussed it, not even within the family. Yet any citizens exhibiting even the slightest connection to the earth were exiled in fear of their power being used to take the throne. Exiled to Doltas Island to die. Years ago, the rulers abandoned the island and left them with nothing. He doubted anyone had escaped. Caellum's eyes roamed back to his father, who glared at his slackened posture. He straightened.

He just needed to make it through the meeting.

***

"Again!" Caellum huffed. He swung the sword, steadying it across his body. Hesitation crossed Sir Cain's features: a significantly bulkier man, who stood across from him in the training ring and knew all too well this was Caellum's method of self-inflicted punishment.

"Prince—"

"—Again, Sir Cain!" He cut his father's commander off and shook the sweat-ridden locks from his eyes. Breathing heavy, pain spread across his lungs and chest, but he pushed through it and braced his stance. Sir Cain struck, but Caellum easily deflected and narrowed his eyes. Despite his strength, the deflection should not have come so easily considering the hours they had spent dueling. His strength and speed were unmatched to those of the other realms, yet he wondered how different fighting would be if he could grow vines from the earth to trap his opponents or blow wind at them like the princesses of Vala.

He readjusted his hands on the pommel, the sweat weakening his grip. *Weak.* He lunged at Sir Cain, reminded of his Father's words, but Sir Cain was prepared: one of only two people strong enough to brace against Caellum's onslaught while trapped in this headspace. A second person flashed in his mind's eye and spurred his anger; Caellum screamed, lunging again in a flurry of movement as the golden sword caught the light and collided with its opposition. He barged ahead with every swing and forced Sir Cain closer to the wall.

Weak, the voice echoed again, and he missed Sir Cain's low duck as he spun from the prince's reach and circled him. Caellum spun to face him but refused to meet his eyes. He knew the pity he would find there.

"Caellum," Sir Cain tried. The prince cringed at the affection in his tone—the affection he wished he experienced from his father even once as a child. Caellum was not done. He swung again, yet this time Sir Cain did not move. In the last moment, Caellum halted, and instead pushed the man to the ground, towering above him with the sword poised at his throat.

Sir Cain gasped for breath as his bare chest rose in the struggle to find balance. Caellum wondered what it would be like to best his father like this and beat the only person stronger than him in battle. In place of Sir Cain's flame-red hair and freckled skin, he pictured dark locks greyed with age and wrinkles outlining harsh eyes—eyes so often fixed in a glower at his children.

Weak. Childish.

"Prince Caellum!" a voice shouted. "Prince Caellum; we must leave at once."

"Cal, breathe." Sir Cain said. The commander's rough accent tethered him back to reality and Caellum blinked at the man lying on the ground, a sword still at his throat. His hand trembled as he tossed the weapon to one side and offered his hand to Sir Cain. Caellum's mind always meandered when rage consumed him, and he opted to force the memories away by battling against the pain. The only method to strengthen himself and no longer be *weak* like his father claimed.

"Prince Caellum!"

Caellum spun to face the entrance of the training ring. Two guards crippled over, panting, as if they had run a great distance at an even greater speed. Cautiously, Caellum strode towards them. He was rarely called for. Worry sparked in his mind. Had his father's anger gone too far; had he hurt one of his siblings?

"It's the Neutral City, your Highness," panted the guard on the left, who glanced at his partner. "It's burning."

"What do you mean it's burning?"

“There's been an explosion,” the guard said. “You can see the smoke in the distance once you exit Hybrook forest.”

My siblings. Caellum had been in the training ring since sunrise and was unsure of who accommodated his parents to the bi-annual meeting of the rulers. He strode to the exit. What would his brothers do? Gather reinforcements, head to the city, and end the threat.

"Sir Cain, ready the guards. Every one of them. Some of the army soldiers, too."

Caellum made for the castle to change into riding gear; he would need to be comfortable for the long journey to the Neutral City.

"Prince Caellum," the guard called. "There's something else."

He turned.

"The guards at the Hybrook watchtower sent a carrier pigeon. In the note, they said," The guard paused, as if fearing Caellum's reaction might mirror his father's. Shame flitted through him. "They said they spotted two Vala Princesses entering the Neutral City after their parents."

Caellum's heart stopped and fear consumed him at the thought of one particular princess, and where she could be.

Chapter Five

Elisara

"Save them all," Elisara commanded.

Slamming open the gilded doors from the advisor's hall, she strode for the grand staircase. There was no need to look back to check the Lords followed: their muffled complaints and the guards' steady footfall carried to her on the wind. Gently enticing the breeze through one of many open windows in the castle, she tried to draw the words to her. While the breeze was not strong enough to deliver their exact protests, she could imagine the colourful terms used to describe her brazen commands as the only royal in residence today—words likely uttered again to describe the chaotic manner in which she had flown into the hall: barefoot and white gown billowing behind her, while curls fell from her half up-do. Apparently, there was a more presentable way to announce an explosion in the Neutral City.

Elisara gripped the front of her gown to lift the hem, granting her naked feet better navigation as she took the stairs two at a time. The group behind would have to find their own way around the train which followed. One floor down; four more to go. This was not productive, but visual evidence was the only way to prove the threat to these old obstinate men. Rounding the corner, she passed the formal dining room, and its powder blue walls blurred as her gaze fixed firmly ahead, sidestepping any staff in her path.

"Princess! If we could just slow—"

"—Lord Adar, if you are not fit enough to run up some stairs," she scoffed, "then how can you be fit enough to rule the Port of

Elvera?" Her breath was unfaltering as she reached the staircase to the third floor. Lord Adar flashed her a scolding look, but reluctantly followed. She rolled her eyes. The Lords cared far too much for decorum, and she was certain Lord Adar would express his outrage to her father upon his return, often running to the King for such petty inconveniences; all it took was Elisara to breathe inappropriately.

"*You may not be Queen one day, Eli, but you will be a wife, and as much as I admire your honesty, others may not.*" She had forgotten the honesty to which her father referred—or the occasion—but luckily, her betrothed favoured such candor, particularly when expressing what she wished for him to do to her in the rare moments they shared alone.

Elisara wondered when she would next see her love. A month had passed, and their last three days together were nowhere near enough. She wished he were with her. The Lords would immediately obey him, even though he was not from Vala. That was how little they valued her opinion, willing to favour a male from another realm. Yet he would likely defend Elisara, too, and her right to command. She smiled at the thought of him, but it soon vanished. Had he attended the Neutral City? The thought prompted greater speed.

When she reached the final steps to the highest point of the castle, Vlad—her personal guard—caught up and nudged her playfully.

"Is this all a ruse? For these men to have heart attacks and clear the way for more forward-thinking Lords and Ladies?" Vlad flashed a grin, the same given to the Lord's daughters whenever they visited the castle: a grin imbued with mischief and suggestion, known to entice many.

"Please, Vlad. We both know if I wanted them dead, I would have thought of something far more fun."

Vlad reached the door to her chambers and pushed them open while the advisors struggled up the final steps. Elisara's chambers were located at the highest point in the castle, far from the rooms of her sisters, who shared adjoining rooms below. Elisara preferred it like this; this way, they would not pester her.

Smoothing her gown, Elisara tucked the stray black curls behind her ear and stormed into the sitting room where the mountains lay before her—another perk of living at the peak of the castle.

As an heiress to the realm of Vala, Elisara relished in the sensation of the air she controlled around her body; so much so, she requested the entire wall in her chambers to be removed, replaced instead with a stone balcony.

The rooms were large, large enough to include everything she required. If she wished it, she would not have to see anyone for days, except when summoning food. They entered the sitting room, which formed a personal library as countless books lined the walls, and plush, powder blue chairs and chaises crowded the rug. Despite the fire burning in the mantel, the stone floor felt cold against her feet, having dwindled in her rush to find the Lords.

Before such commotion, she had sat by the fireplace with her book, beholding the snow-topped city of Azuria and the Zivoi mountains to the east when she noticed the smoke beginning to plume from the most central point of Novisia: The Neutral City. Usually, there was little sign of the city from her balcony, too far inland for the naked eye. The smoke might have come from one of Garridon's forests burning if not for how contained it was: a towering plume of smoke inching toward the clouds until smothering them, blanketing the sky. She wondered if the other realms saw it too or if the castle's high vantage point meant only she could. This was no simple fire. Sounds akin to explosions had pulled towards her on the wind, and in her gut, Elisara knew this was something else.

Reaching the balcony, Elisara rested her hand upon the pale grey stone and schooled her features to disguise the rising anger. This was a waste of time, and she had now proven it by the volumes of smoke rising from the distant city. *Will the other realms also strug-*

gle to send aid? She wondered. Elisara turned to face the advisors now joining her on the balcony: their faces wore a mix of emotions.

"Now, I will repeat myself. Save them *all*. Write only that, Lord Petrov." She drummed her fingers against the balcony before clutching it in frustration. "We do not have time to waste with royal decrees or full reports. As the closest to the Neutral City, you must tell the commander in Vojta: *save them all*." Elisara slightly raised her chin at the Lord, who stared back at her with the eagle on his arm poised to send the message the moment he gave the word.

"Respectfully, Princess, the priority needs to be locating King Arion and Queen Vespera, and your sisters, too." The stout man replied. A weight pressed against her chest as she thought of her parents. Her mother responded calmly to chaos and her father switched from kind to commanding in a second, yet that didn't waver the fear flowing through her now, or the confusion. The Lord must have been mistaken.

"My sisters?" Elisara frowned. "They are at the lookout towers by the Vellius Sea." The placement of the tower to the eastern side of the lake meant it was impossible for them to make it to the city before the destruction took place. They were safe. But if what Lord Petrov said was true, and they were indeed in the city instead, Katerina was likely in a panic while Daeva tried to imitate her father's composure and instill calm among the people.

"No, your Highness. Daeva was asked to detour and attend the meeting with your father as practice." His look was somewhat sympathetic as he continued. "And well, you know Katerina. Anywhere Daeva goes, she wishes too."

Elisara turned from the Lords, not wishing to expose the hurt on her face. It was common knowledge she was excluded by her sister's, yet despite their distance, her heart quickened at the thought that they, too, might be in danger.

"Even more reason for the quick and short message, Lord Petrov." Elisara paced. "We cannot waste time reporting on plans and locations. Who would we be as a realm if we did not consider how to save the residents of the city? My word is final." Elisara concluded. The other Lords bowed their heads as Lord Petrov scribbled on the parchment and sent it off with the eagle.

They had every confidence her family had escaped the Temple of the Neutral City through the hidden tunnels when chaos ensued; after all, that was its purpose: an emergency exit. They had likely reconvened in one of their safe houses while the other royal families did the same. She chewed her lips. But what if the safe houses in the Neutral City were compromised? If they were, the cabins in Vojta would be their next port of call.

Yet something did not sit right with Elisara; little could cause an explosion in the Neutral City, and for it to happen at the bi-annual gathering of the rulers was no coincidence.

Elisara signaled for Vlad to escort the men from her chambers as they discussed tactics for reaching her family. As they left, she gazed out across Vala, her family's realm. The Mountains to the East sparkled in the sun as if it were a normal day. Below, she imagined the citizens of the capital city, Azuria, going about their day as normal, blissfully unaware of the chaos inland. Her father would be calm, so she tried to emulate such emotions.

Closing her eyes, Elisara's palms faced upwards on the stone wall of the balcony. Frost delicately pinched her knuckles, and she breathed in, the cold rush of air soothing her lungs. Her eyebrows strained as she gathered the wind and willed it away, focusing on assembling the sounds from the Neutral City, hoping she would not hear any panic. She sighed. Nothing. Yet this was typical of Elisara's abilities; it was tricky pulling sounds on the winds from such a distance, so the explosion must have been loud to reach her earlier.

Whirling from the balcony, she crossed back into her chambers and closed the book on the side table by the fire. The sheer curtains of her bedroom billowed open as if welcoming her return, though that return would be brief. She had no time to waste as she pulled open the door to her dressing room.

Gowns lined the entire length of one wall and military gear, breeches, and tunics hung on the other. She was grateful all royals of Novisia underwent two years of military training. No one questioned her when she requested to continue training upon her return; as third in line to the throne, no one was concerned about the risks. A memory flashed, and Elisara shook her head, willing her mind to focus.

Reaching for her military gear, she tossed it onto the ivory silken sheets of her bed. She tugged on the two strings holding her dress up at the nape of her neck and began pulling off the dress until an exclamation came from the doorway. Elisara rolled her eyes.

"You could have given me warning, Eli!" Vlad sighed. He placed his hands over his eyes and turned the other way.

"Oh please, Vlad. Enough people have seen me in my undergarments at the springs. Besides, don't act the saint. I know plenty about your adventures with women." She and Helena, one of her few friends, often gossiped about Vlad and his latest conquests. Elisara fastened the night black breeches and pulled the white tunic over her head. The billowing sleeves caught on the delicate gold chains adorning her wrists: a gift from her mother when she turned eighteen. "Now, be the good guard you are, and help me tighten this."

Elisara motioned to the ivory leather corset held to her waist that would house a series of knives, then faced the floor-length mirror. Draping her long black curls to one side, she watched Vlad. His blue eyes were intently focused on pulling the thin ribbons as she held the corset to her figure. If only the ladies saw him now: the dashing young guard with his golden hair and chiseled jawline, helping dress the Princess. Gossip would spread like wildfire. His hands did not linger as he finished and stepped backward.

Elisara glanced at the deep brown eyes of her reflection.

"I am not paid enough for this," he muttered. "What would your betrothed say if he knew a lowly guard was tightening your corset?"

“He would say I can do whatever I wish, providing he is the only one taking the corset off." Elisara tied the top half of her curls back and secured her hair with a golden clip.

"Do I want to ask why you're changing into military day clothes?" he asked, moving to perch on the edge of her bed.

"Because you and I are leaving for the Neutral City."

He rubbed his jaw.

"Of course we are! Why would we stay here while the Commander of Vala manages things?"

"The Vala Commander listens to Lords, who does not believe this to be of concern," she explained, throwing her discarded dress behind the dressing room door. "Round up some other guards, and I will meet you at the stables." It was not a suggestion. Elisara strapped the sword to her waist.

"I cannot exactly complain, can I?" Vlad threw his hands in the air. "At least you have considered taking others rather than heading out there alone." Vlad said, bolting from the rooms while Elisara tugged at her corset and slid the knives into place. She reached for her royal pin—three mountains surrounded by stars—and pierced it through the left of her tunic above her heart. *Everything will be okay*, Elisara assured herself, though the tightness in her chest told her otherwise.

Chapter Six

Elisara

The journey to the stables was quick and unseen as Elisara took the narrow turret of stairs from outside her chambers the entire way, exiting halfway down the mountain on which the Castle of Azuria stood. The castle was built on the highest mountain found in Vala, as it was where the ruling family felt most comfortable when settling on Novisia all those years ago. The only downside being it took forever to reach the city.

She exited the turret, and the bitter winds pierced her face: a welcome sensation. Elisara blew out a gentle fog before marching into the chiseled side of the mountain, sheltering the horses from the cold. In her stall, Molya stood—the horse gifted from her love on her sixteenth birthday. As she reached for the saddle, the rock moved, signalling the guards exiting their quarters through the expertly hidden door. Laughter drifted; many were off duty today because of the royal family's departure to the Neutral City.

The men appeared to chuckle at Vlad's words, then proceeded to the guards' stables. Elisara led Molya to the mouth of the stables and surveyed the city below. Access was provided only by the narrow path unless she wished to traipse the ice caves to the north of the castle. Snow melted on the rooftops of Azuria, yet the further they travelled, the less snow and ice would appear.

I hate summer, she thought.

While it was much colder than the other three realms in Novisia, there was far less of the glistening snow this time of year. Elisara spent many a summer evening gliding her fingertips over the city walls, her power flowing freely while gracing the stone with the thinnest layer of frost and ice. She wished to spend every day keeping the city coated in white and blue. Two more moon cycles and snow would fall again. How her sisters attended countless trips to the other, warmer realms, Elisara would never understand.

The corners of her mouth faltered. A day would come when she would no longer feel the crisp Vala air on her cheeks, instead settling for the cold Garridon rain. She was eager to spend every day with her love, despite the shift from snow-capped mountains to rolling fields of emerald and twisted canopy trees, though it had the reprieve of floral fields. Garridon was beautiful, yet so far from Vala, with the realm of Nerida in between. Even more isolated from the cold.

Though at least she was not forced to betroth a member of Nerida's court, where the warmth of the coastal air and its unfrozen waters would surely suffocate her. Even worse, to marry someone in Keres, where the dry desert heat and red stone rocks would certainly kill Elisara at once.

The approaching guards drew Elisara from her thoughts, and without looking back, she headed down the narrow path. Vlad would likely scold her when they reached the mountain base, for journeying without two guards protecting her front as well as her back, as regulation dictated. Elisara sensed daggers burning into her.

All that mattered was she was obeying her own rules, and no nobles would grace this route to comment on her rule-shirking. The Lords and Ladies of Vala would only be seen in the stately apartments located closest to the castle. This detour would instead journey round the poorest homes of their realm.

***

The journey from Azuria through Vala was quick, a few hours at most. After exiting Azuria through the outskirts, they bypassed the Frozen Forest to instead cross the flatter, clearer lands around Tisova before veering south towards Vojta. Elisara refused to stop unless necessary yet wished to pass closer to Vojta to assess whether the Commander had actioned Lord Petrov's request, and for the horses to have some reprieve in the meantime.

As they reached the Vellius Sea, Elisara glanced over in the distance to where the coastal watchtower stood. She imagined her sisters' infuriating laughter upon seeing Elisara, yet the surrounding air was silent as she reached out to check. In her gut, she knew there would be no laughter.

While the horses refreshed themselves, Elisara scanned the town of Vojta. From the outside, the small town was indistinguishable from the others in Vala: the mountain town of Tisova, the port of Elvera, and the cliff-side town of Marnovo. Elisara observed the identical wooden cabins and brick homes protecting the inner town squares, where the Lord's homes resided. The only significant difference was far less snow settled in Vojta, given its vicinity to the Neutral City.

Little noise graced her ears as she surveyed the town; either the military based there were already in the Neutral City or had not left at all. The men dressed in uniform flirting with a group of women behind the rocks suggested the latter.

"Are you surprised?" Vlad huffed, who had no love for the people of Vojta. Born and raised in a small home in the town square, he requested a transfer to Azuria after only two days' training with Vojta's military. The men did not live up to his standards of the importance of protecting Vala.

"Of course, I'm not surprised," Elisara sighed. "None of those Lords would listen to a woman. The only reason they may listen to Daeva when she is Queen is because they respect my father's decision." Elisara picked a stone from the collection and skimmed it across the lake. "They know their sons will probably take their places as her advisors, thus have plenty of time to mold them."

Vlad nodded in agreement.

"Well, as they aren't surveilling the border to Nerida..." He nodded toward the rowdy men and women. "We should check before we exit the tree line and expose ourselves."

Elisara rolled her eyes but respected his worry all the same. There had been no wars between the realms since the Battle of the Usurper, and even then, it was a civil war in Garridon while the rest of Novisia sat back and watched.

Vlad's right to be safe, Elisara thought. She cursed herself for failing to assess the risks, though she doubted any threat existed outside the Neutral City; by now, she would have heard about it. Similarly, with Nerida's wide rivers gracing the borders to Vala, and the adjacent border to Garridon, any threat that may exit the city could not enter the other realms.

Elisara watched her footing in the thin dusting of snow. As she reached the final boundary of trees, Vlad swiftly held out an arm and took cover. She stared at him, confused, before following his eye line to the border, where the reason for his shock came into view, galloping towards the Nerida Gate to the Neutral City. A rider she recognised instantly by the signature black curls she once braided as a child.

"Shit!" Elisara hissed. She clambered up from her crouched position, fingernails digging into the tree bark to find purchase. Vlad's hand gripped her elbow, balancing her as they both spun back in the direction of Vojta. She pushed what air she could behind them, propelling them forward as they raced back to the horses, leaping over loose tree roots and avoiding patches of ice. The cracks of branches echoed as Elisara pushed them from her path, bursting into the clearing, "Go, go, go!" she called to the remaining guards, who instantly mounted their horses. "Get to the gate immediately!"

Jumping on Molya, she turned towards the route opening from the trees.

"What's wrong?" one guard called.

"Princess Larelle is heading for Nerida's gate!"

The guards stared; eyebrows furrowed.

"She never leaves The Bay, let alone Nerida,'" Vlad announced. Realisation dawned then. Something must have panicked Larelle enough to break the rules of her banishment.

The group galloped out of the trees and down the stretch towards the Vala Gate. As they neared the towering archway, the snow faded on the ground below to reveal worn stone. The muffled sound of hooves echoed now as her group surged on. The open expanse was no longer disrupted by the Vala tree line, offering a clear view of the Zivoi mountains in the north and the fields of Nerida to the south across the river border.

If it was not for urgency, Elisara would have stopped to marvel at the natural beauty of Novisia. Instead, her focus was on Larelle, who tilted her head at the sound of the horses before disappearing through the Neridian Gate. Elisara looked up at the Vala emblem, sat proudly at the summit of its archway. She pulled Molya to a halt.

"Princess, if there is a danger, we should wait for a military force. You cannot access any power in there." The youngest of the men suggested.

"Neither can anyone else," Vlad argued, the only guard to support whatever decision Elisara made. Glancing back at her men, Elisara removed the sword from the strap on Molya's saddle and tossed her cloak aside, strapping the sword to her back instead. The piercing cold of Vala no longer remained to comfort Elisara, replaced instead by a humidity that raised with her anxiety as they approached the city.

"Then it's a good thing I've served my two years of training in the military." She spun on her heel, head high, and marched to the gate in search of answers. Little did she know, the heirs to the other realms approached the other gates with the exact same intent.

Chapter Seven

Caellum

The towering stone archway marking the Garridon Gate loomed over Caellum as he dismounted his stallion, the rhythmic marching of the military halting behind him. Sir Cain approached his side, and the two shared a stoic look while gazing at the smoke rising from the centre of the city and the ash floating in the air. Neither could see the military from either Nerida or Keres due to the large forest borders, planted by Caellum's grandfather to hide Garridon from their neighbours. The towering trees added to the city's darkness.

Whenever Caellum walked into the Neutral City, he was reminded of its individuality within the realm. It was not modelled on the red sandstone of Keres, the woods of Garridon, the polished stones of Nerida or the ornate buildings of Vala. It stood on its own: crafted of pale stone the colour of faded parchment: a mismatched collision of buildings and alleyways, all leading inwards.

Caellum had been grateful for the Neutral City while growing up. He felt inadequate among the other royal children as the only one lacking a connection to the power of his realm. Yet in the Neutral City, where all powers were inhibited, Caellum was an equal. Normally, no danger threatened the city due to restrictions on power. Today was different. He sensed the panic from the lack of welcome from the nearby citizens, and screams echoed from the centre of the city, where layers of smoke emerged. The place his siblings would be.

Caellum stilled. The guards at the watchtower had informed him of multiple carriages entering the city, carrying not only his parents but all his siblings, yet he could not fathom why all but him were there. His mind flickered to thoughts of smoke smothering his siblings; he imagined the screams were theirs. He thought of Edlen and Eve clinging to one another while Halston tried to instill calmness, but most of all, he imagined his father saving himself while his mother screamed for help—screams which morphed to replicate that of a particular princess, as Caellum worried that she, too, was trapped somewhere in the city.

Caellum's panicked eyes assessed the scenes before him. More than anything, he wished to run to the smoke's origin and find those he loved, but ringing pierced his ears, and his pulse raced. Sweat layered his skin, and he realised he was not equipped to deal with such events. Sir Cain shouted orders to the soldiers flooding in while Caellum tried to calm his breathing and centre his thoughts.

The outer circle of the city was mostly residential, aside from a handful of shops. Only a few residents chose to make it their home instead of residing in their born realm. On a normal day, Caellum would enter the gate, greeted by the smell of baked bread, accompanied by the gentle smiles of the elderly from their open windows. As a child, Caellum had often longed to abandon any meetings his father forced him to attend in favour of visiting the quiet homes here.

All remained untouched by destruction. Men dragged the wounded to the herb store, where the best natural healing aids likely resided. As he scanned the sandstone homes now, he smelled no bread and saw no smiles—no, the waft of baking bread was replaced with a pungent stench of smoke tinged with blood. The smiles of the elderly had melted into frowns as they concentrated on bandaging those before them. The door of every home was wide open, with an injured person on every step. It would only worsen the further they ventured. These were the lucky few who had not been near the Temple and were far enough away to run or hobble to some form of aid.

The soldiers made their way along the row of homes, and Sir Cain gathered information from the few men that had reached the outer circle with only scratches to tell the tale. They now helped carry people through the smoke from the inner circles. Caellum's personal guards remained at his side, their hands resting on the pommel of their silver swords, eyes assessing for any immediate threat. Behind him and through the gate was the wide track leading to the Hybrook and Hystone forests; on a normal day, he would ride through the trees on horseback alone or with his siblings.

"Cal!" Sir Cain called. Caellum turned to the Commander of Garridon who walked from a group of men with a grim look on his face. "I've dispatched most of the men further into the city. They will take different streets to look for survivors and anyone else in need."

"Does anyone know what happened?" Caellum asked, glancing at the injured people dragged in from the streets. No familiar faces were among them.

"There was more than one explosion. The first hit the corner entrance to the market plaza, the second at the Temple's entrance, and the third within the Temple itself. I spoke with some men that were outside the Old Ash Tavern, and despite being ten blocks away from the explosion, the entire roof crumbled from the impact. The explosion was far-reaching." He leaned closer, hushing his next words. "But the Temple buildings were the worst hit. No one knows what triggered it. There was only black smoke and people scrambling to flee."

Caellum paced as Sir Cain finished his account. His priority was reaching the Temple to assess the damage and check for his siblings, yet he trusted Sir Cain's judgment of what to do next.

"You three!" Sir Cain commanded the soldiers to his left. "Head to the apothecary on the corner of the 11th Row and ask the storekeeper, 'Do the trees still grow?' They will then confirm if the royal family is above the store in the safe house." Caellum marched towards the street leading directly into the centre of the city. With all the soldiers dispatched, only Caellum's personal guards and Sir Cain remained for the journey inward.

"Are you okay?" Sir Cain asked softly, looking sideways at Caellum. Genuine concern etched his features, and Caellum was grateful to have him by his side for this. He gave a firm but silent nod and allowed the darkness to consume him as he followed the path into the city.

The journey through the outer rows of buildings was easy. Smoke had eased, and no buildings or pathways were damaged, yet the further inwards they traveled, the more signs of devastation appeared. The once bright sandstone was smeared with layers of soot, and the light began to dim as the buildings grew taller, and the smoke thicker. The names of stores were illegible as they passed, making it difficult to determine how far they were from the plaza and the Temple. Caellum's heart ached to witness the destruction of a city known and created to enforce peace among the realms.

At first, citizens from all realms were reluctant to live in the Neutral City, yet it soon became a regular visitation spot for the royal families, who visited to attend meetings to better the Kingdom of Novisia. Thereafter, the appeal was clear; not only were there opportunities for businesses when hundreds gathered for celebrations and meetings, but it offered a fresh start for those who needed it. The Neutral City was exactly that: a neutral zone. No powers, no division, no realm specific rules, no judgement.

Sir Cain caught Caellum's arm as he stumbled, the cobbled ground jutting with fallen debris, and they both looked up to find the Old Ash Tavern. The tenth row. How the men narrowly escaped the falling roof was a mystery, given a substantial portion of the wall crumbled too. The remaining patrons were no longer merry; instead, they clawed through rubble in the search for survivors.

Emotion overtook Caellum as he continued navigating the ruins. Fallen rooftops soon became the collapse of entire buildings, in which screams erupted from inside while their loved ones stood in the streets, crying and unable to get in. His panic spiked with every step, but he was unable to stop. If this was the disaster surrounding the outside rows, what must remain of the Temple...

Quickening his pace, he made his way around the chunks of fallen stone crowding the paths. Bodies lay everywhere: trapped under rock, flung against walls, concealed in thick layers of soot and dust. An eerie silence followed as he drew closer to the Temple, the muffled cries behind him lessening with every step. Caellum tried his best to ease his breathing without consuming mouthfuls of dust, yet nothing prepared him for what lay around the corner.

He exited the street into the plaza. The once beautifully carved, towering temple, a symbol of peace and synergy, was now nothing but a burning pile of stone.

Chapter Eight

Elisara

Elisara could not move. It was as if the heat of the burning ground melted the soles of her riding boots and glued her to the destroyed cobbled street. She held out her hand and glowing embers of ash landed on her palm, yet she felt no pain. Slowly raising her head to the sky, dark smoke circled the air as the same ash descended, almost mistaken as snow from afar. A reminder from the Neutral City, she was not alone, or so she told herself. Dazed, she lowered her head and white residue dotted her black curls, now untamed and hanging around her shoulders. She sensed bodies arriving but was focused only on the Neridian Princess who stood upon the pile of burning rubble, staring into the cavern formed from the explosion.

Elisara usually sensed others' emotions, but with Larelle's back turned, all she could note was her tense shoulders and hands hanging loosely by her sides. She wore no cloak, but only a pale blue chiffon dress cinched by beads of gold at her waist; her feet were bare—something Elisara had not noticed upon first seeing her. The dress was cut at the shoulders and kept her toned arms exposed, a welcome feature for spending time alone on the shores of The Bay, the salt air licking her skin. Larelle raised her arms, tying her locks back with a ribbon while revealing the low back of her dress, baring more of her rich brown skin inherited from her father.

As Larelle circled the top of the ruins, swarms of bodies began arriving at the Temple. Flooding in from the streets to the right of her was the Garridon Military, who piled into formation around the east of the Temple as a group in emerald-green cloaks entered the Plaza, parting to reveal a man who towered above the rest. His light brown hair, the colour of faded bark, fell across his eyes while a velvet cloak flowed behind him, and revealed the toned muscles in his legs that powered into the opening with intent. He paused. The golden crown of vines upon his head dulled in the smoke's darkness, yet he still shone with authority. The Prince of Garridon.

He frantically scanned the ruins and every person in the vicinity, searching, until his eyes locked on hers. Elisara did not realise she was running until she collided with the hardness of his body. Caellum pulled back, cupping her cheeks as he scanned her head to toe, pausing at her lips before resting his forehead to hers. Elisara melted into his hold, calmed by his presence.

"My star," he whispered. "I was so worried." He gently placed his lips against hers, and Elisara sighed at the comfort only he could provide.

"Why?" She stared deep into his eyes, and at the fear settled deep within them. As his gaze flitted to the ruins, she knew who he feared for.

"I was told the guards at the Hybrook watchtower had seen two Vala Princesses enter the city with the King this morning. They could not tell if one of them was you, and then I saw the smoke." He swallowed hard, averting his gaze.

"Caellum, look at me." Elisara cupped the side of his face and brushed her thumb over the scar above his cheekbone, which she had caused as a child. "I am okay; I am with you; I am here." She smiled, and he returned it. A smile that grounded her in amongst the terror winding its way towards her heart.

A deep, arrogant voice cut through their moment.

"If you two are done with your spectacle, I need to speak with each of your Commanders or Superiors to align our reports."

Elisara flinched, refusing to give him the satisfaction of looking in his direction. Caellum understood and kept his eyes on her as he called forward Sir Cain. She did not need to say anything for Vlad to step forward, another reminder the Vala Commander had not obeyed her order.

"I assume that means there's still some bad blood between the two of you." Caellum sighed.

Elisara looked toward the group, now being steered by the Commander of Keres. "You could say that" she muttered, glaring at his back. She picked at the skin around her fingernails.

"The feeling is likely mutual," called a delicate voice. They turned to the speaker, who rested in the shadows of the nearest street.

"And I see you are still choosing the shadows over life as a Princess," Elisara retorted. The voice huffed.

"Like I had a choice in the matter."

The owner skulked out of the shadows. Covered from head to toe in black, stood Nyzaia, the Princess of Keres. Only her amber eyes were visible. She allowed the covering to drop, revealing her grin at the sight of her friend. She adorned black fitted leathers, sheathed with countless knives, and moved her petite frame gracefully towards Elisara, like the smoke in the air. Elisara embraced her, and as Nyzaia stepped away, she removed the remaining fabric from around her head and pulled out her braid. A near imperceptible flicker of movement crossed in the alleyway in which Nyzaia emerged; she had suspicions about who accompanied her.

"How are you not overheating in those leathers?" Elisara gestured to the smoldering ruins, which the Garridon and Keres military had extinguished with gallons of water filtered through a contraption linking to the city's supply. Nyzaia laughed.

"Did you just ask a daughter of Keres how she is managing with heat? I can walk through fire, Elisara. Even if I cannot do it while in this city, I relish in the flames."

They could not be more different, Elisara thought. Ice and fire. Yet maybe that was why their friendship worked.

"I better make my presence known," Nyzaia complained, dragging herself forward towards the Commander of Keres, who stood by the smoldering ruins. No Keres soldier paid her the slightest attention, she rubbed the nape of her neck and glanced down, clearly grateful for the lack of attention. While Nyzaia never chose the life her father bestowed upon her, it was evident the Princess of Keres preferred to keep away from prying eyes and had done for so long, that even the soldiers of Keres did not know her face. The Commander did not bow as she reached him, and Elisara rolled her eyes, having never understood how Nyzaia considered him a friend.

Elisara's remaining guards came running from one of the western streets, scanning for Elisara. When they found her, they shook their heads, their faces stern. Immediately, she knew. Her family were not at the safe house. Elisara tried to suppress the rising fear as she turned back from her guards and to the ruins before her.

Caellum seemed to clock the shift in her stance, how her shoulders tensed, and the unfaltering of her expression. If only he was able to read her mind, too, then perhaps she would feel less alone with her fears. Elisara looked at him in a silent ask about his own family, to which he shook his head. They turned to the ruins, their grip on one another tightening. Smoke from the banished flames curled lightly around the blackened sandstone, and Larelle no longer walked atop the ruins. She sat back on her heels, head down, with her hands folded in her lap.

At the same moment Elisara noticed the Princess of Nerida, the Commander of Keres did, too. He whispered to Nyzaia and unstrapped his golden armour, which differed to Keres' traditional military wares. He wore similar black leathers to Nyzaia underneath; the leather molded to his broad chest like a second skin, emphasizing his stride as he approached the ruins. He readjusted the knot, pulling his dark locks back and tucked a loose strand behind his ear.

The Commander climbed the wreckage, his body swift as he expertly avoided the loose stones rolling in his path. He continued to climb with hands coated in soot until pulling himself atop the ruins into a crouch. Cracking his neck, he loosened his shoulders and walked round to Larelle, but halted as he looked down within the Temple. Elisara assumed it was filled with rock, but grief struck the Commander's movements. His muscles tightened and his jaw clenched, as if struggling to keep his emotions in check.

"Nyzaia!" A half-strangled shout emerged from his throat, and the Princess looked up at him, confused, as the Commander bent to one knee. Elisara's breathing hitched as she watched from below, and Caellum stiffened beside her, jaw clenching as they watched on. Nobody moved, unwilling to accept what they all knew was coming next. Elisara's panic spiked; she was no longer able to suppress her fear. The Commander bowed his head and lifted his right fist, holding it to the left of his chest. Time stilled, the breath on everyone's lips halting, their limbs rooted in place. The Commander was performing Novisia's sign of respect—respect for those no longer living. The silence seemed to last forever, but it was only mere seconds before Caellum and Elisara sprinted to the ruins, and they, too, began climbing in the path Nyzaia nimbly left them as she expertly sped up the stones.

The King of Keres was dead. Elisara felt it in her bones. There was no one else the Commander would show such emotion for—no one else he respected as much. Caellum reached the summit behind Nyzaia and stretched to pull Elisara over the remaining rocks. As she steadied herself, she noticed the tremble in Nyzaia's body, who instinctively reached for the Commander's arm to steady herself while looking into the crevice below. Elisara could not see around the large stone blocking her eyeline, but spotted Larelle on the other side of the opening, whose face was still as she peered down, despite a single tear rolling down her cheek.

Why is she crying? Elisara thought. She navigated around the debris as Caellum fell to his knees, too, but not in respect. His face crumpled, his hand flying to his mouth to contain a sob. Elisara followed his eyeline into the crevice below.

There, in a perfect circle, lay the Royal Chamber of the Temple.

The ruins fell perfectly, allowing sunlight to stream in as the smoke cleared. The enormous solid stone table, which once sat resolutely in the centre, was now cracked in four. Each broken slab fell outwards, and there, trapped under the northern stone, trapping their lungs, and cutting off their breathing, was the King and Queen of Keres, accompanied by Nyzaia's three brothers. Their faces were a mask of peace, as if lulled into a slumber. Elisara struggled to recall their names as a haze clouded her mind. To the East were Caellum's parents, the King and Queen of Garridon along with all six of his brothers and sisters. Her knees weakened as she saw the twins, Edlen and Eve, their sweet innocent faces a picture of peace.

Perhaps they felt no pain, Elisara hoped. Her eyes watered as she recalled the times spent with the twins and Auralia, the sisters Daeva and Katerina had never been. Elisara struggled to look at Caellum. Grief ripped him apart. She rested a hand on his shoulder, then looked south at the King and Queen of Nerida, and their son, his consort, and their child, barely five years old.

She continued her gaze, her heart quickened as her eyes scanned the destruction, mouth drying as she blinked back tears. Elisara squeezed her eyes shut, knowing who would be found trapped under the western stone. She willed it all to be a nightmare, in which the shrill voice of Katerina would soon awake her from. Clenching her fists to control the mounting panic, she slowly opened her eyes. There lay her parents, King Arion and Queen Vespera of Vala, along with her two sisters. All appeared as serene as the other bodies: still, trapped under the stone, with hair spilling around them but no clothing out of place.

Elisara was the final one to drop to her knees, covering her mouth to stop the same strangled cry as the Commander from escaping. She could not do this. She could not allow grief to consume her. Elisara needed to see them, to feel for any air from their colourless lips and know for certain they were gone. Her father raised warriors; he could not be taken so easily. How could she manage her pain without him there to guide her? She needed to check their bodies for signs of what transpired, for anything to help the confusion rattling in her mind as to why all royal families attended such a trivial meeting, and why they were now dead.

The Commander rose, likely to warn Elisara not to do anything reckless, yet she held no respect for his commands. Surveilling the west of the summit, she noted the gradual descent of stone, a staircase crafted of destruction.

"Princess, don't even think about it!" The Commander of Keres snapped, tone laced with venom. Elisara ignored him and stepped carefully over the fallen stone carvings, searching for weak spots but her entire existence could be a weak spot to her realm. Especially if the bodies lying below her did indeed hold no more life, and so she gave caution to the wind. Elisara jumped, and it was as if the air encouraged her forward despite its lack of power in the city. Her military training prepared her for such tactical maneuvers, and she exhaled all worry from her lungs. Yet Elisara's confidence soon slipped as her foot caught on a loose stone. Caellum screamed her name as she wrapped her body in on itself and rolled against the impact of the jagged rocks beneath.

Elisara's body jerked to a stop as something cushioned her fall. She coughed as dust filled her lungs. As it cleared from her vision, she opened her eyes fully, face to face with the ice-blue eyes of her father, not yet faded with death. That was when the strangled cry finally escaped her. Dragging herself up, her hands braced the sides of his lifeless face. No air gently caressed her cheek as she bent down to listen. Elisara's sobs continued as she checked over her mother and sisters, their crowns toppled from their heads and black hair splayed around them. It all fell into place then. Her family was dead. The King and Queen were dead. The heir to the Throne of Vala was dead, and as was the second-in-line. Elisara was the only one left. She screamed and reached for the stone trapping her father, failing to push it from him.

"No!" she cried, batting her fists against it. "No, no, no!"

She could not do this. She could not be alone. Her screams

muffled as Caellum's arms pulled her close, holding her as the grief poured from their bodies. Elisara thrashed against his hold, desperate to return to her father's side, as if staying close to him would somehow bring him back. But there was nothing Elisara could do except watch as the glow in his eyes faded.

She did not know how long she had sat cross-legged in the dust, staring at her family. At some point, the other two heirs descended into the crevice, too, and sat beside their own. Nyzaia leaned against the wall of rock, twisting her dagger into the stone floor while staring at her brothers. Caellum knelt by his youngest sister and moved the hair from her face, while wiping the tears from his own, quick enough that only Elisara noticed. Then there was Larelle. No tears graced her cheeks. Instead, she straightened the clothes on each family member with pursed lips and adjusted their crowns. Aside from the Commander, the people in the room were the last remaining members of the royal families: the only living heirs.

"You left in a hurry," Elisara choked, wiping her tears. She looked to Larelle's feet then their gazes interlocked. She was not sure what to make of the banished princess. Growing up, Larelle was the quiet, levelheaded one, but Elisara knew firsthand how much one experience could change a person. She wondered if the banishment had changed Larelle.

"I saw the smoke."

"How? It would be impossible to spot it from the beaches of Mera."

"I was not on the beaches," Larelle said. She rose from kneeling and brushed the dust from her skirts. "I was at a home positioned at the top of the cliff. Working."

Elisara stared back down at her feet and said nothing more.

"Does the fact I need to earn a living make you uncomfortable, Princess Elisara?" Larelle asked, tilting her head. Elisara cursed internally for questioning someone she did not realize was so blunt.

"Not at all. I just did not expect to see you here." Elisara commented.

Larelle's eyes pierced hers, and Elisara could have sworn they darkened for a moment before flashing deep blue. Elisara knew of the reasons behind Larelle's banishment, and while she had not agreed with the expulsion, who was she to question the King and Queen of Nerida? She wondered if Larelle hated her family after all that transpired.

"Neither did I," Larelle responded. She pursed her lips before turning to inspect the wreckage.

Amongst the silence, Elisara heard the commander's footsteps as he hunted for any signs of the cause—any remains to bring justice to this tragedy. Elisara was no fool. This was no accident. The perfect display of the royal families gathered in the centre of the ruins was an orchestrated affair; there was no doubt. Elisara was unsure why someone would want to kill all the royals—or nearly all of them. No recent tensions existed, and it seemed clear the attack was planned by someone outside of the families. She glanced back at Larelle, who appeared the only one with a motive, but dismissed the thought. There was no chance the calm, sweet girl she once knew would orchestrate such an event.

Caellum knelt behind Elisara, drawing her from her thoughts as he wrapped his arms around her middle. He buried his face in the curve of her neck.

"I am okay; I am with you; I am here," he whispered.

Tears pooled in her eyes again, she allowed them to spill. No one here would judge her for it, except the Commander she was determined to ignore. The three other bodies in this darkness were three grieving children—four young royals now bound by tragedy. Elisara moved to bury herself in Caellum's cloak until the sound of moving rock had her alert. Caellum tensed, having heard it too. Nyzaia looked to the Commander while rising to her feet; he withdrew his sword, searching for the source of the sound, and Elisara followed his lead.

In the tunnel's distance, another sound emerged. Small stones tumbled from the false wall, where beneath it, a tunnel lay—a hidden tunnel to allow the families a chance to escape in case of attack. The tunnel that should have saved them. The attack must have been sudden, for no one to have reached it in time. Elisara stepped forward with Nyzaia close at her side, but the Commander held out his arm. Elisara jumped at his proximity, then tossed him a glare before silently brushing his arm away. He narrowed his eyes, pointedly looking at the cracked floor she had been moments from stepping through. Taking a few steps back, she leaped over the fissures, and landed in a silent crouch. She glanced pointedly at the Commander, though his longer legs allowed an easy step over the cracks until he towered over her.

"You and the others are the only surviving heirs to your thrones. Dim your incessant need to prove your worth and let me handle this before any more royalty dies today," he hissed, then proceeded into the tunnel. Elisara flinched at the truth in his words, but persevered all the same, following close behind. Nyzaia too.

"Don't worry, Elisara. If anyone is going to jump at the chance to end their line, it's me. I don't want to be Queen." Nyzaia's stoic look was devoid of sarcasm.

Her life will be so different now, Elisara realized. She glanced at Larelle behind; she had not followed but was likely considering her own change in circumstances. Elisara had been groomed for life as a royal, and while the reality was yet to sink in, she would adjust, just like Caellum would. As children, they had all attended the same lessons as their siblings, but Nyzaia and Larelle's lessons were cut short, raising questions about their suitability to rule. Elisara and Caellum were the only two the Historian had consistently nurtured and tutored. The very Historian the Commander now pulled from the rubble as Elisara rounded the corner.

Chapter Nine

Nyzaia

Every second Sunday, that was the rule. As a young child, Nyzaia never understood the need to visit the Historian when she had countless tutors in Tabheri. She did not complain, though. It was one of the few occasions to escape the stifling palace that was once her home. She would relish their breaks throughout the day, immersing herself in the Plaza markets outside the Temple and often returning late back to the lesson, always scolded by the Historian.

The Historian devoted centuries to living in books and old buildings and looked exactly as one would imagine. No one knew his exact age, only that he descended from one of the earliest families of Ithyion. The history books explained that all who lived on Ithyion were blessed with a prolonged lifespan. Magic was at its strongest then, which aided in his life's longevity compared to the average lifespan of the present day. Magic faded when her ancestors fled to their new Kingdom.

Nyzaia's father said the Historian was nearing the final stages of life, yet in the years Nyzaia had known him, he had barely aged. The Historian's bright white hair was slightly faded, the lines etched into his face more prominent, and his hunch more noticeable. Despite his appearance, he had the sharp wit of someone Nyzaia's age: a trait he still possessed, it seemed, as she watched him bicker with Kazaar at a distance. He scolded the Commander of Keres for handling him like a child as he tried to pull him from the rubble.

Caellum leaned into Elisara. "I don't think the Commander

knows much about the old man."

"Kazaar does his best to avoid the Neutral City at all costs. He definitely does not know how to deal with Wisp." Nyzaia retorted, glancing at Elisara with a smirk, who did not return it. Nyzaia's own smile faded, realizing her ignorance of her friend's grief. Nyzaia felt grief, but not for her family. She doubted others would understand one could grieve for more than death but grieve for losing the familiar—the loss of life as she knew it, the loss of herself, and all things she expected changing now her parents and brothers were dead. Nyzaia was the last heir to the throne of Keres—a throne she did not want. She preferred to rule the Kingdom of the Underworld instead. No emotional connection tied Nyzaia to her family and had not for years. She resented the word, and at the sight of their dead bodies, she grieved for her own life as it combusted into flames before her. She glanced at the man they dubbed Wisp, who was coughing up dust.

The affectionate pet name was coined by the group whenever stray pieces of hair fell from the nape of his neck: a telltale sign whenever he was angry with them. It was rare for the four heirs to be together in one place, and ever since Nyzaia stopped attending, they had drifted apart, with Larelle banished shortly after. Over the last few years, they had met at inconsistent balls across the Kingdom, yet no one had become as distant as Larelle. Even now, she stood still among the dead bodies, and stared at the setting sun.

"She was always the dreamer." Nyzaia turned to the wise voice beside her.

"Hello, Sir," Nyzaia bowed to the gentle old man covered in dust, his dark eyes mirroring the void behind him. The Historian had successfully shaken Kazaar away and now brushed dirt from his tunic. Kazaar stepped back with a clenched jaw at the dismissal. Nyzaia knew he found this difficult; he hated being anywhere other than Keres, training with his soldiers or lounging with the Red Stones. She smiled at the man she considered a brother, more so than the dead bodies that lay nearby.

"No time to waste, Nyzaia. We must get to the safe houses; your family's is closest. We go there first." he said. There was no need for formalities with her.

Nyzaia glanced at the others to see who would break the news. Elisara looked at Caellum, whose expression was as grim as her own; his eyes, too, were red-rimmed. Nyzaia wondered if he grieved for his parents as well, or only his siblings. She looked back at the old man—the man who helped found this entire land yet knew nothing of the hand it was dealt. Words escaped her as he edged round her. Nyzaia moved to catch the old man, who slipped against the brick as his frail hand reached for purchase, but Caellum was nearer and quick to support him. Nyzaia rolled her eyes at Kazaar's reaction. It did not go unnoticed the Historian did not brush away the prince's kindness.

"I'm... I'm okay." The man's words were barely a whisper, but Nyzaia caught the waver in his voice and the gulp in his throat as he processed the loss of not only the rulers he advised, but the children he nurtured to one day take the thrones. They were family—his only family—and grief hit him as much as it did the others.

Kazaar broke the silence and moved forward, dominating the space.

"I need to ask you some questions, Historian," he stated gruffly. There was no trace of emotion on his face, except the slight twitch of his eye as a strand of black hair loosened from its tie and fell before his dark eyes.

"At ease, Commander. I'll tell you everything I know, but then we have plans to make." The man sat on the stone beside him, eyes fixed on the King of Keres. "Razik." He nodded towards the King, whose amber eyes stared unblinking at them all. "We were nearing the end of our usual discussion of trade when he highlighted reports of civilians loitering around the tunnel exits. He suggested the tunnels could be compromised and asked I checked them. I had no reason to question him, though it was unusual he asked me and not a guard stationed outside. I thought little of it. The Temple is my home. It is my responsibility. As we neared the end of the meeting, I rose to do as he asked." The Historian paused, as if contemplating his next words. “Razik started a conversation with Wren while I entered the tunnel.” He looked briefly at Nyzaia, then Caellum before continuing. “That's when I heard the beginnings of an argument, but what was being said, I do not know.” Nyzaia faced Caellum and noted Kazaar doing the same.“The next moment, there was a ringing in my ear and total darkness. I assumed the explosion was only in the tunnel and King Razik's report had been correct; I thought only the tunnel was compromised. I never... I never imagined the entire chamber would be destroyed and that all..." The Historian trailed off; eyes fixed on the King of Keres.

"His timing of the request is odd, is it not?" Caellum asked.

Nyzaia's head whipped towards him, narrowing her eyes in the way she reserved for her targets. "After all, the King of Keres is known for his love of fire and destruction." Caellum continued. It took Nyzaia seconds to move to Caellum, her face angled sharply upwards to meet his eye. Familiar hands clutched on her bicep as Kazaar silently suggested she step back.

"What are you suggesting of my people, Prince?" Kazaar asked coldly.

"Your people? Last time I checked, *Commander*, you were a bastard, lucky enough to be taken in by the Queen and handed military advancement on a platter. Nowhere in your name is a royal title." Venom laced Caellum's voice, and Elisara pulled at his hand. While Nyzaia was grateful for her friend's attempt to calm him, she wished she did not have to. Nyzaia had never been a vocal advocate for Elisara's betrothal to Caellum, for reasons relating to his ancestor's.

"The people of Keres belong to Kazaar as much as they belong to me," Nyzaia's voice adopted a deadly edge.

"I did not wish to give you reason to doubt King Razik or the people of Keres." The Historian interjected. "One might question if he was protecting me. Perhaps he realized something else was unfolding and wished to get one of us out."

Too many questions, Nyzaia thought, and Larelle voiced the most prominent.

"Why was my nephew here? He is—" She paused. "He *was* five years old. He had no more reason to be here than Prince Caellum's younger siblings." She gestured to Caellum's three sisters and three brothers. Caellum's demeanor shifted then; his opinions of the Commander seemingly forgotten as he glanced back at his siblings with pained eyes.

"Your brother brought Nile with him as his caretaker was sick. Your sister-in-law trusted no one else to take care of him," explained the Historian gently, before shifting his gaze to Caellum. "As for your siblings, your brothers were here to learn strategy meetings while your sisters used the space to practice needlework. The upper rooms were in a state of repair, something that had not been communicated to them prior to arrival." The old man's eyes fell to Vala's princess then, anticipating her questions. "Elisara's sisters always attend these meetings, as do Nyzaia's brothers." Shock flitted across Elisara's face, yet Nyzaia was more concerned the Red Stones had not discovered her brothers' attendance and relayed the information back to her. It was useful to know for placement of her syndicate throughout the realm.

Debris crunched underfoot as Larelle turned from the group towards the body of her young nephew on the dirt-ridden floor. *Would she wish her family dead?* Nyzaia wondered.

"I would like to return their bodies to Nerida as soon as possible. Their bodies need to be soaked in the rivers before we send them to the sea." She knelt and dusted her brother's tunic, though she had already devoted her time ensuring they were pristine.

"Did you bring guards with you, Princess?" The Historian asked.

She rose from kneeling and moved back to the group with

clasped hands. Anyone would think she was destined to be Queen, emulating both authority and patience—someone who commanded respect. And yet they all knew the unspoken history of her relationship with her family.

"No, I travelled alone." She confirmed.

"I can spare some Soldiers, Princess. They can cross back into Garridon from Seley after they have returned your family, if you will allow it?" Caellum offered. A kind gesture, Nyzaia reluctantly thought. It was not wise for Larelle—or any of them—to be alone. Nyzaia feared this explosion was the beginning of something bigger. Larelle raised her brows, yet her expression quickly softened.

"Thank you, Prince Caellum. I would be grateful for the offer. But please, they may return by boat from Trosso to Asdale on the Garridon coast. It will be quicker to avoid the rivers inland."

Nyzaia glanced at the dead bodies trapped beneath the table slabs; her parents and brothers would have to be transported back to Tabheri. She wiped her sweating palms on her leathers, and Kazaar eyed her closely. He gave a stern nod. He would handle it. Nyzaia was in no position to be furiously demanding answers, or to sob endlessly like Elisara. She had to break the news to her true family. She would move into the Palace of Tabheri permanently and abandon the life she had built.

"We will need to spread messages, your Majesties." The Historian rose, and Nyzaia cringed at the title reserved for only Kings and Queens. He began hobbling towards the incline, where they had all descended: the only way in and out of the cavern. Kazaar insisted on climbing first, and Nyzaia followed with Elisara, each supporting an arm of the Historian. Larelle gracefully navigated behind them while Caellum protected the rear. The rocks stayed cemented in place, as if they had accepted this was the new way of things. Accepted that, like the royals climbing from its midst, the Temple would remain broken forever.

Chapter Ten

Larelle

Larelle clutched at rocks as she emerged from the crater of ruin. A hand touched her own, and she glanced up at Elisara, a fleeting moment of shock passing through her as their fingers intertwined. The Princess of Vala assisted in pulling her from the rubble.

"Thank you," she murmured, rising to stand upon the edge of the rocks, until she looked out at the setting sun. Smoke had cleared from the city, and from their vantage point, the four heirs saw the extent of the damage. The central point of the city was gone and no other buildings surrounding the Temple stood intact. The Plaza, once home to the boisterous market, was now an expanse of rubble and stone. Larelle struggled to picture it as it was before; she had steered clear since her banishment. Her only memories were those from her lessons with the Historian.

The Keres soldiers and Vala guards joined Garridon's military in maintaining a perimeter around the Temple, preventing the citizens from coming too close to the ruins. The people made no noise and expressed no anguish; they stood in stoic acceptance, awaiting to hear the extent of the devastation. While all citizens here lived in neutrality, they all hailed from different realms and each respected the rulers of their homelands. All would have to adjust to the changes—or lack thereof—that came with new rule, but Larelle feared the citizens' response upon learning of Nerida's new queen. All eyes below turned upwards to the four heirs, who bathed in the glow of the setting sun, as though the Gods wanted to highlight the dirt and devastation streaked on their faces as they stood shoulder to shoulder, their heads high. On their left, The Historian approached, wasting no time with poetic words and sombre expressions.

"On this grave day, we acknowledge the deaths of King Razik and Queen Nesrin of Keres, and their sons, Prince's Kessem, Amir and Kavean."

Nyzaia lowered to one knee, her hand clutching her heart as she stared straight-faced at those in the crowd who lowered for her and Keres. Numerous citizens bowed, their dark hair, warm skin tones, and loose fabric an indicator of their birth realm. Among the throng of people, it was a struggle to place those from Nerida. Instead, she turned to watch Nyzaia and the Commander kneeling side by side, the Commander's free arm braced around Nyzaia's shoulder. Having never met the Commander before, Larelle pondered the extent of their relationship.

"We acknowledge the deaths of King Wren and Queen Hestia of Garridon, and their daughters: Princesses' Auralia, Eve and Edlen, and their sons, Princes' Halston, Dalton, and Kieren."

Larelle's pain from earlier re-emerged. *How horrible for children so young to be taken so early*, she thought. She hid the emotion from her face, not wishing to take from Caellum's moment. A tear bled from Elisara as Caellum kneeled beside her, and every one of his guards did the same. The guards' movements did not sway the citizens from crossing the boundary, who stood solidified in their united grief.

"We, too, acknowledge the deaths of King Adrianus and Queen Oriana of Nerida; their son, Prince Aalto, their daughter-in-law, Consort Meera, and their grandson, Prince Nile."

Larelle placed her hand over her heart but did not kneel. She held no respect for her family and only raised her fist in a solitary tribute to her nephew. Several citizens kneeled, signifying those of Neridian birth, their faces rife with confusion—confusion about her identity, about her disrespect, and what this meant for Nerida. Larelle stared only at the setting sun.

“And finally, we acknowledge the passing of King Arion and Queen Vespera of Vala, and their daughters, Princesses Daeva and Katerina.” As Elisara knelt on the jagged rock, she blinked back floods of tears, which Larelle suspected would fall the second she was alone. Elisara's emotion spoke to the close bond she must have shared with her family, something Larelle had not known for years.

"In their death, I stand with the honour to represent the people of Novisia until the new King and Queens are crowned. Rise Nyzaia, future Queen of Keres; Caellum, future King of Garridon; Larelle, future Queen of Nerida, and Elisara, future Queen of Vala."

The three heirs rose to join Larelle who remained standing without a trace of regret. Below, the crowd rose. Larelle glanced back at the citizens, remembering those who kneeled for Nerida. Banished for six years, she somehow felt more connected to the citizens of Nerida than she ever would have while remaining as a Princess. After all, she lived their experiences, their hardships, and needs. For Larelle, this moment was momentous for the Neridian citizens to recognise her position as future Queen.

Perhaps she could improve their lives, yet fear overwhelmed all hope. Fear as to who planned this attack and whether more were to come; fear she would now have to navigate life as a new ruler, while protecting her people from the threat posed against Novisia.

"All hail the heirs," called The Historian, at the citizens overcome with emotion.

"All hail the heirs."

Chapter Eleven

Elisara

Caellum wove his fingers through Elisara's hair and down her neck, washing away the reminders of their day. Dirt-stained water glided down her chest and bled into the water, quickly becoming redundant for cleaning. After rising from the broken temple, with the citizens kneeling below, Elisara left Vlad in charge of ordering the remaining guards while Caellum escorted her to Garridon's safe house. She remembered little of the journey, only his muscular arms around her body as her legs gave way to grief.

"Up," he spoke into her ear from behind. She reached for the towel beside him, but Caellum guided her to the second bath instead.

"This is your bath," Elisara said, looking up at him.

"My Queen can have as many baths as she needs until she is well-rested from the day and washed of all sadness," Caellum kissed the top of her head and helped her into the second bath. *His Queen*, Elisara thought, a term she could easily become accustomed to hearing from his lips.

Struggling to focus, she thought of facing her people atop the Temple, flooded with memories of sneaking from lessons and running through colourful tents housing delights from each realm. One of her guards dragged a man from the rubble, and she felt the pain of every citizen who witnessed it. While the rest of the Kingdom stood, their home had fallen, and Elisara did not know where to begin to lead them through such sorrow.

She sunk into the water; grateful Caellum was so attuned to her physical needs as she focused on the heat of the tub rather than the grief pushed to the back of her mind. He reached for the soaps on the windowsill.

"What would you like to smell like, my Queen?"

That name again, Elisara mused. She understood his tactics for avoiding pain, and during her visits to Garridon, she began to learn when the King had hit him, as Caellum often used affection as a distraction—a technique now in overdrive.

"You," she replied softly. He chuckled.

"All in good time."

She waited for him to decide on a scent; he put thought into every decision made for her. Sweet peas, he chose, and she smiled softly at the memory as he lathered up the soap in his palms.

Caellum waited until her eighteenth birthday, as it was *proper* for a prince to kiss his betrothed only once she was of appropriate age. Elisara's only birthday request had been to spend it in Garridon with Caellum before leaving for her two years of mandatory military training. Knowing her love for dancing, he hosted a ball in her honour—the only acceptable display of status a prince could offer his betrothed. He told her as much while imitating his father's words.

Elisara had rolled her eyes, indignant at being told where to be, what to do, and what to wear, but it was all worth it when she descended the floral staircase in the most elegant Garridon gown, crafted of emerald green satin. The off-shoulder sleeves billowed in the breeze, emulating the sway of the grasses in the fields of Stedon. The sweetheart neckline perfectly caressed her chest, and the lack of bone corset freed her curves as the skirts fell like a waterfall around her feet. Caellum had picked it. In the days to follow, she would stand in the sweltering heat of Keres, but at that moment, the only heat was that which flushed her cheeks as Caellum's eyes darkened at the sight of her, shimmering with devotion.

They danced late into the night, avoiding politics to bask only in each other.

At five years old, many suitors for Elisara were presented to King

Arion, but she made comments on all of them—ridiculous, silly names prompting a chuckle from her father. Yet with Caellum, she simply said *he has nice eyes*, and that was enough to save him from the stress of finding alternative suitors. Elisara always wondered why her father cared so much for her suitor when his own marriage held no romance.

On the evening of her eighteenth, her father danced with her once: the only occasion Caellum left her side. As they danced, he told her to take every opportunity to live her life, and so she had. At the thought of her father, her mind flashed to his body, lifeless in the Temple. She blinked away the image.

Elisara had fled the castle before sunrise, guided by Caellum. Whereas he knew the location of every tree root in the Kingdom, Elisara stumbled through them all after one too many sips of Neridian wine. After tripping into the forest clearing, she froze. On the horizon, the cliffs of Garridon met the sea dividing the land from Doltas Island. The sounds of crashing waves reached Elisara, carried by the air, while saltwater speckled her lips. Yet what stopped her short of breathing was the hundreds of acres of sweet peas gently blowing in the wind. The scent floated all around her now, weaving into her memories: flowers the purest of whites, the softest of lavenders, and flushed pinks.

It was there, in a field of sweet peas, Caellum did not just kiss her but told her everything she had ever wished to hear from a man—from him. He loved her. When she leaned back from the kiss, intoxicated by the taste of his lips, they were a light rouge, tinted from her lipstick.

"I could count every petal in this field, and it would still not reflect the number of days I have spent waiting for you." He kissed her again, the morning sun their witness as Elisara surrendered her heart and body to him. Ever since, he sealed every letter with a single sweet pea stem. Even now, two years after her military training, Elisara was certain that memory was the only thing that kept her going. Keres changed her—the *Commander* changed her—and it was the last time she had been her complete self with Caellum. Memories haunted her now, threatening to consume her in the smallest moments of happiness as she feared hurting those around her. To hurt Caellum.

"What thoughts are you lost in?" Caellum asked. The roughness of his hands raised the hairs on her body. She breathed in the scent of him—fresh morning grass and sandalwood with a layer of smoke settled into his skin.

"My eighteenth birthday," Elisara murmured while relishing his touch. Caellum's hands gently washed the remaining suds from her body, running them up her legs, and knowingly stopping short of the apex between her thighs.

"Mmmm, I will harvest that entire field of sweet peas for you, my Queen, and fill the chapel with them on our wedding day." He kissed her foot before placing it back in the water. Elisara stood and walked into the large towel he held, embossed with the golden symbol of Garridon. She knew what he was doing. All these reminders of them and their future were to keep her from wallowing in the day, but Elisara was not a pretty Garridon flower to be swept away with the storm. She created storms and would not be defeated in her grief, yet she smiled at his suggestion, eager to make him happy.

Their relationship had not always held such a level of intuition. As friends, they had known everything about one another, yet navigating their relationship as courting, then betrothed, was more difficult, even more so after her time in Keres. Elisara returned hardened, unwilling to share her concerns or insecurities. It had taken Caellum the past year to break down her walls, or so she convinced him. The reality was they were still there, but she had perfected hiding it, as she now tried to.

Each step taken from Caellum's arms and to the bed by the far window reminded her of each step into the Temple ruins before falling and facing her father. She could not close her eyes for long, as every time she did, his eyes were all she saw—lifeless and pale blue—eyes once so loving and gentle. She remembered the gazes of the citizens before bowing their heads: a sea of mourners, a sea of uncertainty. They were her people now, and she was responsible for their lives. The fire kept the memories at bay as she avoided thinking of her mother and sisters, using it to centre her pain.

Shouts drifted from the street, and Elisara jumped. What if it was another attack? What if more people were dead? With a quickened pulse, she listened, waiting, but no further noises came.

Caellum approached, and she leaned into the curve of his shoulder, focusing on the roughness of his hands against her skin.

"What do you need, my star?" he whispered against her ear, sending shivers up her spine.

"You know what I need."

Elisara's hand gripped his thigh behind her as he kissed the hollow of her ear. He continued his trail of kisses along her neck and down her shoulder, resting his hands on her waist to move closer. She felt his immediate arousal. Shattered ice captured her from the moment. She clenched her eyes shut, yet the memory was replaced with a flash of lifeless blue eyes, now haunted by the present day instead. Her urgency for distraction quickened.

Dropping the towel, the heat from the fire uncomfortably brushed her skin. Caellum groaned as he ravished her bare flesh with his eyes, her curves creating silhouettes against the walls. Focusing on the feel of his fingers, she sighed as they traced tantalizing circles up her stomach until reaching her nipples and squeezing gently. She once relished his worshipping of her, but it was difficult to bear now. She still remembered, and she wished to forget.

Elisara turned in his arms and immediately brought his face to hers with force yet saw only his realisation upon finding his family dead. He still tasted of smoke; the ash not yet washed from his skin. She tried to push the darkness from her mind and home in on the taste of his tongue, the taste of home, of him. Her hand glided over his cheekbones and into the mess of his hair, tugging with desperation. She pressed closer, guiding him to the wooden four-poster bed behind that drowned in green cushions and silks. Pulling his tunic from his waistband, her eyes snagged briefly on the toned muscles of his stomach, and the strength in his shoulders. The back of his knees hit the bed and she pushed him down with more strength than usual. Looking down at him, Caellum leaned up on his arms, and his eyes trailed down her naked form, which now climbed to straddle his waist.

A whimper escaped Elisara as the rough fabric of his trousers met her sensitive skin. She rocked as Caellum guided her hips, but the distraction was not enough. She rose to her knees, and moved to tug his trousers, but was interrupted by his fingers which found her most sensitive spot, heightening her need for him more. His fingers slipped inside, and she moaned, relishing in the sensation.

But it was not enough.

Elisara moved his wrist, allowing access to his trousers which she quickly untied to free the length of him. Guiding her hand up and down, his eyes closed, but shot open when she, unannounced, seated herself on his him, groaning as he filled her. Her head fell back, her hair grazing his thighs.

"Fuck," he groaned.

Elisara rode him at her own pace, relishing every sensation and controlling every moment. His hands gripped her waist to guide her, but after lacking control all day, she wished to regain it—something that would not surprise him; it was always her preference these days. Pinning his hands beside his head. She fell forward with the motion. Flipping her hair to one side, she watched his eyes roll as she rose and fell to chase the building friction. With her hand, she reached down to the space between them and teased the feeling from herself as Caellum's pleasure built. He was close, but she craved release first: a guarantee she might find some peace and sleep tonight. Elisara rose off him and quickened the pace of her own hand as the heat rose within her core. As he saw her come undone, Caellum gripped her hips and pushed her down, allowing her to pulse around him as he culminated in his own pleasure.

She stayed atop him, resting her head into the crook of his neck as his hands stroked her behind, squeezing gently before caressing her back. With a sigh, she rolled off him onto the many cushions adorning the bed. Neither of them said a word, but their hands joined loosely between them. This was often how sex ended with them in recent years. Quiet and quick. The satisfaction of the distraction wearing off. She wondered if she was the only woman to find a lack of passion in it. Comfortable with the familiar safety of a partner rather than the act itself. Her thoughts began to wonder, the lack of control in her life returning. She analysed the objects of the room to keep her mind busy.

The Garridon safe house was not much different to Vala's, designed to blend in with the narrow-terraced buildings of the Neutral City. Whereas the Vala safe house was filled with whites and ice blues, furs and silvers, Garridon's was dark wood, opulent greens, and bursting with flowers.

"Today changes nothing," Caellum finally broke the illusion of normality and gazed out the window into the darkness of the Neutral City. "I still want you as my wife and as my Queen. I want you by my side in fifty years when we have rebuilt this kingdom; I want us to stand in this very city and look back at this moment." He turned to her, but she continued staring ahead.

Elisara wished for nothing more than to live every dream Caellum fed into her soul. She craved the wedding in the chapel full of the sweet peas he promised. She wanted late night dancing on balconies and the air kissing her skin while he kissed her lips. She wanted to forget the pain of tonight and that which had lived in her for the past six years. But deep in her heart, Elisara knew. As prince and princess of neighbouring realms, they could fulfill their fantasies. As a King and Queen, they would be allowed no such pleasure. This moment would not be one looked back on with fondness, but grief as they mourned for their families, and the loss of their first love.

Elisara knew she was selfish, though, instead of voicing what she knew to be true, she turned to him and simply said, “I love you.”

Chapter Twelve

Larelle

Larelle loved the sunrise, relishing the peace and quiet as the waves washed over her feet and dawn slowly broke. She spent the entirety of her childhood forcing her parents awake to take her down to the shore, then most of her teenage years sneaking past the guards to reach it. What started as a way to breathe in the morning, and prepare for the dramas of court, soon became a way to breathe in *him*. His smell, aura, his entire being. He changed everything. Yet what was once a promise of the future was now a reminder of the hole in her heart, the missing piece left in her past.

Larelle was in her late sixteenth year when she met Riyas, and it was love at first sight, though she cringed to describe it as such. She had gracefully descended the stone steps from the castle, not yet coated in water as the tide made its way in to surround Mera, Nerida's capital. The peninsula could be spotted from any coastal point in Nerida as it stretched far from the rest of the realm as if surrendering to the seas. Larelle halted on the bottom step. There, in the usual empty spot in the centre of the beach, sat a lone figure. She almost debated turning back; she did not like to be interrupted when alone on the sand, and this person likely felt the same, but then water gathered around her feet.

Larelle had frowned, peering at the ocean water caressing her toes and slowly climbing her ankles in tendrils, despite the rest of the tide remaining where it was. A small smile graced her lips as she realised the lone figure controlled it, willing the water to dance up and around her calves. Pulling her hands from where they rested behind her, she glanced at the figure on the sand. With a quick flick of her fingers, she directed the tide to him. She had not met many others who mirrored her abilities to control the water. He must have been a Lords son, or someone whose relatives were loosely connected to the royal line in the past. He intrigued her, and her breath caught, recovering from the strength she exerted.

When the water around her legs had retreated, she strode the length of the beach, sand filing between her toes. The closer she stepped to the figure, the more she saw of him. He was around her age, his long legs stretched out as he leaned back, propped on his elbows. He tilted his head back to bask in the rising sun, his shoulder-length brown locks falling behind him. Larelle had never seen him before, but in that moment, she would never forget him. A tug pulled gently in her chest, as if an acknowledgement from the Goddess Nerida herself that this young man was the other half of her soul. No words escaped as she finally reached him; instead, she sat beside him in silence and pulled her knees to her chest, resting her chin upon them. The unknown feeling brewing in Larelle's chest appeared to be mutual as he turned to look at her, pulling the ribbon from her hair, and allowing curls to fall down the open back of her dress.

The water yanked Larelle from her memories as it brushed over her toes. She did not bother to move, but lazily flourished her hand to usher the waves around her instead. One of the minor adjustments in her life now: the ease with which she could control her power. A greater change was that of becoming Queen—something she neither expected nor wanted. Having hidden away the past two days, Larelle assumed the Neridians did not want her as Queen either. How could they, when her own parents deemed her an embarrassment, unworthy of royal life?

The people loathed her brother, and liked his wife even less, so she doubted they would change their views for her.His blatant displays of superiority, and the way he leered at the citizens in passing, were only two of the reasons they abhorred him. The same could be said for her parents, too. Larelle was the only one in the family to not develop such an ego. Despite Larelle and Aalto's closeness growing up, all that changed the moment Meera entered the picture: the daughter of the Lord and Lady of Amoro. With the legacy of the largest and wealthiest wine vineyard in Novisia, Larelle's father was quick to arrange their marriage. Greed initiated their arrangement, and Aalto and Meera became the embodiment of it. Larelle, however, knew she had the right morals to be a Queen, but her strength abandoned her the moment she lost *him.*

"Mumma!" a tiny voice called from behind her. There was the reason for her family's embarrassment, the reason the people might not accept her as Queen.

Zarya—now the Princess of Nerida—bound across the sand, unruly black curls flying in all directions. Her daughter's eyes of midnight blue, *his eyes*, glistened with pride at whatever she had to tell her mother.

Larelle was with Riyas for one wonderful year of passion and love before he was called to the seas. Riyas was a sailor for the Neridian fleet, with the ambition of one day becoming captain. With such a goal, he could not turn down requests to leave for sea. Larelle planned on telling him about her suspicions of pregnancy when he returned from his week-long trip, seeking a trustworthy physician to confirm it in the meantime. But Riyas never returned. Her final memory of him was the smile on his face as he waved goodbye from the ship; she gently rested a hand on her stomach, her soul alight with joy while beaming at the father of her child. In that moment, she had no fear of the repercussions.

But now, here she was, an unmarried mother of a fatherless child, and Queen of Nerida. King Adrianus had ignored her desperate cries. "I love him!" she had screamed.

But his ultimatum was clear.

If Larelle kept the child, there would be no place for her in the royal family. He did not go as far as publicly exiling her, having hoped to avoid further embarrassment. Though gossip quickly spread, and instead, she was given a day to find somewhere to begin her new life.

It did not take her long to seek the only person she trusted. Olden. Riyas' father. Taking one look at the growing bump, he pulled her into his arms and allowed her to cry until she slept. Ushering her awake the next morning, Olden said, "He would want you to see it at sunrise," and she almost broke down again hearing someone reference her love.

Olden had walked out of his small home in the centre of The Bay, with Larelle's hand resting on his arm. They walked along the shore until stopping at a small house at the edge, the last house before the sandy beaches separating The Bay from Mera Castle.The pale stone was much like the other houses neighboring it, all lined up in one neat row. Yet this house looked new, the stone less worn, and the front path less overgrown with moss. The pebble veranda offered a welcome spot to sit and watch the sea. It was perfect.

"He bought it for you the first day he met you on that beach," he told her. "Every day, he would come and work on it: building, painting, until he said it was as perfect as you." Olden handed her a key. "You can stay with me as long as you like, but this—this is where you and his child belong, in a home built from his love."

Larelle did not know what to say. It had been one of their dreams whenever they explored how different their lives would be if she was not of royal birth. She shared with him her wish for a small home at the end of The Bay, so they could spend their afternoons strolling the shops and their evenings drinking wine by the sea, beginning their mornings walking out of the door and onto the beach where they met. That was the home their daughter, Zarya, ran out from now as she charged towards her mother.

Larelle caught her daughter in her arms as she tripped. For five years old, she was a tall child and regularly fell over her feet. Brushing the curls from her face, she stared lovingly into those midnight blue eyes. Larelle had always been mesmerised by Riyas' eyes, a trait Olden claimed came from many generations ago when the families of Novisia still lived on Ithyion, a sign they were kissed by the Goddess of Nerida. How different life might be if her ancestors had never fled Ithyion but remained living on the land of their gods, where everyone could connect with the power of the water, not only those with royal blood in their veins. Yet seeing those eyes the moment her daughter was born was the confirmation Larelle needed. While Riyas was lost to the sea, he was always with her. It was odd Larelle's eyes now matched, eyes which had always been a stormy grey, but since inheriting the full power of her family, they had changed. When Larelle used her power, her gaze mirrored the dark shade of her father's.

"What do you have in your hands?" Larelle asked, watching the way Zarya clutched them tightly to her.

"It's for you. I found the perfect shell!" Zarya giggled and opened her hands, revealing a carefully crafted silver bracelet lined with tiny shells. Larelle smiled. Olden must have taken Zarya's enormous collection and given in to her wishes of making jewelry with her.

"It must be the most beautiful bracelet I have ever seen!" Larelle exclaimed, clasping it to her wrist. "I will never take it off." She promised, placing her hand gently on her daughter's cheek.

In the distance, Olden exited their small home. It was time. Larelle turned, and sure enough, nobles exited the castle in the distance and residents from different regions across Nerida gathered on the beach, all dressed in the dark blue of their Goddess.

Larelle rose carefully, brushing the sand from her dress. She wore the only ceremonial dress she owned, the one worn on her eighteenth birthday when she broke the news to her family and was forced to leave. Now, at twenty-four years old, it still fit, which was unsurprising given the small portions of food she scavenged. Larelle grasped Zarya's hand and walked towards the gathered crowd. She had been in two minds about bringing Zarya, afraid of what the Lords and Ladies in attendance might say. But Zarya was their princess and would one day be their Queen. While Larelle did not have the strength to face more judgment, she had the strength to be a role model for her daughter.

Eyes burned on her as she approached the crowd. Head high and shoulders squared, she demonstrated to Zarya what they had practiced, and the young girl copied. Larelle could not keep the smile from her face as she admired her daughter's behaviour, despite having never learned the ways of royal life. The smile was short-lived, wiped away as she met the eyeline of the crowd. Lord and Lady of Amoro's reproachful looks towards Zarya did not go unnoticed. Her eyes moved, now focused on the five wooden boats sat along the shore, and at each of the faces within. She had not seen her mother for years since her banishment until looking down at her body in the ruins. Her hair was the same pale brown as she remembered, resting above her shoulders. Beneath the stone table, her petite build seemed delicate, her hand clasped in the King's; it had looked so pale against the dark complexion of her father. Not one of her father's braids were out of place, meticulous in his appearance even till the end. His dark blue eyes still appeared full of resentment, yet Larelle felt nothing for her family. Except for the boy. While stories rumored Nile's insolence, she would not wish death on a child. Against their stomachs lay greenery from across Nerida: olive branches and grape vines intricately woven into a bouquet.

Larelle moved around the boats to face the nobles and the crowd in the distance. The crowd was not large, and she recognized most families as those favoured by the King and Queen. Her eyes paused on a younger man she recognized from childhood, the only one who offered a smile of encouragement. Larelle kept her face still and continued searching through the crowds. Few general citizens were present, though that was unsurprising. She nodded to the priest, who began his prayers.

Paying the prayers no attention, she focused on the feel of her daughter's hand and the water behind her. The only happy memories of her family were from before she met Riyas, but Zarya and Olden were her family now. She would not dwell on those who treated her as less or cast her aside as if she was nothing. When five men approached the boats to push them towards the shore, she realised the prayers had concluded. Larelle said no words and turned her back on the crowd, a clear sign of how she felt about her family and the nobles who stood behind.

Eyes seared into her back as the boats entered the ocean. She could almost hear their thoughts, willing her to fail in this, too, and prove she was unworthy. But Larelle, the Queen of Nerida, was far from unworthy. Reaching down to her father's neck, she pulled the talisman from it, and the necklace hummed in her hand, in recognition of its new ruler. When the royal families of Ithyion fled from war to Novisia, each took a talisman created from the land itself. The new lands held no link to their origins, so the four settled rulers decreed to halve their talismans and keep one half hidden somewhere in their realm, and the other around the neck of their King or Queen. Garridon's talisman was carved from the wood of the first tree planted on their land, and for Nerida, the stones from the riverbed. Keres' was metal forged in their fires and for Vala, a talisman carved from the rock of the highest mountain peak. In the same way the four realms were named after the four Gods creating their land, the talismans were sourced from lands blessed by them.

The talismans rooted the royal families' power when they left Ithyion: the only elemental connection left. The talisman amplified the ruler's lineage power, and by placing the other half hidden in the land, allowed those with distant royal blood to access their power too. Most importantly, it fostered the environments of the realms to ensure they lived as they had on Ithyion.

Larelle recited this information from memory, recalling the many additional history lessons her father had forced upon her growing up, explaining the workings of the talisman and how he needed it to balance his power. As she tied the talisman around her neck, and felt it press into her chest, a calm wave overtook her body. Her power swam through the rivers of her veins, flooding her completely until she felt whole, until the talisman recognised her power and amplified it.

Gently, she lifted her hands and outstretched her arms, and, with the smallest movements, the ocean rushed forward and dragged the boats into its clutches. Intakes of breath resounded from behind; they sensed her power. Larelle was strong, but it was not common knowledge; in fact, she always bested her brother when it came to her powers: a fact her father ignored. But now, in their death, all power had passed to her at once and settled into the comfort of her own.

Upon the death of the King or Queen, their power would pass to the immediate heir, yet no one could have ever predicted what was to happen if all rulers and heirs passed at once. Now it was clear. Larelle possessed it all. People respected power, but would they respect the person who wielded it? She assumed not.

Larelle watched as her movements controlled the water and wished for nothing more than to sink the boats now and be done with the spectacle, but some part of her knew not to alienate herself completely. She would need to win the support of some nobles to make her life bearable. The lack of words from her was already insulting enough. She willed the water to pull the boats further into the sea until they were merely dots on the horizon. Then she let go.

Where will they drift to? She wondered. The same thought she had of Riyas' ship, lost at sea. There was a certain irony to her father sinking in the same way Riyas would have, submerging into the depths of the ocean to be consumed by the creatures dwelling in the distant seas.

"Mumma," Zarya whispered, tugging her hand. "My back hurts."

Larelle stifled a laugh, knowing all too well the pain of keeping up pretenses.

"I know, sweet girl. We will go in a moment."

"What happens to the bodies in the boat?" Zarya's voice was

hushed, a girl beyond her years, who understood when to quiet her thoughts.

"Scripture states the Goddess Nerida is looking down upon the sea and will determine if they are worthy, and whether they will be pulled into the oceans of the afterlife, sink to the ocean floor, or be left to wander the world for eternity."

Zarya frowned.

"Where is my papa?"

Larelle's heart clenched. Being killed at sea meant there was no ceremony, thus the sea would have claimed him. But how could she reveal that to her daughter so young?

"Your papa was taken to the oceans of the afterlife, where I'm certain he waits for us." Larelle's explanation did little to wipe the frown from Zarya's face, but she turned back towards the crowd. The Nobles had parted, allowing a clear path to the castle—the castle she had not stepped foot in for just over five years. She wondered how much had changed, if the grey stone was more worn, or if the water had carved away at the foundations of the castle with the grand staircase leading into the ocean. Tomorrow, she would stand on those stairs and be crowned as she descended into the dark depths, reborn as the Queen of Nerida. Nevertheless, the castle was not her home, and neither were these people.

Larelle turned from the formed path. With Zarya and Olden, she walked back to the small home on the edge of The Bay, and as she did, she noted the sneers from the nobles she was now to rule. But that challenge came with the sunrise, and for now, she would enjoy these last quiet moments with her family.

Chapter Thirteen

Elisara

Elisara secured the silver clasp to the back of her hair and pulled the tendrils from her face. She smoothed the skirts of her mother's dress, the signature blue of Vala, and clasped her hands before her. The thick embroidery restricted Elisara's chest and stomach, and while she would be far more comfortable in one of her own gowns, she wished to wear something of her mother's. She wore her father's sigil pin, too, and it glinted on her chest as it caught the light of her mirror. The lords and ladies might respect her more if she appeared as her mother had.

Closing her eyes, she remembered her parents standing behind her as they offered Elisara her own pin. "You wear this with pride, Eli. No matter where you are, you represent the realm. It is your duty." Her mother said. Shewould have plenty to say on the matter of duty now.

Closing her eyes did not remove the image of them. She still saw them, but in their final state on the floor of the temple, as her mother's imaginary words rang in her mind.

"We're ready, your Highness," Vlad called from the doorway. Elisara remained in her usual chambers, despite the entire guard insisting on moving her to the late King's quarters. She smiled softly at Vlad; two days ago, he was joking with her, and no formalities existed between them. Vlad took his duties seriously; he now served a future Queen, not a princess with no ruling desires. Elisara hated the sudden formality, but he was not the only guard acting differently. She nodded, and they exited the chambers: hands clasped by her middle, exactly as she was taught, but had ignored so many times.

The halls were different, colder, as if the air itself recognised Vala's great tragedy. Every servant she passed stopped and bowed, paying respects to their future Queen, but also her loss. She wished they took the route down the narrow stairs of the turret instead, but the advisors insisted she should be seen throughout the castle. The truth was, Elisara hated her home now. Around every corner was a reminder of her family, each room she passed brought back endless memories: fights with her sisters, afternoon teas with her mother, court advice from her father. Every step through the hollow halls echoed an aching reminder of them.

She reached the top of the grand staircase and surveyed the sight below. Her father's advisors stood to the right, the noble families of Vala to the left. A breeze filtered into the foyer through the wide-open, arched doors. The wealthiest citizens gathered beyond the threshold, clothed in the colours of Vala: pale blues and storm-cloud greys. Some adorned flowing fabrics to feel the kiss of air, while others shielded from it, having married into the realm.

I cannot do this, she thought. *There are too many people.*

Elisara could not break in front of them. She could not repeat the mistakes of her past. Vlad nudged her arm kindly, urging her forward, the slightest acknowledgement he was still there for her. Holding her head back, Elisara relaxed, and descended the stairs.

Once she was at eye level with those surrounding her, more guards appeared and the doors to the East Wing opened. Out strode the ushers. White coffins rested upon their shoulders, carrying the members of her family. Elisara stared, unmoving, and as they glided through the doors, her heart yearned to join them. She waited, as instructed, until the ushers reached the citizens; only then did the noblemen follow, then the advisors, and finally, Elisara and the Queen's guard.

A cascade of bodies descended the path, winding around the mountain to the cemetery located at the mouth of the mountain. Rows of headstones carved from mountain rock stood in militaristic lines, protecting the site in the centre which housed the tombs of the previous royals.

Who are they here for? Elisara wondered. Her parents? Sisters? More likely themselves, in the case of the nobles. Only two days had passed, and countless condolences had since flooded in from the nobility, who ended their sympathies with unsolicited advice or requests. She would prefer the advice of her few friends in the city.

Elisara questioned if they might change too. Like Vlad.

Life had slipped through her fingers without her realizing, and this new life—one of constant monitoring—hung over her, like the storm clouds brewing now.

The sky was clear when she awoke, the air crisp as she stepped onto the balcony. Yet the weather seemed to change as she dreaded the day to come. Her mood darkened and the winds rose, the bite of the air sharpening, and the clouds rolling in.

No records existed in history where more than one ruling member or heir died at once. Lord Ader had been quick to inform her of that upon her return to the castle. Caellum, Nyzaia and Larelle likely faced the same problem, too: no knowledge or guidance on how to harness the intensity of the power passed to them.

Elisara felt it nearly immediately, when she had sworn, she heard voices in the wind, even in the Neutral City. It had been confirmed when they journeyed back through Vojta. Once outside the Neutral City, everything was amplified. Every sound was crystal clear, hearing conversations of those in the distance with little effort. The combustion of sounds was deafening, but Elisara had no control of it.

Even now, the clouds above darkened as her frustration mounted. Elisara closed her eyes and saw the flash of crystal blue. She adjusted the itchy collar of her gown, eager to be in thinner fabric to embrace the icy winds on her skin, in reassurance she was not alone.

"Look at her fidgeting. So out of place."

Elisara's eyes snapped to a woman near the front of the procession, who turned with a smirk. Noble birth, it seemed, if the silks of her dress were any indicator. Elisara pulled her hand back from her neck, balling her hands at her sides. She focused on calming her breathing to soothe the anger that had spiked along with her heightened power. She had little time to regain control as the procession fanned out upon reaching the cemetery. Elisara's panic rose as she thought of the last time she lost control, worrying this would be a repeat of the mistakes she made in Keres.

The remainder of the citizens arrived and created a half-circle perimeter which curved around the outskirts of the graves until reaching the mouth of the ice caves beneath the castle. Nervousness etched on their faces—the same nerves she felt when told the rite would go ahead as usual. After the explosion, so many people in one place was concerning. A gathering this large would be a perfect opportunity to target individual realms. Elisara kept her face neutral, a show of bravery to the people.

From where she stood, the stalactites in the caves of the mountain glistened as they melted in the summer air. That same dripping water would be harvested over the coming months for its healing properties and traded across the realm for other items. Little snow coated the headstones, and a sheen of water trickled across the ice mausoleums. The scene only confirmed the unnatural way in which her family had died. A Ruler of Vala always passed in the dead of winter, the exception only being when the death was not natural.

Imagining what her father would do, she stood tall. Tuning out the whispers, she began her walk through the crowd to where the four white coffins lay. She noted the nobles: the skeptics, those who smiled with reassurance, and those who made no point in hiding their disdain. The others were the Lords who had not believed her when she spoke of the Neutral City. She wondered if any of the families may have survived had the military in Vojta been dispatched on her orders. Three reassuring faces peered over the back row of the gathered crowd: Helena, Vigor, and Talia. Her anxiety calmed for a moment. She wished it were a normal day at the tavern with them instead.

Elisara averted her gaze from them as she arrived at the coffins alongside the priest. He faced the crowd as he spoke.

"We gather today in the wake of unimaginable tragedy. We gather to honour King Arion Sturmov and Queen Vespera Sturmov, along with their firstborn, Princess Daeva Sturmov, and their second-born, Katerina Sturmov." His weak voice called. "The rite of death is presided over by I, Gregor Vernir, High Priest of Azuria, and Elisara Sturmov, Vala Queen in Waiting."

The reactions of the citizens, as opposed to the nobles and lords, were not disdainful, but mostly grief-stricken.

"Who would believe she is capable of creating a mausoleum from ice?" A man sniggered under his breath, standing amongst the nobles. But to Elisara, it sounded in her ear. Someone scoffed in the distance, one she could have sworn she recognized. The priest began the rite.

“Queen in Waiting and current Princess of Vala, Elisara Sturmov. Repeat after me.” Elisara nodded. “I, Elisara Sturmov, confirm the deaths of the members of the Vala Royal family. I bear witness to their passing into the distant clouds above, and know they are now at peace following the life they have lived and the death they have suffered."

Elisara's voice was hollow as she repeated the words, distracted, but unable to place why. “In creating and sealing the mausoleums, I hold myself responsible for the safety of their spirits and for their life after death. In Vala's name, I protect.” As she turned to the coffins, a cloaked figure moved in the shadows of the mountain—a fleeting movement, gone with a second glance.

Elisara reached with her power and called the air from the direction of the figure, but there was nothing to be heard on the wind. What if another attack was imminent? She frowned and returned to her duties, but since calling her power forward, all the whispers of the people surrounding flooded in every criticism, every doubt, every pitiful word. She closed her eyes to be met by piercing blue, then forced them open. Words floated to Elisara, too many to focus on.

The nobles watched, and the priest spoke, but his words were submerged amongst the others. He gestured to the coffins. She needed to encase them. The other mausoleums were simple ice buildings, no more intricate than a large block. That was all she needed to copy, but she could not focus, the surrounding voices creating a weight on her as she struggled to breathe. Elisara peered up at the blackening clouds and focused on them instead. It worked.

Wind whipped around Elisara's body as the clouds pulled from across Vala to above where she stood. Darkness fell as the sunlight was consumed by them. People gasped as snow floated from the clouds. Her father had never made it snow at any time other than winter and even then, only lightly. It felt comforting as droplets melted on her skin, but it was more than that; she felt it in her veins. What began as a gentle chill soon became ice cold, and before Elisara knew it, she was struggling to move, as though her entire being was turning to ice, burning, and branding her with it.

This is too much, she realized, at the same moment the citizens did. This was the strength of the power she inherited.

Elisara staggered, her power rippling from her body as pillars of ice bloomed from the ground, growing taller with each breath until standing above her and curving inwards, merging, and twisting. An interlocking barrier of ice was formed, with designs so intricate it was as though they could have been carvings from the temple in the Neutral City, before its destruction. Resting a hand against the pillars, it instantly thickened at her touch. Unlike the surrounding graves encased in thin ice, here stood a masterpiece. The ice stopped forming, but snow continued to fall, landing on the monument she had unwillingly built, encasing it in yet another protective layer.

Elisara stood back and brushed the snowflakes from her neck. She surveyed her creation. No one spoke a word. The voices silenced. Light applause sounded from somewhere within the ice stalactites of the cave, but the guards approached, preventing her from following the sound.

"Engraver," Elisara called, and a young man approached. "Apologies sir, it may take longer than expected with the depth of the ice."

"It is my honour, my Queen," he bowed his head.

"I am no Queen yet," she responded, staring beyond him into the cave.

'"That was no power of a princess, your Majesty. Coronation or not, you are our queen," Vlad responded from her side. Elisara turned to him as he, and every guard surrounding him, bowed, with the citizens of Azuria following suit. She noted the look of the nobles and understood their concern. That was the power of a future Queen without the talisman around her neck. What would she become with it?

Chapter Fourteen

Nyzaia

The Lord of Myara boldly ascended the marbled steps leading to the dais where Nyzaia was displayed upon her golden throne. She shifted in discomfort, knocking her crown from its position, then prodding it through her overly jeweled hair back to where it belonged. As a princess in her younger years, Nyzaia struggled to wear her tiara, but wearing a crown at her coronation she hated more.

Home to the Abis Forge, Keres was known for its intricate metalwork. The carefully intertwined golden flames forming the crown were no exception but served as a reminder of why she never felt destined for this life. The movement captured the attention of the nobles filling the hall of the palace, who avidly watched Lord Israar's approach, grateful someone had been forward enough to greet the Queen they knew little about.

Nyzaia sighed. The same thoughts replayed in her mind, as they had every day since finding her family dead. A week ago, now. She felt nothing at all as they paraded their coffins through the city of Tabheri, and nothing when their bodies burned. Only emptiness, grieving the life she loved and missing the people who she had spent every waking moment with. Her syndicate. Her real Family.

The Lord of Myara's confidence was short-lived as the captain of her newly formed Queen's Guard, Farid, reached Nyzaia first.

"My Queen, would you like me to escort you back to your quarters?" He leaned his head in indication of the Lord, and Nyzaia breathed a sigh of relief. Was it that obvious she needed to escape? Briefly, she questioned what her brothers would have done. It didn't take her long to realize; they had been raised for this role and would not abandon their own coronation dinner. Raised in the shadows, Nyzaia disregarded the opinions of nobles whom she knew everything about. She nodded stiffly to Farid before rising and rolled her eyes as everyone in the room did the same.

Awkwardly picking up the skirts of her carmine red lehenga, painted in golden thread, Nyzaia followed Farid into the cooler, tiled halls. She tensed as she strode the halls of the palace while the footfall of her Queen's guard trailing behind put her teeth on edge.

Now I know how my targets felt.

"Thank you, Farid, that will be all," she stated clearly as they reached the entrance to her quarters. "That will be all," she repeated before he insisted on scanning her rooms.

“Yes, your Majesty,” Farid nodded. “The commander would like to meet with you in the morning; he said it was important.”

Nyzaia nodded.

"Sleep well, your Majesty," said one of the female guards. Farid shot her a look for having addressed her, and Nyzaia left their bickering behind as she entered the chambers.

Closing the heavy door, she kicked the silk slippers from her feet and ripped the crown from her head, tossing them in the cushioned alcove to her right. She walked to the open archways, onlooking her private oasis at the rear of the Palace, backing onto the scorching sands of Tabheri. These were her rooms as a child before she was sent to the Red Stones, unfamiliar surroundings now. Nyzaia unclipped the many gold chains and jewels hanging from every visible part of her body. How they expected her to wear such an exhibit every day, she did not know.

The coolness of the tiles was a welcome relief beneath Nyzaia's feet as she crossed through the archways into the breeze, yet nothing compared to the respite offered as she sunk into the bath on the other side. Her mother would have reprimanded the disheveled pile of clothes she left on the floor as she submerged to relish in the peace and quiet only water offered. While water inhibited her flames, the scolding temperatures made up for it. For once, she envied the people of Nerida who found solace below the water's surface, with the ability to breathe within it. However, Nyzaia's rigorous training allowed her to stay immersed longer than most, savoring the thrill of stretching her breath to its limit. Finally, she rose and pushed away the black hair clinging to her face before it clung down her back.

Silence. Nyzaia relished it, and always had. When her brothers boisterously trained, courted, and learned the ways of ruling, Nyzaia watched. Hidden in the shadows, she listened to everything, fascinated by the inner workings of people's minds and actions. Her brothers lay dead in her memory beside her parents, and still, she felt nothing.

It was not long before the King realised Nyzaia moved unnoticed. Then when she bested her brother in a sword fight, clocking all the places he foolishly left open, her father decided to use her skills to his advantage. Keres' secret weapon. So began her journey to becoming an assassin of the Red Stones.

The Red Stones were notorious not only in Keres, but the entire kingdom. Their roots were founded long ago when the people of Novisia lived on Ithyion. Some said they began as common criminals; others alleged the first King of their realm, on Ithyion, assembled the group to spy on the rulers of neighbouring lands. All Nyzaia knew for certain was they dealt the cards of death, and she was their reaper.

Sixteen—the age she had been when her initial training with Commander Kazaar ended and she moved into the Red Stones Den, hidden in a rock face at the edge of Tabheri. Every soul in the secluded fortress knew who she was, yet not a single one of the Pillars cared—not the Spies, Dealers, or Courtesans, nor the Alchemists, Blades, or Torturers. People began their lives anew with the Red Stones, and in doing so, became rulers of the Novisian Underworld. Nyzaia was special, though. She was to serve the King and was not isolated to one avenue. No. Across six years, Nyzaia trained in all six pillars, proving her worth not only to the Red Stones, but her father too. In the last three years, since finishing training, she had been their ruler.

She hated him for it, for sending her into a world where she was forced to become a woman too soon: a weapon who felt nothing, even as people begged for their lives. But Nyzaia liked who she had become, which made her hate him more. But who was she now?

Nyzaia could be the greatest ruler; she knew all the manipulative tactics and methods to get what she wanted. Yet a small voice within urged her to continue life unnoticed, a trait entrenched in her bones.

Nyzaia felt numb, not just from the missing pieces of her, but from the frigid air rushing in, sweeping across the scorching realm. Leaning back, she allowed her hands to float, willing her flames to rise. The temperature heightened until steam rose from the bath, and as she lifted her hands from the water, flames escaped her fingertips and coated her palms. The blaze danced across her henna-covered hands, and up her arms until they reached the smooth metal talisman around her neck.

Nyzaia could not imagine life without the newly heightened power brewing within her now, having branded her heart and soul. She was eager to experiment with her new strength as an assassin, yet as a Queen, she yearned to display the extent of her power to the neighbouring realms: a glimpse of what she could do. Nyzaia had done the calculations. Caellum likely inherited little power without a true blood connection to the royal line, and while Larelle and Elisara were powerful, Nyzaia was sure her strength prevailed.

While war in Novisia had not occurred since the civil war broke out in Garridon, Keres needed to prepare. Having barely stepped foot back in Tabheri, Nyzaia had dispatched endless Red Stones to gather information. Yet no fresh information emerged, at least nothing The Historian had not shared already.

Despite the argument ensuing between King Razik and King Wren, Nyzaia knew little else. Nothing to implicate the Garridon

King for his involvement in the explosions. She would not be surprised if the man had taken after his father—another way to gain more power, which backfired.She sighed. There was little proof of anything, in fact, though many citizens would use the explosion as an excuse for war, blaming other realms without evidence.

A change of light reflected in the water—the slightest change, but enough for Nyzaia to sense someone in her chambers. She made a loud show of swimming further forward, turning as if to admire her surroundings, but gaining a better assessment of the rooms. Her robe hung from a pillar that made up the archways; it was the furthest from the door. The other pillars marked her vision: each offering a hiding place for whoever had entered. Nyzaia floated towards the towering stone, and while doing so, controlled the flames of the candlelight, which rose, casting more shadows throughout the room.

The slight movement was clear now as the shadows fluctuated behind the second pillar; their scent on the soft breeze gave the observer away. Nyzaia reached for her robe, unable to stop the smile gracing her lips. She hopped behind the pillar, before expertly ducking low, hooking the person's ankle with her foot. The body toppled, and Nyzaia gracefully pinned their arms above their head, straddling their waist.

"Hello Tajana," Nyzaia whispered, smirking. Her eyes met those of the beauty beneath her: eyes of a unique green which shone up at her, framed by dark lashes matching her dark chocolate-colored braid. The faint freckle above the right of her lip rose as Tajana smiled.

"Hello, my love," Tajana breathed, relishing the sight of Nyzaia sitting atop her, whose nipples peaked through her wet, scarlet robe. Leaning in, she planted a soft kiss on her lips. If Nyzaia was now Queen, then Tajana was her throne, and would happily be for the rest of her life. Tajana groaned into her mouth. Nyzaia was an expert in torture, and that was no different when it came to their evening adventures.

"Did you really think you could sneak up on me? You're becoming predictable, Tajana," she whispered, loosening the grip on Tajana's hand and dragging her fingers up to her throat, gripping it to force the woman's eyes to hers. Eagerness glinted within them as Tajana's eyes roamed her face and body.

"This is far too much leather for our kind of evening," Nyzaia said, frowning at Tajana's attire. She began pulling at the dark laces hiding the golden-brown flesh she desperately wished to see. "Maybe we should work on your ability to hide in the shadows, seeing as you've come dressed for a mission and are so evidently in need of training."

Nyzaia shifted and Tajana saw her opening; she propelled upwards and rolled, splaying the Queen below her on the cold tile. Her wet back against the marble made her gasp at the exact moment Tajana swept her fingers between the Queen's legs, back arching.

"Maybe you need to remember to be prepared, seeing as I have crept into the Queen of Keres' quarters undetected." Tajana countered, pushing her fingers into her.

"'Tajana, I am always prepared for you," she mocked. Nyzaia's wetness confirmed her jests, eliciting a moan as she moved against her hand, content with how easily she could become undone by her. Tajana mimicked the Queen's previous gesture, pinning Nyzaia's arms above her who reached to undo the laces of Tajana's leathers.

"Does a royal Queen taste as good as the Queen of assassins?" Tajana pondered against her neck, grinding against her queen's bare thigh. The friction of her leathers provided some relief to Nyzaia.

"Why don't you find out?" the Queen said breathily as she licked up Tajana's fingers. A groan escaped the assassin's mouth as she sat up, admiring the queen laid bare before her. They had been by each other's side for nine years now. Her father would have hated Tajana, though not because she was a woman—no, that was no problem in Keres. He would have loathed her audacious and brash nature.

"As much as I could spend all night between your thighs, the others are outside your chamber door, and I know you cannot keep quiet."

That had Nyzaia's attention.

"Why are you all here? What's happened?" She frowned, shifting into strategy-mode as she pushed back from Tajana to stand.

"From what I heard, a group of Red Stones successfully evaded every guard in the Palace and captured the entire Queen's Guard," Tajana smirked, strolling to the door. Nyzaia groaned.

"Tajana, you didn't."

Tilting her head back to the red ceiling, she sighed before pulling her robe closed and tying it more forcefully, following Tajana to the now open door. Sure enough, her entire Queen's guard stood in the doorway, each with a knife to their throat.

"Ah! Nyzaia!" a booming voice jeered. "I'd bow to my queen, but it would defeat the point I'm trying to make."

The voice belonged to Isaam: an excessively muscular man who now gestured to the captain before him, who instead seemed more concerned for the safety of his Queen. Nyzaia assessed each guard, her syndicate tended to take liberties in the process of disarming. Farid stared only at Nyzaia; his eyes of pale blue held warning, as if waiting for instruction to kill the assassins at their throats. The other guards looked fearful.

"And what point are you trying to make?" Nyzaia demanded; she crossed her arms, covering herself, though more for the sake of her guards than her syndicate.

"You need a new Queen's guard. These fools clearly cannot keep you safe," Jabir chimed in, the leanest of the men. He held the smallest guard effortlessly by the throat.

"Exactly. You have been Queen for only a day! You could have been killed," Rafik chastised, his hands tightening around the shoulders of the female guard he detained. Nyzaia did not know her name.

"Please, you all know I sensed Tajana the moment she entered my chambers," Nyzaia retorted.

"The point is, love, we want you to be safe. The Red Stones are the only ones who can ensure that."

At the mention of the notorious group, Nyzaia glimpsed the shocked reactions of her Queen's Guard. All plans of concealing her previous life were ruined. It was also entirely possible their eyes were widening at the lack of formalities between them all, too, realising their Queen knew the assassins well.

Nyzaia peered between them all; she would never hear the end of this from either group. The Red Stones would persist that she was unsafe in the hands of the Queen's Guard, while the latter would argue her relations with the Red Stones was dangerous. Their naivety was embarrassing, and perhaps that alone suggested they were unfit to protect her.

There's only one way through this, she decided, and the most entertaining one for her. Nyzaia feigned regality for her guards, though knew she would be mocked for it later by her syndicate.

"In this moment, I speak to you not as your Queen, but as Ruler of the Red Stones," The guards audibly gulped, earning scoffs from Issam and Jabir. "Understand this: if what you have learned this evening is revealed to anyone, I will personally kill all of you."

Tajana smirked at their fear. All knew the stories of the ruler of the Red Stones.

"We settle this in the way of the Red Stones. Through trial. Red Stones, you have two weeks to disarm every one of my guards on three separate occasions. If successful, you shall take their place." Nyzaia paused, eyes flitting to Farid, who she trusted would put up the best fight. "Guards, if you avoid being disarmed, you may stay. There are no other rules. This is fair game."

Tajana stared each one of them in the eye; the Red Stones would not play nicely, and the Queen's Guard would fail.

"Do we have an agreement?"

They all nodded.

Nyzaia inclined her head to Tajana, then towards the chamber door. As she turned to enter, the other Red Stones swiftly disappeared, the Queen's Guard left frantically scanning around them. Before Farid could say anything, Nyzaia firmly closed the door in place.

She had not seen Tajana since they left to travel to the Neutral City. Word of the explosion had reached fast through their network. Nyzaia's syndicate were the few people who made her feel something again, but Tajana... Tajana kept the fire from consuming her completely, and now she wished for nothing but to show her gratitude for that control over her heart.

Chapter Fifteen

Caellum

Caellum tried to centre himself, fixating on twiddling the golden ring around his finger, thinking of the tiny star engraved on its underside: a gift from Elisara when they were young. He closed his eyes and focused on his breathing, settling on the image of her in his mind and the sensation of the ring as it twisted. It did not work. Nothing drowned the surrounding noise or the uncertainties running through his mind. When his eyes reopened, he met those of a man on the other side of the room, dressed in dark green: the traditional Garridon colours. Caellum watched as the man turned back to his table and spoke in what appeared to be hushed tones as the rest of the table leaned in, sparing several glances at their new king.

Caellum guessed at what they were saying. He was not fit to be sitting on the golden throne, with the gaudy crown atop his head. He was not fit to be the King of Garridon. And yet, he was. For exactly six hours and thirty-three minutes, Caellum had been King. He had been counting to ease his thoughts. Six hours and thirty-three minutes ago, he stood before the oldest tree in Hybrook Forest with the Lords forming a circle around him. But when the Priest lowered the crown upon his head, it did not feel right, though not because the true crown of Garridon was lost in the civil war. No, it did not feel right because he was alone. The Lords suggested the coronation be private, like the crowning of his father. Caellum had not questioned their advice. They knew better than him.

He glanced back at the table of men, whose whispering relented, as they now drowned themselves in drink. Few friendly faces graced the great hall of Antor Castle. The voices and laughter bouncing off the vaulted ceiling and wooden beams were not ones he recognised. His sisters' laughter and brothers' bickering rang through his mind instead, and he found himself gulping back tears.

Weak.

That's what his people would think if they saw their King cry, no matter the reason for it. While Caellum was acquainted with the Lords sitting at the long table, he felt no fondness for them. Guards stationed the doors, as did Sir Cain, who surveyed the hall.

He wondered if the rowdy people stuffing the hall were citizens or distant relatives of Lords and Ladies. Perhaps they were people selected at random to fill out the room, as who would wish to attend the coronation dinner of a man undeserving of the throne? Halton should be the one sitting here, overseeing the celebrations. After all, he was next in line, and would know what to do. Caellum tried to embody him and straightened, lifting his chin in an attempt to appear regal.

He avoided looking toward the men again, but instead sought Sir Cain's eye, who stood directly by the door which would allow Caellum's swift exit when deciding he had enough. Sir Cain offered a firm nod, one Caellum returned.

It will be okay. Just get through the evening, Caellum told himself. *One step at a time.*

As he turned to survey the rowdy diners, a young girl weaved expertly among the tables. He smiled, reminded of Eve and Edlen yet again, a smile which soon faded as he thought back to the Temple: their green dresses coated in dust and ash, their hair blanketed the same. Still, he did not understand why they had been there. Why was he the only one left behind? Had his father loathed him that much?

Caellum wished desperately to see them again—to speak to them. The only way was in the gardens. His father and mother were buried in the royal crypts beneath the castle walls, as they would have desired. Yet Caellum wished for his siblings to be closer to the light, buried in the western gardens: a line of six traditional grey headstones, surrounded by flowers. Buried in the heart of Garridon. Irrespective of their weakened royal line, they deserved the same respect.

Caellum straightened his jacket and nodded to Sir Cain; he wished to leave. The gardens would be peaceful at this time, and he could be left alone with his thoughts and siblings.

Something wet hit his face as he rose, splattering the black velvet of his jacket. Shock overtook him for a moment as he stilled, trying to fathom what happened. The room fell silent. He blinked back the substance coating his lashes and wiped it from his cheek. *Mud.*

"For the true Queen of Garridon!" A man called. "For Queen Lyra!"

Multiple voices shouted then, echoing the sentiment. Caellum frowned at the mention of the Garridon Queen usurped by his grandfather.

"Take down the usurper!" another yelled. Caellum wiped more mud from his face and his vision cleared, sighting the man who whispered earlier, standing in the centre aisle with his green jacket bold beneath the candlelight. Caellum had no time to think as chaos ensued. More men and women rose from the benches, all dressed in dark emerald, clasping handfuls of mud. Guards flooded in and Sir Cain shielded Caellum as filth volleyed across the room. Dragged to the exit, Caellum looked back at the men and women curled on the floor while the guards beat them senseless. He said nothing as Sir Cain ushered him out and to his chambers.

***

Moonlight flooded in through the windows of the chambers. The Lords insisted he take over his father's rooms, but he refused. He could not sleep in the same place the man who hated him had. All he would hear as he lay in the king-sized bed would be the constant insults from his father on replay, having accumulated over the years. Light framed Caellum's silhouette as he stood before the windows, the darkness of his mind reflected in the long shadow spilling behind.

He rubbed the stubble growing on his jaw as he glanced across the Western gardens. His father never cared for it, and Caellum imagined the view of the plants and trees served as a constant reminder he was not of royal birth. Sir Cain had not allowed him to visit after the disruption of the celebrations, yet he supposed 'celebrations' was no longer the right word. What was there to celebrate? Caellum focused on where he knew the six tombstones stood amongst the wildflowers; even in the shadows of the trees shielding the moonlight, he knew where they were. After all, he had chosen it within the eyeline from his chamber windows, to feel as though his siblings were still here with him.

Mud still streaked Caellum's face and clothes, as he rubbed his hands together, the dried dirt crumbled to the floor. His father would have watched as the assailants were beaten, likely to death. But when Caellum glimpsed the guards and the feet meeting the stomachs and faces of their victims, he saw only himself at the mercy of his father.

His mind cast back to the meeting from before the explosion. Lord Gregor of Albyn mentioned someone wrote 'Usurper' on the castle ground walls. Caellum frowned; he had not realized the volume of Garridon citizens against his throne.

Have I been blind to miss such tension? He thought. He did not question Sir Cain and had no chance to. The second he was escorted to his rooms, Sir Cain left to investigate, and Caellum had been alone with his thoughts ever since.

He wondered how Elisara's coronation went and wished he had been there, but as King of Garridon and Queen of Vala, their own realms took priority. He needed to think of a timeline—a plan—for their marriage. A way to rule both realms while wed to one another. Surely a distant cousin somewhere could rule Vala instead? He could not bear to disappoint his father, even in death, and renounce his throne.

He shrugged off his jacket, the black of mourning adding to the shadows cast around the room as he tossed it on an armchair. He had blown out the candles in the room upon entering. The darkness was a comfort, the moon an observer, as Caellum stepped closer to the mighty windows—a staple in the Castle of Garridon—and stared across the gardens, past the few trees within it and the open fields offering an uninterrupted view of anyone attempting to approach the castle. He squinted, staring into the distance. Something flickered. A faint orange glow appeared past the fields, right where the walls marking the city of Antor began. He blinked. The orange glow contrasted that of the pale moon, a clash of who owned the night, and as the smoke rose, he was suffocating in grief once again, standing atop the Temple, and glancing down at his siblings.

Another attack, he thought. He was not equipped for this; he could not live in fear of another attack, knowing he was too weak to save anyone.

"Guards!" he shouted, whirling for the door. At the same moment, Sir Cain ran in.

"Your Majesty," he said, with a quick bow of his head. "Your presence is needed immediately with the Lords."

Caellum followed him into the hallway.

"No," he countered, "We must make for the city immediately. There must have been another attack," Caellum said, turning left while Sir Cain guided him right.

"The events in the city *need* to be discussed," Sir Cain whispered frantically, releasing Caellum's arm. Caellum peered down at his hand; Sir Cain would not have removed it so quickly if he were still the same lowly prince as before.

"Shouldn't I be there?" Caellum demanded. "Shouldn't the

people's King be seen helping and caring?"

The pair reached the doors to the council chambers and Sir Cain pushed them open; all Lords were present and seated.

"Trust me, your Majesty." Sir Cain told him, drawing out the golden chair at the head of the round table. "The city is the last place you should be right now." He backed away and took a position at the door. Slowly, Caellum seated himself and regarded the Lords of Antor, Albyn, Asdale and Stedon. Lord Alvan of Seley was not present, he noted, and assumed he was reporting to Nerida. Lord Gregor of Albyn gave Caellum a look of reassurance while the other Lords stared skeptically upon their new King, who forced himself not to look away as he recalled the times his father had belittled him before them. He cleared his throat.

"Does someone wish to inform me of what is happening?" he asked, forcing authority into his voice, like his father. The Lords shared a look before Lord Gregor spoke: the only one brave enough to, as he had been with King Wren.

"As you may have realized after the events of the evening, your Majesty." The young Lord fidgeted with his hands. "There are those in Garridon that do not believe you, or any of your family, should be on the throne." When Caellum said nothing, the Lord continued. "That has been the case since King Jorah took it."

"Dear God, boy, get to the point!" snapped Lord Ryon of Stedon, standing from his chair. He began pacing, and Caellum wondered whether to remind him to stay seated while the King did. He decided against it.

"It is a bigger problem than it used to be, your Majesty."

"In what sense?"

"Before, only a few citizens would dare to speak on the matter, but your father would always have them," He paused, glancing at the other Lords, "*dealt* with."

Lord Gregor looked away as he finished. Caellum knew what he meant.

"But since his death, there are those that believe you are an easy target to have removed. Hence why they are rioting in the city."

"Rioting?" Caellum exclaimed, standing from his chair. He walked to the window, trying to detect the orange glow from before, but the trees his father planted to block the view from the chambers showed little.

"Fires, looting, attacking those who openly supported your family," Lord Ryon explained bluntly. "This cannot continue. We need stability. We need to instill faith in the people that you are right for the throne. Otherwise, we will lose it." Lord Ryon approached Caellum, who surveyed his bold stance. The Lord was the closest to his father and held the strongest of opinions. From what he knew from castle gossip, he was also heavy-handed with those who disagreed with him. Caellum turned back to the remaining Lords.

"So, what do you suggest?" he asked, staring directly at Lord Gregor.

"The problem is rooted in the fact you are not of Garridon royal blood," he replied, a tremor in his voice. "But that can be addressed if you marry someone that *is*."

"I am marrying royal blood," Caellum said, his voice adamant. He glanced at Sir Cain standing by the door, who returned the look with sad eyes.

"You need to marry Garridon royal blood, not some brat in Vala you have pined over for years!" Lord Ryon scoffed. Caellum whirled, fury in his eyes.

"Utter one more word about my betrothed, and I will have you removed from your lands. Do you understand?"

The Lord smirked and sat back down. Caellum returned to his own seat, resting his elbows on the table, the wood worn from where his father did the same over the years.

"My father had anyone with a connection to the royal lineage exiled to Doltas. There's no one left to even entertain the idea." Caellum said, trying to reason with them.

"The citizens of Garridon do not view those on Doltas as prisoners. They would accept a marriage to a lady from the Island," Lord Gregor explained, offering a pleading look, as if desperate to end the conversation on a positive note.

"How do we even know anyone is still alive? The island was barren. How would they have survived it?"

Lord Ryon rolled his eyes.

"They were exiled because they had a connection to the earth and a loose connection to the royal lineage. It would have been easy for them to grow what they needed."

The man spoke with such certainty. This was not speculation, and then realisation dawned.

"You've sent an envoy already," Caellum concluded aloud, leaning back in his chair.

"There are two others we know of that have strong royal Garridon blood, your Majesty. You need to consider meeting with them." Lord Gregor tried softly.

"You may all leave," said Caellum, staring at the golden ring on his finger. No one moved. "Now!"

Sir Cain's breathing swallowed the silence as Caellum buried his head in his hands, with no idea what to do next. Yet there was one thing he knew for certain: he must settle the unrest but could not marry another.

Chapter Sixteen

Elisara

Elisara's head hurt, and it was all she could focus on while her father's crown dug into her scalp at her coronation. Her own was not yet ready, and while she insisted her tiara would be fine, the advisors were adamant she must wear the crown of a ruler. So now she sat, trying to focus on food instead of the silver crown hastily adapted to fit her head. The tailor had not thought to ask for measurements.

With a fork, she pushed the bread around her plate, unable to eat it as she wished to, not with all those eyes on her. Elisara preferred to enjoy her meals at the tavern at the lower end of Azuria with her friends, dipping bread in gravy rather than daintily pulling it apart like she was taught. Elisara was now the crowned Queen of Vala, and yet could not even eat as desired, let alone rule how she wished.

The advisors had been constant, from the end of the funeral yesterday until the morning of her coronation, discussing meetings with noblemen and new laws in urgent need of decree. Elisara was losing what little patience she had left; they were advisors, not rulers. Their attitudes would need to change, but she had not a spare moment to comprehend her new responsibilities.

She wished Caellum was here, yet he had his own coronation to attend. It was no surprise all the heirs' coronations had fallen at a similar time, yet she yearned for a friendly face instead of the halls filled with endless nobles, servants, and guards. Vlad was there, but his face was less friendly nowadays.

Elisara's hopes soon came to fruition, but it was not the face of a friend who announced themselves as the great hall doors flew open. Muttering swarmed the hall as women gawked at the male in the doorway, who adjusted his hood just enough for Elisara to confirm his identity. She glared; any panic overwhelmed by anger. The man did not heed the smile of his admirers or nod to the Lords. The flames in the sconces flared along the walls as his glowing amber eyes fixed solely on the Queen sitting upon the throne at the centre of the raised table. Alone. He moved fluidly in black leather, radiating authority as he strode down the centre of the hall, the light of the chandeliers catching on the gold of the blade strapped to his back. The black of his hair and darkness of his clothes were a stark contrast to the soft hues in the hall, the tone of his skin out of place amongst the sea of obnoxiously white noble families.

He did not falter in his gait, nor blink as his eyes remained locked on Elisara's, who unknowingly twisted a blade into the oak table. Several guards approached the intruder in formation. One stepped forward but was disarmed immediately, the towering man in black pinning him to the floor by his throat.

"I will not be disarmed, *especially* not by a guard so inferior they lacked the skill to detect my arrival in the castle." He spoke low, then released the man's neck. Gasping for air, the guard stumbled back into formation.The intruder removed his hood, glowing amber eyes now darkening back to their normal shade as the flames along the walls dwindled. The guards straightened, unsure how to handle the intruder. He slowly rose from his knees and faced Elisara.

"Hello Princess," he smirked, eliciting gasps at his lack of correct title, though Elisara was unsurprised; he had never been one for respect, especially not with her. Placing the blade down, she feigned composure at his presence, and leaned back against the throne.

"Hello, Commander."

The Commander of Keres took no notice of the correct use of his title, but it was not overlooked by others in the room who would commend their Queen's composure despite such rude intrusion. They did not know the reality. His title had been ingrained in Elisara during her time in Keres. Why Elisara's parents had sent her to train with Keres forces, opposed to Vala's, she would never know. It was there she spent two years of her life under the Command of Kazaar Elharar, the most ruthless Commander in Novisia, the King of Keres' personal torturer, and adopted son.

"How inconsiderate of me to ruin your festivities. I forgot you had returned to privilege since your service ended." He spoke with little emotion, while Elisara let out a humourless laugh.

"Are we to talk of privilege, Commander? When you have been fed, watered, and granted your position from the late King himself? Was it not his Queen that took in a bastard child and raised him with the same privilege he now mocks me for?" Her tongue was ice, unthinking of the many nobles and citizens present to hear such spite. Focused solely on him, the Commander was a great point of distraction from the memories threatening to invade.

His eyes narrowed a fraction, having hit him on one of the few things he took personally. In their years of training, she had watched and learned everything she could about the Commander, which made this game they were playing even more entertaining.

"I'll forgive the many laws you have broken by being here, Commander, as an unauthorised envoy of Keres. State your business."

"Forgive me, Princess, but it appears I have broken no laws as I am no longer Commander of Keres."

Muttering from the guests resumed as Elisara frowned, trying to gauge the angle he was taking in their verbal sparring.

"It would appear the Gods do not favour me, the same as your Lords, it seems." He did not bother to look at the men who held strong opinions against him. Elisara glanced at Vlad, searching for guidance on how to diffuse the situation if it were to get out of hand. Vlad appeared stone faced as he nodded to his Queen. He had a plan if she required it.

"It would appear my late King has reassigned me. An agreement was forged and signed with your parents." The Commander paused; jaw clenched. He appeared to dread his next words, as though realizing he could not take them back once they were out in the world. “I am to be Commander of Vala."

"Ridiculous!"

The current Commander of Vala rose unsteadily to his feet and struggled to stay upright. Elisara refrained from rolling her eyes. The man was a renowned drunk and had already fallen lower in her opinions having failed to aid at the Neutral City.

'"I assure you, if there was any other option, I would take it. Here," The Commander handed a parchment to the closest guard, who glanced over it before approaching Elisara. The broken red seal was typical of the King of Keres. She unravelled the parchment.

I, King Razik Elharar of Keres, do by decree upon my death, and the death of the King of Vala, King Arion Sturmov, that Kazaar Elharar, Commander of Keres, be reassigned as Commander of Vala.

The same words were repeated by Queen Nesrin below, and then her own mother and father. Lastly, beneath their signatures lay Nyzaia's, signed by the new Queen of Keres herself. She, too, had approved of her father's wishes. Elisara frowned.

Why would they all agree to this? She thought. Especially her father, who knew of the powerful feelings she held against the Commander since her time in Keres.

The Commander remained unyielding, eyes locked on her: the last possible man she would ever want in her realm, let alone in a position of power. She pictured him stood atop the Abis Forge in Keres and shivered at the harsh reminder.

"Lords," she commanded, rising from her throne, a clear demand for her advisors to follow as she left the hall. The guards escorted her upstairs to a private sitting room, steering clear of the strategy room housing Vala's military secrets. "That will be all. Vlad, you may stay." She dismissed the guards while Vlad stood on alert to her right.

The Commander stood opposite as the Lords filed in to stand on his left, and she handed over the decree, allowing each a chance to read it before arguing ensued. Elisara listened intently to their different deliberations, but her eyes never left the Commander's. Lord Adar feared he was a spy for Keres, while Lord Petrov argued he could be useful to improve Vala's defenses in light of the explosion. Another even alluded to the odd timing may implicate his involvement, but throughout it all, the Commander remained still, arms crossed. Matching Elisara's stare.

"What I'm hearing is we are undecided," Elisara huffed, breaking up the discussion. The Commander's eyes never left her. She tried to match the determination there, but those eyes held so much more. They were a reminder of pain and fear, and the memories that shaped her into who she was now. How could she face those reminders every day? "Nyzaia has allowed this?" Elisara asked.

"Yes," The Commander gave a reluctant nod. "She did not wish to go against one of her parents' final decrees, regardless of whether she understood their reasoning." The leather gloves shifted as he clenched his hands.

"And you want this? You would not rather work below a new Commander in Keres?" she questioned, confused by his and Nyzaia's motives. The Commander uncrossed his arms and leaned forward, placing his hands firmly on the table between them.

"That was not my late King's request, nor that of my Queen. We are not all defiant of rules and decrees, Princess."

Elisara narrowed her eyes, considering his words.

"I would like a moment alone with the Commander," she said to the room. The Lords did not argue upon receipt of the look she gave them. "You too, Vlad." Knowing better than to fight, he left alongside them.

"I'll be right outside the door if you need me." He spoke clearly, ensuring the Commander heard.

"She does not need any guard to keep her safe. I trained her." The Commander told Vlad, though looked only at Elisara. She sensed

Vlad's shock. Everyone knew she trained in a different realm, but not where she trained, or with who.

For a long while, neither spoke, both remembering the night she mounted a horse and never looked back. In those four years, he had aged, his youth fading as he entered his thirties, faint lines forming around his mouth and between his brows, adding to his stern nature. He towered like he always had but now appeared to dominate more of the space, with widened shoulders and broadened thighs. The Commander's hair remained pulled back by a leather band, a similar black leather clinging to him like always—a useful piece of clothing that allowed Elisara to track his smallest movements during training. Her gaze returned to his face, his eyes in clear view. She wondered what assessment he made of her, too, though wished she did not care; she wished the need for his approval was not so engrained in her. She wished he did not stand before her now, threatening to expose her weaknesses and past.

"Do you still hide behind your flames when you're insulted, Commander?" Elisara asked, inclining her chin.

"Do you still flinch at the lick of that fire on your skin, Princess?" he retorted, taking a dangerous step closer. Flames appeared and danced on his palms, the glow of his eyes returning. That habit had been broken early in training, but she took the longest compared to Keres' recruits. Inviting in the wind from the window, she snuffed his flames and the Commander applauded, a familiar taunt.

"It was you, in the caves yesterday." Elisara said, eyes narrowed.

"I have to say, princess, I was both impressed and disappointed. On the one hand, you displayed an immense amount of power, but on the other, you yet again failed to yield control of it, nor detect an intruder like myself." He strode towards the open window.

"I had other priorities on my mind that day," Elisara said, tone lowered. She moved towards him, ensuring a full meter remained between them as they gazed out over the snow-coated city of Azuria.

"My condolences." The Commander stole a sidelong glance at

her, and she could have sworn there was some sincerity in his eyes, but did not allow it to sway her.

"There must be rules if you are to stay here, and if I am to respect my father and Nyzaia's wishes." Elisara said. He nodded stiffly. "First, I do not want to see you unless it is an important strategy meeting. Any general communications can be passed on through your chosen second-in-command. Second, you do not use the same training methods with my military. I will not have them subjected to what I experienced. They are already strong." Before he objected, she continued. "Finally, you will sleep in the west wing of the Castle, not the guard's quarters. I want it known where you are at all times." Elisara turned to leave the room, the restraint on her anxiety already slipping as it began to dawn on her that she had not spent this long with him alone in years.

"Do you still hold such resentment for your time in Keres, Princess?" The Commander asked seriously from the window, turning to watch her. Elisara paused, unsure of what lay beneath his change in tone. As she reached for the handle, she glanced back. In the light of the fireplace, Elisara studied those eyes that had scrutinised her while suffering the flames of his soldiers, and the mouth always curved into a grimace every time she failed him. The way he blew his hair from his face in frustration, and how his entire body tensed when she proved a disappointment again.

"Some scars do not heal so easily, Commander," And with that, she left the Commander of Vala alone in his new home.

***

Vlad said nothing as the guards escorted Elisara back to her chambers, who had no desire to return to the festivities. He ordered the others to stand watch as he followed her in.

"Keres!" he exclaimed, the second the door closed. "Keres, Eli, Keres!"

"I did not realise we were back to informalities, Vlad," Elisara bit back. She swiftly headed to her room to discard yet another suffocating dress and changed into her nightgown.

"Eli, please," Vlad pleaded as she undressed behind the screen beside her wardrobe. "You have to understand this is difficult. The guards already believe me highly favoured; they think Captain of the Queen's Guard has been handed to me on a platter, simply for being your friend."

"I have given you that role because I trust you, Vlad, but I also trust you to treat me no different because of my station, the same I always have with you." Elisara faced away from him: a silent request he remove the jewels clasped around her neck. Vlad held her loose hair while she thought back to their years together, friends from the moment he was assigned as one of her guards upon his transfer to Azuria and remaining so ever since. There had been a time Elisara's mother suggested he move to protect Katerina instead, but the argument which ensued necessitated Vlad stayed assigned to her. She flinched, not wishing to remember her mother in such a way.

"I know, but I need to be respected if I am to keep you safe. That means being proper in front of anyone. You are constantly surrounded by people, and it is impossible for us to have a moment between friends."

Elisara softened, slightly frustrated for not having considered that before. She sighed and walked to the stone balcony, breathing in the cold air dancing against her skin, free at last from the restrictions of decadent fabric. She focused on clearing the clouds to gaze upon the stars.

"So, Keres, that must have been—"

"Let me be clear," she cut in. "I trust you, but I will not be speaking about my time in Keres. I do not even talk to Caellum about it, who was also there, albeit briefly." Elisara held back tears at the mention of Caellum; Vlad's eyes glimmered with concern. He did not push the matter, perhaps he knew Elisara would lose patience or was merely obeying his new Queen's demands. She did not know.

"I understand," he said. "Do you need anything else this evening?"

"Could you have someone bring food and wine? I hardly ate at dinner."

Vlad nodded and left her be.

Four years ago, when Elisara mounted that horse and rode home through the Zivoi Mountains, she vowed to never set foot in Keres again in the hopes of never seeing the Commander. Elisara was subjected to the same routine as any other soldier in Keres, the same living quarters, tests, and punishments—for the most part, she was treated no differently. Yet Keres recruits prepared their entire lives for it, and the tests against fire challenged their natural responses. To Elisara, fire was her antithesis. As a daughter of the cold and descendant from the Goddess Vala, who was said to despise Keres the most out of her siblings, Elisara understood why.

Elisara's mother was insistent on her training in Keres; after all, she was born there and understood the strength of Keres' military and their Commander.

The story of the Commander's rise was notorious. Abandoned on the steps of the Tabheri Palace at only two weeks old, no note or sign was given as to who birthed him or if he was even from Keres at all. Queen Nesrin had been struggling to conceive and was yet to bear any children; instantly, she fell in love with the little boy and named him Kazaar after a noble warrior of Ithyion. King Razik saw how much joy the child brought her, and so he stayed. At five years old, he burned down an entire building, and from that moment forward, King Razik took far more interest in him. No one knew his heritage, and given his power, some guessed he was a bastard child of the king, while others theorised, he was a gift from the God Keres himself. All that was certain was Kazaar would grow to become the most powerful man in Keres.

Having no legal claim to the Keres throne, they assigned him to the military at a young age, and he quickly worked his way through the ranks. Not because of his connections to the royal family but because of the undeniable strength and power of his flame. At age twenty-four, he rose to the rank of Commander. Now, at thirty, his years had aged his distaste for the other realms, yet Elisara knew better than to question him. There was likely a reason for his solitude, his walls, and hatred, but it was not something she was eager to learn of.

Elisara shook the Commander from her mind at a knock on the door. A servant arrived with a tray of food and wine, placing it by the fire. Elisara dimmed the flames, leaving only glowing coals in the fireplace. Picking up a book, she carelessly dipped her bread in gravy and sipped her wine, a sense of freedom washing over her with no eyes upon her.

It did not take long for Elisara's eyes to grow weary. She made her way to bed, sighing at the comfort of the silk, and the gentle breeze blowing in as she peered out at the stars, hopeful her family were watching over her. Elisara closed her eyes, eager for sleep. But tonight, it was not her father's eyes of blue haunting her dreams, but those of burning amber.

Chapter Seventeen

Larelle

Memories haunted Larelle as she walked through the stone halls of Mera Castle to the grand stairs leading to the ocean. Zarya and Olden walked alongside her, having left the house early that morning. She wished to enter the castle before any Lords arrived.

Only three witnesses were needed for a coronation: a priest, a Lord, and a Neridian citizen. Larelle wished to avoid a spectacle; the celebrations seemed tasteless when so many in Novisia mourned those lost in the explosion. A part of Larelle dreaded how her people might receive her, too, thus kept it private. Instead, announcements would be made by the Lords of each town and city within Nerida: Mera, Trosso, Amoro, and Seley.

Olden was the citizen to bear witness to the coronation and woke the priest at the chapel before sunrise. Olden would have been there, regardless. After all, he was family. Lord Alvan of Seley was the Lord in attendance. Seley was a small town crossing both Nerida and Garridon, and Larelle imagined governing a town spanning two realms required an open mind and much patience. She hoped she was right. They were close in age, too, and their parents were good friends. Spending many afternoons together as children, she imagined he was likely a future marriage prospect for Larelle, had she not met Riyas. Yet as they grew up, they spent less time together, and eventually, Lord Alvan's parents were killed in a home fire, whereby he assumed his new role as Lord, and she saw little of him. She hoped he was as kind as she remembered. His smile at the funeral was a promising indicator.

That smile greeted Larelle as she rounded the corner toward the open wall at the rear of the castle, the view of the ocean clear below the stairs descending into the depths. The smile lit up his face and reached his almond-shaped hazel eyes, immediately putting Larelle at ease. He was much taller than she remembered, and she felt awfully small standing before him.

"It is an honor to be asked to bear witness to your coronation, Princess." Lord Alvan bowed and kissed her hand, and as he did, Larelle glimpsed a tattoo under his closely shaved head.

"Please, I have not been called by my title for years," she said, "and I'm dreading '*Your Majesty*' even more. Larelle is fine," She gently pulled Zarya out from behind her. "This will be Zarya's coronation too."

"Well, a princess cannot walk around without her tiara. How about we get started so you can look the part?" The Lord smiled, kneeling to look at her daughter. "I'm Alvan. I knew your father." Larelle and Olden's heads snapped to him immediately.

"You did?" Zarya asked boldly, eyes lighting up. Sorrow flickered in Alvan's gaze as he peered into Zarya's eyes, as if recognizing Riyas within them.

"Yes, he was the bravest sailor I knew. He told me lots of stories about his adventures at sea. Maybe, if your mother allows it, I could tell you them one day." He suggested, smiling gently at Larelle, who returned the gesture, though was cautious in doing so. While kind, they had not crossed paths in years, and Riyas had a small circle of friends. He had never mentioned the Lord of Seley, and it unsettled her to know he kept something from her, however small.

"Please mumma!" Zarya tugged Larelle's hand.

"We can't right now, sweetheart. Maybe Lord Alvan can tell you on our way to your new rooms," Larelle stole another look at the young Lord—a pointed look to indicate her wish to know more too. He smiled and nodded, as if reading her thoughts. Olden squeezed Larelle's hand. Perhaps Goddess Nerida offered Lord

Alvan's presence as a blessing: another connection to Riyas on a challenging day such as this.

"If you are ready, let us begin," the priest said from behind. Larelle jumped, and the small group parted ways as the priest led them down the worn stone staircase to the ocean below. Olden, Alvan, and Zarya stopped several steps down to where the water could not reach them. In silence, they watched as the priest led Larelle further into the water. The ocean lapped at her feet, stretching down the beaches leading to her home and The Bay. To her left was Trosso in the distance, shielding Mera from the cliffs of Garridon. She once believed Mera castle was built at the end of the Peninsula to be as close to the water as possible, protected by the multiple karsts jutting out from the sea to form a labyrinth, should anyone wish to sail there.

Larelle breathed in the sea air.

The night before, Olden had practiced the coronation with Larelle, and the pair succumbed to fits of laughter as he crowned her with a soup pot. Yet today, she trusted her instincts and allowed her feet to guide her down the remaining slippery steps, no longer visible as the water darkened. Larelle paused once she was waist-deep, the priest three steps above.

"Repeat after me," he drawled. "I, Larelle Sevia, Princess of Nerida and second born to the deceased King Adrianus and Queen Oriana, swear fealty to my realm."

Larelle repeated the words, caressed by the water.

"To guard the waters of the Goddess and protect the people born of the seas as Queen." Hesitating, Larelle recited the words, and the weight of them enveloped her like the ocean around her middle.

The Priest nodded, lifting a chalice of water. It was tradition for the Neridian King or Queen to manipulate the liquid, so, without glancing at the chalice, Larelle willed a single droplet to rise and drop onto the crown of her head: a droplet from all bodies of water across Nerida. Finally, she sank below the surface, allowing the water to determine her worth as she calmed her mind and took a breath, at one with the ocean. Eyes open, she stared into the darkness of its depths. Larelle lingered there a moment, savoring the feeling of the ocean's acceptance—welcomed by it, like it was her home. For a fleeting moment, she wished to stay below the surface, cradled by the darkness that enveloped her heart. Larelle whispered a single prayer to Riyas before she rose.

"By the power invested in me by the Goddess Nerida: I crown you, Larelle Sevia, Queen of Nerida. Long may you reign." The priest lowered the crown upon her dark curls—a crown of silver, forged to mimic the waves of the ocean. As he did, Larelle willed the seas to part, revealing the rocky staircase, much to Zarya's delight.

"Long may you reign," they repeated.

Olden released Zarya's hand and gently nudged the young girl down the steps to her mother. Dressed in skirts seemingly too long, Zarya gathered the hems of her dress and curtseyed to the Queen, who accepted her outstretched hand. Steering her down two more steps, Larelle gently allowed the ocean to return and cradle her daughter, then recited the same words as the priest, albeit in smaller portions. Zarya slowly repeated them in her innocent voice.

Larelle felt her own voice tremble as tears threatened to spill. She wished a better life for her daughter, one of acceptance and ease, one at which her authority was respected when she, one day, ascended to the throne. Larelle pledged to create change during her own reign, giving her daughter a realm to be proud of. But where to begin?

She would face those challenges head on and do it all for her daughter.

"I crown you, Zarya Sevia-Zerpane, Princess of Nerida."

Zarya beamed as her mother's old tiara lowered onto her matching black curls. Larelle ignored the Priest's evident disapproval, and glanced to Alvan to gauge his reaction, who wore a smile as genuine as her own.

"Can I hear the stories now, Mr Alvan?" Zarya bounded up the steps, the tiara tilting off her head while the soaked gown dragged behind. Larelle bowed her head in disbelief as Alvan laughed.

"Zarya, what did we say you are to call a man of Alvan's station?" Olden prompted.

"Sorry, Lord Alvan," she said, staring wide-eyed at the man chuckling to himself.

"Don't apologize, Princess. I like Mr Alvan much better." He smiled. "If the Princess would allow me, I would be honoured to escort her to her new rooms." Bowing, he outstretched his hand and waited for Zarya to grasp it, who looked to her mother for confirmation. Larelle nodded and continued up the steps to join them.

***

The castle was breathtaking as they walked through it, listening to Alvan's tales of the sea. Memories stirred as Larelle walked along the halls, yet she praised whoever kept the castle in such good repair. Her father was never one for trivial things. Larelle was pleased when Alvan guided them through a balcony that acted as a hallway, overlooking the sea. She paused, relishing the sound of the waves crashing against the rocks, and bent to remove her water-soaked slippers. With curiosity, Zarya watched as Larelle shot her daughter a mischievous look.

With a motion of her hand, the waves crashed high through the gaps in the balcony and soaked the hallway floors. Zarya giggled, jumping in the small puddles forming—a reminder to Larelle of the happier memories she had in the castle. As a child, she would constantly soak this hallway: a welcome reprieve for the servants on hot days who walked barefoot to cool down and thanked her as they passed. Larelle hoped she could instill that tradition again. She watched the few servants behind Alvan and was filled with hope at their smiles to one another.

The further along the hallway they walked, the more servants they came across, who curtseyed or bowed, their smiles of a genuine nature. This wing of the Castle was busier than most. She realised why when they approached the grand doors to what used to be her bedroom.

"I assumed you would prefer some slight comfort," Alvan said. "So, I had some items brought from your home." Larelle appreciated the gesture but was overcome with anxiety at returning to her childhood room. She froze as the doors opened. "Oh, and I had it redecorated for you." Alvan smiled.

Larelle released her breath.

While the room held painful memories, there was no reminder of them. It was completely different. The room before was extravagant, filled with suffocating gold and silver. Royal blues and dark woods had swarmed it. Now, it resembled the beauty of her understated beachside home, as if Riyas himself had decorated it.

Stepping through the doors, she gawped at the brightness of the cream walls and sandstone floors. Her bed from home had been deconstructed and rebuilt here. Larelle traced the carvings Riyas had spent months creating. A small sitting room was added, too, mimicking that of her true home, making the overall room smaller and more comforting. An enormous stone fireplace stood within it, surrounded by shelves of books and artefacts. Olden's armchair took centre place before the fireplace, and she was reminded of the nights she watched Zarya fall asleep on her grandfather as he read to her. The masterpiece, though, was the view. Gone were the dark blue drapes, replaced with thin white chiffon blowing in the breeze, which framed the glass doors to the terrace.

Overcome with emotion, she removed the hand covering her mouth to clasp Lord Alvan's.

"Thank you. Truly," she choked.

On the terrace, Zarya lined seashells along the wall, hiding them among the purple clematis plant rambling along the edge. The sun settled across the horizon, scattering pinks and oranges across the waters. Larelle calmed the waves, relishing the tranquility it brought.

"Apologies, my Queen. Lord Alvan assumed you would wish to eat in your chambers this evening with your family."

A young servant girl entered, looking at Zarya and Olden with a smile.

"Thank you..." Larelle paused. "My apologies, I do not know any names yet." Larelle continued, afraid of insulting the first of her people.

"Lillian, your Majesty." She curtseyed, her straw-blonde hair refusing to fall from the bun pulled tightly to her scalp.

"Thank you, Lillian. Dinner on the terrace would be perfect, if you do not mind." Larelle smiled at the young girl, trying to place the recognition.

"Of course, your Majesty." Lillian turned to open the doors to the chamber, and in walked an additional three girls; two carried trays of food, while another held several bottles of wine, of which Alvan was quick to take before she dropped them. Awe-struck, Larelle gaped at the lavish foods, accustomed to only simple meals. Then realization dawned. Lillian. The woman at The Bay, collecting leftovers from the market.

"You have a son, Lillian, don't you? Around Zarya's age?"

The young women could not hide her shock.

"I do, your Majesty. Zion. He is about to turn six."

Larelle's brow furrowed. Why would a mother employed at the castle struggle to afford food for her child? Perhaps that was the case for all the staff. "How many of you are working in the castle today?" she asked.

One of the younger girls stepped forward. "Nine of us, your Majesty. The three of us, the cook, two that clean the castle, one gardener, his son, and the librarian. Forgive us, your Majesty. We are a small team today; everyone else will arrive tomorrow."

Larelle cast a questioning look to Alvan.

"I assumed you would not wish for the pressure of the Lords

and Ladies, alongside a full staff and guard. Apologies if I am mistaken."

He was not.

"Alvan, would you escort the ladies back to the kitchens and help them gather the rest of the staff? We shall all dine together tonight. Zarya, Olden, and I will await your return."

Uncertainty crossed Alvan's face.

"I will not dine on lavish foods knowing my predecessors have bothered little to feed their own staff." Larelle was firm, and the girls bowed their heads at the acknowledgement. "I will ensure this is seen to when I attend a meeting with the Lords and the treasury."

Alvan nodded and guided the girls to the door, who whispered excitedly between themselves. Larelle knew what Lillian endured to feed her family, having endured it too. As she eagerly left now, there was no doubt she planned to take the leftovers home to her son. The memory of her brother at The Bay flashed, and his blatant disgust for the poor. It was sickening to think of the extravagance they experienced while their staff starved.

"He would be proud of you." Olden said, planting a hand on her shoulder. She hoped so. Larelle may have grown up with the luxuries of royal life, but meeting Riyas humbled her, especially once leaving the castle and living at The Bay. She had no interest in winning the nobility's approval or following in the footsteps of her mother or Meera. They had become a family of greed caring little for their people, and Larelle was among those. She would happily face the backlash of the nobles if it meant gaining the hearts of her people.

The rest of the evening began awkwardly as the servants arrived and sat crammed around the small table on the terrace. Informality did not come easy for the servants in the presence of royalty, yet Zarya soon broke the ice by asking all means of questions, curious as to how they found time to do everything in a day, how the chef 'magicked' ingredients from across Nerida, how the gardeners watered their plants without powers, and how many books the librarian could provide her at once. Zarya was a breath of fresh air in an aristocracy so stifling.

Laughter commenced as her people shared stories, savoring the additional foods brought up by the cook: olives and sundried tomatoes from Trosso, red and white wines from Amoro, and the most delectable breads from The Bay. Larelle was overcome by flavours, a testament to why Nerida's foods were in such high demand across Novisia. While Keres traded in weapons, Vala in healing potions, and Garridon in building materials, Nerida traded in food and wine. She considered the last time she enjoyed a spread like this, not as decadent in volume, but as delightful in company.

The night before Riyas left.

They had wandered together, down to their spot on the beach, where Olden guarded a wrapped basket then left them be. After helping her onto the sand, Riyas unwrapped the same ingredients before her now, but in smaller quantities. He fed her olives, dipped bread in oil, and filled her glass with wine, insistent on treating her as his princess.

"Before you know it, I'll be home and filling your glass once again," Riyas said. Red wine flowed from the bottle clutched in his calloused hands from endless rope work on the ships.

"It is not pouring wine that I will miss."

"The awful jokes? The snoring? Or perhaps the way I tell five stories in one?" Larelle jabbed her elbow into his side, spilling the wine in his glass, and staining the sand. His attempts at distraction almost worked, if not for the ocean acting as a reminder he was leaving. Larelle leaned into his gentle touch as he ran his fingers up and down her spine.

"It is one week, sweetheart," he rested his head against hers. "This will be the beginning of our future, I'm certain of it. This will aid me in promotion," He raised her hand and kissed each finger, until ending on one. "Then a beautiful band will sit on this finger when I make you my wife." How naïve they had been. But to be naïve was to be hopeful, and to be hopeful was to be madly in love.

A servant mentioned one of the Lords, and captured Larelle's attention.

"What can you all tell me about the Lords and Ladies? It has been some time since I have interacted with them. I know little of who holds what seats and alliances." She sipped her wine again, and so began an evening that would set in motion her upcoming reign.

As Larelle drank, she learned of the untrustworthy nobles and secrets that could end their stations. What's more, she learned the true thoughts of her people, and in one night, Larelle had gone from dreading becoming Queen to realising she had the power to shape her reign however she wished. And what she wanted was to rid Nerida of greed and hierarchy and replace it with the will of the people, for the people were the heart of Nerida and had been trampled on for too long.

Chapter Eighteen

Nyzaia

Eight Years Ago

"You've got to be kidding me."

Nyzaia scowled at the tall girl with wide eyes, standing at the other side of the circle where everyone gathered. Nyzaia scowled.

"Do you think I want to be in a group with you either?" Nyzaia retorted. The girl's eyes narrowed as she sneered, the freckle to the right of her lip rising with it.

This girl is insufferable, Nyzaia thought, watching as she flipped her long dark braid over her leather-padded shoulder.

"Isaam, Jabir, Rafik!" Arjun called. Arjun was the leader of the Spies, a group which formed one of the six pillars making up the Red Stones. The boys groaned in unison, glancing between the two girls who had spent their last year arguing in constant competition.

"Groan all you like," Arjun persisted. "You have been selected as a group for the trials, and how you score in this trial will determine if you pass, but also the Pillar you will train in next." He ticked the names off on his parchment and waved a hand at them all. The five recruits walked out of the circle of bodies, lining up against the red sandstone forming the canyons on the outskirts of Tabheri. Jabir stood in silence and used his dagger to pick dirt from his nails, while Rafik rocked on his heels, waiting for someone to talk. The girl would be the first to open her mouth—she always was.

"So, I think we should—" the girl began.

"—Let us get one thing straight first," said Isaam, his volume cutting across her as he pushed off from the rock. He crossed his arms and glared down at the girls. "You, Tajana," he pointed. "And you, Nyzaia," His finger moved to the princess, who feigned shock, "are going to have us repeating this year."

"I do not lose, Isaam." Tajana scoffed.

"Neither do I," Nyzaia stated. The boys rolled their eyes.

"That's the problem," Jabir said, spinning his dagger before holstering it in a strap on his thigh. "You are both so adamant about proving yourselves, you're willing to put your needs above the rest of the group." He looked pointedly at them; a dark eyebrow raised as he waited for a response. Nyzaia looked away from Tajana.

"We have one week to gather the information and capture a target; can you two get along for one week?" Rafik asked, keeping his arms locked behind his slight frame.

She peered back at Tajana, whose judgemental eyes roamed up and down her leather-clad body.

"Fine," they said in unison.

***

Nyzaia smiled while remembering the first trial undertaken with her syndicate—the trial which had formed their bonds and opened her eyes to Tajana. Trials were a standard form of assessment in the Red Stones, hence why Nyzaia decided it was the best determination of who should form her Queens Guard.

The first trial went as expected. Her Queen's Guard were *not* prepared. Appearing in the dead of night as before, the Red Stones snuck in from the rooftops and disarmed them in a matter of seconds. Nyzaia had not bothered to say anything when she peeked her head out of the door at the sound of dropping swords. She simply rolled her eyes at Tajana's smugness and returned to bed.

The second trial was far more interesting; the Red Stones had raised the stakes, and Farid almost stood a chance. Nyzaia had left her weekly meeting with the Lords early, having discussed defenses based on the probabilities of another attack. All blamed a different King or Queen for the explosion, all of which—as she reminded them—were dead now. Their accusations soon shifted to the new rulers, with many fearing Keres could be next. When the topic altered to hosting a ball in several months, Nyzaia bid them farewell, informing them she would choose who to invite later. She barely turned the corner from the advisor's hall when the Red Stones struck.

Nyzaia thought them foolish to choose a location so close to the Lords, but it made their attempt seem even more impressive. As with the first trial, nearly all the Queen's Guards were disarmed immediately. The surprise came with Farid, who ducked and dodged Isaam's broad form, and reached for a knife kept in his boot. Farid might have stood a chance if he paid attention to the others in her syndicate, not just his primary target. If he had, he would have noticed how quickly Tajana tied up her guard and snuck behind him, holding a dagger to his throat as she bent back his arm, forcing Farid to drop his knife.

"Are you getting rusty, Isaam?" Nyzaia retorted, raising a brow before continuing her walk to her chambers. The entire time she focused on any sounds suggesting the Lords had heard the commotion. They had not.

Nyzaia wished Kazaar was here to gossip about their attempts and had hoped his presence would be the one thing keeping her sane in her new position as Queen. When he showed her the decree found in her father's office, her heart cracked—even more so when he wished to abide by it. She tried to argue but knew better. Kazaar wished to do this for her father, and she could not bear to make him unhappy. *Though he is sure to be unhappy now*, Nyzaia guessed, *working beneath a Queen he despises.*

"Apologies for the delay, your Majesty," said the serving girl, interrupting her thoughts. She placed breakfast upon the excessively large dining table at which she sat—alone.

"Not to worry," Nyzaia said, with a small smile, one she hoped seemed warm.

"Do you require anything else, your Majesty?" The girl clasped her hands before her.

"No, thank you."

As Nyzaia reached for the cup of water, the girl bowed and turned to exit the dining room, bare feet padding on the tiles as she went. One of the female guards smiled at her as she left—a smile of familiarity. It was easy to naturally gather intel from her new position as Queen, yet it was merely household gossip rather than anything of significance.

Nyzaia reached for a piece of sliced stone fruit and brought it to her lips, pausing as a shadow passed in the far corner, yet it was faint, given the room's natural lighting. She looked at Farid and smiled; he had noticed, too. Farid's eyes scanned the room, while his hand subtly reached for his back, where she knew a dagger hid. *Let the fun begin.*

At the exact moment Nyzaia bit into her fruit, leather-clad bodies flooded the room. Figures emerged from behind each pillar, and she wondered who had chosen Farid as their target. Rafik's look of confusion answered her question as he whirled from behind the pillar and found Farid no longer there. She smiled as Rafik turned to her and then the rest of the syndicate. Tajana held a guard by the throat, Isaam had another pinned to the floor, while Jabir tied one up. Pulling two knives from his side, Rafik crouched and scanned the pillars in case Farid hid among them. As Nyzaia reached for another slice of fruit, she glanced upwards. Rafik noted the movement, his eyes following hers.

Farid dropped.

He fell directly onto Rafik, smothering him. Stunned, Rafik was slow as Farid spun him over and pinned his arms behind his back with one hand and used the other to yank back his head.

"I win," he whispered. And there was a smile.

Nyzaia looked Farid in the eye and slowly applauded. "You learn quick," she commended. He simply nodded, blowing a stray piece of dark hair from his pale eyes. Nyzaia looked back at each of her syndicate, they released their captive guards while looking at Farid. Impressed.

"You," Nyzaia pointed at each of her original Queen's guard. "You're all done. Return to your posts as regular guards." None of them disagreed, all ashamed by their failures. Nyzaia rose and left her breakfast, stalking towards Farid. *He's tall*, Nyzaia noted, *he reminds me of Kazaar*. Shifting his legs together, he clasped his hands behind his back as she approached, the stray piece of hair still covering his eyes—eyes such a rare shade of pale blue. She had never witnessed it before in Keres. Standing an arm's distance away, Nyzaia's gaze roamed across him in slow assessment.

"You stay," She decided. Farid said nothing. "But you are no longer Captain. I will consider it one day." She glanced at Tajana. "If you can ever disarm her."

Tajana smirked, and finally, without formality, Farid acknowledged his queen.

"Challenge accepted, your Majesty," he said, the corner of his mouth twitching.

"I like him." Isaam laughed, clapping Farid on the back as he approached. Any hint of a smile on Farid's face disappeared.

"Go," Nyzaia said. "Clean up, and Farid—find the new guards living quarters close to mine."

Farid nodded and turned to lead the syndicate away. Tajana approached and snaked a hand around Nyzaia's waist, resting against the bare skin of her midriff between the two pieces of deep red fabric.

"You do realise I would kill him before I ever let him disarm me?" Tajana whispered in Nyzaia's ear. Nyzaia leaned into the warmth of her body.

"I'm well aware," she said, turning to face Tajana as her hands moved to her back. "Maybe give him a few months at least."

Flames danced at Nyzaia's fingertips as she cupped Tajana's face.

"And where would you like my living quarters?" Tajana asked, voice hushed. She began planting kisses along Nyzaia's neck.

"If you can be discrete, stay with me." the Queen breathed.

Tajana's kisses trailed from her neck to her cheek then paused before her lips.

"Deal," Tajana whispered. Gently, she pressed her lips to Nyzaia's, who instantly felt safe. She missed seeing Tajana every day and looked forward to the comfort of having her permanently by her side. Footsteps sounded, and Nyzaia pulled back. She stepped away from Tajana and brushed herself down. Lord Israar of Myara turned his head from them, a smirk playing on his lips as he left the hall. Nyzaia's stomach dropped, and her pulse spiked. She glanced at Tajana, who seemed unconcerned by his intrusion.

She tried to ignore the dread that formed in the pit of her stomach.

Chapter Nineteen

Elisara

A week had passed since the Commander's arrival, and Elisara was surprised to find he obeyed her three rules. She had not seen him, but her guards confirmed he was staying in the west wing, and it wasn't until the next evening she heard from him. She turned over the small piece of parchment: *Training Yard. Sunrise.*

The ink marking the bottom right corner was the Keres sigil: a clear indicator of its sender. Elisara took a tonic that night, knowing she would otherwise toss and turn in apprehension for whatever the morning would bring. She contemplated not attending at all, given it broke her first rule of not wishing to see him; however, if the matter regarded the quality of her guards and soldiers, then she deemed it important to break.

Elisara self-consciously glanced over her appearance in the mirror, checking her attire aligned with the standards of her soldiers and guards. After all, it could not be one rule for them and another for her. She swallowed the lump in her throat upon realising they were the same clothes worn on her journey to the Neutral City. There was no time to change, so she forced herself to tie her hair in a thick braid and exit the chambers for the training yard.

Azuria Castle did not have its own training grounds, as her father insisted there were no hierarchies of class in battle. Elisara loved training in the communal ring, able to spar with the old or young, male or female, and sometimes, rich or poor. Of course, some of the wealthiest thought too highly of themselves to train with *commoners,* especially women. As a result, the Azuria training yard, like those of Vojta, Tisova, Marnovo, and Elvera, was in the city's centre. Elisara relished the journey through Azuria yet had not visited since before the funeral. Despite the accompaniment of her guards, she refused to let it dampen the spirits the city raised in her.

They strode through the peaceful streets, the stone structures coated in thin layers of ice and snow that had not melted since the beginning of her reign. The bakeries prepared for their day ahead as dough and baked bread wafted through the city gardens: the focal point of Azuria. Citizens from across Novisia made it their priority to visit if they were ever in Vala, and Elisara understood why. Enclosed by intricate black iron railings and gates were snowcapped trees that, once ventured through, would take a person to the most breathtaking sheet of sparkling ice that was the lake. Why it was called the gardens, she would never understand. It was Azuria's own small woodland, where Elisara spent much of her childhood.

Around the railings, bakers moved in their windows with trays of buns, breads, and pastries entering the ovens to cater to those who strolled the gardens throughout the day. She wished she could partake in that joy; what she would give to eat a maple and pecan danish on a bench by the lake. She thought of Helena and Vigor, two of the few people she considered friends. Elisara would often meet Vigor to train, and afterwards, Helena would bring them freshly baked pastries from her bakery. She smiled sadly, wondering what they thought of her now as Queen. She had not visited them, too afraid to find out. Elisara rounded the corner, and her thoughts slipped away as they continued their walk down the main plaza to their destination.

The training grounds mirrored the size of the city gardens, but instead of beautiful woodlands, a series of structures stood for different training exercises, all bordering a large walled arena. The local boys would often rake the snow to reveal the slippery black stone beneath—which Elisara had cut herself on many a time.

The Commander had clearly implemented earlier training routines, as instead of boys removing snow, a range of citizens, guards, and soldiers performed set drills. While the wall blocked their footwork, Elisara watched their movements from the waist up. Never had she seen the training grounds so busy, especially not this early. The guards and soldiers had little choice in the Commander's demands, yet the volume of citizens' training shocked her as they gathered at the end of the arena rehearsing different disciplines. Usually, the citizens favoured the late afternoon.

She stopped on the outskirts to gauge everyone's measure before entering without being seen. The citizens were slow but more skilled than expected, guided by a man she suspected was once a guard or soldier. They were broken into groups: women, men, and children. Hopefully, once more skilled, the instructor would merge the men and women to allow them to learn from one another. At the opposite end, the guards, led by Vlad, practiced defense tactics, and her gaze hovered over the group of soldiers training in the centre, led by the Commander. In only a week, they seemed faster, sleeker, yet still nowhere near the prowess of Keres' soldiers.

The Commander motioned one soldier to step forward and proceeded to talk him through his footwork before beginning their sword fight. Elisara studied the Commander closely. Most of his movements—defensive and otherwise—remained the same as when she had last watched him fight. There were subtle differences, however: he angled his left shoulder further back, twisted his wrist while moving to strike, and most notably, he ducked lower than before—a skill to catch the opponent's ankles, and drop them to the ground. The Commander pointed his sword at the guard's neck.

"Are you observing or partaking?" the Commander called, wiping the slight sheen from his brow. His muscular arms rose to tighten the leather strip holding back his dark hair, wet with sweat. The tattoos covering his body stretched and moved with him as his muscles rippled. The soldiers followed the Commander's gaze, and all quickly straightened before bowing to their Queen; the guards noticed, too, and followed suit. The citizens seemed to wonder of the sudden formality, and excited whispers from the children began while the adults instructed them to bow or curtsey.

Nodding to each group, Elisara released them from their positions, but even then, they struggled to return to normality. She walked through the gates of the grounds, leather-clad in training gear. The Commander's mouth twitched.

"Don't your people deserve to know how their ruler fights? To know if she is capable of battle?" he taunted. He strode to the sword station, weighing each until finding what she knew would be her sword.

"There hasn't been a battle on Novisia since that man usurped the throne!" A little boy exclaimed.

Elisara stifled a laugh as a woman quickly covered his mouth and pulled him back into the crowd. The boy was not wrong. Confined to Garridon, the other three realms had not intervened in the battle. Instead, they sat back and watched to see who emerged victorious; the rulers at the time did not wish to protect one another from internal threats.

"But if an unseen threat were to arrive on our shores tomorrow, would your Queen be ready for battle?" he called back. The use of *your* Queen rather than *our* did not go unnoticed by Elisara. Shrugging off his upper-half leathers, the Commander stepped forward in his black trousers and a loose white tunic. Elisara assessed him before removing her cloak, revealing a similar white tunic held close to her body by a leather corset. Marching towards the Commander, she snatched the sword from his hand without so much as a glance, then spun in the opposite direction. She steadied her trembling hands as memories threatened to explode to the surface. Metal crashing from a swordfight nearby brought her back to the Abis Forge. The two of them standing high above it entered her mind, but she blinked it away, refusing to deteriorate now.

"Rules?" Elisara asked, flicking her braid to her back.

"No magic." he responded, reaching for a sword, and mirroring her stance.

"Glad to see you have accepted you cannot defeat my power."

The dance began. They circled each other as they had done so many times before. Others in the ring stepped forward, eager to watch the notorious Commander and their Queen fight.

"If only that were the case. I do not want to risk the lives of those around us when you lose control of it." He knew the comment would prompt the memories to surface, and she fell for the trap. Elisara lunged. He spun from her sword, but she was quick. Realising his taunt was a trap, she spun at the same time he did, their swords clashing together.

"I would never hurt my people!" She spat before their dance took full force.

The crowd faded out of focus as she homed in on his dark eyes, watching for any sign of where he would move next. He knew all her tactics and met her every time she raised her sword to strike, every time she stepped forward to push him back, and each time she spun or used an elbow to shove him aside. Their dance continued for what felt like hours, sweat beginning to drip down their faces. Elisara made to use one of his newer moves.

As he swung with his sword, Elisara ducked lower and reached out for his left ankle, but he anticipated it; as he fell, he kicked her shoulder, toppling them both onto their fronts, swords flung from their reach. The distance to her sword was too far, so she unsheathed a dagger from the bone structure of her corset instead. At the same time, the Commander pulled a dagger from his boot, and they both spun on their knees in sync. Each held a blade to the other's throats, inches apart. Panting, their eyes locked before he glanced down at her neckline then returned her stare.

"That, Princess, is why you need to allow Keres training methods with your people." he said, so only she could hear. "Because none of them fight me the way you do."

Elisara focused on calming her breathing, which became audible intakes of panicked breath as the distraction of the fight faded. Their proximity was a reminder of all the times they had done this before. His lips pursed while watching her quickened breaths, but with a clenched jaw, he rose and did not offer his hand. Applause slowly erupted as their Queen rose too. Elisara glanced back at the crowd, who had moved closer, forming an impenetrable barrier around them. Many of the guards smiled, evidently impressed with her performance, while the citizens appeared awe-struck. Elisara blushed; she was not used to such positive attention.

"Train the citizens. They could use your knowledge," he said, before turning back to his soldiers. Elisara wiped the sweat from her brow with the sleeves of her tunic and took a moment to regulate her thoughts.

You are here; you are okay. You are here in Vala, not Keres. You are okay, she thought. As the words rang in her mind, they adopted another voice entirely, her mind wandering to Caellum. The words were first spoken when they were young. Caellum fell from the Vala castle wall and cut his cheek as he landed on the branches below. They were ten years old at the time, yet Caellum reassured Elisara with those words, who was near hysterical after watching him fall. He had a faint scar now.

Elisara strolled to the citizens, with the Commander's words in mind. Was he right? Did her guards and soldiers require more intense training? She knew what he *was* right about. There was every chance a new threat could arrive on their shores, especially as whoever orchestrated the explosion was still out there.

Elisara hoped for more answers in the upcoming weeks. Now they were all crowned, the four new rulers had been summoned by the Historian to the Neutral City to discuss the explosion further, so in two weeks, she would depart with her guards and the Commander. She did not wish to bring him, but the Historian requested his presence.

Elisara wished they could meet sooner, but the Temple and Neutral City were rebuilding. However, she was not a patient woman, and if nothing came to light soon, she would begin her own investigation.

***

Elisara was distracted while demonstrating footwork to the women in her group, who had all volunteered to train. As she feigned assessing their movements, she considered the Commander's suggestion of implementing Keres' training methods. She thought back to the tests and approaches used. Where the Keres recruits could withstand the heat while burned for information, Elisara's ice-cold veins fought against it. When they worked as a team to navigate the rope bridge across the Abis Forge, the ropes burned and marked her palms. She did not wish for her people to endure such torment.

The Commander was right, though, as much as she hated to admit it. While at the time it destroyed her, she was unrivalled in battle, and could easily disarm Caellum through tactics over strength. Elisara waved the children farewell as their mothers left to escort them to their other lessons. She jumped up onto the wall, imagining her mother scolding her for such un-queenly behaviour. She did not care.

The last remaining soldiers were defeated by the Commander within minutes. He clapped the final one on the back before returning his sword, and she watched the merriment of men disband from their units and merge with the guards, excited about the prospect of developing their skills. She was astounded they had so promptly taken a liking to the Commander and Elisara couldn't help but question why.

"They are good men and women," the Commander commented, leaning against the wall where she sat. "They just needed a good leader." He seemed careful to maintain distance between them, as he placed a cup of water beside her. Elisara eyed the cup before gulping down the water.

"It is because they are good men, I cannot allow you to impose

Keres methods in their training." The Commander clenched his jaw and made to speak. "Wait before you pass judgement, Commander." she snapped. Hair fell loose from her braid and shaded her eyes. "You need to adapt the methods. They are not born in fire; they are raised with ice, and you must consider that for their tasks and scenarios."

The Commander seemed to contemplate her suggestion.

"Who is your strongest wielder?"

"Other than me? Helena. She's the illegitimate child of a Lord, but we do not know who. She owns the Crescent Bakery on the southern corner of the city gardens. It's unlikely she will help you, but you can try." Elisara thought back to the last time she trained with Helena, who was adamant Elisara was restraining the extent of her abilities. Helena pushed so much that when she stopped wielding her power, the strength of Helena's air blew her right across the frozen lake in the gardens. Helena rushed to her aid afterwards, frantically apologizing, but Elisara pulled her down beside her as the pair fell into fits of laughter.

The Commander would need an expert to reshape his training plan. The pair stood in silence for a moment as Elisara willed the air to cool them.

"Nice party trick."

She did not fall for his taunting, but basked in the rising sun as the remaining soldiers and guards left the grounds.

"Your neck is bare," he said. Elisara looked at him. "You are not wearing the Vala Talisman."

Elisara touched her chest.

"No. I am not."

The Commander cocked his head. "Why?"

She glanced away, and slowly, he nodded.

"For someone so confident they would not hurt their people," he said, narrowing his eyes. "You seem rather concerned to test the strength of your powers with the talisman."

Elisara pursed her lips and refused to look at him. Leaving the truth of his statement to hang in the air, the Commander rose and left.

A scream clawed for escape. The Commander seemed to always know her deep-seated fears. Ever since the funeral, she feared the extent of her powers, with the talisman amplifying it. A slight slip of her emotions could wreak blizzards upon not only Azuria, but the whole of Vala.

Yet there was only one way to learn if the talisman would turn her into a weapon of destruction. Elisara headed for Vlad, who was laughing with the rest of the Queen's guard.

"I need you to take me to the vaults," she said.

Vlad adjusted his sword and nodded, knowing what she was ready to try.

Chapter Twenty

Elisara

Vala's sigil was skillfully engraved into the mountain rock that formed the talisman, smoothed and polished to perfection: one mountain, half of another and one star. Half of one whole. The talisman was once broken into two, the other half hidden somewhere in Vala.

Vlad moved her father's talisman to the vaults the moment they returned from the Neutral City. Elisara wished to be far from it, and even now, it called to her, whispers floating in the air as it urged its owner to unleash.

All the risks and worst-case scenarios warred through her: storms so wild they ripped apart the homes of Vala, torrents of snow trapping her people and starving them to death, or insanity from all the voices carried to her in the wind. Yet she could not stare at it forever, and she needed to wear it soon. After all, the other rulers likely wore their talismans. She would seem foolish to not wear hers.

Maybe I can carry it on my person, but not wear it, she pondered, yet it seemed foolish to carry something of that magnitude without its security around her neck.

Elisara tried to recall her father without the talisman, and whether it changed him. But if he ever removed it, it had not been in her presence. She sighed and reached for the chain, the metal cool like the ice in her veins. She lifted it, turning it in the light. Nothing. Resting the talisman in her hand, immediate power merged with her blood. She dropped it.

"Do you need help?" Vlad called, who stood watch by the door.

"No, I need to decide this myself," she murmured.

Elisara picked the talisman back up, careful to only touch the chain as she placed it in the pockets of her cloak. The lack of skin contact calmed her. She felt no impact. Striding out of the door, without a word to Vlad, she returned to her chamber, the talisman heavy in her pocket. He was certain to follow, and likely remain outside her door until she reemerged.

Elisara hung the talisman on her dresser and discarded her cloak before pacing the balcony in her chambers, peering out across Azuria. How could she test her powers while wearing the talisman when she did not know the extent of her powers without it?

Elisara needed Caellum to ground her, or the help of someone experiencing the volume of power she possessed.

Helena, she realised. While she did not obtain the level of Elisara's power, she was a confident air wielder, and had mastered control of it. Yet how could Elisara go to her, alone, without her Queen's Guard? The problem would be sneaking past them. Vlad knew all her tricks from when she was Princess, and likely had all the exits guarded now, which left only one option.

Elisara peered at the stone railings and contemplated the distance to the ground below. Fresh snow lay at the base of the castle, yet from this distance, she would be falling on solid ground if her plan failed, likely breaking her back.

Elisara made it down two balconies before realising it was not her best of plans. She rose from the crouch, having rolled during landing. Two more balconies stood between her and the path. She unclenched her hands, loosening her knuckles from the strain of hanging uncertainly off her own balcony.

Less hesitation this time, she thought. Instead of lowering, she climbed to the edge of the balcony and stepped off it. She fell through the air until it hit her, pausing her descent—only for a second, but enough to balance her landing on the next terrace. Glancing around, she called on the air again, testing her ability to curl it around her body. She stepped over the edge, this time lowering until she balanced on the balcony beneath with ease. With renewed confidence, she grinned and stepped again—and that was her mistake. This time, the air faltered, and she plummeted to the path below, the mountain of fresh snow cushioning her fall.

She groaned and gradually rose to her feet. At least the coldness of the snow would numb any injuries for now. Brushing the moisture off her legs, Elisara continued her descent, this time firmly with two feet on the ground. She followed the winding path of the mountain down to the city, without crossing paths with another soul.

Elisara navigated the shadows of the wealthier streets belonging to nobles; the buildings were painted pale blue, adorned with white engravings and overhangs. Tall lavish buildings of art changed to mid-sized fixtures, then mismatched streets of different homes: some wooden, some stone. The sigil of Vala embellished every door: a sign of respect and fealty to the crown and their Goddess.

Unnoticed by her dark cloak, she reached her destination swiftly and weaved around the evening revelers who cheered for who knows what. As she entered the quiet tavern, she stole a quick glance around the room. The stone interior was painted several times in soft cream, worn in places from years of drunks leaning against the walls. Wooden booths lined the east and west walls, the benches coated in grey velvet. Round oak tables filled the centre, and far too many people clustered around them. The tavern was popular among the working folk, yet Elisara had never minded the crowds. The influx of bodies added to the comfort of the tavern. It was easier to stay unnoticed too. Something Elisara hoped was still true.

Lowering her hood, she anticipated a change in the mannerisms of those around her, yet no one seemed to even glance in her direction. Elisara wove through the throngs of people; booths of friends shared food, warm breads and meats. The centre tables were rowdy with drunk men and women celebrating the end of the working day.

"Eli, Vigor is getting the next round. Grab him if you want in!" a voice called.

Elisara could not help the grin widening across her face as she turned to the table where her friends played cards. She had not had a moment of joy since the explosion and felt guilty any time she smiled at the reminder of a happy thought. Here, she felt no guilt, because at the Pine Tavern, you left your worries at the door. You left who you were at the door. Vigor turned from the bar and grinned, the smile barely visible through his thick beard.

"Usual?" he shouted.

Elisara nodded and removed her cloak, heading to the booth.

"We wondered if you would grace your old haunts," Helena grinned, embracing her.

"I could not stay away too long; Vigor owes me coin he seems to think is erased by buying me a drink." She tossed a pointed look to the physician as he placed a glass before her and sat beside Helena, their hands entwined. Elisara had never met a couple so in love. Talia sat with them, too: a fierce soldier, one Elisara had fought on many occasions. She met them all the week after her eighteenth birthday. Vlad insisted they needed to have a celebratory drink before she left for military training and brought her to the Pine Tavern—the ever-responsible personal guard. Elisara felt a pang of guilt, then, that he was not with them.

It was there at the tavern Vlad introduced her to the people he coined his second family, who welcomed her as their own, jesting immediately at her royal status. Once she returned from Keres, she spent many an evening alongside them. They had been determined to chip away at the walls she so expertly kept up, even around Caellum. There was the slim chance one of them—likely Talia—would spread what she would share with them tonight, yet the worry she carried was worth the risk.

"By my count of how much you drink when you're here, my debt is well cleared." He laughed, his drink spilling over the sides as he sat down at the table.

"Careful, Vigor," Helena said, eyebrows raised. "Elisara could force you to hand over every penny."

"How?" Elisara asked, a shortness to her tone. "I would never use my powers for my own gain. Is that what you're trying to suggest?"

They all looked at her.

"No..." Helena's wide grey eyes monitored her friend. "I meant that now you're Queen, you could demand he hand over his entire livelihood."

Helena flicked her pale, near-white hair to one side and leaned towards her friend. Next to her, Talia dropped her cards, having sensed the shift in tone. She could not look more different than Helena. Talia appeared as if she hailed from Keres, a distant relative to Nyzaia but taller, with more curves. She had far more bite than Helena too. She was not from Vala, but never divulged her birthplace. They knew better than to ask. "But let's address the other problem you're having." Helena continued. Vigor leaned in.

"I thought we left our problems at the door when we're here," Elisara said, playing with the bent corner of her ace of spades.

"Unless our friend has experienced a significant loss, while also becoming the most powerful Vala ruler in existence." Talia retorted from her usually silent corner.

Friend. Elisara feared they would cut ties the moment she became Queen, and her insistence there was no one to trust had festered from her fears. The truth of the matter was plenty of people in her life loved her, but the fear of disappointing them kept her barriers up. Yet after four years bottling her qualms, where had it got her? In a castle, as Queen, alone. Perhaps it was time to put some blind trust in people that had never let her wallow alone on nights in the city.

"Not here," Elisara said, shaking her head. Vigor gathered the cards in the centre of the table.

"I'm in the mood for a bath, aren't you all?" he asked.

The group grinned, but Elisara could not replicate it. They took the hint and rose, heading for the hot springs—one of Elisara's favourite places. She found solace in the warm water as it clashed with the bite of air. The group, more intoxicated than Elisara first thought, quickly stripped to their undergarments and edged into the water, carrying their drinks from the Tavern. Elisara laughed as they all giggled at their own stupidity.

"Show us the problem, *Snow Queen*," Talia jested. Elisara cringed at the awful attempt at a new nickname but reached for her cloak in a heap along the water's edge. Out came the talisman as Elisara dangled it for all to see.

"Your problem is a necklace?" Talia scoffed. Helena rolled her eyes at her, but Elisara was surprised she did not recognise the talisman. "What?" she exclaimed. "It's just a pendant. A broken pendant at that."

Helena approached Elisara while Vigor jested at Talia's ignorance. She did not touch the pendant, but bent to examine it, pushing the damp blonde hair from her face. Her eyes assessed Elisara.

"You're afraid of it." She frowned, cocking her head to the side. "Why?"

Helena sank into the warmth of the springs until only her head showed.

"You were at the funeral; you saw what happened." Elisara said. She placed the talisman on her palm, and the winds picked up immediately. "You know the harm my power can do without the talisman, let alone with it on." Elisara returned it to her cloak as Helena's face softened.

"Eli, no one saw a Queen who wished to harm them. They saw a Queen destined to protect them—a Queen they could be proud of, touched by the Goddess Vala herself." Vigor murmured his agreement, and even Talia nodded. Elisara peered down at the water, watching its movements as she threaded her hands through it, unable to meet their eyes.

"I cannot control it. Not enough, anyway," she whispered.

"What if I hurt someone?" She looked up at Helena but looked away at the pity on her face.

"Elisara, look at me." Helena said, grasping her hands. "Control can be learned, but your heart and concern for your people is what will make you a great ruler."

Helena reached for the talisman and placed it in her friend's hand, clasping her own around it. "Let it in," she urged. "Start small but embrace it."

Closing her eyes, she felt the smooth stone within her palms. Power exuded from it, absorbed by her skin, and merging with her blood. The rush of air froze her veins, and she breathed clouds into the cold night air, and as air wrapped around them, she willed it to stop. Helena smiled when she succeeded.

"Now, think of how you create snow, and use that influence to freeze the water instead. Try at the edge." Helena gestured towards a rock pool at the verge of the hot springs. Elisara waded to it and dipped her fingers in the water. She focused on the way it moved around her skin and closed her eyes, willing her power to freeze it, yet when Elisara peeped to check, her father's eyes—a piercing blue—stared back in the reflection. That day tumbled back to the forefront of her mind and air suddenly whipped around her as she gripped the edge of the springs and felt her fingers turn to ice. The water beneath finally froze over, yet she held no control.

"Out! Now!" Helena called, using her own strength to blow air towards the others, propelling them to the edge of the spring. Vigor and Talia clambered out quickly; the droplets of water dripping from their bodies froze and fell to the ground, shattering on the rocks. Elisara could not breathe. It was like her throat had frozen, along with her hands that clasped the talisman. Vaguely, she heard Helena's voice trying to calm and instruct her, but it was nothing compared to the sound of the air whizzing past her ears. Elisara's wet hair whipped, lashing against her skin, yet her eyes remained locked on her reflection: at her now glowing crystal blue eyes—a constant reminder of the power she did not want or deserve.

After losing her family, Elisara smothered her emotions, acting as though this hole in her chest did not exist. While she was never close to her sisters, she mourned their laughter. She missed her mother's smile as she gushed over Caellum or while they bonded over their love of dresses. But her father—her father she missed more than anything: their morning teas after breakfast, looking out from his sitting room across the city, his advice, and the way he softly stroked her hair whenever they bid farewell. The memories flooded back as the power formed around her and combusted.

In one clean movement, the small patch of ice Elisara formed suddenly expanded and raced towards Helena in the centre of the spring, whose eyes widened, unable to move. The ice did not change route but entrapped Helena as it spanned the entire spring, stopping only at the last drops of water on the rock's edge. As if exerted, Elisara's power dwindled, and the air slowed. She retreated from her reflection but halted as something hard dug into her lower spine. Elisara turned and saw the sheet of ice entrapping the entire spring. She reveled in its glistening beauty until she saw Helena trapped in the middle as ice encircled her waist. Above the water, her body tinged blue.

"Helena!" Elisara screamed. The woman's arms slowly moved to wrap around herself. Vigor skated across, wielding a large stone to begin cracking away at the ice, trying to make it wide enough to pull her out. Little did he know Elisara had not just frozen the surface of the spring; she froze the waters beneath it too, with Helena's legs trapped in a block of ice. Elisara's fears came flooding back and replayed before her. She had put someone she cared about at risk. Again.

Elisara stared as if something would prompt her ability to fix the mess she had created. Nothing. Air could not be used to retract ice. Talia pulled out her dagger and frantically stabbed at the ice alongside Vigor. Snow fell, and Elisara looked up at the dark clouds gathering.

A storm, she realized. *I have conjured a storm.*

Perhaps she could harness her power to turn the storm into lightning, willing it to crack the ice open. It was dangerous, but Helena's life hung in the balance.

Elisara focused on the clouds and willed them to condense. Electricity ripped through the air as a ripple of thunder spilled across Azuria. She homed in on that sound, the feeling of the energy prickling along her skin. And struck. A bright fork of lightning pierced the ice at the edge of the spring, sending a crack in Helena's direction. Elisara focused, hair static, as she felt currents of electricity roil along her body. She struck again on the opposite side, and the group jumped back.

It was not enough. The cracks broke through the ice, but it was too solid and risky to send a bolt of lightning closer to Helena. Elisara felt drained. Pulling the talisman from her palm, she lowered it around her neck. Elisara lifted her arms and felt the buzz of power connect with her soul. She struck at multiple spots at once, shattering ice and splitting apart trees at the rocky edge. As the lightning flashed, a dark silhouette emerged. Another strike and the ice cracked, flying into the air at the same time a tree, caught in the crossfire, caught fire, and fell too.

Out from the flames walked a dark figure, unbothered by the yellows and reds licking his black leather. Elisara halted the strikes as the figure began to run to the springs.

The Commander.

He reached the group at the same moment Vigor pulled Helena from the pool of shards that were once the hot springs, freeing her from the ice encasing.

Elisara forced her way through the shards, numb to their sharp edges, and focusing only on reaching her friends. The Commander knelt and pushed Vigor to the side. He rested Helena's head on his knees, and his hands on her shoulders while he focused. Amber glowed in his eyes as Elisara made her way through the shards, blowing them out of her way. But this time, a known control supported her movements. The Commander's jaw was tense like the rest of his body. *He's trying to control his anger*, Elisara realized. She swallowed, pushing the thoughts of Keres from her mind. She needed to focus on Helena. Colour was returning to her skin, a layer of moisture across her flesh as the remaining ice melted beneath the Commander's touch. Gently pulling Vigor by the arm, the Commander switched places, so Helena's head rested in her husband's lap. He moved to cup her calves instead, radiating warmth through them.

Elisara watched in awe. She had only ever seen him use his power for death, destruction, and intimidation. Now, staring at those glowing eyes, she knew he had done this before. Elisara knelt before her friend.

"Helena. I—I'm so sorry," she muttered, trying not to choke on her words. With hazy eyes, Helena looked at her.

"Remind me to never get on your bad side."

Elisara sniffled through a faint laugh and wiped her tears. As she raised her head to the Commander, the glow of their eyes connected, and the light in his quickly faded as he removed his hands from Helena. He glared at Elisara with dark fury instead.

"Take her home," he said to no one in particular, but the group understood. Elisara rose to help but was hauled back by his rough hand on her arm. "You. *Stay.*" He demanded through gritted teeth.

Elisara looked on longingly as the group wound their way through the trees back to their homes; Vigor and Talia supported Helena together, each using an arm to steady her body between them. Talia tossed a frustrated look back at Elisara before they vanished into the woods.

Slowly, Elisara faced the Commander, her face as furious as the one staring back at her. Lightning flashed behind him, darkening his silhouette.

"You are a fool," he spat, surveying the damage. "You have no more control now than you did four years ago, Princess. You are still reckless, self-centered, and above all, *dangerous.* Every royal family member knows you need the talisman to centre your power with your soul. Running around with it in your hand only pushed its lack of understanding as to what you wanted."

"Then why didn't you tell me that?" Elisara yelled back, taking several steps towards where he stood at the edge of the springs.

"Because I should not have to!" He roared; fire rose from his hands. "I am a Commander of armies. I am not your babysitter, Princess." He took several steps to her as his voice raised, his glowing eyes a signal of the power coiling beneath his skin. "Did no one tell you these things? Did no one think to teach you to use your new powers?"

"Who would teach me? I have lost everyone!" she screamed. Ice exploded behind him, shards filling the sky and sparkling like the stars watching intently from above. They melted with a wave of the commander's hand, water raining on the two of them instead as though they stood in the middle of their own storm. "I have no one," she cried, a strangled sob emerging in her throat as the water soaked her. The Commander stared, wet hair slicked to his face, panting in rage as his eyes stayed intently on her. Elisara's grief was all-consuming as she finally acknowledged her pain. Her family was dead. Tears streamed down her face and blurred her eyes, her mind flashing to the image of her family in the Temple. How could she have so much power and yet feel so powerless? Looking at the Commander, she thought she found pity in his gaze, if only for a moment. But she did not want it, and Elisara's pain soon turned to rage. Not only had she lost her family, but now his presence was thrust upon her—the last person she ever wished to see.

"Losing people you love is no excuse for endangering others." His response was cool. Matter of fact. "Or endangering yourself."

She ignored the latter half of his comment. He did not care for her, so there was no reason to pretend. The attack stung as she looked at him, pain in her eyes. She recovered quickly, taking a step closer until they stood inches apart.

"You dare speak to your Queen that way."

The Commander stepped closer, towering above her. The

warmth of his skin brushed against the cold air surrounding hers and she tracked the droplets running down his face, dripping onto her chest, suddenly aware she still stood, drenched, in only her undergarments.

"You are my Queen once you earn my respect," he hissed, turning from her. "Go back to the Castle. I will remain here and return the rest of the springs to their original state."

Elisara spun from him, pulling her cloak from the ground and hugging it around herself. She debated turning to have the last word, but he was already at the other side of the spring, melting the ice. So, she left, despite wishing to stay to prove she *was* his Queen and forcing him to bow. But after Elisara's time in Keres, she knew better.

Kazaar Elharar was a man who bowed to no one.

Chapter Twenty-One

Nyzaia

Nyzaia's jaw strained from the constant smile plastered on her face. Absent-mindedly, she nodded at the next citizen who stood before her, while the bangles on her arm jangled as she shifted position. Albeit beautiful, the golden throne made her back ache in ways even the hottest of baths could not eradicate.

The Court of Appeals was a weekly hearing, having existed for as long as Nyzaia remembered.

She stood in the shadows during her father's attendance. It was easier to pay attention to the qualms of the people without the scrutiny of the Lords standing in the wings, misconstruing every twitch in her expression. One of the six Pillars of the Red Stones involved a year as a Courtesan: faking a smile—faking many things, in fact—a skill she never thought would be useful as Queen of the Realm.

In the palace throne room, the floors were tiled in an array of colours and patterns: the walls a deep red, lined with golden arches and columns depicting endless flames. The room was long, allowing for the citizens to maintain an orderly queue as they filtered through. Her throne sat upon a set of steps, framed by an open arch allowing a view across the royal courtyard, while an extravagant fountain trickled in the background.

Whereas opulence described the throne room of Tabheri Palace, mediocre defined the room where she met with clients in the Red Stone's Den. The floor was made of the same red stone concealing their den. Drawings and names covered the walls, while her throne was a simple black chair stolen from a Lord's house. Yet she would trade this for the Red Stones in a heartbeat. Displaying wealth was not a quality of the Red Stones, who preferred simple lodgings. Many spent their money on supporting their families remaining in the city or other settlements in Keres.

"He said that the licensing process would be reviewed, my Queen?"

With a smile still plastered to her face, Nyzaia looked at the man standing at the base of the steps. She chastised herself for not paying enough attention.

"Is it still being reviewed, my Queen?" the man asked again, hands clasped before him.

"Yes, sir. It is being reviewed. I will provide you with an update next week if you would kindly attend court once again." She inclined her head to the man, who bowed and thanked her before exiting the hall. Nyzaia tapped her left wrist three times, and in her periphery, Tajana nodded to Isaam and Rafik by the doors. They paused the queue of citizens and directed those who remained through the exits. Nyzaia rose, smile remaining, and she inclined her head to the Lords, who upon her signal, left the room. As the last door closed, Nyzaia collapsed with a groan on the throne—a poor move, however, given it still caused her pain. She prodded at her jaw while her newly formed Queen's Guard smirked. Farid too.

There was too much to focus on, not least the next leader of the Red Stones. Her responsibilities as Queen meant she had little time to spare now. In fact, she had even questioned disbanding the Red Stones. After all, she now had the power to make changes across the entire realm, including the Underworld. But the Red Stones was a way of life. Entire portions of her people could lose trade with the communities across Novisia and Doltas Island.

"Do not laugh at me. This is exhausting. How am I to do this every week?" She complained, pulling up her skirts and kicking the shoes from her feet, allowing them to breathe from their constraints.

"You underwent how many years of training? Not to mention, you completed countless missions exerting your physical and mental limits, but this—sitting on a chair and being polite to people—is your undoing?" Tajana smirked.

"Of course. She never did have any patience," Jabir joked. A split second later, he dodged the hair pin thin knife tossed at his throat, and Nyzaia glared at him. "See, I've made my point." He laughed.

"Please tell me one of you was listening," She sighed, still watching Jabir: a skilled assassin, but also the Keeper of Books for the Red Stones. He rolled his eyes.

"Of course, I did. For the most part, there is nothing for you to action. Most complaints were aimed at the Lords who stood idly by. The only one you will need to investigate was the last man's request. He wants the entire licensing process for the spice market reviewed; he said it favours only those that can afford bribes." He leaned against the wall, twirling the knife she had thrown between his fingers.

"The King kept a record of all the requests in his office." Farid spoke up from his place at the back of the group, far from the eyes of the syndicate. "You will likely find more notes on the man's request there. Good luck getting the approval of the Lords, though."

"I am a Queen, Farid. Who said I need approval?" Nyzaia rose from the throne and Tajana extended her arm, a gesture she ignored. She did not wish to appear weak, not even in front of family, but she also knew a servant could enter any moment and gossip would soon spread.

Lord Israar had said nothing of Nyzaia and Tajana's kiss, yet his silence was concerning. Nyzaia was still trying to determine who she was as a ruler and what her people thought of their Queen; she did not wish for her relationship with the Captain of her Guard to become public knowledge, nor for anyone to start digging into Tajana's past and uncovering her role in the Red Stones. Farid clocked the movement but said nothing. Sensing Tajana's coldness, Nyzaia immediately sought to rectify it.

"Tajana will escort me to my father's office. Find other duties to attend to in the meantime." She did not allow room for any arguments. Swiftly exiting the throne room, she took a sharp left down the corridor and into the west wing.

"Have you been down here since..."

Nyzaia shook her head. Those who knew her understood she shared a complicated relationship with her father, while she believed they had no relationship at all. Her relationship with her mother was no different, and the last time she saw them both alive was during Kalon's assassination.

Perhaps only Larelle understood Nyzaia's management of her grief. The Neridian Queen had likely seen her own parents less than she had.

Tajana escorted Nyzaia down a dark corridor void of lanterns, as if it had never belonged to the King of the Fire Realm. A chill lingered in the air, and flames erupted on Nyzaia's palm. She allowed it to swim up her arm and bathe them both in warmth. Tajana admired the gesture as they walked side by side, her fingers grazing the flames.

With this new power in her veins, Nyzaia was able to control who the flames burned, as if it recognised those she cared for, and they welcomed Tajana with more welcome arms than Nyzaia had of late.

"Here we are," Tajana announced, upon reaching a grand door in the centre of the wall.

She removed a key from her side to unlock it, and with a forceful shove, the door opened, a layer of dust erupting from the disturbance. Nyzaia coughed as the dust settled. She peered into the room before crossing the threshold. She did not recognize it.

It was unlike the other rooms in the castle. While most rooms featured open archways, her father's office was lined with tall glass windows, and shielded the humidity from outside. Positioned on the highest floor of the castle, it offered uninterrupted views of the rocks forming the Abis Forge, with the peaks of the Zivoi mountains beyond.

"Is it just me, or is it unnaturally cold in here?" Tajana asked. Nyzaia frowned in agreement and made her way to the fireplace. She traced her hand over the engraved sigil before kneeling in front of the hearth. The flames danced on her hand but did not take to the wood within it. Turning, she directed a flame at Tajana, who dodged it; instead, it burned the armchair behind, setting it aflame. Nyzaia attempted the fireplace again while Tajana extinguished the blaze.

"It's as if the hearth is made from something that cannot catch alight," Nyzaia said, rising to survey the rest of the room.

"For a King of Keres, it seems the man was not fond of his God-given powers." Tajana murmured, rifling through the remaining papers on the desk. Nyzaia circled the room, attuning her instincts. Two armchairs overlooked the view, a small table between the two. Water rings stained the wood from the rise and fall of goblets.

He had company, she mused. The goblets still contained remnants of dark red wine, though this did not surprise her. The Red Stones often reported the King's visitors.

"This one is locked," Tajana declared, tugging at a desk drawer. Nyzaia left her to continue unlocking it while she persisted with her surveillance. The bookcases lining the walls appeared untouched, each leather-bound copy smothered in dust. A copy caught her eye on the centre shelf, harboring significantly less dust than the others. Nyzaia made a beeline for it, and gently, she brushed over its spine.

Myths and Lies of Ithyion by Caligh Servusian

As she made to pull the book from its shelf, a clatter sounded from behind, and she whirled to find Tajana braced against the wall, a splintered drawer in her hand.

"Graceful, Tajana. Very graceful," Nyzaia said, joining her in a crouch to collect the papers having fallen from the drawer. The skirts of her lehenga pooled as she switched to sit, instead, letters in hand.

"Iahabi," she read. "Who do you think that is?"

"Given the content of these letters, I'm going to assume it's his lover," Tajana said, scrunching her nose as she skimmed through another. "It's not a name I've heard, though."

"I do not need to learn about my father's love life outside his marriage."

Nyzaia flung the letter to one side and began filtering through the rest. Any addressed to Iahabi were added to the pile without a second glance. Her parents' marriage was once a happy one, so she had been told, though she had never seen it herself. It seemed their love dwindled before she was born. Her brothers often suggested it was because of how the King used Kazaar, turning him into a weapon. An affair was unsurprising.

Filtering through the other letters, each joined the rising pile as she deemed none of importance. Some general correspondence appeared between the King and the other lords of Keres about tithes.

Of course, Nyzaia thought. *All he cared about was money.*

An occasional letter emerged from another ruler, though it was simply discussions regarding the coordination of balls or delayed shipments. The only other letters were from Kalon, often filled with information about the Lords and others of position in Keres. The contents were not new to Nyzaia, and all contained information she had sent in her own correspondence. She wondered where he kept those letters, or if he even bothered to.

"This one is addressed from someone in the Red Stones,'" Nyzaia announced, squinting at the parchment.

"How do you know?" Tajana continued flicking through the scattered parchments that had fallen under the desk.

"The parchment. I recognize the texture. The ink is red, too, few others use red outside of the assassins or royals." She turned it over and lit a flame, casting light on the parchment. The symbol of the Red Stones embellished the top right corner: a sign only those in the Stones would recognise.

"Who would communicate with my father that I did not know about? His assignments were all directed to me."

"Maybe it's a minor job. What does it say?" Tajana asked. She stopped rifling through letters and moved to sit across from Nyzaia.

Perhaps he sent someone to spy on me, she pondered, a thought that ignited fury within her. Or maybe Tajana was right.

"Ready to burn."

Three simple, clearly coded words. Tajana frowned, as if trying to decipher them.

"Maybe he was trying to get rid of you," she jested, and laughed at her own mocking. While no love existed between Nyzaia and her father, she did not expect him to have ordered her dead, yet *what would he need to burn?* She thought back to the Historian's words: her father had argued with King Wren of Garridon moments before the explosion. Was her father capable of killing so many?

"Tajana, this is serious. Someone was sending coded messaging to the King of Keres without my knowledge."

"Well, are there any others? If there are, we can figure out if it was an ongoing communication or merely a random message with no meaning."

Nyzaia turned, collecting the few remaining parchments from her side of the desk. She landed on another in red writing, but this one was her father's script.

"He never sent it," she said, turning the paper and reading it again. *"'Understood.'"*

She looked up at Tajana.

"That's it? That doesn't help at all."

"There's no date?"

"Of course not. It's a coded message."

"You're uptight when you're playing Queen," Tajana jested, though Nyzaia sensed the seriousness hidden in her words. "Rajan could test it and provide a rough timeframe."

Nyzaia nodded; she had not anticipated returning to the Red Stones so soon. It was her home, her family, but how could she face them after so quickly being ripped from their arms? Tajana read the emotions on her face.

"They will not judge you, love," she whispered, cupping her cheek. "You are their Queen either way. They will still hold the same respect as they did before." Smiling, she planted a kiss on Nyzaia's lips.

"But the public may have something to say if they see me entering Red Stones territory. Our dwellings are not exactly secret, and I do not think they are ready to accept their Queen has been one before."

"We go at the most welcoming time then. Nightfall. Do you still have your leathers?"

Tajana laughed as Nyzaia pulled a face. Of course she did. She gazed at them longingly every time she opened the wardrobe door, now home to hundreds of lehengas, sarees, and kaftans instead.

"It's a date." Nyzaia kissed her before standing. "The rooftop? Midnight?"

"A date." Tajana smiled. Familiar butterflies filled Nyzaia's stomach at that smile, and all concerns of being seen together disappeared as she focused on her love.

"Are you coming with me?" Nyzaia asked, heading for the door.

"I'll stay and tidy these up. Farid will be at the end of the hallway to escort you to your chambers."

"Thank you, Tajana. For this," Nyzaia gestured at the room she had not dared enter alone. Tajana gave her a soft smile and returned to tidying as Nyzaia left the room. Giddy with excitement, she walked along the dark hallway. Tonight, she would don her second skin and return to the underworld—*her* world. And she hoped it would welcome her with open arms.

Chapter Twenty-Two

Larelle

Suppressing the sigh in her chest, Larelle clenched her hands in her lap to avoid rubbing her brow. Poised, she sat in the council chambers of the east wing turret overlooking the ocean to one side and the City of Mera to the other. She glanced at the clock to her left and then back at the closed wooden doors. The doors would eventually open, and the men on the other side would see Larelle sitting in the place her father once had: the steel throne, with the windows behind perfectly framing her position of power. Her delicately woven crown was arranged atop her curls that were pulled tight behind her into a low bun.

Stern, unwavering, and unforgiving. That was the look Lord Alvan advised. A look far from their perception of a young, unruly, and unwed mother. Larelle had scoffed at the need to possess such male characteristics because God forbid, they respect a woman who has *lived.*

Deep laughter echoed down the hallway and Larelle glanced at Lord Alvan, whose own brow furrowed at the blatant disrespect. They both knew the other Lords wished to dispute her rule, but to be an hour late to the first council meeting was impertinent. Larelle returned her gaze to the door and allowed her power to manifest, the seemingly calm waters around the turret crashing against the walls. The laughter abruptly stopped.

"Letting her emotions run away from her..." Someone murmured as the doors finally opened.

Larelle was a relatively calm, patient person, who did not relish in conflict, but these men could incite the drowning of the city.

How wrong they were to think her emotions controlled her; she was perfectly in control of the waves outside, and she manipulated every molecule in a demonstration of her power.

"Tell me, my Lords. Would you call the anger of my father the simple act of his emotions running away from him?" Larelle asked, voice cold as they filed in. The men were vaguely recognisable, though older since she had last seen them, their stomachs filled out from age, and the years of sitting in judgement of others. None met her eye, but disgust flitted across their faces. They moved their chairs. "I do not recall permitting you to sit."

Her eyes assessed each man in turn. The male at the end, directly opposite Larelle, scoffed and sat down, matching her stare.

"Lord Leto, isn't it?" Larelle rose from her place, the skirts of her Neridian Blue gown twisting with her movements. The man did not acknowledge her. "Do you all remember how my father's power manifested when he was angry?" she mused as she circled the men. "The waters would darken, liquid in glasses and jugs would bubble and spill, waves would crash..."

Boredom etched the men's faces.

"Can someone tell me," Larelle asked, "if my father could create water?" She reached the seated Lord and placed her hands on the back of his chair. None of the others answered, as if her question was an idiotic one. Lord Alvan's mouth twitched upwards, and the ocean crashed higher, droplets landing on the floor of the tall tower. The men exchanged glances.

"Do you think it is possible, Lord Leto, for someone—a descendent of the Goddess Nerida herself—to *create* water?"

Lord Leto opened his mouth to answer or retaliate, but no one would know for no words escaped. The man clutched at his non-existent neck with thick fingers clad in silver, his bug-like eyes bulging further from his skull.

He gargled, clawing his throat for breath as he tried to rise from the table. Larelle pushed him back into his seat by the shoulder while the others looked silently on as sea water spilled from the man's lips and onto the table before them. As his face paled, the water stopped, and Larelle retreated to her chair. With a small motion of her hand, the spilled water formed a sphere. Lord Leto flew backwards as it slammed into his chest. The other Lords watched in stunned silence.

"It is clear none of you have any respect for me, and if you do not have respect for your Queen, it makes me wonder... what *is* your purpose? Why should I keep you here?" Larelle asked, leaning back into her throne. The silence persisted. "You have wasted my time this morning and so I will waste yours. This meeting is over. You are dismissed." she said firmly, remaining seated as they rose and left the chambers.

The second they did, Larelle approached the windows, eager to feel the saltwater air on her skin, a calming sensation. She was past caring about the Lord's opinions, no matter what Alvan advised. If her birthright was not enough to sway them, nor the strength of her power, then they were lost to her. She could not be advised by men who would never respect her rule, for their values did not align. But she knew simply stripping them of their seats would alienate them, and the other wealthy citizens, too.

She sighed, calming the waters below as the colour lightened. Alvan approached from behind.

"So, creating water is new," he hummed.

She glanced over her shoulder at him and smiled.

"Zarya asked me if I could last night, but I had never considered it. It didn't take long to fill a whole chalice." She turned back to look across the sea. "I have always been powerful, but this is new waters. While I am learning as I go, it terrifies me."

"What terrifies you?" he asked.

"The feeling of it. I can feel the power flowing through my veins, and I do not tire. It is as if my wells are endless, but no one should have an endless amount of power."

Alvan did not answer, but appeared deep in thought as he cracked his knuckles.

"Riyas would say something profound in a moment like this. '*The depth of your power only aids your decisions, influenced by the depth of the love you have for your people*," he mimicked Riyas' voice, earning a gentle chuckle from Larelle. It was nice to speak with someone else who remembered Riyas like she did.

"You're yet to tell me how you knew Riyas," Larelle said. "Zarya was too enamored with your stories about him I forgot to ask."

Sadness appeared to plague Alvan then as he gripped the windowsill and looked out to sea.

"I had just taken over as Lord of Seley, and in the chaos of it all, I could no longer care for my younger brother as much as I wished." He peered down at his feet. "My brother always wished to become a Captain for the royal fleet, so I said he could enlist to train at The Bay. I took him there, and it was Riyas who signed him up." Alvan smiled. "He joked that as the Lord of a town across both Garridon and Nerida, I had surely lost any connection to the sea. He told me I needed to train as much as my brother." Alvan turned from the ocean to lean against the frame and crossed his arms. "That was it. I met him every two weeks, and he trained me on the ships. We formed a friendship fast. The people of Seley often conduct business in Garridon, so they do not miss my absence."

"He never mentioned you," Larelle said.

"He mentioned you a lot," Alvan laughed. "But I am sure those are stories for another day."

Larelle smiled at the thought of Riyas talking about her and glanced sideways at Alvan as the haunting question resurfaced again.

"What do you know of that trip?" she asked.

"Not a lot. All I know is, one day, they assigned him to a trip, which he seemed convinced would aid in promotion," he said. "I can go to the docks, if you like, and see what information I can gather."

His knowledge did not differ from her own.

"No," Larelle shook her head. "I am stifled being kept in this castle. It would be nice to return to familiar surroundings and walk amongst my people again. I will go."

"You should take guards with you. I can prepare a carriage," he said, walking away.

"Alvan, I do not wish for this to be a royal event of grandeur. I will visit on horseback, but if you have the time, I would appreciate the company."

"Of course, my Queen, I will have the horses readied to meet you at the stables." He bowed and left Larelle to pace the room.

She longed to be back among her people in the city where she raised her daughter, to assess how they were all coping after the events in the Neutral City, yet she hoped her return would not bring all she knew of her life into question.

***

Alvan laughed as he finally caught up to her after having raced along the shore on horseback. Larelle relished the salty air and ocean spray mingling with her hair, flowing freely behind her in the breeze. It took them a mere hour on horseback, the land flat and quiet. The beach between Meera and The Bay was renowned for its peacefulness, as no buildings stood between the two, only the beach, the ocean to one side, and open fields to the other. Larelle wished Zarya was with her and felt like she had seen little of her daughter since becoming Queen. Though she vowed to bring something back for her, to make her smile.

"I did not realise you were so competitive!" He laughed as they both slowed their horses to a standstill before dismounting.

"Maybe I simply like horse-riding at a fast pace. I believe this speaks louder as to how *you* feel about competition." She chuckled and led them towards the home overlooking the sea, tying the horses up outside.

"He did a beautiful job," Alvan said, marveling at the humble home.

Larelle nodded, a sad smile crossing her face. While it saddened her to think of him, the house held many happy moments. She had lived a quiet life there, but one filled with joy as she, Zarya, and Olden became a family.

She led them past the house, admiring the other homes lining the narrow strip. As they walked in comfortable silence, water filtered into The Bay, and contentment washed over Larelle as they reached the dockside and began weaving amongst the many food stalls. Most days, she visited the food stalls as the sun set, when the remaining items were discounted. Yet on days when funds were better, she treated Zarya to an item of choice. She smiled upon reaching her favourite bread stand.

"My Queen," greeted Orlo, his moustache seeming to curl from shock. He wiped his hands across his apron, leaving dusty white handprints behind.

"Orlo, please. You are Zarya's favourite stall. Continue to call me Larelle."

Alvan drew closer as those around seemed to whisper, having heard Orlo's address.

"And how is the little princess?" He grinned, revealing two golden teeth.

"I think she would be happier if I brought her back some of her favourite focaccia," Larelle smiled, remembering her daughter's excitement whenever Orlo handed over a tiny chunk of it: all she could usually afford.

"Olive and sundried tomato?" He did not need to ask. "I've just taken a fresh one out. Would you like it?"

A range of emotions overcame Larelle then, who could now purchase her daughter an entire loaf of bread, when only weeks ago, it was a delicacy to have a bite-sized piece.

"That would be wonderful." Larelle handed over a bag of coins, which Orlo reluctantly accepted. "How have things been? Since..." she trailed off, and Orlo gave her a sad, knowing smile while wrapping the focaccia in paper.

“I was lucky. I didn’t know anyone in the city. I so rarely leave The Bay,” he told her. He handed the wrapped bread over and placed his hands in the pockets of his apron. “People are unnerved though; they worry Nerida is next.”

Larelle listened intently, nodding in agreement with him. She glanced at the faces of the citizens trying to listen in.

"I am meeting with the other rulers soon, as well as the Lords of Nerida. Please trust me when I say I will do all I can to keep us safe.” Her words incited whispers from those gathered.

“There’s no one I would have trusted more to take over,” Orlo said with confidence. She smiled before bidding him farewell, navigated by Alvan through the crowd. Word of the Queen's arrival had spread fast in The Bay, and Larelle sensed Alvan's confusion, having clearly expected a different response from the public, who all bowed their heads as she passed. There was a familiarity between them.

"Did you ever visit The Bay with my father or brother?" she asked as they exited the edge of the crowd and descended into the heart of the docks.

"Once with your brother," he said, walking with his hands behind his back.

"Let me guess: several guards kept the people away from him while he perused the stalls to simply turn his nose up and leave as quickly as he came."

"You missed the part where a small child tried to run up to him, and a guard pushed them away."

Larelle stared at him, the disgust clear on her face.

They passed sailors along the dock, many stopping to bow as she passed, some of whom she recognised from evenings in the tavern with Riyas. Upon reaching the Captain of the Royal Fleet’s quarters, Larelle took a deep breath and stepped over the threshold, in fear she would soon learn the truth, which may change all she had known about the departure of her beloved.

Chapter Twenty-Three

Caellum

The riots in Antor lasted three days and three nights, confined only to the capital, he was told. Antor was home to the wealthiest of Garridon and housed many of his father's and grandfather's supporters, yet the further one travelled from the city, the quieter the towns became. Little commotion was cited elsewhere.

Caellum would have never expected the people of Antor to riot: a city famed for its peaceful nature. Yet as the capital, it welcomed many visitors from other realms, and Caellum wondered if the exposure to other citizens had contributed to the more radical opinions of his right to the throne.

Over the past three days, Sir Cain and the Lords assured him all was being managed in the city. While he had tried to request specifics, he was repeatedly reminded that, as an inexperienced ruler, he should focus on finding a suitable marriage to better the throne's relations with its people. But Caellum refused to listen any further to such absurd proposals and could hardly believe the Lords when they discussed potential matches. Instead, as the King of Garridon, Caellum took matters into his own hands.

With a handful of guards, Caellum set out on horseback to make amends with his people. Neither the Lords nor Sir Cain knew of his plans, but he was not willing to hear their objections. He had decided. He was going into the city.

To settle the unrest, he needed to understand firsthand the thoughts of his people, and prove he was not his father.

"Two guards will stay here with the horses," a guard informed

Caellum, who nodded as they reached the low wall marking the entrance to Antor.

Resting his hands along the divider, Caellum scanned his eyes over the city outskirts as the guards secured the horses and discussed their plans. Wide strips of multi-colored wildflowers separated him and the wall from the first buildings of Antor. Their plan was to enter the west of the city closest to the castle, where most market stalls were located—the home to many tradesmen. Whereas the east housed the simpler homes, the wealthiest in the city lived in the centre.

The city appeared untouched. Caellum was eager to discover where the riots were contained to assess the extent of the damage, but more so to ease the people's worry.

He began walking through the fields, careful to follow the small path fashioned from footfall over the years and avoiding the flowers where possible. Two guards were quick to rush around him, disregarding the path to protect his front. He frowned; he was not used to entering the city with protection. Often, he visited alone, or with Elisara, and largely went unnoticed: insignificant to the people as one of King Wren's many children. But that was before.

His mind wandered to Elisara. They frequently visited the city together, with Caellum collecting bunches of wildflowers for her before returning to the castle, content with one another's presence. He felt that absence now as the air lifelessly brushed his skin. The Lords' advice loomed. It spurred him ahead, and Caellum ushered the guards to quicken their pace.

The patchwork structures of the buildings came into view as he approached the back of what he knew to be a butcher's shop. Walking to the left of it, he entered the wide walkway leading deep into the city. The first thing he noticed was the volume of people. There were many more than he expected, yet they continued as normal, despite the events of the last three days.

Nothing appeared out of place, which urged Caellum further into the city, but three steps was all it took for his presence to become known. Several citizens halted as odd whispers dotted the silence, and every head in Caellum's eyeline turned to face him. His step faltered. Everything in his body urged him to turn and leave. Disgust was evident in the faces of his people; others marked with fear and hatred, while some with mild, wary intrigue. His guards halted, too, waiting for further instruction. Despite the dark thoughts and doubts warring in his mind, Caellum took a breath.

"Continue to the city centre." He commanded.

Forcing his head high, a soft smile graced his face as he nodded in acknowledgement to those appearing the least likely to murder him. Every step on the paving seemed to echo, announcing the unwanted King's arrival in the city, and as he continued his journey behind two of his guards, a crowd began to merge behind him. He swallowed. With so few guards, visiting the city during a time of unrest seemed a profoundly stupid idea now. But he needed to do this—to find a way to speak to the people, and for them to see reason. Caellum glanced around for a podium of sorts: somewhere to be seen. There was none.

"I know this is an unstable time," he called, the crowd barely acknowledging his words. "But I assure you, I wish to rule in your interests." The wide promenades of the city narrowed as people filtered in, and all the while, as the guards held out their arms to keep people back, Caellum continued walking. Whispers heightened as he felt bodies pushing closer, and the guards picked up the pace as shouts tore from the crowd.

"Usurper!"

"Tainted!"

"Find the fallen queen!"

Caellum's head spun at that, trying to locate the voice, but there were too many faces among the crowds. One of the guards behind had an arm poised around his back, and Caellum bowed his head as people began throwing anything and everything into their path. The guards shouted at one another, but he could not make out their words. He was pushed forward as the guards guided him round corners and alternative paths, his only view the paving under his feet.

It soon darkened with soot, and Caellum's head snapped up, catching a glimpse of the smoke-stained buildings before a guard forced his head back down. Chest tightening, and breath quickening, he pictured Edlen and Eve laid across his path, covered in ash. Auralia's peaceful face. The limp bodies of his brothers. Unable to breathe, he stumbled from his guard's grip, his head colliding with the path. Pain flashed through his skull, almost as strong as that in his heart. Caellum rose unsteadily to his feet, head spinning.

"Cal!" Someone shouted. Hands grabbed him from all angles as the faces of his people blurred before him. "Cal!"

Caellum turned, disorientated, as Sir Cain fought his way through the people. The guards pushed citizens back, landing punches as they went.

"No," Caellum murmured, trying to hold himself up amid the jostling. "Don't hurt them!" Air refused to flow through his lungs. It was all too much—the noise, images, the thoughts of his family, the struggle to breathe. Sir Cain almost reached him and withdrew the sword from his side. He screamed at Caellum, who frowned, confused as to what he was doing. That was when he felt it—the knife driving through the back of his shoulder. He looked down silently, at the silver blade protruding from him. He looked back up, eyes wide, as Sir Cain approached.

Caellum did not see who Sir Cain held by the throat as he plunged the sword into their stomach, though whoever it was had tried to kill him. People fled the chaos and there were no more bodies to hold him upright as he fell to the floor.

"I've got you, Cal."

Caellum looked up from his position on the ground, and for a second, thought his father held him. He blinked, but his Father was gone, and when he blinked again, there was only darkness.

Chapter Twenty-Four

Larelle

The salted air reminded Larelle so much of Riyas: the exact scent lingering on him whenever he returned from work. The only thing missing was the note of citrus he naturally retained. Larelle turned from those bustling throughout the sailors' quarters to school her emotions, drawing away the added moisture pooling in her eyes. The building's interior mimicked that of a ship, with only small windows for daylight to emulate the portholes. She feigned interest in the map on the wall whilst levelling out her breathing. Alvan introduced himself to the sailors, buying her time to compose herself. The few sailors flitting in and out to the docks greeted him with warmth. All dressed casually, their exposed forearms covered in tattoos. As their conversations concluded, it was time for Larelle to present herself as Queen, and not the heartbroken partner of a dead sailor. The men bowed low as she turned. She inclined her head with a smile.

"Please. Rise," she said softly. A look of knowing sadness passed between the men, who knew her not only as their new Queen, but as Riyas' beloved. The mother of his child. The recognition was clear in their eyes as they beheld Larelle.

"Larelle, my sweet girl," a voice boomed from the doorway. That voice, she *did* know. Captain Thain. The man looked no different from the last time she saw him six years ago, when she swore never to return to the docks. He often jested the Goddess kept him young in gratitude for keeping her seas safe, and she was inclined to believe him. Now in his early sixties, the captain looked not a day over forty, with his long black hair tied low at the nape of his neck, and no grey in sight. His arms were as dense as the younger sailors, ropes tattooed onto his forearms, and reaching his hands, the wrinkles there the only sign of his aging. His smile was broad and skin sun-kissed from countless days at sea.

"Captain Thain. It is good to see you," Larelle clasped his hands as he moved towards her, taking her in as if ensuring she remained in one piece. She remembered the last time she had seen him. The day he broke the news her true love—the father of her unborn child—would not be returning. The seas had claimed him. Thain held Larelle as she broke down in his arms, staying huddled on the old wooden floors together as the sun set and moon rose, neither uttering a word.

"You should visit more often," he said with a grin, his one gold tooth glinting under the dim lanterns. Yet the memories of Riyas were the sole reason she did not visit; she did not need any reminders of the pain in her heart.

"Sadly, life as a Queen limits my ability to go out to sea." She smiled.

"Nonsense!" He exclaimed, ushering her towards a private room. "You are Queen! If you want to live at sea, you can!"

Larelle did not want to live at sea. It was difficult enough calling to the oceans that had taken her love; how could she live atop the waters that killed him? Larelle's heart raced, and her lungs constricted. Alvan pulled out a small wooden chair for Larelle and stepped forward to introduce himself to the captain. She removed the thin cloak from her shoulders and folded her hands in her lap: a habit of a Queen she could not seem to break, even in familiar company.

"If you do not wish to visit the seas, then what do I owe this pleasure?" Thain asked.

"I would like to see the schedules from the week of Riyas' last trip," Larelle requested, head high. She refused to let the tears defeat her, though the pity in his face was clear, as if she were a helpless widow unable to abandon the past. She could not abandon it, however, and that was the problem. There was something wrong about how Riyas was taken. She felt it in her gut.

Thain reached behind him, tracing a finger along a shelf of large leather-bound books. His hand paused on a red leather copy.

"This should be it. You'll have to squint your way through my awful handwriting to find the relevant dates." Captain Thain dropped the book, the seashells on the desk vibrating with the impact. "I'll be on the docks inspecting the ships if you need me." With that, he exited his office, and returned to the communal area, leaving Larelle and Alvan to sit in silence.

"I can leave as well, if you wish. I understand this is sensitive." Alvan said. She shook her head.

"No. You are welcome, Alvan. I may need someone to listen to my rambled thoughts as I read over it." Larelle's shaking hand reached for the bound cover, pulling it back to reveal parchment lines with names, dates, and descriptions.

Tracing a finger down the list, Larelle paused whenever she saw his name, with each line referring to his usual training duties. She continued looking for the date engrained in her mind, and it did not take long. There it was.

Riyas Zerpane. 26th August, the 115th Year of Novisia.

Assigned to the Royal Maiden. Scouting mission to the outer border at request of the King.

"At request of the King..." Larelle repeated, head slowly rising to look at Alvan. She did not understand. She did not know what, or where, the outer border was, let alone why Riyas would be requested to attend it so unexpectedly.

"There's nothing unusual about that. Perhaps he was hand selected for missions a lot. He never gave many details," Alvan said. She glanced back at the book and turned the pages, stopping every few turns to read. Larelle repeated the motion until she was back at the first page. She slammed the book shut.

"Training duties." She declared. "Every week, every shift, every *day*—training duties! The only task he was ever assigned to."

Larelle rose, frustration and anger building as the room darkened. Clouds roiled outside, blocking any light from entering the portholes.

"He was skilled, and great with the younger lads. It makes sense for him to have been training new recruits," Alvan reassured her.

"Then why was he selected, at random, for a King's mission?"

"Maybe he was just one of the few men available," Alvan said. "The men are assigned to ships months in advance, and most stay on them permanently. It makes sense only a handful of people would be chosen." Stepping away from the wooden wall, he began to pace, as if digesting the information. "The king was not to know the ship would not return."

"Was he not?" Larelle snapped, rising from her chair. "We do not know his motives. What if he knew about Riyas before I told them? What if this was his way of getting him out of the picture?" Quickly, she became frantic. Larelle had always wanted answers, yet the answers raised more questions now.

Pushing back from the desk, Larelle stormed from the building. Rain descended in sheets and lashed at her face, but she did not care. She did not bother controlling her emotions or calming her power; she needed to feel the sting of rain lashing against her skin, to feel the same pain Riyas would have felt once the storm struck his ship—the ship her father purposefully assigned him to.

With the rain pouring, everyone had vacated the docks in search of cover, allowing Larelle an uninterrupted march back to her horse. Had her pregnancy started showing before she realised? Or soon enough for her father to have planned something to rid Riyas from the picture? Perhaps he hoped Larelle would give the baby up if Riyas could not be there to help her raise it. Her mother's maids likely spied on her, too, so what if one had put the pieces together and told her? Unable to think straight, the pain clouded her memories while the rain blurred her vision.

Flashes of storms appeared as she envisioned Riyas' last moments. Larelle thought she had closed the door on such pain, but she relived it all now as she mounted her horse and turned in the direction of the castle. Had he drowned? Did lightning strike him? She would never know, and that was the worst part, the guilt of those that remained after the death of another. In all the fury, she had not even stopped to focus on what the script meant by 'outer border.'

Earlier today, she raced Alvan to The Bay, and now she raced to return in search of more answers, more proof of her unending heartbreak—and the reason Zarya had no father—was because of the malice of her own family. Or was Alvan right? Was Larelle merely looking for reasons to keep this at the forefront of her mind, to keep Riyas in her mind? Had her mother known her father's plan? She had no doubt that her brother did, content with causing her despair. The tide pulled further back into the ocean the closer she reached the castle, the height of the waves ascending. She did not care. The water would never harm her. If only the same could be said for those she held dearest.

As she dismounted at the castle steps, a blur moved across the pouring rain, Alvan, racing to catch up to her. She did not want him near; she wanted no one near as she confronted her pain. Servants stopped to check on their Queen as she powered through the castle; her dress was soaked through, highlighting the shape of her figure, and her loose hair plastered to her face, arms, and back. Yet still, she did not care, leaving a path of water in her wake.

Growing up, she was forbidden from her father's strategy room. Only Aalto had permission, along with his military commander and those overseeing the sailors, including Captain Thain, who she had thought was her friend. Down she went into the darkest depths of the castle into a room built into the rock foundations, with only a wall separating it from the ocean.

Larelle stopped in the doorway, and stared at the giant table that formed a perfect depiction of Novisia. She circled it until reaching Nerida. And there it was.

The Outer Border.

Two engraved rings surrounded the oceans of their land: one marked the Novisian Border, stopping just past the Unsanctioned Isle marked to the north of the map. The second ring—further out—labelled the Outer Border. Miles of ocean rested beyond it. 'X' dotted hundreds of places across the map, and Larelle's brow furrowed, confused as to what they signified.

The rest of the room was largely empty, and she wondered where they kept their records, books, historical notes—anything related to strategy. There were no bookshelves. The only other items in the room were a fireplace, a stack of rolled maps, and a large tapestry of the Neridian sigil.

Was she destined to never know the truth behind Riyas' disappearance? Tilting her head, she looked at the tapestry, and the bottom left corner which appeared worn over time. Her brother had never been creative with his hiding places. She chewed her lip, wondering if he inherited that trait from their father. Pulling the tapestry aside, a door lay behind it. Larelle rolled her eyes.

Foolish, she thought. *Even more so for not locking it.*

A round room lay beyond, seeming to form part of a turret. Like the room before it, it remained below the water, but there was something different—something eerie—as if the room itself knew her presence was unwelcome. As she stepped further inside, and closed the door behind her, she was mesmerized by the four portraits spaced evenly around the wall.

The southern wall bore a resemblance to her own reflection and those of the other women in her family line. The woman had dark skin, yet darker than Larelle's, given her mother's pale complexion. She had the same black curls, too, but more tightly coiled; a silver tiara of waves pulled the hair back from her face, her eyes an enticing blue. Larelle stepped closer, peering at the golden name plate on the frame.

Nerida, Goddess of Water.

She staggered, spinning to look at the other three portraits. A woman with silver hair and ice-blue eyes that matched those of

Elisara's father; a male with skin the same bronze as Nyzaia's, with a strong brow and dark lashes framing amber eyes. Finally, a man she did not recognise. His hair was the brightest blonde, and freckles lined his face, but those eyes—those were eyes of pure emerald. The original ruling family of Garridon.

Nerida, Vala, Keres, and Garridon. She stood surrounded by the Gods themselves, and wondered if they were in any way accurate. There was no one alive who would know for certain, though she saw the resemblance of the citizens in each God. She was content with this imagining of them. The real question was, why did the King of Nerida have a shrine to all four Gods?

Recovering from her surprise, Larelle glanced around the rest of the room. A short bookcase sat below the portrait of Vala, and below the portrait of Keres was another fireplace. Below Garridon's was a collection of rolled maps and beneath Nerida, a writing desk. She stepped towards it and sat where her father would have, trying to conjure the inner workings of his mind.

Proof, she reminded herself. *I need proof of his involvement.*

She pulled at the desk drawers, but none budged. She ran her hand across the unique imprint embellished on the front, though it did not appear like any lock she had seen before. On closer inspection, she realised it was the sigil of Nerida. The same size as her talisman. Unclasping the chain around her neck, she breathed in, and closed her eyes, channeling the water thrashing in her veins as she pressed the talisman against the imprint. It was unhappy being taken from her neck. Hearing a click, she pulled the drawer open and returned the talisman to its home on her chest.

The drawer was a mess, not like the usual rigid organization of her father's chambers. Spilled ink covered stacks of parchment, weighed down by seashells and stones.

Larelle lifted the stack from the drawer and began to investigate. The first few lines meant nothing but were merely random scribbles of which she could not decipher. Then, she spotted it. The proof. A list of names, enough to crew a ship, and right at the top—underlined—was Riyas. Larelle sat back in her chair and looked up at the Goddess of Nerida.

"How could you let the waters take him?" she whispered.

And how could a father break a daughter's heart?

She expected a sense of closure upon discovering the truth, but the pain remained, as did the fury. She needed to speak with the Historian to discover more about the mission, and whether her father had known it would fail and end in death.

"Larelle?" Alvan called from outside.

"It's open," she called. The tapestry clearly fooled no one.

"No, it's not." Alvan said as the brass doorknob twisted. Larelle frowned. She had not locked it. She rose from her seat and pushed the door open, where Alvan stood. No lock.

"Try again," she said, closing the door in his face.

"Hello to you, too," he responded before turning the knob. Nothing. It would not open for him. Larelle pulled him inside and exited the room, standing where he had been moments ago.

“Let me guess, try to open the door to get out?” he jested, turning the knob. “Are you purposely locking this somehow?”

“No, it seems it only opens for me."

Larelle glanced back at the door, then returned to the desk. "I supposed my father was not as foolish as I first thought." She murmured, folding the list of names and placing the parchment to one side. She was not ready to discuss the events with Alvan, and he assumed as much as he silently took in the contents of the room while rifling through the remaining parchments.

"Huh. I did not expect Garridon to look like that," He finally broke the silence, returning to the desk to lean against it, facing Larelle. "Anything interesting?"

“My father wrote this,” Larelle handed the parchment over.

V,

The most recent location presented the same barriers as before. The same walls hold us. Prepare to release the waves.

Adrianus

"Release the waves. What does that mean?"

"Some kind of code, but I'm not sure what for. Have you ever heard of the Outer Border?" she asked. Alvan's confused look answered her question. "The map outside has a ring for a Novisian Sea Border and an Outer Border. The logbook in the captain's quarters referenced the destination of Riyas' mission was to the Outer Border."

"Why would we need a border? We neighbour nothing."

"Or do we? There's been no mention of any other kingdoms or lands since Ithyion, but that doesn't mean they don't exist," She peered up at her Goddess. "The marks on the map outside. What if they are linked to the border?"

"Like a physical border keeping us in?"

Returning to the other room, Larelle's dress trailed rainwater as it clung to her skin. She shivered, goosebumps lining her forearms as she paced around the map, stroking each of the different Xs.

"Or keeping something out?" She wondered. "What if this is to do with the explosion?" she paused and rubbed her arms. "What if he was trying to make sure whatever these barriers are, were intact to prevent whoever set the explosion from getting in?"

"Which would mean it might not have been someone from Novisia," Alvan finished. Larelle nodded and considered how much of their findings she should share with the other rulers.

Chapter Twenty-Five

Nyzaia

Standing on the rooftop of the palace, the moonlight shone upon Nyzaia's black leathers that intricately molded to her curves. Her hood stayed up, though no one would recognise her up here. She played with a dagger between her fingers, while the other hand danced in flames, as she relished the sensation of her two powers becoming one. If there was a goddess of darkness and shadows, she would pray to her right now for the comfort she provided her.

She glanced at the constellations above. The skies were always clear in Keres. She wondered if Elisara felt closer to the darkness, living so much higher on the mountains.

"What a sight you are," Tajana said from behind. "I forgot how delectable you look in your leathers." She wrapped her arms around Nyzaia's middle, resting her chin on her shoulder. Nyzaia relaxed into her hold. No one would see up here. She treasured the moment of peace, as these days, the stress was unavoidable.

"You forgot, did you? I'm wounded, given how many times you've ripped them off me." She leaned into her touch, laughing with Tajana, who stroked Nyzaia's stomach, and planted playful kisses along her neck. "We could just stay here." Nyzaia whispered, eyes fluttering closed as Tajana's hand grazed her chest before moving into her hair. She pulled, tilting Nyzaia's head back, and silencing her gasp with a deep kiss.

Stepping back then, Tajana gazed longingly into her eyes—a look she so often gave Nyzaia, one that stared into the very depths of her soul.

"The others are waiting, scattered across the city in case something goes wrong." She traced a thumb over Nyzaia's plump bottom lip. "We should go."

Nyzaia retreated several steps, her back to the city.

"In case something goes wrong?" She repeated, cocking her head with a smirk. "Have you forgotten who I am?" And with those words, Nyzaia threw out her arms and fell backwards off the top of the palace. She fell with a smile, spinning midair as she prepared to land on the rooftop below. Nyzaia rose from her perfectly executed landing and brushed the red dust from her hands, turning to check Tajana was behind before they took off into the night: two shadows of a flame gliding through the darkness on the rooftops of Tabheri.

The rest of her syndicate could likely see the pair leaping from building to building, their laughter gentle in the stillness of the night. Nyzaia reached the corridors of tents that made up the market and dropped through an opening between two brightly coloured fabrics. Scents of spices lingered still. What she would give to wander through the stalls in daylight: tasting every treat imaginable, admiring the metalwork stands, buying flowers for Tajana.

She did not worry about being seen. No one would recognise her, though citizens rarely visited the market at night, it was commonly known as a meeting place for the Red Stones, though tonight it was empty. Tajana waited up ahead, leaning against the wall. Smirking behind the black fabric covering her face, she signaled with her hand, pointing upwards. Tajana held up three fingers, then counted down. Three. Two—

She sprinted, returning to the rooftops, but Nyzaia was a second behind and cursed at not having chosen a quicker exit.

This had been a common game for them on quiet nights: a race back to the den, though Nyzaia was out of practice. Back onto the rooftops, they headed from the lavish city homes to the clustered streets of the outer city. She monitored Tajana, only two rooftops away, until she dropped below, vanishing from sight. Nyzaia continued on the rooftops, confident in her route. She passed over the drinking establishments as the last few stragglers filtered onto the streets.

"*Shit,*" she cursed, skidding to a stop. The next roof had caved in. Boarded off for repairs. That explained Tajana's change of route. Nyzaia dropped to the floor below, not happy with having to glide along amongst the alleyways, there was every chance some Red Stones could be lingering. She did not want anyone to know she was visiting until she was ready, so she stuck to the shadows. She weaved through the last small homes until reaching the towering stones bordering the city.

Nyzaia assessed her surroundings, yet there was no sign of Tajana or her syndicate. Slipping into the gap in the rock—their usual meeting point—she regulated her breathing.

"I win—"

Grasping Tajana's hand from behind, she twisted Tajana round to face her, who dropped her dagger in the process. But she pushed back, pinning Nyzaia against the wall and pulling down her hood.

"I still win."

She kissed Tajana deeply, though scolded herself for not having checked further back, ensuring she was alone before announcing her win. All self-criticisms melted at the touch of Tajana's lips. Nyzaia was flame, and Tajana was smoke, the taste of which lingered on her. Nyzaia relaxed in the moment—moments that were becoming far less frequent since her return to the palace. Her hands grazed Tajana's sides to pull her closer while Tajana gripped Nyzaia's face, as if scared she would disappear at any moment. Tajana groaned as Nyzaia bit her lip.

"I hate to be the one to break up the party," Isaam called from outside. They turned and there stood the syndicate, respectfully avoiding the gaze of their Queen.

"Don't lie, Isaam. We all know you'd love to join the party." Nyzaia smirked and pushed off the wall, Tajana behind her. The two walked further down the rocks, waiting for the large crack which signaled the entrance to the Red Stones Den.

She stopped when they approached and motioned for the syndicate to enter first, filtering in one by one. Taking a breath, she followed, inhaling the scent of old blood having settled on the walls. Some thought the group was named the Red Stones because of the notorious architectural designs in Keres. Others knew the truth of the name—in reference to the amount of blood sprayed across areas of the Den from years of torture and death.

The narrow corridor widened, forming a more open foyer carved into rock. The group nodded at the two men guarding the entrance to the common hall, while Nyzaia remained hidden. The men tensed at the syndicate's return to the underworld.

As they strode through the archway, fighting reached Nyzaia's ears: a typical sound in the hall. Often fights occurred over petty things—sometimes for entertainment or failed bets. The group entered, but no one stopped reveling at the unrest. A stocky man—a Blade, Nyzaia knew—dove for his female opponent, one Nyzaia recognised as part of the Torturers. Their fighting styles reflected their pillars. Where the stocky man was on the offensive—his moves bold and forceful— the female was light and nimble on her feet, ducking and diving while stabbing with a needle-thin blade. She would easily bet they started the fight over an argument about who was better with steel.

Her syndicate fanned out, leaving Nyzaia to walk forward as the two fighting rose from the floor to face one another. Unsheathing a dagger from each leg, Nyzaia twirled them until they sat comfortably in her hands.

In one silent motion, flames coated the blades as they flew at the fighters, grazing each of their tunics before embedding the wall behind. The fire still blazed as silence fell. Everybody turned to face Nyzaia, her syndicate fanned out behind her. The reaper and her scythes. Flames licked up her arms as she pulled back her hood.

"Is that the kind of fight worthy of my attention?" Nyzaia asked, dimming the flames. Upon recognition of her face, every member of the Red Stones dropped to their knees. She scanned the group as representatives from all six Pillars showed their respect. "I'm not that kind of Queen here, idiots," She rolled her eyes and made her way to the bar that was set up in the corner, pouring herself some liquor—the heavy stuff, the kind the palace lacked. The silence lingered, and when she turned back, she found they remained kneeling.

"Get up or I'll put the place up in flames," she snapped. That seemed to work.

"Are your flames really that powerful now?" a voice called.

Bold, Nyzaia thought. *I like it.*

She looked at the speaker: a petite girl, no older than ten, dressed in dirtied clothes. An Alchemist apprentice. A woman behind scolded her interruption; she was dressed in sheer skirts that revealed her long slim legs beneath, and golden chains draped across her body. A Courtesan. Most of the Red Stones were present, scattered throughout the Den. It was likely a day off for most of them. They mingled freely rather than in their pillars: the black leathers of the Blades, the blood-stained arms of the Torturers, the covered faces of the Spies, the lavish dress of the Courtesans, and the formal dress of the Dealers.

Flames jumped from the ground and licked up the walls, surrounding everyone. No one screamed or balked. Instead, they cheered, mesmerized at the blaze. This—*this* was home. Where people relished the flames. Respected them.

She downed the rest of her glass and left the flames burning.

"I want to see a much more entertaining fight next time," she said, glancing at the two fighters once again, who were still mesmerized by the daggers in the wall. She nodded to Tajana, and the group fanned out to engage with their members. In the meantime, Tajana joined Nyzaia in heading through to the Alchemists' quarters in search of Rajan. She hoped he could offer some form of information on the letter hidden under her leathers.

"Can you do that with all weapons?" Tajana asked as they walked. Nyzaia shrugged.

"Probably. That was the first time I've done it. Sometimes my power just speaks to me and acts like an extension of my mind."

Tajana glanced sideways at her, as if only now grasping the immensity of Nyzaia's newfound power. It was not merely the power of flames she possessed. Nyzaia embodied power in every way. From her stature, her looks, and even her very being—it took one glance at Nyzaia to feel the presence of her power. Though Tajana was not intimidated like so many others. People moved aside, standing flush against the walls, heads bowed. She was formidable.

Nyzaia refrained from coughing as they entered the carved, domed hall that formed the Alchemist's chambers. Smoke from their creations lingered in the air, creating a haze the Dealers so often came to relax in. The Alchemists' created many substances, largely drugs and poisons, but their skills were advanced enough to create more if required: healing potions, explosives, markers. Nyzaia passed rows of worktops, mostly empty at this late hour. The only people left were the apprentices, forced to carry out petty labour such as measuring and cleaning under the supervision of whichever poor Alchemist drew the short straw that night.

"Just the intelligent young man we wanted to see," Tajana called. A thin boy's eyes bulged, and he lurched down the corridor to the left of his worktop. Glass jars and vials vibrated from the speed at which he pushed back his chair. It fell to the floor. Nyzaia and Tajana exchanged a quick look. Nyzaia nodded.

Tajana took off in a run, Nyzaia walked swiftly but with intent. She must appear to always be in control of a situation, never panicked. Following the sound of Tajana's footsteps, Nyzaia rounded a corner into a narrow corridor that led to the sleeping quarters. Only two candles lit the space, flames dimmed. Tajana stood with a knife to the boys' throat.

"No, no, no! She said it wouldn't come back to me!" The boy cried while Tajana repeated her question, scattered with a few colourful threats.

"Tajana!" Nyzaia barked.

The boy looked to his Queen, the fear clear in his eyes as she inclined her head towards the door at the end of the corridor. His bedroom. Nyzaia made it her business to know where everyone slept in the Red Stones, to ensure they could be found at short notice. Tajana opened the door with one hand, the other held the knife at Rajan's neck. She grabbed him by the collar and threw him in, Nyzaia following.

Tajana pulled the wooden chair from his desk and forced him to sit down on it. Standing behind Rajan, she rested her hands firmly on his shoulders to keep him in place. Nyzaia assessed his thin body, who had no chance of bypassing Tajana or his Queen. They all knew it, Tajana only wishing to scare the boy.

"Now, Rajan. What are you so scared of?" Nyzaia asked, leaning against the metal chest that likely housed his clothes, given the small nature of his room and the lack of any other available surface.

"She made me make a special ink," Rajan said, glancing frantically between the two women. "She asked me to make something that wouldn't be detected—something so good that if someone asked me to trace its age, I would not be able to."

"And when were you asked to do this?" asked Tajana.

"About a month before the explosion in the Neutral City," he cried, wiping the tears from his eyes. When it came to Nyzaia's father, she was not one to believe in coincidences. The man was meticulous with his plans, but could he really have something to do with the explosion? He was vile, greedy, but she did not think him capable of killing the ruling families.

"Huh, that was much easier than I expected." Tajana shrugged, but Nyzaia said nothing. "Who asked you for it?"

"Isha." He sniffled.

Nyzaia raised her brows.

"The girl kicked out of the Courtesans?" she asked. On Nyzaia's final mission for her father, she spotted Isha exiting the most expensive brothel, covered in blood, later learning the head Courtesan had her removed.

"Yes, she moved to the chambers across from me and began as an apprentice to the alchemists instead." he said.

"And do you know why she was in contact with the King, using an *apparently* untraceable ink?" Nyzaia propped her elbows on her knees and clasped her hands. The boy nearly fell off his chair.

"The King?" he spluttered. "She never told me it was for the King!"

"What did she tell you it was for?" asked Tajana.

"She said she needed to get a message to someone powerful, and that if anyone found out, she could be killed, and I would be next."

That explains his reaction, Nyzaia thought, rising. Perhaps her father had been familiar with Isha during her time in the brothels. Could she be the Iahabi referred to in the letters?

"Where are you going? What will you do to me?" he asked.

"Nothing. You gave us what we needed with ease. I'm going to pay a visit to Isha," Nyzaia took a step towards the door.

"Wait! You can't!" Rajan shouted. Tajana tugged him back down into the chair as he tried to stand.

"You think you can command your Queen?" she hissed. The boy flinched.

"No, of course not. It's just," Rajan was flustered, bouncing his feet on the floor. "She went missing on a mission last night." He wiped his nose with the back of his hand.

Slowly, Nyzaia turned.

"How convenient," she murmured, locking eyes with Tajana: a signal to leave the room.

Striding purposefully for Isha's chamber door, Nyzaia kicked it open with force, ensuring any lock on it was broken. She stopped to remove her hood, hoping to find some sign of the girl's location, or at least more communication between her and the King.

"Any chance she was just crazy?" Tajana murmured.

Before them, hundreds of drawings covered the walls in clusters.

Each wall represented each realm, and sigils were sketched onto each. A collection drawn repeatedly. Nyzaia inspected the wall of Keres sigils and sniffed at what appeared to be the newest drawn, the metal tang distinct.

"Is that blood?" Tajana asked, having done the same thing.

Nyzaia nodded.

"Maybe she was some kind of loyalist," Nyzaia murmured.

"Then why have representations of all four realms? Why not just the symbol of Keres? I have never heard of anyone devoted to all four realms like this."

Nyzaia trailed her hand across the papers on the small desk beneath the wall. Hundreds of pages repeating the same thing over and over.

"The flame has burned."

"I didn't think your father's letter was sent." Tajana said, peering over Nyzaia's shoulder.

"It was not. She must have known what this code meant regardless," Nyzaia checked the remaining parchments for anything different but found nothing else.

"What do you think it means?"

Peering around the room, Nyzaia answered.

"I think it means either my father knew something about the explosion, and Isha was involved, or there is another conspiracy within the realm," Nyzaia said.

She hoped, for her realm's sake, it was the latter. She did not wish for Keres to face the wrath of the other realms; but supposed in the instance that it did, she would go down in flames with them.

Chapter Twenty-Six

Nyzaia

Arms stretched above her head, Nyzaia clasped her hands together before stretching her upper body to each side. As her arms lowered, she cracked her neck, and released her breath, locking eyes in the mirror propped against the carved wall of the Den: The Red Stone Queen staring back at her. Nyzaia had forgotten that look, becoming so accustomed to uncertain eyes, luxurious fabrics and layers of gold adorning her body, her hair loose and curled. She preferred the reflection now, of the woman with kohl-lined eyes and dark hair pulled into a tight braid. Thin black fabric hanging around her neck to soon mask her face.

Stepping away from the mirror, she continued her old rituals, and walked the perimeter of the room that acted as her quarters. Nyzaia flicked her wrist to heighten the flames on the scattered candles throughout, casting a bright glow against the red walls. Her eyes trailed to the blood splatters on the floor, now more prominent, as if the ground was deliberately painted to appear that way. Crossing quietly to the desk—a luxury Tajana stole for her from the house of an old man she was assigned to kill—she trailed her fingers over it, stopping at each knife lined up in a row. She straightened the thinnest of the ten, ensuring they were perfect, and made her way around the desk, taking a seat and pulling herself close to it. Voices emerged from outside the door. Drawing the black fabric from her neck, she secured it across her nose and mouth, leaving only the eyes of the Assassin Queen visible. Hands clasped, she rested them on the desk, ready and waiting. A single wooden chair sat poised against the wall to her left.

Let the fun begin, she thought, as the voices grew louder, and the door opened.

Her eyes locked with Tajana's, whose features were concealed by the same dark fabric. Tajana's eyes were Nyzaia's favourite feature, capable of both looking into her soul and having her undress in seconds. The fabric rippled, and she knew beneath it, her love smiled back. Nyzaia returned her face to one of quiet neutrality as Tajana guided a blindfolded female into the room. Dirt covered the girl's linens and marred her golden skin.

"Look who we've brought home," Tajana declared, pulling the blindfold from her captive's eyes. The girl's short hair was disheveled as the blindfold tugged roughly against it. Nyzaia said nothing as she looked into the eyes of Isha. She expected to see fear there, at being captured and dragged here, but saw only defiance. A girl unafraid of her Queen. That would have to change. Nyzaia allowed the silence to stretch between them for several minutes in case Isha's expression faltered. It did not.

Nyzaia rose slowly, accentuating every movement as she prowled toward the small wooden chair. She curled her fingers around the seat, watching Isha from the corner of her eye. She turned the chair on one leg until it was poised behind her, and it screeched as she dragged it across the floor. There was the one gap in Isha's armour—the slightest flinch. She would know the stories of the Torturers, having heard the screams of those brought in for questioning. Isha would know the fate to be bestowed upon her by the Queen—the Queen she should have been loyal to, as opposed to the late King, for reasons which Nyzaia was intent on discovering.

"Sit," Nyzaia said.

Tajana pushed Isha forward, who stumbled but corrected herself, straightening with some nameless pride as she moved toward the chair and turned to face Tajana. Tugging back Isha's arms, Nyzaia cut the ties from her wrist, allowing the girl a moment of hope she would escape torture today. As Nyzaia pushed Isha by the shoulder deeper into the chair, she anticipated a gasp or groan—an audible signal of shock or pain. Nothing. Tajana crossed her arms and adopted a wide stance. Through the open door, Isaam stood, flashing Isha a taunting grin before it closed, leaving the three women alone.

It had not taken long for her syndicate to find Isha. She had dispatched them three hours prior, upon leaving her bloodied artwork-filled room. Nyzaia was yet to learn where she was found, but she preferred to figure it out: a game. This time, it was easy. By the dirt-stained boxy linens, sandy feet and cropped hair, and the darkened tan of her skin, Isha had been hiding out, disguised as a male, likely at the orphanage on the outskirts of the city before it stretched into the Ashun Desert.

"I didn't know you were an artist, Isha." Nyzaia began. Her captive's head turned, an almost indiscernible gesture. The question threw her off. Smiling, she walked back to her desk, making a point of playing with the knives laid across it.

Always start with a question they will not expect, Kazaar had instructed. Many years ago, now.

Nyzaia picked up the thinnest knife and stalked back to Isha, rounding the chair so they faced one another and forcing the girl's eyes to hers.

"An interesting style and topic choice, though." Nyzaia continued. An array of scars covered Isha's arms. "What happened?"

Isha glanced down at them then back up, eyes narrowed.

"You know what happened," Isha said emotionlessly. "I saw you on the rooftop the day it happened." Nyzaia's face remained neutral as she remembered Isha, covered in blood, exiting the brothel. The scars were from then—*not from creating the artwork*, she thought. She was surprised when Isha spoke again, voluntarily.

"Did you not find the art to your taste, *my Queen*?" she spat. Nyzaia raised a hand to stop Tajana, who stepped forward.

"I'm used to seeing art related to Keres in *my realm*."

"The realm does not belong to you, and neither does this Kingdom. It does not belong to *any* of you." Isha hissed; voice raised.

"Are you referring to the other rulers?" Nyzaia asked, twirling her knife between her fingers.

"This is bigger than all of you," she said, eyes frantic. Nyzaia knelt before Isha, who averted her stare. Pressing the blade flat against Isha's cheek, she forced her to face her Queen.

"What is?" Nyzaia asked, eyes daring Isha to answer. The girl paused, as if battling with what to say or do. "The explosion?"

Kazaar would scold Nyzaia for raising the issue so quickly, but she was trusting her gut. *The letters*, Nyzaia reminded herself. *Do not forget to ask about the letters.*

"Perhaps if you and the other rulers saw yourself as an entire Kingdom, opposed to four separate realms, you could figure it out." Isha said, tone lowered.

"That's why you had paintings of all the sigils?" Tajana scoffed. "You're just some hardcore royalist that believes in abolishing the realms?"

"Tajana," Nyzaia warned, but Isha laughed.

"You're not listening," said the girl, looking between the pair.

"And was the King good at working with the other rulers? Did you ever ask him that in your letters?" Nyzaia drew Isha's focus away from Tajana and back to her. Her lips drooped at the mention of the King, as if suddenly consumed by genuine sadness.

"Your father understood better than anyone," Isha said, holding back tears. Nyzaia could not keep up with the girl's ever-changing emotions.

"Understood *what*, Isha?" Nyzaia tried a softer approach as the girl looked down, tears silently falling. "What was 'ready to burn'?"

Isha's head shot up so quickly she did not expect it. Her dark gaze seared into Nyzaia, who found herself lost in them, trying to decipher the thoughts in her mind. Since being cooped up in the castle, Nyzaia's foresight had slackened, so she did not anticipate Isha's speed as she head-butted Nyzaia and grabbed the knife. She laughed, waving Tajana off who moved to help her. Nyzaia pushed up into a crouch while Isha remained seated. The girl raised the knife to protect herself.

"You're forgetting knives are not my only weapon," Nyzaia hissed, placing her palms on the floor. Flames burst from her fingertips, snaking their way towards the base of the chair, but Isha glanced down, unfazed. She wished she could decipher the girl's constant-changing thoughts and feelings. Flames licked at the legs of her chair. Isha glanced at Tajana then back at the Queen of the Red Stones.

"When darkness returns, sacrifice is made." Isha declared, before slicing the knife across her neck.

"No!" Nyzaia shouted, rushing towards Isha.

The only person with answers now gargled, choking on her own blood. Isha's head fell back, blood gushing from her neck and adding to the patterns on the floor. Nyzaia clutched the girl's head, staring into her eyes as life faded from them.

"Trust only the other rulers," Isha sputtered. "*No one* else."

And with those last words, the girl died.

Chapter Twenty-Seven

Elisara

"That's officially attempt number five," Vlad chimed.

Elisara glared at him, shaking snow from the skirts of her gown. The pale blue silk layers glistened beneath the rising sun, though the shine was swallowed moments later by the heavy clouds now appearing. The temperature dropped. Vlad glanced upwards, then shot her a pointed look. She sighed, focusing on breathing until the clouds cleared and the sun re-emerged.

"What if she doesn't forgive me?" Fiddling with the talisman around her neck, she paced in front of Vlad.

"Well, if she doesn't, then maybe you'll think twice before sneaking out without me." Vlad shot her a sarcastic smile, but she looked away. She did not need to repeat their argument. After stomping back to her chambers, she found Vlad stationed outside her door, face enraged as he realized she had left without him noticing.

"I'm kidding, Eli." He nudged her leg. "You've learned your lesson, and now your guards have doubled."

"I am Queen," Elisara's voice bordered on obnoxious, "I could just command you all to leave." She peered at the different guards stationed on the street corners and those in the distance.

"So why haven't you?" he asked, cocking his head.

She hated him sometimes and hated his ability to read her innermost thoughts. She agreed to the extra guards on the condition they stayed a reasonable distance away, but she had not put up a fight. The night would have ended a lot differently had Vlad been there—the voice of reason. When Elisara said nothing, Vlad broke the silence.

"She won't hate you, Eli." He sighed. "Which you would know if you just spoke to her."

Grabbing her shoulder, and spinning her round, Vlad gently pushed her towards Crescent Bakery. The displays were empty, as she deliberately asked Vlad to visit before the store opened, a decision she was happy with as peace filtered through the streets. Those training would already be at the training grounds while everyone else stayed home or prepared their businesses for the day.

The soft ivory of the painted shop front beckoned her forward, promising comfort within—a feeling she often had during visits to Helena's bakery. Guilt overshadowed the worry nagging in her stomach. A heavy sigh escaped her lips as she walked forward and reached for the handle for the sixth time that morning. She pushed the door open before any doubts stopped her, but blocking the entry was a wall of back muscle, an arm casually outstretched to keep the door ajar.

"I've no doubt that I'll be back next week for the same order!" A familiar voice called, one she recognised immediately, despite its uncharacteristically positive tone.

"Not a problem, Kazaar," Helena's sweet voice said back. "Vigor is watching the store for me tomorrow afternoon, so I'll meet you at the training yard."

The Commander then did something unheard of. He *laughed*.

"Great," His laughter was richer and more genuine than Elisara expected, a sound that rippled through the air to her. "I'm looking forward to being told I am not as good as I think I am. Yet again."

Helena laughed.

"Well, maybe put up a better defense!"

Elisara could not see past the Commander's broad back but sensed the friendly teasing in their exchange.

"How can I defend when all your methods are cheating?" accused the Commander.

"Get a move on or those cinnamon buns will be cold by the time you get to the training yard." Helena scolded.

The Commander chuckled again and turned in the doorway, slamming into Elisara. The smile on his face vanished, but Elisara had glimpsed it. A smile changed him, though his usual grimace and tensed jaw had returned.

Something is different, Elisara pondered, and it was not simply the drastic change in his character. He was dressed differently, too. Relaxed. While he wore his usual leather trousers, his chest was covered by a loose white tunic, the sleeves rolled to reveal countless tattoos and prominent veins gracing his forearms. The Commander clenched the box in his hands, his knuckles paling. The tunic ties hung loosely by his chest, revealing enough skin to expose the continuation of all his tattoos. Elisara leaned forward to examine the brown leather cord around his neck, where a smooth black stone hung. She had never noticed it before, or perhaps had never seen it beneath his fitted clothing. Regardless, she was drawn to it, the smooth black stone seeming to taunt her. She had flashbacks to the talisman in her hand during the chaos of last night and leaned back, toying with the chain around her neck in the process.

"Princess," he acknowledged. He stepped aside to get out of the doorway, forcing her to step back in the same motion,

"Commander," she replied frostily, reminded of his comments from the night before, that he did not respect her and refused to call her Queen until she earned the title. It could be worse, Elisara decided. He could respect her as little as his second-in-command once had.

She considered asking what he was doing here at the bakery—anything to offer an outlet to the awkwardness. As he looked down at her, the sun brightened the flecks in his eyes, but before she had a chance to speak, he stepped around her and walked away. Elisara watched him leave, waiting to see if he would turn back. He did not. Shoulders tensed, he headed for the training yard. The encounter did nothing but worsen her mood, and she turned back to the bakery and stepped inside.

Warmth immediately smothered her. The table was piled high with loaves of breads, ready to be moved to the window display. The bell above the door jingled, and Helena glanced from behind the counter amid placing strawberries on delicate jam tarts. Elisara scanned her from head to toe, checking for injuries, but while a few scrapes traced her arms, she looked in one piece: the same, calm Helena in a flour-covered apron, white locks piled in a bun on her head. Clasping her hands, Elisara opened her mouth to speak but found herself speechless as Helena gave her usual warm and friendly smile. No hint of resentment or fear.

"Helena I—"

Helena stepped out from behind the counter and pulled her into an embrace, one she was quick to return. She held her friend tightly as if fearing Helena's mind would change at any second.

"You do not need to apologise, Eli." Helena pulled away. "I know you did not mean to hurt me."

"But that's the problem," Elisara responded. "I caused that amount of danger by accident. I cannot control the extent of my powers, and I fear I am a risk to everyone."

"But once you had the talisman on, you stopped it." Helena said, stepping back to the counter. "Kazaar said without it, your power was unstable." She placed another strawberry on a tart. "Now you're wearing it, your power will recognise the natural Vala magic in the talisman and be at one with it."

Helena smiled, but Elisara was focusing on the notion of the Commander *justifying* Elisara's actions. How could he be one way with her but another with Helena?

"What else did he say?" Elisara asked but closed her mouth abruptly. She was not sure why she felt the urge to enquire about him.

"Not a lot. He lost a bet with the guards he is training. Cinnamon buns were their requested prize. I have begun helping him develop new training plans." Helena placed the tarts onto a tray, glancing at Elisara before clearing her throat. "He also asked if I had seen you today." Helena began moving the breads, with an unreadable look in her eye. Why would the Commander care where she was, let alone ask Helena her whereabouts?

"I'm glad you're contributing to the training plan. I trust you to be far less harsh than him."

"I don't know what you have against him, but he seems to have your best interests at heart, and he is highly regarded by those he trains." She passed Elisara some bread to position on the display, who turned the words over in her mind.

"I am your friend, Elisara," Helena pressed, "and I think you need to begin accepting others into your circle. Otherwise, you will find your new life as Queen difficult." Elisara's back was to Helena while listening to her friend's advice. *Friend*. Smiling, she turned and faced her again.

"You will need to visit Talia at some point, though. She was less inclined to forgive after last night."

Elisara sighed but was not surprised. Talia had always been the harshest of the group.

"I have to visit the Neutral City with the Commander, but once I return, I will visit the tavern." Elisara smiled. "I'll try and speak to her then." Helena nodded.

"Now, help me finish setting up the store before you return to your Queenly duties." Helena commanded.

Elisara laughed, grateful to have a friend so understanding. She reflected on Helena's words about the Commander and wondered if she could ever overcome her past with him—to see in him whatever everyone else did.

Chapter Twenty-Eight

Nyzaia

The sun beat across the backs of Nyzaia and her Queen's Guard as they exited Tabheri on horseback. Nyzaia insisted on wearing her usual leathers and would change into the monstrosities of royal attire the closer they were to the Neutral City. Tajana reminded her that leathers would draw the eye of the people, she would instead need to wear more common, relaxed clothing. The common clothes Tajana provided were a blessing: the loose fabric billowing around her legs and cuffing at her ankles, while the lightness of her short tunic exposed her midriff to the sun. She left the city unnoticed, proving Tajana right. The people did not recognise her. The elusive Queen of Keres.

The calls of the market and the scents of spices faded as they travelled through the sky-high archway forming the city boundary. They would ride through the outskirts of the Ashun Desert and camp under the stars before journeying through the Nefere Valley to the Keres Gate of the Neutral City. They could have risen early and made the journey in one day, but her Queen's Guard insisted she needed to be well-rested for the days ahead. She tilted her head to bask in the sun's glow, free of the palace confines. The last month had been draining, and while she was used to daily training and midnight missions, nothing compared to the exhaustion of holding court. If only Kazaar were here.

Nyzaia straightened on her horse, squinting at the dust clouding the Ashun Desert. Sand blew gently, creating a haze across the gentle slopes before them. Frequently, Nyzaia had been dropped in the middle of the desert as a survival exercise: a typical trial in the Red Stones. She missed it more than anything, but at least she had her syndicate.

Glancing at the surrounding group, she smiled, grateful for the familiarity before spending days with the other rulers. Nyzaia had not heard from any of them since the day they all stood atop the Temple ruins. Yet given the endless funerals and coronations, she was not surprised. But she wondered if any had gathered as much intel as she.

"You'll give yourself wrinkles," Jabir joked. She turned to him; eyebrows raised.

"Do I strike you as someone who cares about appearances? We live in the hottest realm where the sun seldom sleeps. Wrinkles are inevitable."

Jabir rolled his eyes and urged his horse forward to reach the others, as Tajana tucked in close.

"You do look worried though," Tajana said, dropping the reins on her horse's neck and reaching for Nyzaia's shoulder. She gave it a comforting squeeze.

"I'm still thinking about Isha," Nyzaia explained.

Trust only the other rulers.

"Why was she thrown out of the Courtesans?"

"The other Courtesans complained," Nyzaia glanced at Tajana, and wiped sweat from her brow. "Only recently I was told they walked in on Isha holding a knife to the throat of a man, while whispering in his ear."

"That doesn't exactly sound unusual for a Courtesan mission," Tajana frowned. Nyzaia cleared her throat.

"Then he started screaming uncontrollably, grabbed the knife from her, and plunged it into his throat. It turned out he was not a target, but there purely for pleasure."

"Gods above, what did she say to him?"

"Nobody knows, but after he killed himself, Isha began painting her body with his blood and chanting. No one knew what she said, they escorted her from the brothel. The other Courtesans were not comfortable with her staying." Nyzaia paused before seeking Tajana's advice. "Should I tell the other rulers about it?"

"Will they divulge what they have come across?" Tajana asked.

Nyzaia did not answer. She did not know. She supposed she would have to decide whether to reveal all she had found in the meeting tomorrow.

"Why did you allow her to stay?" Tajana pressed. "And move to the Alchemists?"

"No one really knew her background. She was found on the streets, so I assumed she was just a girl with a traumatic past. I hoped the skill, precision, and focus required with the Alchemists might help centre her. I did not challenge it when she started working of her own accord," Tajana barked a laugh at Nyzaia's response.

"I don't think it worked," Tajana commented. Nyzaia shoved her arm.

"Do not disrespect the dead. She could genuinely have had a troubled mind," Nyzaia scolded.

***

A night beneath the stars was a peaceful affair, and the next morning, the group rode the final distance through Nefere Valley to the Keres Gate. The group dismounted their horses while Tajana helped untangle Nyzaia's lehenga she had changed into that morning. She straightened the skirts reluctantly, looking up at the carvings on the Gates of Keres. Flames licked the stone and wound around the pillars. This was it. The first meeting of the new rulers and a chance to gather more information.

The Neutral City was in the process of rebuilding, yet there was much to do. The outer streets remained in-tact, but homes towards the centre were overcrowded, as the citizens had taken in those who needed shelter. As they walked through the streets, they observed the remaining damage. Rocks and dust had been cleared, yet a haunting quality remained where buildings once stood. A sadness overtook Nyzaia as they passed what used to be the spice market, now nothing but an empty stone road.

No one was sure what to expect when they reached the Temple ruins. The Historian had been adamant to meet there, not wishing to break tradition, and as Nyzaia walked into the light of the Plaza, she halted. Not a speck of dust remained in the open space, the light sandstone having regained its brightness beneath the sun. The usual shadows from the many buildings were gone. The citizens had cleared the remains of the stores and homes from the inner circle, leaving a much larger space in its wake.

The Temple remained a ruin, yet the rocks were tactically moved to create a towered entrance into the pit, now the heart of the building. Nyzaia admired the citizens' will to create normality amongst the chaos.

Hidden in the shadows, Nyzaia watched. That had been their plan: arrive last to assess for any danger or oddity. Larelle arrived with a small group of guards, who waited outside the ruin as she walked into the darkness of the Temple. Yet Nyzaia's only intel was an unsurprising find: Elisara and Kazaar *loathed* one another.

Elisara stormed ahead, shouting something back at Kazaar, who rolled his eyes, fists clenched as he followed. He paused then tilted his head, as if sensing Nyzaia's presence where the others had failed. A rare grin filled his face. She approached him, Tajana extending an arm to stop Farid's intrusion. They wanted a moment alone. Kazaar looked the same as ever: black leathers and brooding stare. She was not surprised he had not allowed himself to be forced into a Vala uniform yet. Yet a weariness lingered in his eyes. Something troubled him. Though she knew he likely would not tell her about it and only deflect if she asked.

"Look at you. Maybe you should have left the Red Stones earlier. I am sure Tajana is enjoying the vision of you in all these jewels," he said. Nyzaia punched him yet was soon pulled into his embrace.

"You need to work on your right hook. I barely felt that."

"I miss you," she murmured when they parted. He nodded.

"I'm starting to wonder if your father was sane when he wrote that decree. I cannot possibly imagine what he and King Arion gained from a partnership between the realms through the Princess and I."

"Have you found any sign in Azuria as to why they planned this?" The look he gave her said he had not.

"I can only assume I must have wronged the Gods to be placed with her. She is insufferable, Nyzaia."

She chuckled. Elisara was not insufferable, though Nyzaia imagined the pair together were. They were similar in character, yet too stubborn to see it.

"Some would say the same of you, Kazaar." She nudged him, and he shoved her back before clearing his throat. His mask returned as her Queen's Guard approached, led by Tajana. Nyzaia smiled, watching Farid survey the area in silent assessment of the guards from the other realms who circled the Temple. Ever the cautious one.

"Commander. It's nice to see you again," Tajana nodded.

"Tajana," Kazaar repeated the gesture. "I hope she has not been too much of a handful for you." Before Tajana could make an inappropriate joke, Nyzaia entered the Temple ruins; Kazaar to her right, and Tajana to her left. If these were the only moments to share with him now, she would cherish them.

"Nice of you to finally join us, Commander." the Historian scolded, lowering onto a chair. Kazaar muffled profanities beneath his breath as the only one to be reprimanded. Nyzaia did not know for certain why the Historian appeared to hate Kazaar so much yet was thankful he was the only Commander allowed to attend today's meeting, unable to withstand so many egos in one room had the other Commanders been present. Yet why the Historian allowed him to remain, she was unsure. Perhaps because he was the only Commander present when the bodies were found.

Light from the opening above shone into the crevice and centered on the large stone table, now melded back together. The cracks were still evident, a permanent reminder. Nyzaia took her seat and grimaced at the thought of her father sitting there. Behind each ruler hung a banner with their sigil: Vala's pale blue with three mountains and stars; Garridon's green with three trees and a soaring hawk; Nerida's deep blue, a ship with three sails, and finally, Keres, a deep orange with three dancing flames across two crossed swords.

Three seemed a ridiculous number. *Should it not be four? There are four realms,* Nyzaia pondered.

There was likely a reason for it, but when her ancestors fled Ithyion, many of the history books were left behind. Ever since, stories and truths passed down through generations, repeated in ink. She wondered about the Historian's exact age, and how many stories he could verify as truth from fiction.

In only four weeks, change had shaped the rulers. Elisara looked exhausted; dark circles haunted her eyes as she twirled the talisman around her neck repeatedly as if monitoring its presence. Elisara, too, dressed in finery today, opposed to her preferred military wear. She wore her staple dress: billowing sleeves and flowing skirts and a neckline cut down her chest. The colour today was the palest of blues, so pale it was almost white. Her crown glistened, silver twists holding the diamonds proudly in place. The daintiness of it matched her light jewelry. A concerned look passed between Elisara and Caellum. Nyzaia must have missed some news while outside.

Caellum always looked the part, but that was unsurprising; his father had trained all his children—the paranoia of a man whose father usurped the throne. The king had so many children for that exact reason, Nyzaia suspected: his own personal army, and a guarantee his line would live on. Caellum seemed uncomfortable, the dark velvet of his finery blending with the shadows cast by the lanterns. He flinched as he moved his left arm. The clothing by his shoulders seemed bulky.

Bandages, she realized, wondering what happened.

His crown was his father's: the traditional gold woven branches with no emerald in sight. Rumours in Garridon whispered they could no longer mine emeralds since the usurper took the throne. The last mined gems were within the lost Garridon crown that disappeared upon the death of the original Garridon line. She wondered how similar to his father Caellum would be. She was wary.

Larelle intrigued Nyzaia the most, and only knew a brief history of her life: romance, death, a child. Few spies were based in Nerida, so she knew little of Larelle's transition from pauper to Queen. Royalty suited her. Larelle retained an air of grace, an infectious calmness. She did not need jewels as her beauty shone instead. The lilac off-shoulder gown complimented her darker complexion and the ebony of her hair.

The Historian cleared his throat, shifting a pile of dusty books before him. Nyzaia's eyes skimmed the spines, *The Lineages of Ithyion, The History and Practices of Wiccan, Caligo: A study of Darkness.*

"I asked you all here for the inaugural meeting of the royals, where traditionally, discussions are had on future trade, concerns, and prospects. But as you are all aware, we have a more pressing issue." He coughed deeply before sipping from a cup of water at his side. "It is with great sorrow I must inform you all my concerns were correct. I fear there is indeed an old threat approaching the shores of Novisia."

"What threat, sir?" Caellum was the first to speak.

"To understand, we must trace our steps in history of how Novisia came to be."

Caellum's face gave away his frustration, while Nyzaia suppressed her own.

"Our ancestors fled Ithyion from the threat of war. The warriors of night invaded and forced a choice: fight and lose or flee and rebuild." Caellum summarized, but the Historian cut him off.

"To understand, we must trace our *full* history," he repeated. "The one only *crowned* rulers may know the truth of." Coughing again, he opened the largest book before him.

Nyzaia's frown mirrored that of each of her fellow rulers, as well as Kazaar. It was clear, as they all drew the same conclusion: their parents had kept secrets from them all.

Chapter Twenty-Nine

Caellum

"In the beginning, there was Chaos. An entity of darkness and destruction. He waited, but what for, no one knew. Centuries went by, and over time, Chaos evolved until his power condensed and formed what became a body. Chaos chose a different form each time, yet always favoured strength above all. For centuries, this continued: Chaos making and unmaking himself, until he wondered whether he could craft more than just a body. Endlessly, Chaos tried to create a land to call home: a place to create and destroy. Each time, he failed." The Historian paused, taking a sip of water.

"One day, he awoke on hard solid ground, different to the pit of nothingness to which he was accustomed. It was not long before the real creator of the land revealed herself: a beautiful creature that had formed a body, too, but favoured elegance and peacefulness above all else. She introduced herself as Order."

Caellum glanced at the other rulers. He could not believe they were entertaining a history lesson at a time like this. They should be preparing. Strategizing. He looked to Elisara, who was glaring at Kazaar. Learning the news of Elisara's new Commander had come as a shock, yet now he realized how little they had communicated over the past month, despite their few letters.

Kazaar was blatantly ignoring Elisara, picking at his nails while the Historian spoke. Nyzaia slapped his leg, then returned her confused gaze to the old man. Larelle seemed the only one interested in what he had to say.

Shifting impatiently in his chair, Caellum flinched at the pain ripping through his shoulder. Travelling to the Neutral City was the first time Caellum had been active since the assassination attempt. The wound missed any major arteries, and luckily, he had avoided infection. Bed rest. That's what Sir Cain instructed while assuring him they had regained control of Antor. It seemed that way, too, after they passed Antor on their journey. Sir Cain insisted he remain in Garridon to investigate, to ensure the assassination attempt was simply a heat of the moment attack, and nothing more sinister. The compromise? An army of guards must accompany him.

"Order had watched Chaos, who was born from his failed attempts at creation. From afar, Order watched and built their own mind and body until it was perfect enough to build more land. Order created the world soon to become home to thousands, but she did not do so without learning from Chaos' failed attempts. Chaos was skeptical of Order, and anyone who believed themselves more powerful than him. But Order slowly warmed the pit of his soul, and a heart was born: one with feelings and understanding for others. Together, Order told them they could shape the world: Order creating, Chaos reshaping. And so, they did. But they could not do so alone."

"Respectfully, sir, we know the creation story," Nyzaia interrupted, with kinder restraint than Caellum could have managed. The Historian seemed unfazed by the interruption, and simply waited for silence. Elisara urged him to continue. She had always been respectful towards him.

"The thing the two struggled with the most was balance." The Historian continued, as if no interruption had occurred. "Chaos always fought for more darkness, arguing it needed to balance the light. Together, they decided two others were needed to control and balance the concept of time. From the essence of themselves, Chaos created a daughter: Sitara, the Goddess of Dusk. Whereas Order created a son: Sonos, the God of Dawn. Sitara would wake as the skies began to deepen and sleep when Sonos rose. This is how the world began." The Historian cleared his throat, ignoring the impatient looks from Caellum, Nyzaia, and Kazaar.

"Chaos reveled in having a child, having someone to whom he could pass his strength and power to, his thoughts of destruction. What Chaos did not account for was love. Sonos and Sitara remained separated for centuries until one day, Sonos rose later than usual, and in doing so, met Sitara. Love at first sight, if you will. But that love was cursed. They were destined to never spend more than a few fleeting moments together—a destiny controlled by their creators. Order, loving her son, was willing to sacrifice her human form on this plane to become the entity she once was: a deep slumber of which her presence could be felt, but not seen. Chaos was less willing for such sacrifice, but Sitara pleaded, and her father agreed. Yet Chaos was the first being and would not have his presence wiped completely."

"So did Chaos and Order sacrifice their form to allow each of their children living bodies instead?" Larelle asked, allowing the Historian pause. Caellum rubbed the shoulder of his wound, aching for having sat for so long.

"Exactly, Larelle. That point is often overlooked in historical retellings. Order sacrificed her form for her son, Sonos. Chaos sacrificed his form for his daughter, Sitara. With both in a slumber, Sonos and Sitara bound their own essence to their bodies, allowing them to wield their power rather than be controlled by it. In doing so, they could live a life together. And they did for centuries, until eventually, they birthed four children, born from their love and power. Two daughters, Vala and Nerida, and two sons, Keres and Garridon. The four children barely resembled their parents but took on appearances of their own as the essence of Sonos and Sitara evolved within them and became their own being."

"While the family lived together in harmony, they had a desire to create, so others could live in their greatness. So, together, they created. They created water and lands, mountains and caverns, rain and snow. They built a world for themselves and named it

Ithyion. Ithyion grew over the years alongside the four children who learned the extent of their powers. Nerida had an affinity for water. She could create it, control it, banish it—which she rarely did, for she loved it too much. She was a gentle soul, who favoured the calm of the rivers but could rage a war from the sea when her siblings incensed her. Garridon was stubborn and spent most of his time slaving over nature, wishing to create the most for Ithyion. He grew fields and trees, flowers and bushes, but rocks and dirt when angered. He, too, could manipulate the earth, twisting vines from the soil to entrap his siblings, and levitating rocks in the air. And with nature came the emergence of insects and animals."

Caellum refrained from calling the history lesson a waste of time. He did not want to listen any longer, as it only served as a reminder that he did not belong. Garridon's strength and relationship with the earth was something Caellum could never envision in himself.

"Keres was strong and ambitious; his power having grown from his jealousy toward Nerida and Garridon at their abilities to create such beauty. One day, in a fit of rage, he created fire and burned an entire woodland Garridon had created. In the realisation of his power, he learned to control the flames and temperatures around them. With his power, Keres melted natural materials to craft weapons to keep himself strong, and formed pits of lava underground and in mountains, to protect his family from any threats. Vala, however, was balanced and understood democracy. While she understood Keres' jealousy, she could not sit and watch him wield the potential to destroy what they had created, so her power manifested as air. She could extinguish fires, freeze Nerida's waters, and blow Garridon's plants to dust. Vala held the peace amongst the four, and as her own power grew, she wielded clouds and created weather patterns, striking with anger when needed."

Caellum glanced over at his love, whose power had always been stronger than his. Yet never had he witnessed the gifts the Historian now described. But her determination would ensure her capable if she tried, especially now she possessed the power from her entire lineage. Balanced, however, was not a trait she possessed. In fact, she had a much shorter fuse than Caellum, and her impatience reminded him more of the Historian's description of Keres.

"Together, the four siblings created a home to be proud of. Their parents were proud, too, as they watched their children create while they controlled the rise and fall of the sun and moon. For a while, Ithyion was enough for them, but living with only their family grew tedious. They yearned to learn something new, to have new beings to walk their world with. The siblings built their essence until humans formed from that power. The first humans.

"The siblings loved their humans, even more so when they learned to build on what the four siblings created. It was not long before they showed signs of their creators' powers, wielding it to build more for Ithyion. Slowly, the world developed. Knowing the story of Sonos and Sitara, the four siblings desired love too, so built homes for families to live. However, with the growth of the population came the need for more land, and the people soon divided. Those whose powers mirrored that of Keres wished to live only on a land of warmth and sands, where heat beat down on them while they worked with the lava. Those with an affinity to Nerida wanted to live by seas and rivers, while Garridon's people thrived in nature, wishing for green lands and woodlands to surround their homes. Yet Vala's people had become cold, tired of providing balance to the others; they wanted a land of ice and snow—mountains to stand upon to feel the air whip around them.

"With the essence of their power, the four siblings split the existing land and added to it. They formed four separate homes for their people, a narrow sea dividing them from one another. Yet to ensure communications remained, the family decided to build an island: a neutral home for the four siblings and their parents to attend once a month. And eventually, when the siblings were sure their humans could manage without them, they left for the neutral island and slept while their power remained in their lands, the people worshipping them as Gods."

"As Nyzaia said before, we know this already." Kazaar said.

"Have some respect, Commander!" snapped Elisara. "There is likely a reason he is explaining it again."

Caellum regarded Kazaar's sharp look, monitoring the intensity of their glares as they faced one another. Nyzaia cut in.

"We do not need to hear of how our Gods disagreed. It is not uncommon for people of different realms to argue." She moved to push her hair back, but one of many golden bangles tangled in it. Caellum scoffed as she yanked it free.

"Especially with those in Keres, where the people deem themselves above anyone from elsewhere." Caellum countered.

"It's not hard to be better than the grandson of a usurper." Kazaar retorted, with a sour smile. The Historian sighed and rubbed his wrinkled forehead. Caellum refrained from standing but sent a pointed look to Elisara. The Historian interrupted before she had a chance to speak, though Caellum was not sure she had ever intended to.

"All will become clear if you allow me to continue," said the Historian.

"Please," Larelle leaned forward and offered an encouraging smile. "Continue."

"Ithyion was growing, and with it, the presence of Chaos and Order did too. While there was no physical body for Chaos or Order, their presence floated throughout the world, and tempted the humans. Chaos' influence caused arguments and wars, Orders' caused diplomacy and agreements. And while the four Realms of Ithyion grew in prosperity over the years, they also faced hardened times.

"The rise and fall of ruling families came and went, yet there was always an heir to inherit the power of their parents, passed down over the centuries from the God or Goddess of their realm. Distinct orders formed within the realms depending on the powers possessed by the citizens, if any at all. The only exception was the ruling families who retained all powers from their God.

"Over time, the people of Ithyion forgot they had once lived in harmony. While the realms traded and political agreements formed, tensions rose between different rulers over the years, with Keres often initiating wars over petty disagreements." Caellum sent a glare in Nyzaia's direction. "But rulers came and went, and with each new ruler came different ways of life. It was in an age of harmony when the threat emerged. Over time, the people of the four lands had dispersed, some eager to see what else lay across the seas of Ithyion, while some never returned. The creatures came at sunset. Black-winged beasts with teeth sharp like daggers, and skin as tough as steel. They were disfigured creatures, that looked as if they had once been human. They craved the blood of children, but why children, no one could be sure. Some speculated they ate them, while others said they returned them to their master. The latter appeared to be the truth. Nothing killed the creatures. Every wound leaked darkness but did not kill. Keres and Vala began working on a weapon to kill such beasts, infused with the power of fire and lightning. They never got the chance to use it."

Caellum tried to process the twist in the tale, having never been told of such nightmares. The prospect of such creatures existing terrified him, and while he had not been close with his father, he was surprised something so immense was kept from him and his siblings. An outburst erupted from the four new rulers as they all talked over one another.

"That's not exactly a *simple* war," Elisara exclaimed.

"If Keres and Vala created a weapon, how could that be kept from Elisara and I?" Nyzaia demanded.

"What if those creatures were behind the attacks on the Neutral City?" Caellum asked.

"Let him continue." Larelle said, remaining calm among the interruptions. Caellum's mind was a flurry of thoughts, as images flashed of mythical monsters kidnapping children. While the emergence of an old threat made sense, an explosion differed greatly from missing children. Winged creatures that feasted on adolescents did not seem capable, or likely, of resorting to explosives. The Historian continued.

"Months passed, and every sunrise, the realms fought off the monsters landing on their shores. Then one day came, when they did not attack. They hovered over the seas across every inch of all realms, and multiplied until the horizon was an ocean of black, waiting and watching, until finally, they dispersed. Their threat proved successful. The rulers met, yet they were outmatched by the creatures. If the beasts chose to attack, they would lose their realms.

"They decided to flee without any idea of where to go. So, they called on their Gods, and pleaded for a safe haven to hide their people. The Gods granted their wish and created a new land. Novisia. They called upon the Wiccan: a race that surfaced over time as different races across the realms merged. The Elder graced the land and surrounding islands in its vicinity with a spell to seal it from sight.

"The power of the people were linked not only to their leader, but to the lands. And so, each God created a talisman to take with them: a piece of Ithyion's land to amplify the power of their people. Therefore, at sunset, the rulers—with their talismans—fled to Novisia with their families, bringing as many citizens as they could with them. Never to return to Ithyion again, for it was lost to darkness."

Caellum tried to gauge Elisara's thoughts, yet her confusion mirrored his own. They spent their childhood learning Novisia's history, always wishing to know more of the war that encroached on the shores of Ithyion, yet never told. Caellum had never predicted this.

"Novisia was a shock to all the rulers, for it was small. They were accustomed to their own separate realms and their individual ways of managing their people, yet here, they had a blank canvas. But old habits were hard to break. They divided the realm into four and named them after their Gods: Keres, Vala, Garridon, and Nerida. They aimed to model them as close to their homeland as possible, finding comfort in the familiar. They lived in peace, acknowledging that there were bigger threats to their world and that they must stay together should those threats ever return.

"Patterns emerged: exports were traded, and meetings regularly occurred, as all wished to discuss any signs that suggested the creatures of Ithyion had returned to our shores. Rulers passed and new ones rose, and each took on the burden of the potential threat that loomed. On one particular meeting, King Errard and Queen Lyra Mordane—the rulers of Garridon, at the time—made the mistake of bringing a Lord with them. Lord Jorah. When Jorah was dismissed so they could discuss the creatures, he used the escape tunnels to travel back to the Temple, hiding outside the door. Jorah was a proud, selfish man. He listened, learning about the old threat hidden from the people of Novisia. He cared not for the citizens of the other realms, but only for those of Garridon, who he believed to be the true creators. The truth angered him, and he believed he was more capable of dealing with such a threat. So, he began planting seeds of doubt regarding Errard's capability and turned the other Lords against him. Eventually, Jorah usurped the throne, killing the entire royal family and the last of the legitimate Garridon line, Queen Lyra."

Caellum thought back to his Lords' suggestion he marry someone of Garridon Royal lineage, but who could he have meant? If the Historian's words were true, only those very distantly related to the royal line would be left.

"They never found a body, though," Elisara said. "Lyra's body." She looked to Caellum.

"It is said Jorah had so little respect for Lyra, for having married Errard, that he drowned her in the ocean. She was not provided a traditional burial, nor was Errard who burned at the stake in Antor's town square." Kazaar voiced.

Of course, he would be the one to reveal the gory details.

No one said anything, as if waiting for Caellum's reaction. Avoiding their eyes, he looked pointedly at the Historian instead, urging him to continue.

"Jorah had no intention of creating panic in his realm, nor did the other rulers who agreed not to challenge his reign, provided he kept the secret of the creatures from his people. And so, the rule of Novisia continued with no changes or threats to report. Yet if they ever challenged King Jorah's rule, he would reveal the truth and tell the people of the creatures."

"I have had enough of this." Caellum stood from his seat.

"Cal, please." Elisara pleaded, eyes gentle. She knew how difficult this was for him. Reluctantly, he sat and avoided the eyes of the other rulers. Caellum stared at the Historian, suppressing his fury at the involvement of his family once again. His grandfather was a hero and took the throne because King Eddard was a greedy monarch. This—*this* was vastly different to the stories he grew up with, and he did not know what to do with the information.

"My apologies," Caellum said through gritted teeth. He could have sworn, beneath the wrinkles, the old man hid a smirk.

"The rulers became wary," The Historian continued. "While they had heard of the fall of Ithyion, they were not alive when such a threat encroached the shores. But one day, King Adrianus called an emergency meeting, and when Adrianus walked through the doors of the Temple, no one expected to find his son—and his most trusted captain—carrying the body of a black-winged creature, once human but now disfigured. Only one creature. No attack, no flock, just one solitary being, hidden in the caves by Mera Castle.

There was much panic as the rulers debated what to do and what to tell their people. They decided on forming a scouting mission. King Adrianus would send a warship out to the Outer Border to scout for any sign of the creatures and Ithyion, though no one knew what remained of the land since the creatures invaded.

The King sent the Neridian ship out, but it did not return. A month later, the ship was found by another fleet. Blown to pieces. The wreckage had sunk to the bottom of the ocean along with body parts." Caellum noticed Larelle's features slacken and her face pale. "Yet what was most surprising, was that was the last they heard of the creatures."

Chapter Thirty

Elisara

"The ship. What was its name?" Larelle cut the silence. It seemed an odd question, but the Neridian Queen appeared moments from tears. Elisara frowned at Caellum, who shook his head. *Do not ask*, his look read. Then Elisara remembered.

The father of Larelle's child. Lost at sea.

"The Royal Maiden," said the Historian gently.

Larelle's face crumbled, but only for a moment. As if sensing the eyes on her, she regained composure, and averted her eyes downward, avoiding the others. A single tear fell. Perhaps Larelle had clung to a sliver of hope he was alive—lost, but alive. Larelle's self-control was admirable, and Elisara wished she possessed it as her frustration mounted. Pushing back from the table, Caellum rested his hands upon it, directing his fury at the Historian.

"Our parents kept this from us? *You* kept this from us?" he shouted. His eyes narrowed at the old man before him as he slammed his fists against the table. The weighted stone trembled, and rubble fell into the crevice. Elisara's eyes widened a fraction, careful to school her surprise; Caellum had not revealed his newfound strength. While he possessed more strength and speed than the others, he had not divulged how it had amplified since the explosion. The other rulers stared, evidently shocked at the obvious display of his power.

It's not possible, Elisara thought. *Powers are inhibited here.*

"We must tell the people!" Caellum demanded. Behind Nyzaia, the Commander scoffed.

"The apple doesn't fall far from the tree," he muttered.

Caellum grabbed a rock and hurtled it at him with unnatural force and speed, yet he underestimated the Commander, who caught the rock inches from his face, and turned it in his palm before throwing it back.

"Enough!" Elisara shouted, rising too, slamming her palms onto the stone. They all froze, their attention fixed not on Elisara, but to the rock now floating midair, halfway on its path between the Commander and Caellum. Gasping, Elisara sat back down, the rock falling in the same breath. As it connected with the table, a layer of ice quickly spread and spanned to the fingertips of the rulers, who pulled back at the approaching attack. The ice stopped short of the edge. All exchanged a look while the Historian leaned back in his chair, curiosity clear on his wrinkled face. Larelle's eyes, rimmed-red, widened like the others. It was Nyzaia's turn to test the waters.

Lowering until she was eye-level with the ice, Nyzaia appeared to assess its depth before glancing at the Commander. He nodded. She extended her fingers, newly marked ink from her coronation climbing up them and over the backs of her hands: the burning flowers a tradition for all rulers of Keres. Lowering her palm to the ice, she flinched at the piercing coldness of it biting into her skin instantly. It did not last long. As Elisara watched Nyzaia flex her fingers, the ice soon melted—slowly at first, until a light flame crawled across the table and danced across the water, eventually dwindling. A pool now lay before them, reflecting the sun from the open cavern above. Nyzaia sat back down, mesmerised by the golden flames dancing across her palms. The Commander squeezed her shoulder, and she extinguished the flames. A nameless emotion flickered in Elisara while watching the Commander's preferred station beside the Queen of Keres.

No one spoke. Instead, all turned to face Larelle, who shifted uncomfortably in her seat before raising her head—a Queen commanding the attention of her peers as she effortlessly glanced at the water. Small droplets rose from the table, swimming in the air before them. Elisara was mesmerised as Larelle's eyes glowed a deep blue, resting her hands neatly in her lap. Carefully, she lowered the droplets then cleared her throat when, still, no one spoke.

"Your turn, *Prince*," the Commander sneered. Caellum's eyes shot to him.

"This *King* has already exhibited his power, from the force in which the rock nearly hit you," spat Caellum.

"Let's focus on the word *nearly*." The Commander uncrossed his arms, eliciting an eyeroll from Elisara. While she was quick to defend Caellum, she would not involve herself in childish word play between two grown men.

It was clear that the passing of power had not granted Caellum any access to the earth, his power remained as simply heightened strength.

"It would seem the rules of the City no longer apply to the four of you," The Historian finally said. Slowly, he looked each of them in the eye, the emotions behind his gaze unclear.

"Is it possible these creatures have re-emerged?" Nyzaia asked. "And they have somehow interfered with the spells inhibiting powers within the city?"

"Commander," the Historian looked to him. As the only non-royal present, he was to test Nyzaia's theory. Jaw tensed; the Commander laid his palm out before him. No flame ignited.

Looking to Kazaar, the Historian's eyes glinted. "Those with powers, but no crown, still cannot use it within the city, but remember the story," he continued. "In death, the lineage of power is passed to the heir, as it has done ever since the Gods and Goddesses created the first humans. With the death of so many in your lines at the exact same moment, you have inherited more than the Gods ever intended. As a result, your power is unmatched in the history books by none other than the creators themselves."

"I am no God," Larelle said, though the look in her eyes argued otherwise. The Historian gave her a long look.

"No, my dear, you are not. But you are the closest thing to the Goddess Nerida that has ever existed." He smiled at the Queen, and Elisara frowned at the weight of the revelation that befell her too. Elisara's immense power had not been seen since Vala herself last walked the lands and graced the air. She tried not to spiral as she thought about her lack of control, and the damage her powers could do—and *had* done. She may not have dented the well of power within.

The Commander watched her intently, but she looked away, not wishing to acknowledge his disrespect with his station beside Nyzaia rather than his new Queen.

"It is almost as if the Gods planned this, as if we are designed for the destruction of these creatures," Elisara finally said. All eyes turned to her. "If these creatures are re-emerging, is it such a coincidence that a crime was committed resulting in a manifestation of power this immense?"

"Perhaps," The Historian seemed to ponder it. "Perhaps those very creatures orchestrated the events. To leave Novisia ruled by inexperienced and naïve rulers. What better way to infect the minds of the people by casting doubt on their leadership?"

Elisara was unsure whether to feel insulted at the insinuation, or concerned such depraved creatures had the minds and means to enter the Kingdom undetected.

"So, we should begin preparing for an attack? Is that what you're saying?" Caellum asked.

"That's exactly what he's saying." The Commander looked grave. "And I assume that means I'll be journeying to the Unsanctioned Isle." He locked eyes with the Historian, who tilted his head. Elisara suppressed a sigh at the Commander's suggestion he knew something they did not. As Vala's Commander, he should have informed her. Elisara knew nothing of the Isle, only that it was equally divided between the Vala and Keres borders and was abandoned when no decision could be made as to whose jurisdiction it fell under.

"What do you know of the isle?" asked the Historian. The Commander began to pace, his hands clasped behind his back. Elisara scoffed at his air of arrogance.

"I know that five years ago, King Razik had me enter the Isles undetected, tasked with finding an apparent weapon with great historical significance—a weapon he said his father had hidden long ago, designed for a dormant threat." He stopped short behind Elisara's chair, as though contemplating the preciseness of his words. "Except the Isle would not grant me passage. It was as if someone was controlling the oceans surrounding it, preventing a safe channel through." As he gripped the back of Elisara's chair, she tensed at the closeness of his hands to the nape of her neck. "When I returned, it was as if King Razik never cared about the weapon. He explained he was merely making a point to his sons." Elisara glanced at Nyzaia to sense her reaction at the mention of her father. There was none.

"What does this have to do with anything?" Caellum snapped. His eyes lingered between Elisara and the closeness of the Commander's hands.

"I imagine this significant weapon is the one the Historian referred to. The weapon created from those of Keres and Vala lines, but never tested. It would be foolish not to bring it to the new lands when they fled." His eyes locked with the Historian who, for once, did not look at the Commander coldly, but with intrigue.

"You are right," he confirmed.

"Then why did we not recover it sooner? When this threat first emerged?" Larelle questioned.

"It is but one weapon." The Historian explained. "Heavily guarded by the same magic that guards the city and keeps Novisia hidden. As the unsanctioned land between Vala and Keres, only two of those lines may enter."

"Then Nyzaia and I will go." Elisara was quick to volunteer, anything to protect her people from her instability. Nyzaia agreed, but the Commander did not.

"Absolutely not! It is too dangerous, Nyzaia." He argued, striding towards her.

"Oh, but it is all well for your current Queen to go and risk her life for the Kingdom?" Fury rose in Elisara, her glare clear to all. "What is so dangerous about it?"

"It is too dangerous for two rulers to go—for two rulers to risk their lives. I was only on the shores for a moment, but I could sense the darkness there. Free of ruling and control, the beasts there are untamed, and the magic grows in its own ways, unrestricted in its abandonment." The Commander leaned against the table, staring directly at Elisara, who scowled at his patronising manner.

"It is just as well then, that the Queen of Vala now has a Commander who hails from Keres. Two lines, and one with strengthened power against the old magic." The Historian's eyes twinkled, as if knowing the nightmare Elisara would soon endure. She clenched her teeth, but Caellum was quick to object. Elisara listened to his arguments, but it did not matter.

She should do this for her people—her Kingdom. Yet the thought of spending even a minute with the Commander, let alone *days*, filled her with dread. Elisara caught Larelle's eye, who had not engaged in the debate, having focused on her instead. A silent look passed between them, and a gentle nod on Larelle's part encouraged her to take on the task. One Queen to another. Elisara respected her quiet way of things.

"I will go," Elisara broke the argument with the clarity in her voice. She looked to the Commander. "*We* will go."

While the Commander appeared reluctant, he was likely thankful to not be risking the life of someone he cared about. Elisara wondered if she would ever gain his respect. Caellum said nothing, but his disdain was clear as he tried to catch her eye. He knew better than to disagree with her in public, but an argument would likely ensue between them once the meeting ended.

"We will need to plan the most effective route." The Commander switched into strategy mode and reached for the large, rolled map stored in the corner. As he splayed the map across the table, his fingers grazed Elisara's bare arm. She leaned away and cleared her throat, placing a rock across the map to flatten it. No one knew exactly what this weapon looked like or what it could do, but they supposed they would soon find out.

Chapter Thirty-One

Larelle

The second the strategy plans to the Unsanctioned Isle finished, Larelle left. She did not wish to speak to anyone. The city was stifling, and she felt desperate to escape it, to find water in the hopes it would calm her racing heart and mind. So focused on the revelations, she forgot to mention what she found in her father's battle rooms.

The Neridian Guards she had brought with her ushered people out of the way, sensing their Queen's urgency. If Larelle had it her way, she would have attended the city alone, though it was perhaps unwise whilst more attacks could be imminent.

"Make way for Queen Larelle of Nerida!" A guard yelled at the front of their small precession.

Larelle could not bring herself to look at the people of the Neutral City as she rushed to escape it, her mind consumed only by Riyas. Tears welled as the pain rose, and the Nerida Gate blurred into view. She could not take it.

Launching into a run, Larelle passed the guards, who did not question her, but trailed behind as she passed through the gate. A sob threatened to escape as she mounted the waiting horse tied to the wall. She did not look behind as she urged the stallion into a gallop, swiping at her eyes as the wind rushed past.

Larelle steered further towards the border of Vala, continuing the gallop until she was far enough from the gate to the Neutral City that she would not be seen. The river bordering Vala was calling to her. She turned to look behind, her vision tainted by the hair having fallen from her updo.

"Wait here," she commanded, though she wasn't certain if they heard her.

Larelle did not bother to tie up the horse as she dismounted but allowed it to rest and roam in the grass. Stumbling towards the riverbank, the meadow brushed against the thin layer of blue chiffon making up the skirts of her dress. She felt the urge to kick off her shoes and soak her feet in the moisture of the grass. She tried to focus on the way the water felt soaking into her skin, but all she could think instead, was how did the cold water of the oceans feel to Riyas when his ship exploded.

Tears fell fast from her eyes, and with no one around, she did not draw them away. Her vision blurred as she stumbled the final few steps to the edge of the water, the ground sloping upon meeting the calm river's edge. The second the water submerged her feet; she released the pain.

Larelle screamed—a scream so heart-wrenching anyone near would have thought she was the one dying. She screamed again and again while slowly collapsing into the water, her hand gripping her chest where the few remnants of her heart rested. Tugging the crown from her hair, Larelle tossed it behind as the water soaked her skirts, darkening the blue so close to colours of mourning. And as she shrieked, she relinquished all the control she held so tight on herself and her power. The water swirled and moved, rising into the air to cocoon around her body, as if seeking to protect her from all pain. Conflicted, she fought against it.

The very water she connected to—the water she ruled—tried to soothe her, yet served only as a reminder of what took her love. The father of her child. She was suffocating, drowning in grief.

"LEAVE ME ALONE!" She screamed. "I just want it gone." She sobbed then, the salt of her tears another reminder of the unyielding oceans yet again. "I want the pain gone." The water did not listen. It was as if it had a mind of its own, desperate to comfort her in any way it saw fit. She gave up trying to make it listen.

Six years Larelle grieved, trying to come to terms with her

loss, but a small part of her always wondered—always hoped—he would return. But hearing the Historian reveal the Royal Maiden was found blown to pieces offered a finality to her loss. Riyas was dead.

The Neridian Queen was oblivious to how long she sat in the river, crying as the water shielded her from sight. But as the tears dwindled, and the pain numbed in her heart, rage returned with a vengeance. Someone had destroyed the Royal Maiden, and though she was uncertain of who was responsible—whether it be those creatures, or whoever planted the explosions in the Neutral City—she was sure of one thing.

Her father put Riyas on that ship. It was his fault the other half of her soul was gone.

Larelle wanted revenge, and the only thing left to symbolise all her father stood for were the Lords he left behind. The glutinous, selfish Lords, who increased taxations despite their people's struggle for survival, and disrespected their Queen in their first ever council meeting.

They were everything her father had been, and he cared more about his Lords than the happiness of his subjects, his daughter—her people. Her father had been willing to inflict a life of pain upon his daughter for the simple crime of falling in love: stripping her of her titles and sending Riyas to his death.

But Larelle had a title now. Larelle was Queen and could take from the men who had stolen her everything.

She bowed, staring into her reflection, and the deep-blue eyes so like the Goddess Nerida's. Wiping them, she reached for her crown and placed it back atop her curls. Larelle raised her head and stood, and as she did, the cocoon of water fell. Turning, she found the guards all standing by their horses. Drenched. Dark clouds roiled above, and she frowned, wondering if they had always been there. A guard approached to offer her his arm and help her up the now slippery riverbank.

"I need three riders. One for The Bay, one for Trosso, and one for

Amoro." Three guards stepped forward at her command. "Gather the Lords, they meet me at the castle in Mera *immediately.*" She said nothing more as they all nodded and prepared to leave.

The next steps were clear. Larelle would return to her home, to her castle, and to the family she had remaining. She would dismantle all her father stood for.

Chapter Thirty-Two

Elisara

Elisara had been on the boat, watching the horizon for merely an hour, and already she regretted agreeing to spend so much time with the Commander. She also regretted having little time at the meeting to talk with Caellum, their only conversation being his reluctance to admit what happened to his shoulder. She was not surprised by his cold demeanor. The distance between them felt real now, but she wished he accompanied her instead.

They made quick work of readying their horses and packing for the journey. Given the secrecy of the mission, only the two of them could attend. Despite Elisara's trust in Vlad, the Commander was adamant.

The notion that he feared the trip too dangerous for Nyzaia, but not for his Queen, was not lost on Elisara. Yet she trusted when faced with danger that her powers would protect her.

They had left in the dead of night for Elvera, the only port town in Vala. Everyone they came across was paid handsomely by the Commander, while Elisara kept her hood up, not wishing to raise any questions as to where their Queen headed. They had only one captain: a man Larelle claimed could be trusted, per a close Lord's insistence. The captain travelled up from Mera the evening prior, waiting patiently for their arrival. He reminded her of Talia: stern and quiet. And while Elisara spent the first moments of the journey trying to converse with him—anything to avoid the Commander—it soon became apparent the captain felt the same about small talk as he did.

The sun rose over the ocean as Elisara stood to watch the glow reflecting off Vala's snowy mountain shores, light painting shadows across its crevices. The Unsanctioned Isle lay north of Vala and Keres, the last land before the Novisian sea border.

Elisara sighed, eager for the shore of the Isle to appear in the distance to finally end her torment. Yet several hours remained.

She wondered what creatures might lurk across the Isle, and what the weapon might be. Weapon training was her favourite, having exercised with everything from swords and daggers to bows—and the occasional axe whenever Caellum trained her. Yet her least favourite weapon was that which coiled within her blood.

Elisara had always been at one with her powers growing up, confident in the gentle pull of the air to listen to whispers of socialites, casting a gentle frost at her touch, but it had never been something to wield in attack, that had only ever happened twice in her life, both in Keres. Her father had been a powerful King but was never capable of what she could conjure recently.

She needed to practice wielding it, yet the last time she used her power as a weapon, she put Caellum's life at risk. Elisara glanced at the Commander, who stood at the opposite end of the boat, warming his hands with a gentle flame. She hated that flame.

Focusing, she willed the cold to calm her. She needed to practice and control her power like Larelle if she was to ever make a worthwhile Queen. Rationally, she knew she could do it, having done so at the springs, and would need it if she had to defend herself against the Commander, or someone worse like his second-in-command.

Beginning with air, she lightly drew on it as she listened to the captain's hums. She detected the rustling of trees on the shores of Vala, the rise and fall of the Commander's breath. Closing her eyes, she focused on draining the surrounding symphony of sounds. She strained, but to no avail, and when her eyes reopened, the waves crashed higher against the boat, and the sails struggled to stay upright in the wind. A hand touched her shoulder and she jumped, pulling from her power, and cutting off the storm.

"It won't listen to you if you won't listen to yourself," said the

Commander. His tone was even as he stood behind her. Elisara pursed her lips. He moved to her side, placing his hands beside hers on the railing. Warmth radiated from him—a warmth she wanted to move away from, yet for whatever reason, settled the chill in her bones. "Every time you use it out of choice, you're worrying about damage. But how can you expect your powers to be gentle when you are so hard on yourself? I do not believe you have smiled once since becoming a queen."

That caught Elisara's attention, and her head spun to him. His face remained unmoved, staring out at the sun now settling across the horizon.

"What is there to smile about when you're handed a position you never wanted, or expected?" She sighed.

"The ability to shape what you and your people become."

She looked away from his gaze but turned his words over in her mind. The profoundness of them surprised her, yet she supposed he must motivate his soldiers somehow, though she never expected to be on the receiving end of his advice.

"I never wanted to be Commander," He continued looking at her until she met his gaze once again. At those words, she did, tilting her head. "The King recognised my abilities and strength and forced it upon me. He concluded it was what I would become: a torturer, a leader, a weapon. But I never asked nor expected it. From an early age, I assumed the position would go to one of Nyzaia's brothers." He tore his gaze to the light ice unknowingly cast along the railing and willed his flames to lick gently at it. "So, you see, Princess. I know everything about being handed a position I never wanted or expected."

Princess. She suppressed an eyeroll, her gaze remaining locked on the Commander: analysing, surveying, determining whether the ruthless man before her spoke the truth or if this was a test like the ones she endured under his so-called leadership in Keres.

"What is your legacy then, Commander? You say there is the ability to shape what you and your people become, so I ask: what is that?" Elisara's tone sharpened. "Where I stand, I see a man who grew cold despite the fire in his veins. A man who relished in the torturing of his soldiers. Despite being thrust into a position you did not want, you play the part well, molding your people into ruthless killers that care little for the minds of young soldiers... or a young princess."

The Commander looked away at her words, but Elisara would not allow him to disregard any acknowledgement of her experience in Keres.

Suddenly she was back there, light framing a dark silhouette walking into the cell that was once her room. She sat up, preparing to be taken to another midnight task, but froze as the body drew too close too quickly, amber eyes searing into hers, while a wide-toothed sneer broke across his face. She shook off the memory.

"On my first day, you had all recruits line up on the edge of the Abis Forge, with our feet almost in the lava, and left us. You left us there for twelve hours to bake in the heat. Now for the recruits of Keres with distant royal blood, they could learn to manipulate the heat and direct it elsewhere, but where do you think they directed it? At the Princess of Vala who did not belong, the princess who had no strength to cool—let alone freeze—the heat thrown at her." Elisara did not look away as she berated him. "When we were dumped and blindfolded in the middle of the Ashun Desert, instructed to find our way back to the training ground, it was a lesson to test the recruits' ability to work together and find the lines of lava below the desert leading back to the forge camp. For me? A test in ignoring a tirade of insults, while maintaining an undetectable breeze around myself."

"Enough," he commanded, but she would not be silenced. Finally, she let her words flow freely. His shoulders tensed and his grip on the railing tightened with every word. Elisara hoped he was as uncomfortable as he looked, finally realising the agony she endured under his command.

"In my first torture session, I was made to sit and hold my tongue as your second-in-command doused my arms in flames with lit rags, to heal and break them repeatedly until I gave up the information I was instructed to hold as part of our mission. For a recruit of Keres, it was a test of overthrowing the flame with their own or for those with no power to control their reaction to the heat. For me, it was a test of how much pain I could tolerate before I blacked out."

"Those tasks taught you endurance. They tested your ability to strengthen your temperature control. But instead, you lost control and killed my second-in-command, and now you carry a weight stopping you from wielding your power correctly."

He said it. The words that remained unspoken between them from the moment he found her that morning, and the hours which followed when she left Keres. She flinched away from him as she recalled his hands picking her up from the floor, his feet crunching on the shards that she could not tear her eyes from. The words hung heavy in the air.

Elisara straightened and turned to look directly at him, cold as the ice walls she kept up.

"The weight I carry is because I almost got Caellum killed when the Garridon recruits joined us on a mission. I was so furious at *your* assignment that my power caused him to blow over the side of the forge. It has nothing to do with the second-in-command you believe still deserves *respect*." She inched closer as the ice bloomed from her fingertips, trapping the Commander's hand against the railing. "I did not lose control with your second-in-command. I relished in his pain as I froze the water on the floor of my room and guided the ice up his body, around his chest, and shattered him into millions of pieces. In fact, I commended myself for breaking a man—who had just tried to force himself on me—into a shower of ice shards." At her final words, the Commander whirled, eyes roaming her expression, as if looking for any signs of a lie. She was not lying, and he realised.

"I blame you for everything," she hissed. "For the training methods, the attitude of your second-in-command, for Caellum's near *death.*" Her face was inches from his as she confessed all that haunted her, having never spoken the words aloud, having never acknowledged any of it. If she kept it all hidden, none of it happened.

The flames erupting from his arms quickly melted the ice she entrapped him in. Pivoting, the Commander strode for his quarters below deck, where Elisara was left, breathless, trying to force those haunting events from her mind. The only reprieve from their argument was her ability to retain control, despite such torment. She touched the melted water gently and turned it to ice.

Had what happened to Caellum resulted from a lack of control? The Garridon recruits were sent to Keres for a joint training exercise; as an heir not in line for the throne, Caellum had joined.

The exercise was simple: a Keres recruit would be paired with a Garridon recruit to fight until one yielded, no powers or weapons off limit. Elisara and Caellum were paired together. Naturally, she had argued with the Commander, citing it unbecoming for two people—a betrothed couple—to fight in such a way. The punishment for her insubordination? Elisara and Caellum would fight on the galley, the area reserved for teaching a 'lesson'. Keres recruits were immune to the heat of the lava flowing below, should one fall in. The same could not be said for Elisara and Caellum.

After months of torture, that had been the last straw. She had summoned all her strength, the winds erupting furiously around her, before propelling it toward the Commander to make an example of him and push him from the edge. But before the air reached him, Caellum jumped in to defend her honour, not realising she was readying a storm—a storm that ran its path right towards him and blew Caellum over the edge and into the Abis. While Elisara had ran immediately to him, the Commander stood, arms crossed, and watched as she reached over the Abis to where Caellum, thankfully, clung to a branch, close enough for her to pull him up. Standing on the sidelines, the Commander called her what she was: a flight risk. A princess with no control who would get her loved ones killed.

She marked the Commander as her enemy ever since, for his command, for his tests, for his inability to acknowledge the evil around him. For the silence when he found her there and did nothing but guide her from the room and prepare for her to leave Keres.

Elisara lost control when she feared hurting those she loved yet held nothing but control when it came to men believing themselves above the rule of women. She would kill the second-in-command again if she had the chance.

Chapter Thirty-Three

Larelle

"Mumma!" Zarya's sweet singsong voice called from the terrace of the chambers she shared with Larelle, and Larelle's fury subsided as the light of her life bounded towards her, barefoot across the sandstone, wet imprints in her wake. Her unruly black curls trailed behind as she ran, the oversized tiara lopsided in her hair. Bending down, Larelle caught her daughter and enveloped her in her arms. She breathed in the smell of her hair, the familiar rosemary and salty air. Olden joined them, and she offered a soft smile over Zarya's shoulder at the look of concern on his face. He could tell she had been crying.

She would need to inform him of Riyas without disclosing all she had learned at the meeting. That had been one of the hardest things to consider while the Historian spoke. How could she not tell Olden? She wished to tell Alvan, too, who she found herself trusting easily.

"How have you been, sweet girl?" Larelle asked, pulling back to stroke Zarya's hair. The little girl grinned.

"I ate FIVE pieces of focaccia," she said, holding up five fingers. Larelle laughed.

"And did you learn anything in your lessons?"

"Yes! I learned that if I asked for five more pieces, I could have had TEN!" Zarya raised her other five fingers, and Larelle's heart warmed. The door behind her opened and Lillian stepped in with a smile, one which seemed permanent since Larelle took the throne. Lillian's cheeks were plumper, too, and her dress no longer fell from her shoulders. It was now mandatory for all staff to be fed throughout their working day; their wages had also increased. It made her heart sing to see the difference. Lillian bowed in the doorway.

"Your guards said you wished to see me, your maj—Larelle," Lillian corrected. The Queen had requested none of the servants use her royal title. Larelle rose.

"Olden, could you ready Zarya for dinner?"

"But mumma, I want to stay with you!" A stab of pain entered Larelle's chest; since becoming Queen, she had lost precious time with her daughter.

"We are going to have dinner together!" Larelle said animatedly. "You need Olden to help you choose the best dress from the wardrobe!" That comment quickly had Zarya running for the adjoining door to the bedroom. Her daughter had quickly developed a love for dresses, now she had endless to choose between. Waiting until Olden closed the door, she continued her conversation with Lillian.

"We have not known each other long, Lillian," said Larelle, "But I know I could trust you if I asked you to do something to better the realm."

"Of course!" Lillian said eagerly. "You have already made such a difference. I would be honoured to help more if I can!"

Larelle stepped towards her and clasped her hands.

"I want the Lords gone," she said simply, though it was not what Lillian had expected, given the shock on her face. "I cannot do it quickly without causing unrest with the wealthiest of Nerida, so it needs to be gradual." Larelle squeezed Lillian's hand. "I plan to meet with the Lords in the morning and inform them of a change to improve our ways of making decisions in the realm. To do so, I need people I can trust to return to their homes to support the plans I have." Larelle looked earnestly at Lillian. "Is that something you would do? Zion can stay at the castle while you are gone. It should only be for a few days."

Larelle did not have to wait long for an answer.

"Absolutely," said Lillian. "I would do anything for you." Lillian returned the squeeze while Larelle informed her of the details she would share with the Lords the next morning.

***

Larelle waited in the small sitting room connected to the advisor's chamber in the castle turret. She would not be left waiting for the Lords to arrive like last time. She straightened her dress, having chosen a deep-Neridian blue gown with a high-necked collar and short sleeves, leaving her arms bare. A silver pattern of waves climbed their way up the skirt. The stiffness of the fabric mimicked armour—appropriate, given this was the start of a long battle ahead. A plethora of voices passed by the door she stood behind. Unsurprisingly, they were late, though not as late as they had been before. Alvan's two quick knocks at the door signaled they were entering the chambers in the adjoining room.

Larelle straightened and waited a full three minutes before nodding to the guards standing either side of the doors. Light from the windows of the turret streamed in, framing Larelle's body as she paused, looking into the chamber, waiting for the Lords to rise. Alvan rose immediately, smiling. The other Lords did not rise so quickly, but when they saw Larelle had no intention of entering the room until they did, they reluctantly pushed back their chairs.

Larelle glided with grace and self -assurance as Alvan moved to pull out a chair for her. She nodded to him before taking a seat.

"Be seated," she said calmly, noting their lack of enthusiasm as they did as she asked.

"We'd like to discuss the taxes you have lowered," Lord Leto began. Larelle looked to him, unsmiling.

"I would like to remind you that *I* called you here. There will be no conversation on the taxes," Larelle said to each of them. "My decision on that matter is final."

"Then why are we here?" asked the Lord of Trosso. Larelle cleared her throat.

"It has become clear to me that neither my father, nor most of you, care about the people of Nerida. You care only of money." The men said nothing. "So, it seems logical to enforce a better system, one which understands the needs of the people in which your seats govern." Alvan offered a smile of reassurance as she looked at him.

"When you leave today, I will send some of my staff to your towns. Their purpose is to engage with the citizens and nominate a spokesperson for each of your holdings. If I cannot implicitly trust my Lords, then I will place that trust elsewhere, with the people who know the hardships and needs of others." She assessed each Lord, each struggling to hide their feelings. The display of her power at the last meeting appeared to have scared them into some submission.

"A spokesperson to do what? Take our jobs?" Larelle looked to her left. *Not yet*, she thought.

"No. To help bring the voice of the people to the forefront of our decision-making," she answered.

"You cannot replace Lords with common folk. They do not know how to get the job done, and while they may have their 'needs,' they have no idea how to implement them."

"And that is what we are here for." Larelle stressed. "To support them and get things done with your assistance."

"Do you trust these people because you have lived amongst the commoners?" The Lord of Trosso asked, though his voice held no malice.

"Indeed. Do you not trust those *you* live with?" She tilted her head at him.

"Interesting, and yet you lived with your family and your father was the least to be trusted when it came to the events in your life." The corner of his lips lifted, as if knowing something she did not.

But Larelle knew all too well what her father had done.

"My father is dead," she said bluntly. "There is no need for us to talk about him again." The waves crashed high against the turret walls. "While I know you likely disagree, I will not entertain a debate." Rising from her chair, they reluctantly followed suit. "You will return in a week."

She strode from the wall and down the corridor, her skirts trailing behind, while a victorious smile crossed her face. And so began the plans to abolish all her father held dear.

Chapter Thirty-Four

Elisara

The Unsanctioned Isle was desolate. The land was long and narrow, not like any land she had seen before. Elisara had expected either the sands of Keres or the snow of Vala, yet there was neither. Something was wrong, like the air did not know who it belonged to. She expected humidity, given half of the island aligned with Keres, but she sensed something else. It was as if the air was alive, assessing her. Elisara stilled, allowing the air to roam her skin until tightening around her neck and brushing down her back. For once, she was thankful for the tightness of her leather corset. Trapped against her skin, there was no way for this strange air to invade her space.

"You feel it, don't you? Its wrongness," said the Commander, shifting in place. "I did not get this far last time. Whatever the magic on this Isle is, I don't think it wants us here."

"Maybe there's nothing wrong with it. Maybe this is what natural air should feel like. Air without the control of magic talismans forcing it to change and bend to a master."

Elisara turned to assess her surroundings. The Isle was wild and untamed from the lack of human control and influence. The sand was like ink, a quality she had never seen before. She wondered if it was natural or influenced by the coal and ash of Keres. Bending down, she clasped a handful, gaping as it fell through her fingers, the light refracting in the sun. It was not completely black as she initially thought. As she watched the dust fall from her hands, she caught the specks of white and silver, like diamonds colliding with the darkness. Would there ever be anything as beautiful as this in her own world of darkness?

The Commander did not interrupt her as she repeated the motions: lifting the sand, and letting it slip through her fingers. He watched from the edge of the shore, water lapping at his boots. She felt his eyes on her; sensed his inquisitive gaze. She shifted under it, uncomfortable having not spoken about her admissions on the ship. She dropped the sand again, but instead of scooping it into her hands, she rested her palm on the surface and closed her eyes. She focused on the difference in the air, wondering if it would respond to her the same. It did not. It was even more eager to please, like it immediately felt at home. Elisara found it quick to call upon her gifts since wearing the talisman, but the thought barely formed before the air responded.

Elisara's eyes glowed against the darkness of the sand which no longer lay thick at her feet. The sand danced: shimmering plumes of black floating softly in tendrils. She directed them in different directions: Elisara the conductor; the sand, her orchestra. A cocoon of sounds floated in her ears: the whistle of sand, the whipping winds, the rustling tree lines. It was raw, free, and above all, beautiful. She had never felt so at peace. Her eyes lost their glow as the grains floated like feathers to the ground, dusting the Commander's shoulders.

"I rest my case," Elisara said, the corners of her lips lifting. "This is right." She gestured to the air and then turned to assess the trees. The beach was narrow, yet the forest floor did not seem capable of flooding whenever the tide washed in. The trees were different to any she had ever seen, and as the betrothed to the King of Garridon, she had seen many. The towering trees bathed her in darkness as layers of garnet leaves formed a canopy above. The trunks and branches bore years of age and wound in countless directions. She was unsure where she was headed as her feet trod a clear path across the forest floor, deeper into its core. She felt a natural confidence on the Isle, and what at first appeared to be desolate, now came to life.

The Commander did not speak—something Elisara was glad for. He followed behind, alert and ready to draw his sword at the slightest sign of danger. Yet there was no danger; while the island felt dark, it was at peace, unfazed by the two wanderers interrupting its slumber. Elisara had been walking for less than an hour when the forest thinned and light streamed through, cutting the darkness into fragments. She shielded her eyes as she stepped from behind the last tree and stared at the land before them.

In the distance stood a mountain, carved so meticulously by the elements, it resembled a castle. A glistening lake surrounded the rock, similar to the Vellius sea in size, but instead of dark waters threatening to entrap you under layers of ice, it sparkled. The palest of blue to contrast the mountain's darkness. If Elisara was younger and more spontaneous, she would run for the shore and dive deep into its depths. Instead, her hand lowered from her mouth to rest on her chest as she breathed in the crispness of the surrounding air.

The Commander approached on her left, and even he could not wipe the amazement from his face. Light bouncing off the lake seemed to reflect in the dark pools that formed his eyes. He pushed his hair from his face and tied it back, as if preparing for danger. Elisara scoffed internally.

The only danger of this Isle is I may never want to leave, she thought. Following behind the Commander, they trailed down the small incline directed to the lake. Before they reached the edge, Elisara spun slowly, assessing, but nothing appeared changed about the tree line.

She felt more certain here, her feet and soul in sync. The grass welcomed her every step, the longer stems threading through her laced black boots. While nature in Garridon always welcomed her, she assumed that was Caellum's influence, and wondered if nature took on a life of its own here, favouring whoever it desired.

The water of the lake sang in ripples as she reached the shore, an answer to her questions. Up close, it was clear. Pebbles and blue shards—of what, she did not know—called from below, and as she reached to grace the water with her fingertips, the Commander grabbed her wrist.

"Do you remember nothing from your training days? Approach anything as a threat." He released her, and they both looked back at the water. Crystal clear.

"You're right, Commander. I should beware of the deadly, invisible creatures lurking within its depths, ready to drown me." She unlaced her boots.

"You cannot walk all the way to the mountain. You will end up having to swim and drench yourself." He scolded.

"Then it's a good job my commander has fire in his veins and can dry the moisture from my skin." Elisara turned her head back and waded into the lake. She sighed as the ice-cold water soothed every ache she had, similar to the stalactite potions of Vala.

Droplets clung to her fingers as she lifted them from the surface, another similarity to the stalactites. Frowning, she pulled a small dagger from the structure of her corset and sliced her finger open. Droplets of blood spilled and entered the lake, but within moments, the water healed the cut shut. Elisara swung her head back at the Commander, whose frown matched hers as he mimicked her actions, his own blood spilling for a mere second before closing.

Distracted by one another's concern, it took several moments before they noticed the water change. The clear shimmering liquid now merged with a pooling of black, radiating around them until stretching across the lake. Elisara watched with mixed emotions: awed by its beauty while fearing the unknown. Despite its darkness, it was breathtaking. It contained similar qualities to the sand they had arrived on. Closer inspection revealed streaks of white and silver swam through the pool.

"Are you still happy to be in the water now you cannot see into its depths?" The Commander mocked, yet before she could respond, the water took on a life of its own. She scurried onto the grass, and the Commander reached for her arm urgently. The water pulsed, creating waves resembling the darkness of the Vellius Sea.

With every movement, the waves heightened, yet remained contained within the lake. The pair stepped back as the darkness grew until they were no longer waves at all. Instead, the water parted to form a clear path along the pebbles leading to the mountain. Elisara had been right. Centuries of no interference had allowed the Isle's magic to regain its own control. Clearly, it had its own intentions for the Queen and her commander.

Elisara was not typically one to wait for instructions, but she wished to avoid drowning in case the two pillars crashed at any moment. Looking to the Commander, it was clear he sensed the doubt in her eyes, and Elisara was surprised by the lack of judgement she found in his own. He nodded and stepped in front, striding toward the unknown. While she hated him for her experiences in Keres, she admired his confidence and respected his duty to protect her. His Queen or not. She ignored the cautious voice in her mind and followed, her feet crunching along the pebbles and shards below. They did not look blue anymore but pearlescent. She picked up a pebble and placed it in her pocket, wishing to retain a souvenir as one of the few people ever to step foot on the Isle.

Elisara stepped through the walls of water, and darkness slowly crept in, blocking the sun. Though there was not the usual rush or trickle of water. It was like a song—a melody—played within. Carefully, she trailed her fingers along the wall. One moment the water felt ice-cold, the next scorching hot, as if unable to decide which descendant to emulate. She paused and investigated the depths of the black water instead; she could have sworn she heard her name whispered amongst the white tendrils swirling through its depths.

"What are you doing?" the Commander asked sharply, staring at Elisara whose hand rested against the wall.

"I thought I heard something." As she lowered her hand, the water protested. They spun to look behind them as the wall fell inwards. They didn't need to tell one another what they were thinking as they broke into a sprint towards the mountain.

It had been a long time since Elisara had run so fast or hard. Summoning the air into her lungs, she willed it to the Commander too, who glanced sideways at her in surprise as his breathing eased. She focused on keeping her stride steady as they reached closer to the mountain, where a gaping mouth appeared to be waiting for them, as dark as the wall of water crashing at their backs.

The Commander grabbed her hand, pulling her with him as he jumped over the rocks toward the mouth of the mountain. Upon reaching the darkness, the Commander pushed Elisara behind him and raised a wall of fire across the entrance, yet the flames didn't get their chance to battle with the water, as the darkness stopped its attack. Elisara watched as the final plume crashed down just before the ledge they had jumped upon, and it calmed into its original tranquil state. She steadied her breathing while the Commander stood at the edge of his flames, peering out at the water below. He stood rigid, his fists clenched. Elisara could not decipher the look on his face. Contemplative and angry all at once.

Leaving him to wallow, she surveyed their surroundings. The lack of light made it difficult. The stone warmed beneath her touch as she trailed her fingers along the wall. Flames burst across it at the contact, and she leapt back, still mistrustful of fire, given her experiences. These flames glowed differently, a usual mix of reds and oranges casting light across the rocks but blue and white interspersed the flames, making her feel somewhat at home.

"I did not know you could change the colour of your flames." Elisara called over her shoulder. She felt the Commander's breath by her neck as he approached.

"I cannot," he said, waving his hands through the blaze. "They feel different."

Elisara approached to test his theory. Holding her breath, she placed her hands in the flames and then withdrew. Nothing. She tried again, slower this time, yet the flames did not harm her at all. Instead, they caressed her hand, only singing the hems of her sleeves. It felt both wrong and right. Common sense told her it should hurt but her soul took comfort in the rare moment of being kissed by the heat; for once, she did not feel uncomfortable or crave the cold. She felt balanced.

The Commander watched, his face the same mix of contemplation and anger from earlier.

"I know you dislike me, Commander, but there is no need to make it so obvious." Elisara scolded, turning her hand within the flames.

"I dislike that I have to care for a Princess who just, without a doubt, stuck her arm into a fire."

He began examining the walls.

"You said they felt different. What was I supposed to do? Not find out for myself?" She barged past him, and as their arms collided, he roughly spun her, gripping the loose fabric on her arms as he pushed her against the wall, trapping her in the flames. Elisara forced her eyes to meet his as the flames engulfed their bodies, cocooning them in what should have been raging heat. The Commander must have retained some control of the flames as their clothes remained unsinged. The only warmth piercing through them was that from the grip of his fingers and the strength of his body against hers. Realizing his position, he released her, but kept both hands on the wall on either side of her head.

"That's exactly what you were supposed to do. My job is to keep you alive, and I cannot do that if you insist on doing whatever you want. You hate being told no, too used to men abiding by your every whim." His voice was low and threatening, his breath tickling her skin. Placing a finger under her chin, he roughly turned her head to the side, where a dark hole lay by the wall. If he had not grabbed her, she would have fallen in. Elisara turned back as he gave her a look that said *I told you so.*

"I am Queen. That is my place. You cannot tell me what to do," she retorted, willing the flames to turn blue as they licked ice up the leathers of his arms.

"Princess, you would be surprised at how easily I could make you obey me if I cared enough to try." Suggestion laced his voice as he whispered before pulling back, the flames retreating with him. Elisara stared at his back as he crossed to the opposite wall. She ignored the heat burning in her chest at his words, cursing his ability to control the flames.

As Elisara stared at where the flames had singed the wall, small symbols and engravings were carved in their place. She had studied what few texts had travelled to Novisia from Ithyion, but she recognised none of them. The farther she walked into the mountain, the more appeared. Hoping to avoid another confrontation with the Commander, she waited for him to come to the same conclusion and follow, but as she turned, she realised he was already storming ahead. Frowning, she tapped into her power, unsure why his steps and movements had not carried to her on the air. She was beginning to feel wary of its ability to do as it pleased on the Isle. As she followed Kazaar, her eyes wandered across the markings until she slammed into his back and cursed.

Before she could curse more strongly, she peered around his body and noticed the reason for their sudden halt. They stood at the edge of a cliff, where before them lay what could only be described as nature's throne. And in it was exactly what they came for.

Chapter Thirty-Five

Nyzaia

Nyzaia stared into the towering flames dancing on the tiled floor. The longer she did, the more adamant she became they could understand her thoughts before she understood them herself, always carrying out her command with the slightest thought. She nodded to Isaam who closed his eyes and pushed his hand into the blaze. He was grinning when he opened them again.

"I can't feel it," He laughed, waving his hands in and out to demonstrate.

"Okay. Next test then," Nyzaia hardened her stance. Since returning from the Neutral City, three things were on her mind. One, how had she never known the truth about Ithyion? Two, had Kazaar and Elisara made it to the Unsanctioned Isle? And finally, where did the well of her power end? Having uncovered too many truths, any intentions of discussing Isha went out the window.

Trust only the rulers.

Something about Isha's erratic nature felt honest to Nyzaia. She believed her. So, when the tests of their powers manifested within the Temple, she decided to wait until the Historian was not present to discuss Isha with the others. How Nyzaia's flames skated across Elisara's frozen waters played in her mind and had her questioning—more than ever—how much she could do with it. A thought leading her to now.

Nyzaia nodded to each of her syndicate: Tajana, Isaam, Rafik, and Jabir. All stepped forward, a single line of solidarity by her side, clad in their leathers. She glanced at Tajana to her right, who nodded in encouragement, then glanced behind to Farid, who guarded the door into the royal gardens. He inclined his head. No sound came from the other side. Nyzaia took a breath, her fists clenched. Slowly, she exhaled and unclenched her fists, watching the flames deepen.

"Now," she commanded, and held her next breath. Each of her syndicate took slow and synchronized steps into the flames. She paused, waiting for a dreaded scream or cry. There were none.

"Okay, so can you promise we'll always be able to do that?" Isaam called from the other side of the flame. Nyzaia released the wall of fire to find them all stood, grinning in one piece.

"How do you feel?" Tajana asked, stepping forward. "Tired?"

She shook her head; she felt no different from before but was running out of ideas on how to push her power to its limits. Farid coughed by the door. Someone was coming. The syndicate fanned out, stationed by different trees, plants, and archways. Nyzaia perched on the edge of the fountain and picked up a random book pulled from the shelves of her chambers; she fixed the maroon skirts of her lehenga, checking for any signs of ash clinging to her body. She needed new clothing. Enough red existed in her previous station, albeit not in fabric. She could not stomach wearing the colour every day as Queen of Keres. Nyzaia nodded to Farid as a knock sounded at the door, revealing Lord Israar of Myara on the other side.

She avoided glancing at Tajana when the Lord's dark eyes found hers. His golden sherwani glistened in the sun as he stepped from the covered alcove by the door, complimented by the blood-red fabric draped over his shoulder; the waves of his voluminous black hair appeared freshly oiled, as did his beard. She was wary of his smile as he approached and knelt before her, extending his hand, which she politely accepted. The warmth of her skin was shocked by cold from the many golden rings cladding his fingers. He kissed her hand briefly before rising.

Nyzaia had not seen him since he spotted her kissing Tajana in the dining room, nor had she tried to find him. Nyzaia was not one to fear a man—or anyone, for that matter. Yet her curiosity burned as to what he would do with such information, and whether she should be concerned.

"Lord Israar," She plastered on a fake smile. "What a surprise." Nyzaia rose from her seated position, and he stepped back to give her space.

"I had business to attend to in Tabheri. I would not be a loyal Lord if I did not visit my Queen while in her city." He glanced at the syndicate, who watched with stony stares. "Perhaps we could take a more... *private* walk around the gardens?" He leaned in to whisper, glancing in Tajana's direction as he did.

So, I will finally learn his intentions, Nyzaia thought. Tajana made to step forward, but as she did, Nyzaia turned.

"Farid, would you be so kind as to accompany Lord Israar and I around the gardens?" Farid's pale blue eyes glinted as he nodded. They began their stroll down the pale-yellow tiles of the garden. Israar placed a gentle hand on her arm but removed it quickly when Farid stepped closer.

"Perhaps the larger gardens? We could stroll around the water," he suggested. Nyzaia tried to determine his angle. Why suggest the public gardens opposed to the private grounds? Other Lords had advised Nyzaia she needed to be more seen. Thus, she took the risk, willing to face outrage from her syndicate later. Nyzaia nodded, and they instead turned left down the pathway of palm trees until reaching a gated archway that Farid opened for the pair.

"It would be wise we appear to be in good friendship," Lord Israar advised, offering his arm as they walked through the gate. Nyzaia cautiously met his eyes and then peered down at his arm before accepting it politely, careful to avoid her bangles catching in the threads of his sherwani. She glanced around the entrance to the public gardens, and while public, only the wealthy seemed to visit, who now strolled arm in arm in a similar manner.

"I imagine you have been wishing to speak with me, your Majesty," he said. She glanced at him and feigned confusion. "You can drop the act. I know you saw me walking past you and the captain of your guard at breakfast the other morning," he said, voice calm.

"And what were you doing in the palace in the first place?" Nyzaia asked, smiling at those who bowed as she passed.

"I am Lord of the only port city in Keres. Tabheri is the easiest place to meet with the other Lords to discuss imports."

Honest, she thought, though she would need to have Farid speak with the other guards and advise them to inform her whenever a Lord arrives.

"Speak plainly, Israar. I have no patience for digressions," she declared, her own tone far less friendly. He sighed.

"I do not wish to be at war with you, your Majesty. I offer only advice, as is my role as a Lord." He steered her towards a bench among the bushes of green overlooking the lake. "Continuing your relationship with Tajana is unwise, especially given you are new to ruling." He sat beside her on the bench, while Farid watched closely.

"And why is that?" she asked, twisting to face him. "Because she cannot provide an heir?"

The Lord laughed and raised his hand.

"Gods, no. My apologies, I do not mean to laugh at you, your Majesty. You know full well the people of our realm do not care about such things. Hell, if we did, then Lord Arnav of Khami would not have his seat."

Then why is he so opposed to Tajana? Surely, he is not considering I marry already? She feared. Israar leaned closer, and her stomach dropped. Perhaps *he* wished to marry her.

"What do you think the people of Keres would think if they knew their Queen was sleeping with a Red Stone Assassin?" He asked, tone hushed. Nyzaia drew from him, analysing his expression to check if he was bluffing. "Do not insult me by lying, your Majesty."

Lord Israar smiled and leaned back to look across the water.

"How do you know?" she asked.

"She killed my wife."

"Is that what this is, revenge? You wish a different outcome for her?" Nyzaia asked. The Lord's laughter was cold this time.

"No, your Majesty. It was I who requested the assassination." Nyzaia did not expect that response. "I have nothing to fear in telling you this. I do not believe you will tell a soul. After all, I could reveal how it is your very lover who did it." He clearly did not know of her own role in the Red Stones. "My late wife, Anika, was the heir to Myara. Once I knew her father was dying, I pursued the marriage. We would inherit everything in a matter of years; I just had to be patient."

As Queen of the Red Stones, she had seen and heard many things, but something about the coldness in Israar's voice made her uncomfortable. As if devoid of all emotion.

"Why kill her? You had the power of a Lord once her father died." Nyzaia enquired.

"Because she was barren," he said plainly. "I wanted legitimate heirs, and she could not provide that. Plus, she was a bore." He turned to his Queen. "There is something about you I believe is good for this realm, your Majesty, so I am honest when I say your relationship with Tajana will not help your rule."

"You suggest I turn her away?" Nyzaia scoffed. "You do not know the stubbornness of those in the Red Stones." Lord Israar rose from his seat and straightened his sherwani.

"I suggest you think about it. Take a month or so." He smiled down at her. "Any longer, and who knows what information might get out."

And with that, he walked away.

Her inability to place the Lord's intentions unnerved her. Rising from the bench, Farid stepped to her side.

"We could kill him," he said stoically. She burst out laughing, surprised at the statement from a man who said so little. His pale blue eyes watched her, the corner of his mouth twitching.

"You would have been good in the Red Stones, Farid." She said, smiling.

Nyzaia pretended not to notice the way his eyes darkened, and how his features tensed at the suggestion. Or how quickly he turned to resume his post of surveillance. Nyzaia had the impression there was a lot more to Farid than he was willing to share. She turned back to the royal gardens, turning over Israar's warnings, and contemplating what to tell Tajana.

Chapter Thirty-Six

Elisara

Centuries of incontrollable nature carved the throne room. They stood at the edge of the cliff, and to their right began a steep, winding staircase of stone coated in ivy and inky roses flowing from the staircase toward the ground of the circular cavern, creating a blanket of green. It slowly thinned as it reached a set of low steps, wide enough to almost fill the width of the space. Elisara gasped at the demonstration of nature's power.

Atop the steps sat two thrones. Behind, a cascading waterfall towered and gushed black liquid. Where the streams met the rock, the water had frozen, a glistening effect cast across it. Pillars of marble encompassed the waterfall, wrapped in the same orange, blue and white flames witnessed in the mouth of the mountain. Elisara had never seen one place in Novisia where the power of all four Gods convened in such harmony.

The harmony continued to a tomb in the centre: a tomb of ice wrapped in burning vines, surrounded by a pond. It was as if the Gods themselves guarded the weapon they knew sat within. Protruding from the ice was a dull silver sword where someone before them had tried to chip away at it. Magic entrapped it now.

Elisara was eager to explore every inch of the throne room and experience every element that appeared intent to greet them upon their arrival. She glanced at the Commander, who assessed every inch of the room. Turning to Elisara, he nodded, and gestured at the staircase. While she had not earned the respect to be his Queen, he understood his place against hers in a room clearly intended for royalty.

Elisara descended the steps which, upon closer inspection, appeared to be a war of onyx and white marble, as if the designers of the room argued over which materials to use, and compromised on a sharp contrast of both. It appeared that way throughout the entire room. The only exception was the thrones, which stood separate. One throne of onyx, another of marble.

A light scent travelled through the air from the flowers, and as she admired them, she took note of the large thorns hidden beneath the petals and withdrew her hand from the railing. When she reached the final steps, the ivy moved. Vines retracted from their place of slumber and redirected themselves to the edge of the room, weaving up the walls to free the floor of their presence, allowing Elisara a clear path inward. With the vines absent, Elisara noted the four symbols engraved on the ground. She did not recognize them. She checked the Commander was behind before continuing.

The height of the room was magnificent, carved so deep into the mountain the sun was barely visible through the round opening above. They bypassed the tomb to assess the waterfall, ice, and flames behind the thrones. Everything hummed, as if the Isle was content she and the Commander had found this slice of purity. The power was raw, too, like the pure essence of the elements rather than a manifestation wielded by the royals.

They stopped in front of the thrones: exquisite, equal in size and elegance. Elisara's hand traced the marble, her fingers pausing over an image of the sun at its base. The onyx throne etched with its opposite. The moon. The elements had created a shrine for their own gods, Sonos and Sitara, as if one day they hoped the beings would rule again.

"It matches your eyes," the Commander commented. He stood with one foot raised on a step, his arm resting on his thigh as he watched her.

"You must be blind, given my eyes are the darkest of browns." She responded, tracing the coldness of the stone thrones. She glanced behind her as he drew closer, and her eyes locked on the

Commander's unrelenting stare. She looked away first, flushed beneath his scrutiny. She could not read him.

"Naturally, yes. But since the coronation, your eyes glow pale blue whenever you use your power and seem to lighten each time. Here, they are a glowing silver—nearly white—the colour of Sonos' throne." He moved to stand beside her, placing himself before the onyx. Shifting on her feet, she wondered why he had watched her so closely, and what purpose it served him. Discerning things she had not about herself.

"Then, I suppose yours matches the colour of Sitara's throne." She returned.

"Do you often spend time assessing the colour of my eyes, Princess?" Elisara's arm brushed his, but he did not move away, forcing her to step back under his gaze.

"No," she flashed him a sarcastic smile. "I just know that unless you're using your power, they're the same darkness as your heart and soul."

The Commander tilted his head, eyes focused on her lips, reminding Elisara of his comment that she never smiled anymore. She wondered why he had noticed.

"Why do you think the King of Keres did all this?" She asked, backing away and down the steps.

"What makes you think Razik had this made? It possesses all the elements."

"He asked you to retrieve the weapon from here, so I assume he must have visited before."

"Or his family had told him of it." Kazaar countered. Elisara pondered the suggestion. He could be right, she thought, but would not admit it. Elisara had never interacted with King Razik; what little she knew, she heard from her parents. Yet they spoke more of the families in Nerida and Garridon than Keres, hence why she was quick to assign blame to a King she knew little about.

"Regardless, the Keres line has kept this a secret. It makes me question why." She continued toward the tomb.

"He is not the only royal to keep secrets and was not the royal awaiting my arrival the last time I was here." The Commander crossed his arms, and Elisara glanced up at him.

"You lied," she said. "At the meeting, you said the Isle did not allow you access."

"I did not think it would be appreciated for me to reveal that someone's parent had been on the Isle and turned me away," he said plainly. "But it was not Razik who expelled me from the Isle. But the person delivered a message in code—a code only used by King Razik." The Commander appeared to survey her as he spoke, a cautious look in his eye. Elisara gently prodded at the vines encasing the tomb.

"Who was it then? A Nerida royal? The Garridon King?"

"Your mother."

Elisara whirled.

"My mother would never keep something like that from me," she hissed.

"Really?" He asked as he stalked the final steps to reach her. "She kept the nature of Novisia's creation from you, and the threat that could resurface. Why would she not keep the content of the Unsanctioned Isle from you as well?" He kept his eyes locked on her.

"She was not from royal lineage. My father was. It was not her place to divulge such information, but my father's."

"You are contradicting yourself, Princess. You're trying to defend her, but the truth is: you did not know her as well as you thought."

"She was my mother. Of *course*, I knew her." Elisara spun back to the tomb to find a distraction from the power roiling in her veins.

"Of course, you did. *Star*." He smirked, moving to face her on the opposite side of the tomb. "That's the name your parents used for you, isn't it? Their star? It is also the name she used for you before casting me from this Isle."

His hands gripped the fire coated vines and pulled, all the while assessing her reaction. Elisara would not meet his eye, would not let him see the pools of doubt that lived there. No one outside of her family knew their pet names for one another. Her mother must have spoken with the Commander, but would she have come to the island?

"Why would my mother speak of me to *you*?" Elisara bit, calling his bluff. The Commander averted his gaze for a second but then returned it, his eyebrow raised.

"She asked me what changed you in Keres," he said plainly.

A lie. His eyebrow raise was a telltale sign she learned while analysing him during their years of training. Before she could probe further, he cut her off.

"That was not the only time I saw your mother," he continued.

"Well, of course not. She attended royal gatherings, as did you." Elisara snapped. She began attempting to shatter the ice of the tomb, mimicking the Commander's half-hearted attempts on the vines as they both now stood ankle-deep in the surrounding pool of water.

"Does she often spend royal tours of Keres sneaking through the streets of Tabheri in commoner's clothing?"

"You're lying," Elisara sneered, though he was not. But she was not willing to accept that yet.

"What reason would I have to lie about a deceased Queen?" He grunted, snapping one of the vines having formed around the ice.

"You have no respect for your current Queen, so why should you have any for the dead?" Elisara stormed around the tomb as the Commander advanced.

"I have little respect for you because you have not *proved* yourself as Queen. What have you done since your coronation? Even as a princess, what did you ever do for your people? For others? You are selfish, and while you have a heart and I know you care; you are too transfixed on your own worries to help those around you. When you were training, you were too worried about hurting people to even try and save them."

"I am not selfish. I only worried about hurting people because of your stupid tasks!" She shouted.

"You could have completed the task, but instead you chose to lose control with me. And even now as you begin to understand your power, you keep yourself from the well inside you. Too scared to find out who you really are." Elisara's eyes glowed at his words, the white of her irises reflected in his gaze, which lost their darkness as the glow of amber emerged.

"You have no idea what it's like to have this much power! To live in constant worry that you might become feared." Elisara screamed to be heard over the wind whipping throughout the throne room.

"I am feared!" the Commander yelled, and flames engulfed him. Elisara did not balk. "My entire life, I have been raised to be feared, to incite fright rather than respect." The inferno blazed, his eyes glowing the signature burnt gold of Keres.

"You know how it feels not to be respected, and yet you insult your Queen?" Elisara screamed. He had just scolded her for contradicting herself, yet now he claimed to understand. "You resent your life, Commander? A bastard raised with a silver spoon in his mouth. What you really resent is never being good enough for Razik to see you as a son."

Elisara flinched at the look that crossed his face—the closest thing she had ever seen to hurt. It soon vanished, and in its place stood the Commander everyone across Novisia feared.

Elisara ducked as he shot his flames at her with speed, breathing heavy as he did. She rose from her crouch, the disbelief clear on her face. She soon forgot his disrespect, instead wishing to show him the extent of power she possessed. Elisara's hair whipped behind her as the wind picked up around them and lightning crackled in the room. She glanced upwards, yet no clouds rippled in the sky. She created the lighting from nothing.

"Do you think I cannot be feared, Commander?" Lifting her hand, he rose with it, floating midair while encased in his flames. She rose with the wind, eye to eye with him. The colours flickered from orange to blue as Elisara willed air to pierce through the fire. He countered, orange flames dousing her entire body. She did not feel its pain.

"I know you can be feared, Princess. I was just trying to get you out of your cage." He smirked and struck with a ball of flame, quickly met with one of ice. A flash of white light tore through the room as their powers collided, and they fell to the floor, both expertly landing on their feet. Neither released control of their power, the magic building and gathering between them.

Silver formed where their powers met, growing until it inched along the threads to the owners of the power. What could only be described as raw magic crawled along the flames and ice towards Elisara and the Commander. She would not yield but probed deeper into the well within. It was all-consuming. Her head fell back at the same time as the Commander's as magic overwhelmed her. She sighed, as if realising she was incomplete until this moment. Now, she was whole. Her power sung in response, like it had been waiting for this its entire life. Elisara opened her eyes to watch as the glow of their power darkened before disappearing completely, with the two left panting on the floor.

Elisara called the air to her lungs, and it arrived instantly, like it was seconds ahead of her forming thoughts. She took a moment of solace in the darkness as questions stormed her mind. Eventually, she rose to find the tomb shattered. The Commander kneeled, rummaging through the ice. He could barely see in the darkness, *but it's midday*, Elisara thought. She turned her gaze upwards at the hole in the mountain, and there, blocking the light, was the silhouette of a winged, dark creature.

"Commander, how close are you to reaching that weapon?" Elisara asked, stepping towards him. Her eyes trained on the creature above.

"I'm trying, princess, but it is difficult in the dark and I've likely expended too much power."

"I hate to be the bearer of bad news, but you might need to check if you have any power left." The Commander looked at her then and followed her eyeline.

The creature descended, landing so hard that a crack split through the ground. Its wings remained tucked around itself, resembling torn leather. Not a stranger to battle, it seemed. The Commander rose and unsheathed the sword from his back at the same time Elisara did. They watched, horror-stricken, as the creature spanned its wings, revealing the dark creature within. It bore the same bodily design as a human, except elongated and disfigured. Holes existed for eyes and teeth flashed as long as daggers. Elisara and the Commander dropped into a fighting stance, but the creature did not care. Throwing its head back, it wailed—a high-pitched scream that reverberated throughout the room, propelling the Commander and Elisara to opposite sides, swords flung from their grip. Elisara yelped as a sharp rock struck her calf.

The creature stalked toward the Commander, its long tongue flicking across its teeth as if readying for a feast. The flames erupting from the Commander's palm blazed a bright white, the same as the magic consuming them earlier. It blinded the creature momentarily but did little else as the beast refocused and continued stalking its prey. The Commander's eyes narrowed, and the creature burst into flames, as if Kazaar had simply thought it and it happened. What had the raw magic triggered in their powers? The creature shook off the flames, unfazed.

They would need the weapon.

The creature focused on Kazaar, its back to Elisara, who redirected the sound of her footsteps as she limped her way to the remains of the tomb, containing shouts of pain with every step as blood leaked from her calf. She glanced back at the creature. The Commander had found his sword and was distracting it with a flourish of unnecessary movements, buying Elisara time. When the sword caught the creature, black liquid leaked from the wound, which only angered it further.

A glint of gold caught Elisara's eye. It lay in the remains of the ice, the vines having completely burned away. Elisara reached for it, but in doing so, the pile of ice shards shifted and alerted the creature. It whipped its head and stretched its wings. Elisara moved quickly—too quickly—forcing her leg out from under her. She yanked on the hilt in her grip and withdrew a sword, gold from hilt to blade.

"KAZAAR!" Elisara screamed. She willed the sword towards him with a gush of air, and he caught it as the creature turned back to him.

She scrambled for a distraction but could not find her sword, and the daggers in her corset would have insignificant impact unless she got up close. Her eye caught the hilt of the dull sword protruding the ice earlier, left by the last stranger on the Isle. It would have to do. Pulling it from the shards, Elisara used it as a crutch to stand back up and swung it in the air to shake off any residue, the sword a perfect mirror to her movements. The creature shifted focus and prowled towards Elisara. She ducked as it swung a clawed talon, and as it lunged, she rose, swinging the sword up in an arc and slicing off its wing. The creature screamed again, but there was no force behind it. Its wing dropped to the floor, black tar spewing from the stump left in its place. Elisara prepared to cut off the other wing as it advanced again. She froze. The stump was no longer, as a wing slowly regrew.

"Elisara!" Kazaar called.

As the creature backed her into a corner, she swung at its legs. Kazaar made to jump at the creature. Elisara directed the air to aid his movements as he swung down and pierced the golden blade into the creature's back. The creature did not scream. It groaned, looking down at Elisara. Her eyes locked with its empty sockets, and she could have sworn her face reflected in them—for only a second—before the creature dropped face-first. With the dull sword still in her grip, she swung to sever its neck. The head rolled, leaving a trail of red blood behind. Human-like blood.

Kazaar moved quickly, hands rough against her cheeks as his eyes roamed to check for any wounds.

"Are you okay?" he asked, his hands remaining on her face. The danger that hung over them seemed to pause, as though the Gods had frozen time for this moment. A moment to breathe. A moment with him. Elisara swallowed at his eyes. Something was different. Where she had only ever noticed amber before, she now saw specks of shadow and light: white embers amongst the flames. She blinked, and they were gone, his eyes fading to their usual brown. She was unsure how long they stood like that, frozen in a moment seeming to last an eternity. Concern imbued his gaze as he assessed the grazes on her cheek. The pad of his thumb stroked over them, lightly smearing the blood as he did. His eyes narrowed, as if imagining killing the creature all over again. Her breathing hitched; he had never been concerned before—not for her. She cleared her throat.

"I'm fine," she said as her leg gave way. He caught her, engulfing her in the warmth of his body as they connected.

He glanced down at the creature while keeping an arm firmly around her waist. Elisara opened her mouth to thank him, interrupted by screams that tore from above.

"We need to hide. Others may come for it." The Commander grabbed her arm and draped it around his shoulder as he clasped her hand and looked around them. She held on tight as he helped her to the waterfall. "This is a throne room; there has to be a hidden exit somewhere."

And as he said it, the black waterfall cascading down the mountain opened to reveal a wide crack in the wall. The Isle was on their side. Kazaar helped Elisara over the gap where the water fell, and they entered the darkness together.

Chapter Thirty-Seven

Elisara

They were not in darkness for long. The hidden path entered a smaller carved room: a bedroom, it seemed. This room was less overwhelmed by nature, clearly furnished by humans. The floor was the same contradicting onyx and marble, and an immense rug sat in the centre. A four-poster bed occupied most of the room, layered with thick-white blankets. To the left sat an empty stone fireplace with cushions scattered around, and a wooden writing desk littered with paper, as if the last occupiers quickly fled.

Elisara let go of Kazaar and hobbled into the room, leaning on her new sword for support. Many symbols sketched the papers strewn across the desk, and she picked up a page.

"Do you recognise these?" she asked, but when she turned, Kazaar was nowhere to be seen.

"Commander?" she whispered. "Kazaar?"

Elisara peered back through the pathway they had emerged from but saw only darkness. Movement sounded, and she spun to find Kazaar re-emerging from behind a tapestry. He beckoned her to silently follow.

How does he keep evading my hearing? She pondered, following him into the hidden opening.

"There might be more to the Isle and the explosion than we thought," he said grimly as they emerged into what could only be described as a shrine. The room was similar in size to the bedroom, but in each corner, a statue stood. Elisara ambled around the room, glancing at each statue. A woman with tightly curled hair and waves lapping at her feet, a tall man covered in vines, a stern woman with long straight hair standing atop mountains, and a man brandishing a sword, flames running up its blade. She looked at Kazaar.

"Are these?"

"The Gods. Nerida, Garridon, Vala and Keres." He confirmed. She turned her attention to the statue in the middle.

"So, this must be..."

"Sitara and Sonos," he nodded, approaching. The two stood side by side as they beheld the artwork before them. A naked woman carved in onyx, with hair skillfully masking her modesty while her arm encircled Sonos' hip, carved from marble. His hands cupped her cheeks as their foreheads rested together. At the base of the statue was an engraved sun and moon, interlocked. Silence fell as the pair admired the details.

"They look..."

"In love," Elisara breathed. "Completely and utterly in love." She felt Kazaar watching her, so she moved to circle past the other statues, then reached the one that intrigued her most.

The Goddess Vala. Elisara bowed her head, but as she examined her ancestor, she found little similarities. The statue was cold and unmoving: a Goddess tired of playing peacekeeper. Elisara wondered if that was where the gift of lightning had stemmed from—anger and frustration. She glanced at Kazaar examining all the statues and noted the similarities he shared with Keres: the strong jawline, broad shoulders, but most notably, the air of arrogance. Yet Elisara was more transfixed with Sitara and Sonos: how Sonos clasped his lover's face, while she gripped his hip. Sitara's right arm was bent slightly, as if gesturing across the room. Elisara followed the line of her finger to a large mirror propped against the wall.

Having been so focused on the statues, they had not noticed the mirror. It was ornate and lined in gold, depicting all the elements, with the same sun and moon at its crown. A thick layer of dust obscured it. Elisara reached to smear the dust away, and with one wipe, words appeared. She continued wiping until most of the mirror was cleared, glancing past the words at her appearance, tired and exhausted from the day. Kazaar was not much better as he appeared behind, squinting at the words painted before them.

"I would have thought it would be in an unfamiliar language, given all the symbols," Kazaar murmured. He was right. Elisara could read it too.

"Look closer. There are still some symbols, but they seem to be carved into the mirror rather than painted on." Staring intently, he reached his arm past Elisara and pointed, leaning closer as he did. Her eyes met his in the mirror and her breathing paused. He stepped back. She averted her eyes before stepping closer to the mirror, tracing the symbols similar to the ones on the floor in the throne room, but smaller and more intricate. The paint of the words was worn slightly, causing her to squint as she read them aloud.

'With those of white and those of black
The spirit of the first makes their way back.

When the darkness returns, sacrifice is made.
In the wake of disaster, the return of the blade.

When light meets dark in the rarest of times
When all that is left is the last of the lines.

The power to awaken that of old lore,
Lies in the soul of those with all four.

Only together can they defeat and restore,
Only together can they gain so much more.'

"What do you think it means?" Elisara asked.

"I can't be sure of all of it, but it looks like it's missing some lines. Look." He gestured further down the mirror to where the words appeared chipped, leaving small dots behind that must have once formed letters.

"Some here as well, " Elisara pointed to small paint marks in amongst some of the wider spread lines. She barely noticed Kazaar leave for the other room, too focused on the markings. He returned with paper and ink and began writing two copies of the words down. Elisara took one more glance around the room before she returned to the bedroom with him, accepting the paper he handed over.

She collapsed onto the bed, crying out as pain tore through her leg. He closed the distance in seconds.

“It’s fine, just a cut,” she said, shifting her calf.

Despite rarely willing to be so close to Elisara, he knelt before her, his hands warm as he grasped her calf to inspect it closely. She flinched at the sudden contact, but he was silent as he ripped a piece of silk from the bedding, his hands uncharacteristically gentle as he began wrapping her leg. Elisara tried to form words of thanks, yet the tenderness of his movements halted her, as did the realization of how oddly natural it felt to have him near. Once he finished, he moved away silently and made himself comfortable in the chair by the desk.

Perhaps King Razik had visited the Isle before and sat where Kazaar did now. She pictured her mother sitting at the desk, too, pouring over the words on the mirror. Perhaps she had come to the Isle seeking answers after the dark creature landed on the shores of Novisia all those years ago. Her mother had always been inquisitive.

Elisara refocused on the mystery of the words. It was no story. The lines resonated too deeply with the events of the present day.

"You have surprisingly neat handwriting for a man," Elisara commented.

Kazaar did not look up as he responded.

"That's rather sexist of you, princess. Why must men have un-neat writing?"

"Well, traditionally, the men of Keres are not taught perfect cursive, but the perfect fighting form."

"The King was adamant I take part in the same lessons his sons and daughters did." Still, he did not look up.

Elisara often thought Kazaar's relationship with the King was an odd one. Raised as if he would be a noble Prince or could even become a King but forced into the military from an early age. She supposed it was likely because he outmatched the King's actual heirs when it came to power. She had seen Kazaar use his flame before in Keres. It outmatched the Keres heirs, but it was still nothing compared to what she saw in the throne room. He matched Elisara's power—a power Elisara obtained only from her lineage.

"The blade must be this," Kazaar lifted the golden sword with ease.

"But who is the 'spirit of the first?' The first spirits were Chaos and Order, but what if it means the first Gods? Sonos and Sitara? Or the first elemental Gods?" Elisara asked. Kazaar made a noise of agreement.

"That part may be difficult to determine immediately." He continued reading. "'In the rarest of times, when all that is left is the last of the lines—"

"The explosion," Elisara said, finishing his thought. "I cannot think what light and dark refer to, though. The dark creatures, maybe. But what about the light?"

"Old lore could be anything. Our history goes back through Ithyion for centuries. We would need to look through the Historians' books to determine something there." He stood and began pacing.

"The soul of all four." Elisara contemplated. "Could that mean someone who owns all four of something—four things to defeat whatever this old lore is?"

She noted Kazaar's face shift, almost imperceptibly.

"Together has to mean Novisia: all the realms, all the rulers," Kazaar said, deflecting the question.

"You're not telling me something."

He looked at her, surprise flitting across his features.

"I cannot be certain of some things, and I do not wish to lead us down a path we are not certain on." He returned to stare at the words again.

"Kazaar, don't make me pull rank." She shuffled up onto the bed, studying him closely. He sighed and approached the other side, the mattress dipping under his weight as he sat on the edge across from her.

"This Isle has a natural presence of all four elements, and you saw the way they reacted to us. Maybe the soul of all four has something to do with this Isle?" He rested his head against the pillow as she contemplated his suggestion.

"But an Isle cannot have a soul?" she said, though it was more of a question. "The mountain retains the powers here, but I cannot see how it would trigger the return of an old lore." Sitting in silence for a moment, the two turned over the words in their minds.

"I do not think we will decipher this until we have the full picture. There are lines missing on that mirror." He sighed. "Can you think of anywhere else that's as old as here? Somewhere that may have hidden scripture?"

Elisara shook her head.

"Only the Temple, but that's going to be a dead end. What about one of the royal castles? You said yourself, my mother has been here, so maybe another ruler has too. Perhaps there is a part of this prophecy they want hidden." She turned to face him, but he was already watching her.

"Do we share this with the others?" He asked.

"We have to. *Together* is emphasized, and who would I be as a Queen if I did not aid the entire kingdom in preventing an attack?" She checked his expression. "Would you disagree?"

"No, you are right. The strategist in me wants to keep it to ourselves until we know more, but we cannot put any others at risk. At least we know the blade works." He glanced at the gold glinting against the wall. "But I am not sure how much use one sword against an army of creatures will be."

Elisara worried the same. The creature's strength and ability to regrow limbs was a terrifying defense. She dreaded to think what an army of them could do. She looked at the sword she had found, propped on the wall beside her.

"You are not seriously keeping that?" he asked, the faintest chuckle escaping his lips. Elisara feigned hurt and raised a hand to her dust-covered chest dramatically.

"What on earth do you mean? It's the most beautiful sword I have ever seen, one fit for a Queen." She laughed. "But on a serious note, it has value. It signifies the first real thing I have done for my realm since becoming Queen. I want to keep it as a reminder of the time I escaped near death and helped gain a weapon for our Kingdom."

A soft smile graced her lips, and Kazaar responded with a smile of his own.

"What?" Elisara asked, shifting under the intensity of his gaze. She was reminded of his visit to Helena: the first time she had ever seen him smile. She was as enamored by it then as she was now.

"You laughed," he said. "I've never heard you laugh."

She considered it, and he was right. While she had smiled little since becoming Queen, she had not laughed at all.

"You're right, I must be delirious from expending so much energy saving your life."

He scoffed and made himself comfortable on the bed, gazing at the canopy above. Elisara copied his actions, relishing in the moments of silence. No noises carried to her from the lack of wind, allowing her mind a moment reprieve. Though she never expected to experience such serenity with Kazaar on a bed beside her.

It prompted her mind to lying beside Caellum, who she had

not thought of at all since heading to the Isle, as if her mind was protecting her from the inevitable heartbreak to follow once she called off the engagement. Despite her love for him, she knew what Vala needed.

"What has turned you so serious?" Kazaar asked, only his head turned towards her as his arms lay by his side. She stole a glance at him, a film of water coating her eyes. He frowned.

"The sacrifices one must make as Queen."

"You are Queen. You decide your fate. What could you possibly need to sacrifice?"

"Love," she whispered.

"The prince?"

"I see you have no respect for him, either."

"I never have," he retorted.

"I have loved Caellum for as long as I can remember," Elisara said. "I wanted nothing more than to marry him and build a life with him, even if it took me from Vala." She rolled to meet Kazaar's eyes. "But I am all that is left to uplift my people. Marrying a King of a different realm is not the right way forward."

Kazaar's eyes roamed her face.

"You want to do what is right for your people?"

"*Our* people, Kazaar. The people of Vala. The people of Novisia. I cannot do that married to a King who will need to prioritise his own realm." Tears fell then, and Kazaar cautiously raised his hand to wipe them from her face. His hand rested on her cheek momentarily before removing it. Elisara's stomach fluttered at the gentleness of his touch—a touch she expected to flinch from, not lean into.

"He was never the love for you anyway, Elisara." Her breath caught at the gentle use of her name on his lips. "He is a good soldier; I will give him that. A man respected by his friends and a man who would do anything for you, no matter the request. But you, Elisara, deserve someone who will challenge you, who will meet you head on and bring out the best in you when you think only of your worst. That often takes a firmer tongue than the prince possesses. He supports you and comforts your needs, but he does not drive your growth."

Elisara's brow furrowed, and he smiled.

"You need a love that matches the power in your veins. A love that defends, but champions you. You need a love that lights your soul on fire, not one that cradles your heart in vines." He turned back to gaze at the canopy, and she did the same in silent contemplation of his words. "Or you just need someone significantly better in the bedroom. He cannot be that good if you will turn your back on him so easily."

Elisara leaned over to smack him across the chest, her hair spilling onto his shoulders as he laughed.

"Did the terrifying Commander just utter a crude *joke*?" She exclaimed. He laughed again, and it was infectious; she could not help but laugh too. There was that look on his face again, as if in awe of the sounds escaping her lips. Kazaar reached for her hair and played with it amongst his fingers.

"I am right, aren't I?" He peered up through his lashes, a grin on his face, and she could not tear her eyes away. The smile changed him. Elisara swallowed and pulled back, suddenly conscious of the fact he was joking about her betrothed.

"You are unbelievable," she retorted, rolling back over.

"So, I have been told."

Elisara rolled her eyes and began unlacing the back of her leather corset.

"Undressing for me already, Princess?" He rolled over and propped himself up on his elbow.

"I do not need to undress myself when a man can do it for me, Commander." Elisara froze as he pulled the final lace for her. She had felt his touch already that day but there was something unplaceable at the simplicity of his action. She swallowed and chastised herself for the comment, thinking of Caellum instead. It had been so long since he had undressed her.

"We're back to 'Commander' are we?" His hand paused on her back, a feather light touch she could not tear her attention from.

"Remember, I am your Queen. No matter the jesting, I am still betrothed." She removed the knife-filled corset and lay back down, facing away from Kazaar this time.

"Mhmm," Kazaar pondered.

Closing her eyes, she hid a smile as she relished their rare moment of civility. Elisara did not know if she could be friends with her Commander, yet she was beginning to come to terms with the fact he had not caused all her pain in Keres. She needed someone to blame, and his demeanor made it easy. Yet she was wary. After all, she was still Queen, and he, her Commander. A heart of ice while his was one of flames.

She did not wish to get burned.

Chapter Thirty-Eight

Elisara

All was silent in the throne room when Elisara and Kazaar reemerged the next morning, neither speaking of the fact she awoke with his arm around her. There were no traces of the dead creature: no blood, no body. Yet dispersed ice and vines scattered the room, a sign other creatures, or someone, had arrived shortly after to carry the body of their fellow beast away from the Isle. The waterfall was clear again, as was the lake when they surfaced from the mouth of the mountain. The water was tranquil and remained so as it parted to form a walkway for the pair: this time, not two towering walls of black, but two separate waves of clarity.

They emerged from the lake, but before it fell back into place, Kazaar picked up a blue shard and placed it in his pocket.

"A memory," he murmured, back to his usual surly self. She smiled at their similarity. The Isle's nature kissed them farewell as they wandered through the forest and back to the shore, where the ship remained anchored in waiting.

"Did you see anything while you waited?" Kazaar asked the captain gruffly. He shook his head.

"Nothing. Some odd sounds in the distance, but I anchored further out to sea, so I couldn't see much." Kazaar nodded then boarded the ship before Elisara, an action not unnoticed by the captain as he stepped back, motioning for the Queen to grace the ship before him. Elisara frowned, uncertain as to Kazaar's sudden return to coldness. The pair sat in silence for the journey back to Elvera, silence which remained for the horseback ride to Azuria, too.

However, Elisara's mood brightened as they reached the courtyard of the Castle. Sat outside was the royal carriage of Garridon. While she knew of the inevitable conversation to be had, she was eager to see him. Their feelings for one another like the love Sonos and Sitara shared. Elisara noticed Kazaar glare at the carriage as he helped her from the horse, careful not to knock her leg.

"He had sweet peas with him," said the stable hand, coming to collect the steed. Elisara found her smile again. He was always so thoughtful.

"Do you know where he is waiting?" she asked, passing the reins to the boy.

"I think he was seen in the gardens, your Majesty." The boy bowed as Elisara thanked him. She would have liked to have changed before seeing Caellum, but the dirt-ridden tunic and military leathers would have to do. Elisara contemplated what colour sweet peas he may have brought her today, and where in her room she would place them. Perhaps she would have one of her ladies dry the petals: a permanent reminder of their years shared before the engagement ended.

Elisara's smile vanished from her face as she rounded the snow-covered wall into the gardens.

There, under the arch of snow speckled dahlias stood her betrothed, lips interlocked with one of her ladies, who held a bouquet of sweet peas. Elisara stilled as, silent as she watched Caellum kiss her the same way he did when they were together. Every rational thought of ending their engagement left Elisara. Instead, her heart simply cracked. Doubt tainted every moment ever shared with Caellum. All those promises he gave her, had he said them to another? Perhaps to the woman she watched him with now? Elisara stumbled back into the bust of a stone ancestor positioned on the pillar behind. The statue toppled and shattered in tandem with her heart. The only difference being the statue could be glued back together.

The noise abruptly stopped Caellum and Lady Relena, who at

least had the sense to feign remorse as she straightened her dress before scurrying into the castle upon seeing the Queen. Caellum's face was unreadable.

"Do not dismiss her on my account," she spat as Caellum headed toward her.

"Star—" he stopped himself. "*Elisara.*" His tone was firm.

She raised her chin at the sudden formality. Caellum had called her Star for as long as she had known him, from the first time he tried to speak her name when they were young. "Elistara," he had said.

"I do not want to hear your foolish excuses," venom laced her voice as air began to swirl and quicken around her.

"Control it, Elisara. That's your preference these days, isn't it? To be in control of everyone and everything?"

The wind stopped. Hurt choked Elisara, who no longer recognized the loveless eyes of the stern-faced man before her. Caellum's near silence at the meeting suggested he was struggling as King, but she could not think why he would turn on her like this. "I do not have an excuse. What you saw is one of many ladies I have been with over the years."

She struggled to tame the tears at his blunt admission.

"Why?" She ground out. Was he purposely trying to hurt her?

"Why?" He yelled. "How about because you left for Keres, despite me telling you to fight your parents on it? Or the fact when I visited you, you barely spoke to me aside from apologizing for having nearly *killed* me in the Abis? Or maybe because when you returned, you barely wanted to be touched or to even have me near. When you started opening up again, everything was on your terms, and I abided your every whim!" He stepped closer, anger rife on his face.

"You do not know what I went through in Keres," she spat, enraged her trauma drove his betrayal.

"Of course, I do not! You never told me!" She flinched; he had never raised his voice at her before. The air seemed to engulf her like a gentle cocoon. "You are selfish! You lack control and you are emotionless when we are together. Why would I want to spend my life tied to someone so incredibly draining to be with?" He stood inches from her, to where she now pressed against the garden wall.

"But you always wanted to marry me," she whimpered. Servants stopped to watch the drama unfold, a group of ladies having formed at the edge of the gardens. She would not cry in front of them. In front of *him*.

"Because they forced me to!" Caellum shouted. His hand moved to grip her throat, to force her eyes to his, but in a single blink, a blur passed in Elisara's vision, a knife pressed at the throat of the man she loved. Caellum peered down at the hand wielding the blade, at the Keres Sigil ring on his scarred fingers.

"Are you threatening a King, Commander?" Caellum spat at Kazaar, who stood firm as stone behind him, his hand gripping the knife so tight his knuckles were white. His eyes glowed as they locked onto Elisara's, those flecks of white returned, deep within his gaze and grounded her.

"That depends, *sire*," he hissed. "Are you threatening my *Queen*?"

A flicker of emotion crossed Elisara's gaze as she held Kazaar's stare: a moment of recognition shared between them. In a single moment, Caellum had caused her to fall apart, and with two simple words, Kazaar pieced her back together. She was worth more than this moment. He nodded, and she nodded back. Straightening then, she raised her chin, shifting her gaze to Caellum. It was as though Kazaar's presence motivated her to keep strong, like his thoughts intertwined with her own. Removing the knife, Kazaar stepped immediately to Elisara's side. A flurry of wind propelled Caellum away as he fell back into the snow, rolling as he landed.

"For someone so unhappy having been forced to marry, you did an outstanding job of faking it."

"I did not fake all my feelings. I just never wanted you as my wife," he said, dusting snow off himself as he rose.

"You are done, Prince." Kazaar stepped forward, hand on the pommel of the golden sword at his waist. "Your carriage remains in the courtyard."

"You dare command a King?" Caellum whirled, but as Elisara squeezed her fist, all air left his body. Caellum gasped and clutched his neck. Her hand tightened and the colour of his face morphed to purple. Her hand gripped the pommel of the dull silver sword from Isle, strapped to her hip. Some dark part of her wished to wield it now.

"My Commander speaks for my safety. If you are deemed a risk, then yes, he commands on my behalf." Elisara unclenched her fist, grateful Kazaar had not intervened. Caellum gasped for breath, looking up at her through watery eyes. "*Leave.*"

Elisara did not look at him while uttering the command but instead at the sweet peas crushed in the snow. He took one last glance at her and then at Kazaar, before storming past them towards the courtyard.

"Elisara," Kazaar's soft voice called from behind, and she sensed his hand moving to reach her.

"Don't," she whispered, stepping towards the flowers. "You were wrong, Kazaar. I did not have vines cradling my heart. It appears I had poison ivy blinding my vision." She froze the petals of the sweet peas before shattering them in her hands.

"Setting your heart on fire would burn both away."

She smiled in spite of the pain.

"Then it is unfortunate a shield of ice now sits in its place." She dropped the remaining shards of sweet peas to the floor.

"You should have seen his attack coming," Kazaar said, walking towards the castle, shoulders tensed. "Training grounds. Sunset. We need to work on your close combat." Elisara turned, exasperated. Training was the last thing on her mind.

"It's like you said," he continued. "When it comes to your safety, I can make demands."

Kazaar did not look at her as he strode the lavender lined path in the direction of his chambers, Elisara staring after him. This was his way of providing a distraction, she realized. Whispers came from the hedges, and Elisara turned to find a group of servants gossiping.

"Could one of you politely inform Lady Relena that she is no longer welcome to visit the castle? While one of you does that, I need the other to prepare the baths in my chambers. I expect it to be done before I get up there." Elisara's tone was harsh as she made her commands, but she needed them to understand.

She would not be disrespected in her home.

Chapter Thirty-Nine

Caellum

"It is done?" Lord Gregor of Albyn asked.

"It is done," Caellum confirmed, turning the golden goblet.

He had dreaded this meeting ever since returning from Vala. Confirmation to the Lords that his betrothal had ended, his first love no longer. The Lords' discussions of next steps were lost to Caellum as he gulped his fifth cup of wine that afternoon. Wine seemed to be the only thing to keep Elisara's image from his mind, after replaying their encounter endlessly on his journey back from Vala. Each time, the crack in his heart expanded at the pain in her eyes. Never did he think Elisara would not be part of his future, but that was the hand he was dealt in becoming King of a realm untrusting of his family line.

To end the engagement, Elisara needed to hate him because any hope—any slight indication of a future—would have broken his resolve. He could not risk his realm falling to civil war once again. So, he broke his own heart, and hoped someone would pick up the pieces of hers.

"Your Majesty?" Lord Ryon called.

"Hmm?" Caellum raised his head, met with critiquing eyes.

"We leave tomorrow at first light. Is that agreeable?"

Caellum stared, gaze empty.

"For Doltas Island, your Majesty?" prompted Lord Cormac of Asdale to his left.

He nodded. The information revealed by the Historian had not been the last of the revelations for Caellum. Upon returning from the Neutral City, his Lords sat him down and revealed a great secret only known by the King and his Lords. Queen Lyra—the original Garridon heir and wife of King Errard—was alive. She escaped to Doltas Island during the chaos of Errard's murder. Jorah assumed she would die there, cut off from the realm, yet it appeared the Garridon line were not so easily ripped from their roots.

"Yes, yes. Tomorrow. Excuse me."

Caellum left the room, avoiding the pitiful glance of Sir Cain as he did. He did not know where he was going as he wandered the halls of the castle that now felt like a shell surrounding him. The dark walnut paneling appeared to close in as he navigated the Castle, the vaulted ceilings offering little reprieve from his rising suffocation. The eyes of his servants followed him through the halls. The gossiping had begun already. Some accurately retold the events at Azuria castle, while others claimed Elisara realised she needed more from a King. The common theme throughout all the claims was this: he was not good enough. A feeling he was acquainted with from when his father roamed the halls.

His sullen wandering guided his feet into one of the many gardens of the estate. This had been his favourite spot in the castle once; the doors to the grounds spanned the entire width of the wall, offering an uninterrupted view of the outside world. The walled garden had always been the favourite of his two youngest sisters, and Elisara too.

The gardens were beautiful, but nothing compared to what they once were, or so he had heard. He was too young to notice the deterioration. The gardens now compared to any well-kept garden in the realm, but that was unexpected for the gardens of Garridon's Royal Family. One would expect grandeur and flowers unmatched by any other.

Everywhere he looked, Caellum was reminded of his failure as a King and as a partner. Sweet peas climbed the archway around the wooden door that led to the taunting small lake that whispered

Elisara's name on the winds.

"You," he called. A man tending the roses raised his head before bowing to his king. "I want that door permanently locked. No one enters without my permission."

The man nodded and left to find a lock and key. Caellum wanted no memory of his moments with Elisara. Behind that door, firsts were had, and dreams were shared.

He hoped Elisara would find someone to help her forget the pain he had caused. Caellum, on the other hand, deserved to never experience love again, to be forever punished for the words forced from his mouth in the snowy gardens. As he watched the gardeners cut down the sweet peas at his request, he vowed to ward his heart from any other. His only other regret being he would force his new bride into a loveless life as well.

The Lords had sent convoys in recent weeks to Doltas Island, without his knowledge. It seemed survival on Doltas Island was not as difficult as Caellum, and many others, had assumed. His father had apparently sent convoys, too, yet were turned away on every occasion. They had been told a visit would be agreed once the time was right. That time was tomorrow. King Caellum was to meet with Queen Lyra's granddaughters.

It was said the sisters would not be parted and a place must be found for both within the Castle, a request which he had agreed to. As daughters of the Garridon line, he would offer them that respect. Reluctantly, Caellum turned from the gardens to inspect his new bride's quarters as the last sweet pea was cut.

His bride would be placed in the room overlooking the same garden he now walked from, given it obtained the largest variety of flowers and was the perfect place to watch the sunrise.

Forest green graced the room, from the bed to the armchairs sat before the grand fireplace. He could do little about the room's standard interior, but he ensured it was filled with flowers from some of Garridon's best specimens. On the writing desk, he left a gift, hoping to welcome her to the realm. Perhaps he was overcompensating for his guilt, knowing he could not give a bride what she would expect.

He wondered if they resented him as much as he imagined their grandparents did. If the people of Garridon were any indicator, he imagined the answer was yes. But Caellum did not want a bride to love him. The best he could hope for was a reasonable acquaintance with whom to share his life with and bring peace to the realm. Perhaps she would take the ruling burden for him, and their roles would reverse. What a relief that would be.

Chapter Forty

Elisara

Elisara enjoyed her baths, but there was something strange about this one. Usually, she preferred the tub once the temperature weakened, yet as she entered the bath upon arrival at her chambers, she relished the water's burn against her skin. Elisara could lower the temperature if she wished, but since returning to Vala, she found she was not opposed to it. She had always savored the cold, refusing to wear a cloak when she could, but there was something soothing about the temperature of the water and the flicker of the flames in the fireplace.

The heat was a welcome distraction from her thoughts, as she created mini whirlpools in the water. A knock came from the door. Assuming it was one of her servants, she called for them to enter, but as a deep cough followed, she spun to find Kazaar analysing every inch of the ceiling.

"You should have said it was you!" She scolded, crossing her arms over her body and sinking lower into the water. "You are also disobeying one of our rules."

"Do those rules still stand?"

"I am not having this conversation with you while I lay naked in a bath!" she exclaimed. Elisara did not hear his steps approach, but Kazaar covered his eyes as he handed her a robe. Frowning, she rose, alarmed as he wrapped the robe around her with his arms. Watching through wet lashes, she found him studying the whirlpools.

"A distraction technique," she said, gliding her hand through the water to break up the movement. "What did you want, Kazaar?"

Gliding back into the sitting room, she fell into the armchair by the fire, watching the snow fall outside. She gestured for him to join her, and hesitantly, he did.

"How do you stand being exposed to the winds?" he asked, warming himself from the fire on his palms.

"It's all I know. However, I am learning to appreciate the other elements since experiencing their kindness on the Isle," she said, gazing into the flames.

"I thought we could train here instead," he said, the flames bouncing from him to the arm of her chair. Elisara smiled as she waved her hand through it.

"Why?" she asked. The flame extinguished as Kazaar closed his fist.

"There is already gossip in the city."

She rolled her eyes.

"Of course, there is. Lady Relena is renowned for her gossiping; you do not need to shield me from hurtful words," she said, eager for the flames to return. They did at once.

"I know. But that does not mean it won't hurt," he whispered, placing two daggers on the table before them. "Now, are you sparring in that robe? I must say, that is a rather good torture technique against a man."

She laughed and exited for her changing rooms, returning in casual trousers and a tunic to allow greater movement. Kazaar leaned against the stone railing now, staring out across the view of Azuria.

"Even a man of Keres can admit it is beautiful, right?" she asked beside him, surveying her realm. He glanced down at her as she tucked a lock of hair behind her ear.

"Beautiful indeed," he murmured, his eyes softening. "I suppose I will have to find it beautiful now it is my home." His eyes seemed softer, his body more open, as though he genuinely felt more at home.

"What do you like most about it?" she asked.

"Don't push it."

She smiled up at him. She was enjoying their verbal sparring from the last two days.

"I have a proposal," Elisara said, and Kazaar turned to face her, his black leathers contrasting against the snow. "A change of rules."

"And what rules are you suggesting?"

"One, you remain in your chambers in the castle, but you may visit me as often as you feel necessary. We do not need to pass mandatory communication via notes or servants."

He nodded.

"What do you deem as *necessary*?" he asked, a playfulness in his tone that she ignored.

"Second, I want daily updates on the new training regime with the military and guards. I want to attend one of the group trainings weekly, and I want one day a week dedicated to my training."

"I can abide by those. What do you wish to train?" he asked. Elisara gazed across the rooftops and the sun setting in the distance as the wind gently traced her hair.

"General physical training, but mostly my power. I want to better understand it. While you do not wield a talisman, you are the most powerful person I know outside of the royals."

"That sounds wise," he said, seeming to contemplate his next words. "I have one additional rule, if you would hear it?"

She nodded.

"Once a week, we have dinner. Here, and after evening training," He cleared his throat, his awkwardness clear.

"Why would you want to dine together?"

"I know a lot about Vala, but you know more. It gives me a chance to learn about my new home, my people... my *Queen*."

"I can agree to that," She nodded, failing to hide her smile. "It gives us an opportunity to study the historical texts from the library, too, and the prophecy from the Isle before we meet the other rulers. I will send word we have found the weapon and require a meeting place. Perhaps Nerida would be best?"

"I agree, though your fellow rulers may be conflicted with their lords and ladies if they discover only one realm has the means to defend themselves."

"Then we better hope they all keep their word not to divulge the threat," Elisara said, unable to suppress a yawn.

"I will leave you to rest. We will have our first training session tomorrow at sunset, followed by dinner."

Elisara did not argue with him as he made his way to the door, but followed, leaning against the doorway as he left.

"Sleep well, my Queen."

Kazaar lowered his head to bid goodnight, leaving Elisara alone. Plagued with nightmares of the black-winged creatures.

Chapter Forty-One

Caellum

Caellum could count on one hand the number of times he left Garridon by boat, favoring the abundance of horses that roamed the wild fields instead. Every experience resulted in him leaning overboard, and this trip was no different. He wished Sir Cain was with him to distract him like he so often did when Caellum was struggling. But the Lords decided it may be viewed as a threat for the Commander of the Military to accompany him.

The journey to Doltas Island did not take long, but they had no intention of staying the night. They left the port town of Asdale before sunrise and aimed to leave the moment the agreement was signed. The seas were choppy as they sailed around the coast, passing the clifftop town of Albyn before rounding the coastline into the open seas. Caellum wondered if Larelle was having a particularly dreadful day, given the rockiness of the ocean. Did the depth of her powers stretch to the seas of other realms? As neighbours, it was possible.

Caellum stopped retching over the side of the fleet once Doltas Island appeared. Dark clifftops loomed, silhouetted by the rising sun. How they were to gain access to the island, he did not know. Still, his captain seemed well adverse in the journey, turning the ship and sailing to the land's edge, where a small wooden port revealed itself, and behind it, an unimaginable number of steps stood, ascending into the tree line above. It was a blessing he at least had the power of strength. The ship pulled into the dock, and very few people greeted them.

The dock comprised a short wooden walkway and appeared as

if a child had nailed it together. The island loomed and towered so high above sea level that he wondered where the citizens lived and how they reached their homes. Greenery concealed nearly every surface surrounding the edge of the island, the forest appearing to expand the higher it grew, hiding whatever lived within.

Three unruly looking men stepped forward. Beards consumed their enormous faces, and all three bore the same hairstyle: braided at the sides and pulled into a bunch at the back of their scalps. They wore brown leather and fur, yet not enough to cover their large bodies or the muscles of their arms and legs on show. For the second time that morning, Caellum was thankful for his strength. He imagined nobody else in his company would fare well if this deal ended badly.

"Our Queen will see you on the edge of our grounds," said the man in the middle, voice gruff. The Lords envoys had not been specific on who Caellum would meet first. Would he be meeting Queen Lyra, who must be close to death now, or her daughter, Queen Ellowyn? He presumed the latter.

"Will the King and princesses be joining us as well?" Caellum assumed Ellowyn had married on the island to father the princesses soon to return to Garridon. He smoothed down his tunic and cloak yet felt exceedingly out of place beside the men.

"The King is dead," said a man to his right. "As is his wife, and her mother."

Caellum glanced at the men in his company, but no one spoke a word. Their entire plan was formed on the notion of meeting with Queen Lyra or Queen Ellowyn. While he knew little about either, he did know Ellowyn had two daughters: Soren and Sadira. If they were preparing for the unknown before, there was little more they could do now.

"Soren is now Queen. You will be meeting her instead." The men turned and led the way up the winding steps into the forest. Despite the concerned looks from his guards, Caellum followed.

The new Queen and princess could not be far from Caellum's

age, so what had killed their parents? Queen Lyra must have passed with age, yet the parents should have been in similar health to his own. His questions were answered once he reached the summit of the island, stepping through the forest and into the ruins beyond.

The fallen family were true to their name. The edge of the grounds was nothing more than a crumbling wall, with numerous holes exposing the lack of whatever home they had within. A handful of men and women roamed, tending to fires, skinning animals, and grinding plants. In only a glance, Caellum witnessed every role within the fallen families' limited household, the Queen's parents likely passed from sickness, aided little by scarce shelter or primitive medicines. He noted no medicinal plants on his way in, and no matter the extent of their power, one could not create from nothing.

Caellum jumped as one of the men blew into a carved horn, the sound echoing across the island. Trees shielded light from all areas except the crumbling wall before him. Loose remnants of ivy hung from the wall as if the people of the island had simply stopped caring. The trees were certainly well cared for, with not a leaf out of place, and thick roots unraveling across the ground. Birds chirped overhead; the sounds swallowed by the dull thuds of hooves arriving fast from the opposite direction.

Through the trees burst two horses, the colour of deepest night. Grey wolves flanked the stallions, then circled the entourage before sitting in a protective line, like soldiers ready for command. Only upon seeing the feminine wall of muscle atop the tallest horse did Caellum realise the wolves were not protecting the horses after all, but their Queen.

The woman did not dismount. Instead, she remained seated and scanned Caellum like he did her. She was as wild as the island, her blonde hair an unknown mix of braids and tangles. Atop her head sat a woven crown of thorns, which appeared fresh as red stained the tips, like she had ripped it from its roots and fashioned it only moments ago. She wore similar leathers and furs to her male counterparts, though her attire was more pristine.

At least she takes some care of her appearance, Caellum thought, aside from the lines of mud streaking her face and arms, highlighting the colour of her eyes—the darkest green, the likes of which Caellum had never seen.

"King Caellum of Garridon," she greeted. Despite her unruly appearance, her pronunciation was pristine, unusual considering her life away from court. He bowed his head to her.

"Forgive me, I know little of your family, and do not know whom I address." Caellum raised his head and met her eyes, which did not move from his gaze, unable to tell if she was insulted. Her face was unreadable.

"Queen Soren: Fallen Queen of Garridon and Ruler of Doltas Island, and all who grace it as its home," called the men in unison.

Why anyone would endure the discomfort of gracing this island as their home, he did not know.

"Your Majesty," Caellum bowed again, not wishing to insult his potential new bride, who clearly believed herself to be the true Garridon heir.

"Do you ride King?" she asked plainly.

"I do. Garridon is famed for its horses." A look flitted across her face at his words, though he could not place it. Soren tilted her head at the horse beside her. The wolves lowered their heads and growled as Caellum stepped towards it. As hostile as her, it seemed.

"*Enough,*" she commanded. They stopped immediately and settled on the ground. Schooling his surprise at her skill with the animals, he mounted the second black horse.

"They stay," she said, nodding to the guards and Lord Gregor.

"Very well."

Caellum needed this woman to trust him if he was to welcome her into his home. They exchanged no words as Caellum followed Soren through the forest, surrounded by endless trees in every direction. Doltas Island seemed a vast place, and the trees towered over the pair as they rode, thickening until barely any light bled through.

They cantered until reaching a clearing, before breaking into a gallop. He could not remember the last time he rode so freely with the wind rushing past. Just like that, at the thought of the wind, he was sent crashing down to the reality of his heartbreak. Elisara's face flashed through his mind at his betrayal. The pain in her glowing pale blue, then the fury as her emotions changed and her eyes morphed to white. Slowing the horse, the Queen halted at the edge of the cliff as the pair dismounted and left the horses to roam. He peered over the cliff edge. A precarious move, given she likely had eyes on his throne.

Melancholy swallowed Soren as she stared out past the sea. He directed his gaze to follow hers, falling on the distant line of forests surrounding Garridon.

"Did you know the trees were grown to stop my grandmother from seeing her home?" she finally said. "From seeing the seat of her power?"

A pang of guilt festered within Caellum at the actions of his ancestors, yet Soren showed little emotion but was merely factual in her statements.

"I did not," he replied. "You have never seen it then? The realm?"

Soren shook her head.

"Tell me," he probed. "Are your intentions simply to be reunited with your lands or something more?" Finally, he voiced the suspicions of his Lords. Soren pivoted to face him, as if affronted by such an accusation. He said no more on the matter, though he did not regret the ask.

"So, am I to marry the great Queen Soren of Doltas Island?" he jested.

"I have been Queen for too short a time to be called *great*," Her face darkened. "But no, King, you need not worry. You will not wed me. My sister is far more genteel and suited for a role beside a preened King." Caellum took insult at the jab, though lacked any right to be defensive. After all, Soren's upbringing would have been the same, if not for his grandfather.

"Will I be meeting Princess Sadira?" he asked, fidgeting with the ring on his finger.

"No, she is busy," she said flatly. "But do not worry, King. She is beautiful enough. It won't take you long to fall in love."

Caellum let out a humourless laugh. He did not believe himself to be capable of love after losing Elisara. Or deserving of it.

"I do not intend to subject myself to such pain again," he murmured, and for the first time since they arrived at the cliff edge, Soren looked at him. *Really* looked at him.

"You are perhaps wiser than I thought," she smiled. "I hope you are also wise enough to accept my additional terms."

"Additional terms?" he repeated, returning a forced smile.

"I wish to join my sister, but as you may have realised, I am not one for pretty dresses, tending flowers, or organising balls. I am better suited with weaponry and scouting." Her words did not surprise him. "I wish for a position in your military—a position of high rank. While I am not the right person to rule by a King, I believe I am best suited to keeping the realm safe." Her eyes bore into his, confident of her claim. That information would have been useful to know before he had arrived; after all, he did not think all the soldiers would want to be ruled by a woman, let alone an exiled princess. But the change could be beneficial, if only to keep Soren—and Sadira—happy.

"You may be Captain of the Queen's Guard." he said. "Once Sadira is crowned. Until then, would leading the female ranks suffice?"

Soren scanned the horizon, expression unreadable, until finally, she nodded.

"Then it is agreed. Many women are emerging in our armies that would benefit from a female lead to take the men down a peg or two. But I warn you, it is not an exciting position. We have no threats."

She raised her brows at that. "So, an explosion did not kill off every royal family member aside from the most inexperienced heirs? Would *that* not be deemed a potential threat?"

Caellum's eyes narrowed, struggling to understand how she had acquired such knowledge. Though gazing across the oceans and lands, it was not implausible to have seen the smoke from Doltas Island. How much more did she know?

"What potential threat?" He asked.

"Somebody wishes the people of Novisia dead. Is that not the message the explosion delivered? I saw the smoke of the ruin from this very spot."

"The other rulers and I have the situation under control. You will not be privy to that, regardless of the position in my armies." He countered before she could argue. She pursed her lips, smart not to push the issue further. Soren did not seem angry, but stubborn, and he imagined the topic would be raised again in the future.

They stood in silence while Caellum waited to see what she would say next, the only sounds from the crashing waves crashing below.

"So, we have an agreement. My place in your armies and Sadira's place as your Queen."

"We have an agreement," Caellum said, offering his arm. She stared, as if contemplating the decision that would alter her life forever. She grasped his forearm.

The deal was done.

"When will you and your sister arrive?" Caellum asked. He inclined his head, sensing Soren's wish for a moment of privacy with the lands she had only ever known as home.

"Tomorrow," she confirmed, striding past him to her horse. He did not argue. Upon seeing the ruin of their home, he was not surprised by her urgency to leave.

They mounted the horses and rode again in silence, back to where his guards remained. No villagers marked his journey through Doltas Island, only the handful of people who he met upon arrival. Either there really were few inhabitants in Doltas Island, or the Queen was hiding the true force of her following.

Caellum hoped it was the former; he dreaded to imagine what would come of Garridon if he was forced to kill this Queen for treason.

Chapter Forty-Two

Caellum

Caellum was exhausted, having arrived late back in Garridon. Yet he rose early the following morning to oversee the preparations for his new bride's arrival. Letters were sent to the Lords the second they arrived back, along with public notices shared across the realm. Shouts and cries rang from the City of Antor and citizens were reported to have lined the royal mile from sunrise, awaiting the arrival of their new Queen. The path leading to the castle gates had been sanded in preparation for the event; guards stationed to keep the people at bay, while a spot was marked to locate where Soren and Sadira's carriage would halt to allow them to walk amongst the people before meeting him at the iron gates guarding the castle.

Caellum sighed, toying with the crown before placing it on his head and fixing the curls falling into his eyes. Straightening the green jacket, Caellum fixed the Garridon pin to his right breast and judged the man staring back at him in the mirror. How could he give the smallest part of himself to his bride when he didn't like any part of himself? The self-deprecation would have to wait as he turned from his reflection and made from the castle, bypassing the gardens to follow the line of trees.

The Lords waited at the beginning of the steps leading from the sanded path up to the gates, and he inclined his head as they bowed upon his arrival. A smile plastered on his face, he waved to the crowds lining the path, the majority cheering. This was a significant moment for him and his people, reuniting Garridon once again.

How would the crowd fare upon the sisters' arrival, dressed in clothes worse than the commoners here to greet them? Hair full of knots and personalities devoid of decorum: wild, free, and uncaring. The ladies-in-waiting would most definitely judge his new bride, and he questioned how long it would take for her to become accustomed to a more luxurious way of living. Caellum knew what was expected of him: smile the entire afternoon, look respectfully upon his bride, and have everyone believe he was in love and fully committed to this marriage. Though the woman to emerge from the carriage would hold no light to the Queen of Vala.

Caellum did not wait long before the carriage approached, towed by two black stallions handpicked for their likeness to Soren's horses. A flash of fur blurred past, and soon wolves flanked the carriage.

She's brought them with her.

Caellum spared a glance at the citizens, yet no fear marked their faces, only intrigue, and excitement. After the explosion and riots, this was the morale they needed. With a deep breath, Caellum readied himself as the carriage drew closer, the horses whinnying as they pulled to one side and positioned the carriage until the door faced Caellum. People scrambled to peer above one another, hoping for a glimpse of the Fallen Queen and Princess. Caellum nodded to the servant placed beside the carriage, but before his hand touched the golden handle, the door swung open; and out stepped Soren. The Fallen Queen. Many gasped as Soren emerged, and Caellum schooled his impression upon realising he had, too.

The woman stepping from the carriage was far from the wild Queen of Doltas Island. The silver armour of Garridon replaced furs and leather, the sigil etched across the chest plate. She did not don the helmet; instead, her clean blonde hair was plaited in many braids falling down her back. Soren cast her eye over the crowd before meeting Caellum's stare. A sly smile broke across her face. She whistled, beckoning the wolves to her side. With a brief motion of her hand, wild roots emerged from the ground beside each of her feet, crawling high and stretching behind her to reach for something. The people of Garridon were not disappointed as the roots resurfaced with the most magnificent sword. Three green emeralds encrusted the base of the blade and the gold handle gleamed beneath the sun. The Lost Sword of Garridon. The people murmured amongst themselves, gaping at the sword in Soren's hands as she secured it to her hip and made her way forward.

Caellum struggled to process the onslaught of emotions rushing through him: betrayal, embarrassment, anger. After all, she merely displayed the relics that were rightfully hers, all the while demeaning Caellum's claim. Soren's actions reminded him of his father, belittling him for all to see.

Caellum's guards—the females amongst the rank—shared a look. Queen Soren continued her walk, and as she did, roots wove across the ground at her side, building a structured walkway to the castle. The wolves kept close. Caellum ground his teeth at the Queen's boastful display of her natural Garridon power. Cementing her position as heir.

"King Caellum," Soren bowed low. "I thank you for the comfortable arrangement and the most gracious welcome." She smiled and waved to the crowd, who had recovered from their shock, and eagerly waved back.

"Queen Soren, you look fit for a warrior queen," he said, eyeing her pristine armour. The wolves growled, and he tried not to flinch. A motion of her hand quieted them.

"Ah, this? Yes. It is such a shame you had to rush from the island. Doltas has much to offer." She smirked, confirming Caellum's suspicions. It had all been a front, after all. Soren turned to address the crowd. "People of Garridon! It is my greatest honour to return home. May I present to you, Princess Sadira of Garridon: your future queen."

At her final three words, she looked at Caellum, who turned to train his eyes on the open carriage door. Having seen the way Soren presented herself, Caellum was curious at the appearance of his bride-to-be.

Beauty and power stepped from the carriage, and Caellum almost found himself compelled to copy the crowd, who all bowed and curtseyed as Sadira emerged. Sadira was dressed in green—not the dark emerald of Garridon, but the palest sage—gracing the abundance of fabric around her, the sleeves hanging loose from her shoulders and highlighting the smoothness of her skin, sun kissed from her time outdoors. The dress cinched in at her waist while the bodice accentuated her chest just so; fair hair fell in loose locks down her back, as golden as the wheat fields of Seley. Fabric gathered in her hands as she stepped from the carriage, and when she released her hold, she raised her head to smile at the crowd. Upon her head was an emerald crown. The Lost Crown of Garridon. The crowd cheered.

The sisters' intentions were apparent.

Motioning with her hand, Sadira took her first step, and pale pink petals rained from the treetops into her path. The crowd applauded as she walked amongst the petals, often stopping to kneel before the children and grow flowers at their feet, their youthful laughter a melody. As Sadira continued in her stride, she clasped the hands of the people, who stood mesmerised by her presence.

As Sadira reached Caellum, he suddenly remembered himself and offered his hand. Her fingers were delicate as she accepted, glancing up at him, eyes a perfect, incomparable shade of green.

"Your Majesty," she curtseyed, eyes still on him. He swallowed.

"Caellum, please."

"Sadira," Her voice was melodic.

Caellum helped her up the steps, where they stood to wave at the crowd, their arms interlocked. Though Sadira smiled, there was glassiness in her eyes, as if holding back emotion from him and the crowd. He peered to where Soren watched her. Sadira followed Caellum's gaze and tensed.

"You made a mistake letting her into your home," Sadira whispered, smiling still. Despite her catching him off guard, he did not look. If Soren's own sister did not trust her, it made Caellum wonder: who had he brought into his realm?

"A small price to pay to bring Garridon to unity, and have a Queen by my side," he whispered.

"I'm sure you will learn the price to pay with time." She looked sadly at him as the guards opened the gates into the grounds. With Soren close on their heels, they entered, sharing common pleasantries on their stroll.

"I wish to show my future Queen the walled garden. We would like some privacy, please." Caellum nodded to the guards positioned outside the entrance. "Sir Cain, please show Soren the training grounds. She will be leading one of the female ranks until the Queens Guard is formed." Soren glared at him but did not argue; she likely thought it unwise to cause a scene so soon after arrival.

Sadira's arm relaxed in his as she looked up at him.

"That will probably be the only time she does not refuse your commands," Sadira said, "particularly when it comes to being alone with me." Despite the sadness in her smile, Caellum could not deny she was beautiful. Her bright green eyes were captivating, urging him closer.

"Then I suppose we best take this rare moment to get to know one another," Caellum gestured to the entrance to the walled garden before walking through together. Abruptly, she stopped at the sight. Light in her eyes returned as she recovered from her shock and began walking among the flowers. Sadira trailed her hands over the petals, infusing them with greater life. Never had he seen such an affinity for Garridon's power, and while this was only a sliver of her strength, he was confident in the extent of her gifts compared to that of the other rulers.

But how?

Caellum brushed the thought aside, choosing to relish in Sadira's joy at returning to her homeland.

She paused at the cut stems of sweet peas beside the locked archway and reached to regrow them.

"Please," he interrupted. "Leave them."

Sadira frowned but nodded, as if recognizing the pain in his expression. She rose from kneeling and gazed at the barren space along the wall where hundreds of sweet peas had once been.

"I hear that until a week ago, you were engaged." Sadira played with the stems at her fingertips.

"I was."

Her soft smile wavered, the look in her eyes changing to one Caellum recognized, having seen that look every morning in the mirror.

"Did you love her?"

He nodded, unable to speak.

"You agree to this marriage only for your realm then?" She continued. Caellum tried to phrase his response so as not to offend his new bride. "Please, Caellum. Do not insult me with half-truths. I know what it is to sacrifice for others. I do not hold that against you nor against the true Queen in your heart." Sadira walked to him, placing a delicate hand on his arm. "I ask only that I may gain a friend from this arrangement: someone familiar in the unknown—someone I can trust when I am not sure I can trust myself." He frowned at her words. "And maybe one day, you will let me grace that wall with new flowers: a testament to friendships and new beginnings."

"I would like that very much."

"I would like to take a full turn around the garden and assess what more I can do with it. Could I meet you by the glass doors in a moment? Perhaps then you could show me to my chambers; I am quite tired." Sadira was already hard to refuse.

"I will wait for you."

Caellum headed to the glass doors, allowing Sadira an illusion of privacy as he watched from the stone pillar. He was not sure what to make of the princess: a woman evidently raised for a position of high standing, yet seemingly unhappy with the prospect. There appeared to be more to his bride than she would reveal: a sadness behind every glisten in her green eyes and a carefulness in her words.

As Sadira roamed the gardens, one thing was obvious. She was at peace amongst nature, and Caellum commended himself for arranging the flowers she would find in her rooms. Sadira's gliding around the garden halted as she hunched over a small patch of roses. She kissed her fingertips, whispering as she closed her eyes and held her hand above the soil. A single moss green flower emerged from the earth streaked with veins of black. It was unlike any blossom he had ever seen. Sadira's composure returned as she rose, appearing to wipe a tear before returning the smile to her face and heading back to Caellum.

“I hope you like flowers inside as much as you do outside,” he smiled, a smile which Sadira returned before he led her into her new home.

Chapter Forty-Three

Larelle

Larelle paced the entrance to her castle, attempting to release the last of her anxiety at hosting the rulers at their first congregation outside of the Neutral City. It was also her first time hosting a ball, too, at which all the alienated Lords and Ladies would be in attendance.

Carriages filtered into the courtyard as the sun set over the ocean. Larelle stopped her pacing. She was dressed in a soft lavender chiffon gown, her staple thick curls weaved atop her head, where stray pieces framed her face. The updo allowed for her back to be accentuated by her open dress. Long pieces of fabric twisted into straps before falling down her back and winding around her waist like rope. The gown was like her day dresses, but endless amounts of additional chiffon piled up in the skirt—a dress Zarya would likely wish to steal one day. Her mother's old jewels graced her neckline, and the Neridian crown sat proudly upon her head. Larelle straightened under the weight of it as the eyes of the Lords and Ladies fell upon her when the carriage doors opened. She scanned the crowd filtering towards the staircase. Her staff were among them, too, arm in arm with representatives chosen from the towns and cities. She smiled.

Queues of people trailed up the steps, and she greeted each of them, exchanging small pleasantries as the guards ushered them into the castle. Larelle embraced Lillian as she approached and ignored the unimpressed murmurings at their Queen's interactions with the staff. Lillian rolled her eyes, having heard the murmurs too.

As the last of the queue filtered in, the royal carriages appeared. Tradition expected Larelle to be awaiting her guests in the banquet hall, where she would sit upon the throne. Yet given the secrecy of the conversations soon to be had, Larelle deemed it better to meet somewhere more secluded before enjoying the festivities.

Night black horses pulled the crimson-red carriages of Keres into the courtyard first. Queen Nyzaia stepped from the carriage, aided by the Captain of her Queen's Guard: a woman dressed in leathers. Queen Nyzaia was beautiful, despite her discomfort as she fidgeted and pulled at the red fabric hanging over her shoulder. The light fabric was perfect against the tone of her skin as tiny intricate designs and jewels threaded across it. It was broad across her shoulders, one large piece of fabric tied at the waist, a hint of silk red skirts flashing beneath as she walked up the steps to join Larelle.

"I will never understand how anyone can spend more than a minute in a tiny box like that," Nyzaia said, repositioning the crown on her head. "It jerks over every stone it rolls over!"

"Please, do not take a carriage at my expense. If horseback is your preference, you are welcome to arrive a day prior next time and change in the evening." Larelle smiled and Nyzaia returned the gesture.

"Trust me, I would take that offer in a heartbeat, but my Captain of the Queen's guard insisted for my safety." Nyzaia rolled her eyes, inclining her head towards the woman climbing the steps behind.

"Is she complaining about me again?" She asked, the corner of her mouth lifting.

"Of course not! I am merely praising your dedication to keeping your Queen safe," Nyzaia smiled then faced Larelle. "Queen Larelle, this is Tajana. My newly appointed Captain."

Tajana bowed.

"A pleasure. You are welcome to wait by the entrance for the others to join us. It would offer us a moment to catch up before joining the ball." Larelle hoped her meaning was inferred, and

Nyzaia nodded, heading for the side door. The light brush of Tajana's hand on Nyzaia's back did not go unnoticed by Larelle, who smiled, keeping the information to herself. The rest of the Keres guards filed up the steps, yet Larelle was drawn to eyes of the palest blue as the last guard passed her. She smiled, and the man gave a polite yet stern nod of respect. Something about his eyes drew her in, home to a pain she recognised.

"I hope we are all prepared for the explosive arguments of ice and fire," Nyzaia returned to Larelle's side as Vala's carriage arrived. Tearing her eyes from the guard, she gave Nyzaia an inquisitive look. "The Commander is notoriously difficult and stubborn. He and the Queen of Vala do not get along."

Vala's guards dismounted from their horses and stood to attention while waiting for their Queen to emerge. The Commander exited the carriage and hastened to the door. Larelle was surprised at his attire, having expected him to arrive like Tajana—black fighting leathers at the ready. And though he wore black fitted trousers tucked into his boots, his shirt was pale-blue and fitted against his chest, the sleeves rolled up to his forearms. The Commander appeared to struggle between the attire of either realm, the splash of Vala colour and formal wear contrasting the combat nature of the sword strapped down his back.

Nyzaia laughed at his new apparel, yet her chuckles halted upon noticing the smile he offered Elisara while helping her from the carriage. Nor did anyone expect to see Elisara smiling in return.

Kazaar appeared hesitant to release her hand but stepped aside once he did, allowing Elisara to walk ahead, whose gaze lingered on him before she lifted her skirts and strode to the other royals. Elisara's gown was the same blue as Kazaar's shirt, contrasting with the black of her hair. Her sleeves were off the shoulder: an intricate pattern of jewels dwindling into icicles from the neckline down her chest.

"Queen Elisara, you look breathtaking," Larelle said, reaching out to grasp her hands.

"I could say the very same about you, Larelle."

"Since when did you learn to smile, Kazaar?" Nyzaia called, earning a stern glare from the Commander.

Instead, he asked, "Is Caellum here yet?"

"Kazaar!" Elisara scolded. Everyone stared between the two as Kazaar's eyes met her. "We *talked* about this," she hissed, though not quietly enough.

"The King of Garridon should be here shortly," Larelle broke the tension, using Caellum's correct title to retain the formalities she felt were slipping. It did little to lighten Kazaar's mood.

"I know this may be difficult for you," Nyzaia said to Elisara.

Larelle had received word about the ended engagement, so it was no surprise Nyzaia also knew of Caellum's betrayal.

"Leave it, Nyzaia." Kazaar grumbled.

Elisara shot him an exasperated look.

"Thank you, Nyzaia. I will be fine. He has shown his true colours, and I have no interest in associating with him for any matters outside of the Kingdom." She smiled regally and straightened her back as the carriage of Garridon arrived. Larelle spotted Kazaar's quick glance at his queen, monitoring her carefully.

The temperature plummeted as Caellum exited the carriage, along with the most elegant woman Larelle had ever seen, with an emerald crown upon her head. Lightning struck close by as clouds moved to shield the moon. Kazaar bent to whisper in Elisara's ear. The woman who emerged seemed to notice Elisara's anger yet did not appear jealous of Caellum's most recent love.

The clouds soon parted, the temperature returning to normal. The pair complimented one another in forest green as they climbed the steps to join the others.

"May I introduce, Princess Sadira Mordane." He gulped, his face pale. He stole a glance at Elisara before looking away. "My *fiancé*. The future Queen of Garridon."

No one said anything until the unfamiliar princess chose to break the tension.

"Queen Larelle," she bowed. "Thank you for inviting us to your home."

Larelle scrambled for a way to diffuse the building tensions. She had not invited this Princess to her home and knew nothing about her. Mordane, however, was a familiar surname, though she could not think why. Then she placed it.

"You are most welcome," she finally said. "Do you descend from Lyra Mordane? The once Queen of Garridon?"

She glanced at Caellum as she asked, uncertain how mention of the usurpation would sit. But he smiled and opened his mouth as though to answer on Sadira's behalf.

"She's Queen Lyra's granddaughter," chimed a second voice. "A fallen princess returned home." A strong blonde emerged from the carriage too, donned in silver Garridon armour. The rulers all took an involuntary step back at the pack of wolves skulking by her side. "Soren Mordane. Queen of Doltas Island and heir of the Garridon line."

Nobody said anything, too shocked at her proclamation as an heir. Suspicion masked the features of a large man with ginger hair, standing beside the carriage. The Commander of Garridon, she realized.

Larelle's only knowledge of Doltas Island was its use as a prison once their ancestors fled to Novisia; she had not expected anyone to live there, having presumed them all dead long ago. Elisara glared at the couple standing before them, and Kazaar stepped forward.

"Now we are all here, we have important matters to discuss." His dark eyes lingered on Caellum a second too long until Larelle gestured for the group to follow.

She led them inside, while suggesting Alvan show Soren and Sadira the castle. Taking an immediate right, away from the festivities, Larelle steered the royals down an open corridor facing out to sea. Olden stood guard at the end, with Nyzaia requesting Tajana to do the same on the other side.

"The ocean should muffle our voices," Larelle said as they all turned expectantly to Kazaar and Elisara.

The pair shared a look, one that indicated this was not the good news they hoped for. The Commander looked to his Queen, who nodded. Intently, they watched as he reached to unsheathe the golden sword at his back. He held it out before them, laid flat on his two palms.

"The weapon," Elisara confirmed.

The rulers analysed the intricate sword. Larelle had never been one for weapons, having never even carried a knife for safety, but there was no denying the sword was spectacular. Gold brightened the space now darkening from the evening skies, and most intriguing were the unfamiliar symbols engraved down its centre: *a lost language of Ithyion*, she presumed.

"'How can we be certain it does anything different from a normal sword?" Nyzaia crouched at eye level to the metal, assessing its structure.

"Because we used it," Elisara said. Caellum's eyes shot up from his feet to Elisara's face, his concern clear.

"What do you mean by that?" asked Larelle.

"The location of the sword was heavily protected by magic and when Kazaar and I broke it, the outbreak of power seemed to call to a creature in waiting. A creature we believe the Historian told us about." Elisara explained.

"What do you mean? Are you okay?" Caellum stepped forward, as did Kazaar.

"She is fine," he said. Elisara rested a palm on the Commander's arm until he stepped back. Caellum's eyes narrowed between the two of them. The change in their dynamics did not go unnoticed.

"She saved my life." Kazaar said.

"And he mine," Elisara glanced at him. "The sword killed the creature. Our powers did not work against it, nor did regular steel." A look of despair passed between the group at the realisation the threat was indeed real. "More arrived while we hid, but we do not know how many, or where they went."

"Then what are we supposed to do now?" asked Nyzaia. "This sword cannot defend an entire realm. Surely, this is not the only weapon?"

Kazaar and Elisara shared another look.

"There is more," Elisara continued. "We found a room with stone statues of the Gods and a mirror containing a prophecy." Kazaar handed Elisara a rolled piece of parchment from his pocket, and she read the words aloud. At the sound of voices, Larelle turned to where Soren and Sadira stood conversing with Tajana. They must have left Alvan to find the royals. A weighted glance passed between the sisters while Elisara spoke the prophecy until Soren pulled Sadira away, and Tajana resumed her guarded stance.

"We have deciphered some of it. We thought we could gather in the morning and see if anyone has any thoughts or ideas from what they may have heard from their parents." Elisara handed the parchment back to Kazaar.

"That is wise. We can meet in my advisor's chambers after breakfast tomorrow," Larelle confirmed. "But tonight, we need to put on a united front. Revel in festivities for the people."

Caellum cleared his throat, and they all turned to him, Elisara with a forced face of indifference.

"On that note," said Caellum. "I would like to invite you all to my engagement ball in Antor. Sadira suggested we wait a few weeks while she becomes accustomed to the castle, but once she is, she would love the opportunity to get to know you all." He smiled a somewhat genuine smile despite the circumstances.

Larelle broke the tension first and agreed, with Nyzaia following suit, and then Elisara, who nodded, jaw clenched.

"I think it is time we all had a drink," Kazaar suggested, immediately steering Elisara from the hallway and back into the depths of the castle. Caellum's gaze followed the queen, a reminder of the look she gave Riyas on the day he sailed away.

Longing.

Chapter Forty-Four

Elisara

"Breathe," Kazaar murmured, his hand resting on Elisara's back as he guided her past the entrance to the ball, winding through the hallways until the other rulers were far behind.

"I have control. I am fine!" she snapped; her anger misplaced.

It was true—she did. The temperature did not drop; the winds did not change. Elisara stopped pacing as they reached a balcony overlooking the sea, and resting her hands on the sandstone, she bowed her head, and closed her eyes. She could not process her feelings, overcome with jealousy, and rage all at once at Caellum having found someone so beautiful to wed in so little time.

It was unsurprising. The second their betrothal ended; Caellum became the most eligible bachelor in Novisia. Elisara had seen Caellum with another woman, but for him to have a new bride hurt more.

Did he court her throughout our engagement? Elisara feared. She did not think he would have but had no trust in him anymore. Knowing the fallen princess had grown up on Doltas Island surprised Elisara, who knew little of the people residing there—or that any still did.

A political move, she decided.

"Maybe he was right," she said, wiping a tear from her cheek. "I am too selfish and wish to control everything. Maybe I was too emotionless."

"Don't," Kazaar said from his guarded position under the archway. "Do not let his words eat away at you, especially as he only thinks those things because of what you experienced under my poor command in Keres." Looking out across the sea, he appeared unable to face her at his admission. He was right. Ultimately, Kazaar influenced her experiences, yet there was no use dwelling on that now. He had since proved he was loyal to Vala—to her.

"We learn from our experiences, Kazaar. Let us put it behind us."

She sensed him step from the archway.

"I cannot," he said, eyes firmly on her. "Every time I see you doubt yourself; I know I am to blame. Every time you lose a little control, as we all do, I remember the look on your face atop the Abis when I said those things to you. Every time you flinch when I am near, I picture the fear you must have felt when a man I trusted thought himself above my rules. I will never forgive myself for the part I have played for the self-doubt that manifests in one of the strongest women I know."

His words pierced the ice encasing her heart, and more tears fell before Elisara looked away. Kazaar reached her in a single stride and spun her to face him, wiping the tears from her cheeks, his hands gently cupping her face.

"I understand you hate me. I hate myself too, for everything I played a hand in and for that which I knew nothing of, but should have. When I arrived in Vala, I was not cold because I hated you, Elisara. I was cold because it was the only way to protect my pride after knowing I had damaged a Queen. I will spend my entire time as Commander—my entire *life*—trying to undo the pain you suffered. I will spend every day reminding myself I am not good enough to be your Commander after failing to protect you at your most vulnerable." Kazaar panted from the speed of his admission while Elisara stilled, eyes searching his, as if inspecting his soul for the inexorable truth in his words. The tranquility of the ocean was no more as waves crashed against the castle walls. And as his hands clasped her face, she felt the warmth of his power against her skin and his breath across her lips. There was something familiar in his touch, as if the power in his veins called to hers, sending sparks through her body.

"Thank you," she whispered.

"Do not thank me for an apology that should have never been needed." He removed his hands from her cheeks and peered down at his fingers. "My loyalty is with you."

The golden signet ring, the sigil of Keres, glinted as he slid it from his finger, and held it to her. "I am not a Commander of Keres."

He placed the ring in Elisara's palm, who was speechless. She had never seen him without his ring. A month ago, the idea of Kazaar offering any gift to Elisara was inconceivable. Yet here they were. She clasped her palm around it.

"I suppose I better have a new ring made for you then," Elisara's smile was soft while their hands remained entwined. Upon realizing, Kazaar released her and turned back to look over the ocean.

"I have never had my air force water before, other than in a bath" she said as the waves resumed their tranquility. A frown flitted across Kazaar's face before he changed the topic.

"Do not think our time away from Vala gets you out of our evening training. Or dinner." He grinned.

"Do you expect me to fight you right now? In this dress?"

Kazaar's eyes skimmed her figure, following the pattern of jeweled icicles crawling down the chest of her gown. She suddenly felt bare.

"No, not in that dress," he said, jaw clenched.

"Do you not like this dress?" She mused, twirling for him.

"You would look better in red,"

"You just gave up your claim to Keres. You will never catch me dead in it," she said. The corners of his mouth rose.

"A man can dream." She rolled her eyes. "Are you ready?"

Offering his hand, Elisara nodded, and placed her hand in his as he led her from the balcony. She did not let go once they reached the doorway of the ballroom, the dances in full swing. In a corner, Nyzaia sat sipping wine, choosing to steer clear of any attention.

Tajana stood close behind, nostrils flared and posture stiff. Elisara was glad Tajana was the newest Captain of Nyzaia's guard; they had met on few occasions during Elisara's time in Keres, or whenever she visited her friend all those years ago.

Larelle sat upon her throne, feeding a young girl Elisara assumed was her daughter. She could not help but smile at the grin on the princess' face. Larelle made a wonderful mother.

Then there was Caellum, who smiled as he offered Sadira a drink. Elisara ignored the rising pain from seeing him happy with another so soon.

"Would you like to make him jealous?" Kazaar leaned in close as he spoke, his hand moving to the small of her back.

"What would you suggest?"

"Find one of the most handsome noblemen in the room and dance with him." Kazaar said; his hand moved from her back, but she grabbed it again and began walking towards the dance floor.

"What are you doing?" He asked, wary.

Elisara placed a hand on his shoulder and one in his palm, his hand instinctively returning to the small of her back, locking them in position.

Elisara looked up at Kazaar as the next song began, and that same feeling returned: the electricity in her veins, the familiarity of his touch. She felt her power crawling under her skin, as if wishing to draw nearer to his. Caellum's eyes appeared to scan the room until landing on the pair, his expression faltering.

"Dancing with one of the most handsome men in the room," Elisara answered, beginning to move. Kazaar's face remained serious, as if in quiet contemplation, yet his years spent with King Razik's sons had clearly paid off as he moved like water with Elisara across the dancefloor. She tried not to focus on the warmth of his hand on her back or the intensity of his stare. He looked over her shoulder.

"I think it is working," Kazaar whispered. He spun her, allowing Elisara a glimpse of Caellum, who watched the pair intently while

Sadira whispered in his ear. She revolved back into Kazaar's chest, marveling at the fit of their bodies, as if destined to be by one another's side. Elisara could become accustomed to having him as her Commander. Trying to relax, she embraced the moment of peace until disrupted by the touch of cold landing on her shoulders.

Snow was falling.

Elisara glanced around to find the snow fell only above them as they spun across the near-empty ballroom floor. They continued dancing as the flakes melted to a light drizzle of rain. She beamed at Kazaar, who observed her questioningly until his face changed at the sight of something behind them. A tap landed on her shoulder as the music came to a natural end. The drizzle of rain stopped.

"May I have the next dance?" Caellum asked, his body rigid.

"No," Elisara answered firmly. She shook her hair, a light mist of rain coating her curls.

Caellum stared, face one of disbelief; not only had she rejected him, but a fellow ruler before a crowd. Elisara seemed to realise too.

"The Commander and I have a regular meeting at this hour, so I will have to take my leave." She bowed, offering Caellum some reprieve from the embarrassment. She did not stay to hear his response.

"I guess you will need to find us some food. Looks like we are having that evening dinner." Elisara grinned up at Kazaar as they left the ballroom.

Chapter Forty-Five

Elisara

Elisara awoke exhausted after spending hours on the beach with Kazaar, reciting the history of the Lords of Vala while he shared ideas for improving the distribution of healing potions across Novisia. He sought her advice on his proposed changes to the military's training regime, and listened intently when she gave it. By the end of the evening, it was apparent the pair worked well together.

Elisara dreamed of the creature that night. Her mind was a prison, and there, encaged alongside her, was the creature. She waited for it to stalk closer or strike or open its mouth to reveal its sharpened teeth, but it only ever sat and stared. All Elisara could do was stare back in the darkness at the black leather of its skin, the shredded holes in its wings, and the hollows where its eyes once were. She shook the image from her mind as she readied for the meeting, having risen too late and missed breakfast. This was essentially a military meeting, so she donned her fighting wear and tied her leather corset as best as she could, sliding her daggers into its structure. The dull grey sword from the Isle rested against the door and she strapped it to her back: a comforting reminder of her strength.

Elisara opened the door at the exact moment Kazaar's hand raised to knock. In the other hand, he tossed her an apple.

"I missed breakfast too," he said.

She nearly dropped it, distracted by the fit of his fighting leathers: a thinner version than the attire tailored to protect against the freezing air of Vala. It clung to his muscles, accentuating his movements. Elisara thanked him and took a bite as they navigated the hallways to the advisor's chamber in the castle's turret. They were the last to arrive, finding the other royals seated around the table. Arguing. Elisara was quick to realise over what.

"What are they doing here?" Elisara asked, pointing to Soren and Sadira by the window. Sadira blushed while Soren raised her head with a sneer.

"My mother attended with my father. It only makes sense Sadira does too," Caellum answered, refusing to look at her.

"Oh, my apologies. I did not realise you had already wed in secret," Elisara exclaimed.

"Elisara is right," said Larelle, sitting at the head of the table. She remained in a royal gown, unlike the fighting leathers worn by the others. "Until you are married, we cannot trust additional parties to be privy to such information."

Nyzaia glanced down at the table, but said, "Even if you *were* married, that does not explain why Soren should be here."

The blonde queen inclined her head to the Queen of Keres. "I am a Queen in my own right, and I will also be head of Queen's Guard for Sadira. I am here for her *safety*." Soren hissed.

"Caellum does not have a guard with him. Why should Sadira?" Elisara added, but Soren looked pointedly at Kazaar.

"Will your Commander be leaving then?"

"That is different. He is the Commander of Vala, not a royal guard. He also played a large part in what we are to discuss."

"Yes, yes. He has the Sword of Sonos." Soren rolled her eyes, yet her words captured the attention of everyone at the table. Caellum looked at Sadira, who avoided his gaze. "I suppose you do not want to hear the other part of the prophecy or what we know of the sword and the creatures then," Soren said, striding to the door.

The royals exchanged a look until Kazaar sighed.

"Sit down," he said.

Soren flashed a cocky smile and pulled a chair out from the head of the table. Elisara averted her eyes as Caellum rose to pull a chair for Sadira, who thanked him gracefully and sat by his side, green eyes examining the room. Elisara folded her hands in her lap as she felt Kazaar's presence emanating from where he stood behind. He unstrapped the golden sword from his back and carefully laid it on the table.

"Speak," Kazaar commanded, his dark eyes fixed on Soren.

"What about? The sword, the prophecy, or perhaps the fact I knew all your families were going to die?"

Shocked silence fell before chaos ensued. Nyzaia was the first to rise from her chair, slamming her fists onto the table as flames ignited on her arms.

"You knew," she sneered. "You knew all the royals would die? You knew we could have prevented it instead of being forced into this *hell*?" Nyzaia shouted now, the flames creeping along the walls. Elisara flinched at the heat that felt so different from Kazaar's.

"Careful, Nyzaia. We would not want your flame to ignite anything." Soren smirked, and Nyzaia's flames wavered. "The people from Keres are all so hot-headed," she continued. "It makes for a fantastic time in the bedroom, though. One of my best nights was with a beauty called Isha—" Larelle waved her hand and the water drowned Nyzaia's flames, splattering Soren who shot daggers at the Queen. Quietly, Nyzaia sat, with a calculating look.

"I lost my father," Elisara choked; Kazaar's hand rested on her shoulder. She was not sure when he had moved so close. "We all lost people we loved." She glanced around the room, yet the expressions did not match hers, except for Caellum, who mourned his siblings. The others did not care for their parents; perhaps Elisara was the only one to have grieved this entire time.

"How are we to know *you* did not orchestrate the explosion?" Nyzaia declared. They all turned back to the sisters. Sadira remained quiet, staring down at her hands in her lap. Soren's smile was a smug one, clearly enjoying the unfolding chaos caused from her own doing.

"Explain," Kazaar commanded, giving Elisara a comforting

squeeze. "From the beginning."

Soren glanced at Sadira, who finally looked up and nodded.

"As a Queen of Garridon, my grandmother knew of the creatures. She knew of the reasons why our people fled Ithyion and rebuilt Novisia. When she fled for Doltas Island, she saw no reason to protect the secrets of the kingdom. Doltas Island was abandoned by all your ancestors, and nobody cared to reach out to my family." Soren looked each ruler in the eye, and Elisara could not help the rising guilt. Her ancestors should have never sided with Caellum's grandfather, not that she had ever voiced that whilst with him.

"From an early age, our grandmother told us of the creatures. She and my mother would tell us stories of them at night for us to fear them." Elisara noted how Sadira bowed her head at the mention of her mother and grandmother. "I suppose when you are raised as an outcast, you do not fear those that are different." She glanced at Caellum, her resentment against his line clear, despite the feigned niceties. Elisara thought him foolish to have allowed such a person into his home. "It is unclear what they are, but my family had their theories."

"Are you going to share those theories?" asked Nyzaia.

"I will, provided no one interrupts me," Soren stated.

Nyzaia opened her mouth to challenge, but Kazaar shook his head, and she leaned back, disgruntled.

"There is one theory that they are an evolution of interbreeding amongst realms over time, potentially an additional race we know not of. Yet there is another, likely theory, that a correlation exists between the creatures and children."

"Presumably they eat them, given the size of their teeth," Elisara added. Soren glared at the interruption, and Elisara pressed her lips into a firm line at the blatant disrespect. Kazaar's knuckles tightened around Elisara's chair.

"You would be wrong, Elisara."

"*Queen*," snapped Kazaar. "*Queen* Elisara."

"I see none of you are paying me the same courtesy, so why

should I?" Soren asked.

"By laws, you rule no lands. Doltas Island—while rarely visited—is still under the jurisdiction of Garridon, of which you are *not* Queen." Kazaar answered plainly.

"I am the rightful Queen," Soren rose at the hurtful reminder while Caellum clenched his jaw, twisting the ring on his finger. Elisara peered around the room. While she was right, no one seemed inclined to agree.

"Soren!" commanded Sadira. "I find you are mistaken on who is to be Queen of Garridon and if you are struggling to remember your place on the mainland, I can arrange for your travel back to Doltas."

Sadira was firm in her ruling—unexpectedly so—the surprise clear on Soren's face at her sister's show of position. Soren began to speak but was cut off by her sister again.

"You will remain seated and silent throughout this meeting after making it clear you cannot converse with rulers in the proper way."

Soren closed her mouth and sat, her arms stiff across her body. Caellum smiled at his betrothed, urging Elisara to wonder how Sadira's level of control was any different from hers. Sadira straightened and looked confidently at each ruler.

"The additional theory is that magic was performed on the children to turn them into those creatures," Sadira continued sadly, "Which is why they only ever targeted children in Ithyion."

"Who could perform that kind of magic?" Nyzaia asked, frowning. "That does not align with any of the powers from Ithyion."

"How much do we really know about Ithyion?" asked Sadira. "I descend from Wiccans, and yet I know little of what their magic entailed."

"So, Wiccans could have done this?" Nyzaia narrowed her eyes. "The people you declare to descend from?"

Larelle shot Nyzaia an exasperated look while Sadira smiled softly.

"That is not what I am saying. It is merely an example that

there is lots about Ithyion we do not know, that may aid our understanding as to what created the creatures."

"Thank you, Sadira." Kazaar inclined his head. "But that does not explain the attack on Queen Elisara and I at the Unsanctioned Isle."

"No, that would be because of the Sword of Sonos. I fear someone on Novisia has been watching you all and had you followed to the Isle. The creatures knew that a weapon was created all those centuries ago. It makes sense they would seek it out before it is turned upon them." Sadira tucked a golden lock behind her ear as the rulers contemplated her words.

"Why the Sword of Sonos?" asked Larelle, her eyes skimming the golden blade.

"I thought those of Vala and Keres created it?" continued Nyzaia.

"Indeed, but it is said to be blessed by the God Sonos himself, imbuing it with light to counter the darkness." Sadira answered.

"*When light meets dark in the rarest of times.*" Kazaar recited from the parchment in his hand. "Could that be what the prophecy is relating to? The sword meeting the creature's end, like when I killed it?"

Caellum rolled his eyes.

"Perhaps," Sadira confirmed. "But there are so many ways to interpret light and dark: a literal sense, spiritual, metaphorical."

"How does all of this relate to the explosion?" Elisara probed, frustrated with everyone's indifference about the act that killed their families. Sadira seemed pained, as if choosing her next words carefully. She shuffled her hands in her lap, glanced sadly at them all.

"The prophecy," she said. "*When the darkness returns, sacrifice is made.*" Elisara frowned, confused until Sadira spoke again. "Your families *were* the sacrifice. They needed to die to trigger the prophecy."

Endless thoughts bombarded Elisara then. What would they

have gained from triggering the prophecy, and why did it need to involve her family?

"*When all that is left is the last of the lines,*" Kazaar said. The others looked at him as realization dawned.

"The prophecy is telling you plainly. Only one heir from each line could remain," Sadira continued. "As the only remaining heirs, you all had to be crowned for the prophecy to move forward, and for that to happen," Sadira looked sadly to Caellum. "Your families had to die." Nyzaia sunk at the weight of the revelations while Caellum reached for Sadira's hand to give it a gentle squeeze.

"Presumably whoever set the explosion is also responsible for these creatures, if it is all linked to the prophecy." Caellum said. "And whoever that is has an outcome in mind that we do not know of yet, but the prophecy does and speaks in riddles about it."

"Then how do we begin to understand the prophecy?" Larelle pushed. Soren removed a parchment from the leather pouch strapped to her side and threw it in the centre of the table. "You likely did not have the full prophecy," she declared. "Otherwise, you would know where to look next." She looked between Elisara and Nyzaia, the former reaching for it and reading aloud.

"The door to the soul bears all to hear
Multiple generations is the rule of the sear

With those of white and those of black
The spirit of the first makes their way back

When the darkness returns, sacrifice is made
In the wake of disaster, the return of the blade

When light meets dark in the rarest of times,
When all that is left is the last of the lines

The power to awaken that of old lore,

Lies in the soul of those with all four.

From fire and ice, the King and Queen must hide
Secrets from the past, the heirs must find

Only together can they defeat and restore,
Only together can they gain so much more

The Gods may whisper and help them on
Only if all possess that from Ithyion'

The group sat in silence once Elisara finished.

"It would appear your parents had something to hide," Soren said, with another pointed look at Elisara and Nyzaia. Elisara glanced at the Keres Queen, turning over the words. Fire and ice. That much was clear. Her mind wandered to her mother; while she trusted her, Kazaar's confession of her presence at the Unsanctioned Isle made her wonder how much she had been hiding. Elisara's eyes roamed over the others, who passed the prophecy between them and pondered the passage. There was so much to decipher, but the next step was clear.

"Are you ready to return to Keres, my Queen?" Kazaar peered down at Elisara, who turned her head up to look at him, countless emotions swimming in her eyes.

"It would appear we will need to do some investigating." She agreed and prepared to face the realm she had not stepped foot in for four years.

Chapter Forty-Six

Caellum

Twisted trees formed a canopy above the path towards the castle gates. It felt suffocating. Having been in Nerida the last two days, returning to Garridon felt unsettling. Even while riding on horseback, Caellum felt in desperate need of space. He dismounted at the gates to the castle grounds and looked behind at Sadira's carriage pulling to a stop. She had requested to exit at the gates to pursue the rest of the journey on foot, wishing to tend to the walled garden on the way. It melted some of the ice encasing Caellum's soul to think she found comfort in her new home.

He approached the carriage, pulled open the door, and immediately offered her his hand.

"I hope your journey was enjoyable, and you were not too lonely," he said, helping her from the carriage as she lifted her skirts with her free hand.

"Of course not! It was nice to be alone with my thoughts. I enjoyed exploring the countryside of my homeland." Caellum hoped her words were true. During their journey to Mera, the speed at which they came to an understanding of one another surprised him. It was if they both recognised the obligation of this marriage yet could profit from a relationship as friends.

"Unfortunately, I will have some matters to attend to," said Caellum regretfully. He released her hands to place his own behind his back as they turned to the gates.

"Do not worry, I am certain the gardens will occupy me this morning."

"Would you be open to an afternoon together?" he asked.

"What did you have in mind?" She smiled at him, raising her hand to block the sun from her vision. Caellum stepped further aside, his body creating a shadow to help her see.

"It dawned on me that you have seen little of Garridon other than the Castle Estate. I would like to take you into the city," he said as he reached his horse.

"I would very much like to see Antor, my King."

"What did we agree?"

Sadira averted her gaze with a smile.

"*Caellum,"* she corrected, "I will see you this afternoon, Caellum." Sadira curtseyed.

He smiled before turning his horse and riding through the gates up the pathway to the castle. Only when he reached the courtyard and glimpsed Sir Cain's curious expression did he realise he was grinning. Caellum rolled his eyes at Sir Cain, who turned back to speak to the guards, leaving Caellum to head to his chambers and change from his riding clothes.

His shoulder twinged as he thought of his last visit into Antor, yet after witnessing the citizens' reactions to Sadira, he hoped attending the city with her on his arm would help ease tensions. His new bride would make his rule much easier.

Bride. Once the wedding transpired, he would have to cut all ties with Elisara. He recalled how she acted with Kazaar, unable to decipher the shift between them. She seemed relaxed in his presence—a forgotten trait since her return from Keres. It was like she had finally let her walls down, but why? They hated each other.

Sadira quickly sensed Caellum's love for Elisara while watching the pair dance, but despite it, she remained by his side the entire evening, devoid of judgment as he explained what happened between them. He had been surprised at her honesty as she reprimanded his lies to Elisara yet understood his motives.

At first, Caellum felt guilty for bringing Sadira and blindsiding her and the others, but that guilt eased as the evening progressed. She seemed happy, given the circumstances, and as the hours went by and Sadira remained at his side, he found it was the first time he watched children play and did not immediately think of his siblings. For once, he found there was a sense of calm cradling the darkness and self-doubt in his mind.

He wondered if that same calmness would comfort him on his afternoon with the future Garridon Queen.

***

"I haven't seen you smile like that in a while," Sir Cain jested, nudging Caellum's arm. "Maybe I should tell her she has finally brought you out of your sulk."

It was during his journey to meet Sadira that Sir Cain accosted him.

"Do not even think about it," Caellum warned. "Do you not have somewhere else to be? I seem to remember suggesting days ago that you try to meet with Sor—" His attention faltered from Sir Cain as he paused. Overlooking the walled garden, Sadira stood. The sun bathed her in light, and closing her eyes, she smiled up at it, a look of contentment across her features. Sunlight caught on the small diamonds encrusting the flowers on her dress, and Caellum recognized it as one of the dresses he asked to be made, to be left in her armoire for when she arrived. A soft lavender chiffon gown with a simple neckline and bodice synched at her waist, cascading into billowing skirts, and scattered with countless flowers that grew in volume the closer to the hemline it reached.

He could not place the odd feeling in his chest upon seeing her so... at home. Sir Cain chuckled at his side, and Caellum kicked him.

"Princess Sadira," Caellum paused, the princess turning at the sound of his voice. He stilled, unsure of what to say as the beauty of her smile caught him unawares. "This is Sir Cain, Commander of the Garridon Armies. I was just advising him on meeting with your sister. I thought she may offer a fresh pair of eyes to our approaches and fighting styles."

"A pleasure to meet you, Princess," Sir Cain bowed.

"And you, Sir Cain. A fine idea. We have many fighting styles on Doltas Island. I am sure she can provide some thoughts," Sadira offered a smile that soon faltered. "A word of warning, Sir. Soren is a brutal fighter. If you find yourself sparring with her, look out for the opening she leaves at her left knee."

The man laughed, and Caellum was surprised Sadira had enough interest in fighting to have noticed such a thing.

"Thank you, Princess. I will heed your warning." Sir Cain bade farewell to the pair and continued down the corridor. Caellum cleared his throat.

"You look beautiful, Sadira," he said, blushing. "I hope you do not mind riding in a dress. I thought we could make the brief journey by horseback."

"Oh, but of course! That sounds wonderful." He offered her his arm as they walked comfortably through the castle and down the steps to the stables.

"I realized you do not have your own horse," he smiled. "I hope you don't mind, but I have chosen one for you. A gift," He gestured to the horse standing beside his own deep chestnut stallion. Sadira's mouth fell open at a beautiful dapple grey. It whinnied as she approached, shorter than Caellum's horse, but majestic in its movements. She reached out to gently stroke the horse's neck while it nuzzled the horse beside it.

"I had Oak choose her for you," Caellum said.

"Oak?"

"This handsome gentleman," He patted his own horse's neck, and she laughed—the gentlest noise to ever grace his ears.

"And how does a horse choose another?" she asked.

"Horses are sacred in Garridon. They are a part of the nature we cherish. Three years ago, Oak found me, and he matches what some might call 'my aura'. I was confident if I let him out into the fields, he would choose one that matched him," Caellum looked down, doubting his next words. "And as a result, you and I." Perhaps he was being too candid. He felt Sadira's hand land on his arm.

"Thank you," she said sincerely.

"Is it okay to lift you up?" he asked. She nodded. He could have sworn a blush graced her cheeks as his hands wrapped around her waist, fragile beneath his hold. Sadira's hair brushed his cheek as he lifted her, the sensation soft as silk. Her fragrance floated to him: roses, sugar, and morning dew. Caellum helped to fan her dress atop the mare before stepping back to mount Oak.

"Would you say Antor is your favourite place in Garridon?" Sadira asked as they rode through the gates and down the path through the trees.

"It had the best atmosphere when I was growing up: the bustling people, shops and shows—but no." Caellum stared ahead while reflecting on the past. "My favourite place is on the outskirts of Albyn. There is a field of flowers as far as the eye can see, which stops at the cliff edge. You can stand, surrounded by the scent, and look out to sea. It is so tranquil, so calming."

"It sounds wonderful. I would very much like to visit one day."

Caellum averted his eyes at the suggestion, awash with sadness at the memories of sitting amongst those flowers with Elisara. He pushed the thoughts aside and continued idle conversation as they rode, asking of her upbringing on Doltas Island while she quizzed him on the different Lords and Ladies of Garridon. It was not long before they met the ivy-covered stone wall marking the entrance to the city.

They dismounted their horses and left them with a guard at the wall while the rest of the procession joined them on their stroll. Caellum was thankful they gave them some provision of privacy. He watched Sadira's mesmerized expression as they entered the city.

"I have never experienced someone's first reaction to Antor," he said.

"Not even Elisara?" she asked.

He let her name wash over him, not wishing to ruin the experience.

"No. We met when we were young. If I was present when she first experienced it, I do not remember." He stopped next to Sadira as they reached the market stalls. Guards moved to scatter through the city while others remained close behind. The citizens in the market turned to them, and he breathed a sigh of relief at the lack of anger or disdain in their expressions. It was nothing like before. Instead, they whispered and smiled, pointing at Sadira.

"Perfumes!" Sadira exclaimed. She grabbed his hand, tugging him to a nearby stall. His heart jolted at the feeling of her hand in his. It felt cold when she let go.

"Do you not wear perfume?" He frowned, remembering her distinct smell from earlier.

"I dabble in creating my own.," She picked up a delicate jar and inhaled.

"Pick one," Caellum told her. He pulled a bag of coins from his pocket, but before she could answer, a scream for help tore in the distance. Sadira was quick to turn and run.

"Sadira!" Caellum yelled, grabbing her arm. She spun to face him. "The guards will inspect it and call a healer, if necessary," he said, trying to direct her away from the gathering crowd.

"I will not stand by while one of my people needs help," she said boldly, with a raise of her chin. Sadira tugged her arm free of his grasp and ran in the direction of the parting crowd.

Shit, he thought, as he ignored the memories of his last visit and ran into the crowd after her.

Chapter Forty-Seven

Nyzaia

Nyzaia peered across the desert sands as the wind picked up to signal the Queen of Vala's arrival. Elisara left Keres on a bad note the last time she visited, and Nyzaia wondered how she was coping as she passed through the Zivoi Mountains and across the Abis Forge. Swirling storms of sand in the distance confirmed her suspicions.

She sensed Tajana's step forward from her guarded position by the pillars, signalling the Lords had finally left.

"I hate the way they speak to you," Tajana said, hand on the pommel of her sword. Nyzaia avoided her gaze; in fact, she avoided many interactions with her love since meeting with Lord Israar.

"They do not know me, Tajana. I spent most of my life hidden away by my family. Gods, I have *killed* people they know and love for the sake of my father." Nyzaia sighed as the spiral of dust dwindled, the Vala procession now crossing the rocky nature of the forge. Nyzaia had requested the steel workers halt their work to allow the temperature to drop as the parade traversed.

"That does not mean they can disrespect you. You are their Queen."

Nyzaia scoffed.

"I am their Queen, and yet I know nothing about what has been going on in my *own* realm." She faced Tajana. "I know nothing of who has been plotting things, or still could be!"

Tajana frowned and tried to reach for Nyzaia, who turned her head to stare at the mountains in the distance.

"What do you mean?" Tajana asked with a tone of caution.

Nyzaia revisited Soren's words at the meeting and the arrogance in which she spoke.

"Soren." Nyzaia spat. "She said she knew Isha."

Tajana's eyes widened.

"There are likely many people with that name in Keres, love."

"It is too big a coincidence. We had no idea where Isha came from, perhaps she had a connection with Doltas Island. Given her involvement with my father, she likely knew secrets we do not." Nyzaia reeled. Soren had sent Isha to Keres—she must have. The true heir to Garridon likely was more involved with the mainland than they realised. "The envoys they sent from Doltas... Did you ever meet any of them?"

"I always delegated the task and watched from afar." Tajana answered, reaching for her again. "It was always straightforward; they handed a list of things they needed, and we provided. In return, they offered a hiding place if we ever required one." She relayed the agreement Nyzaia already knew.

Tajana placed her hand atop Nyzaia's on the balcony, but the queen cleared her throat and removed it, feigning to examine the scars on her hand.

"There is no one here," said Tajana firmly.

"I know, and I am not ashamed of you—or us—at all. But I am new to my reign, and while I know I can do as I please, I do not need to disrupt the way of things with the Lords. It would cause uproar if the Lords discovered their Queen had a guard as her lover." Nyzaia shook her head, trying to find a way to reveal Israar's threat and his belief she needed to separate herself from Tajana.

"Is that all I am? A lowly guard whom you take as a lover?" Tajana asked, staring out across the balcony.

"You know the answer. I wanted to wed you and take you as my Queen Consort, to rule by my side." Nyzaia faced Tajana, her expression softening.

"Wanted?" Tajana repeated, her pain visible as she examined the emotion in Nyzaia's eyes.

"That's not what I meant," Nyzaia said. "I *want* to marry you," *but I am unsure if I can.*

"And if I do not want to be a Queen?" Tajana tested, playing with the tip of a knife drawn from her leathers.

"You do not wish to marry me?"

It would be so much simpler if Nyzaia was still Queen of the Red Stones. When it did not matter what people thought: a time when her family were alive, and the ridiculous prophecy did not exist.

"I do not wish to live a life of royalty, Nyzaia. I was born and made for the shadows the flame creates, not the light itself." The dagger pricked her skin and Nyzaia watched as red welled on the tip of her finger. She wiped it against the stone.

"Neither was I, but sometimes we must accept the hand the Gods deal us. This is my life now, Tajana. Whether you are here or not, I am Queen." Nyzaia took a step closer to her as if pulled by some magnetic force; she combed her hand through the dark lock of hair, having fallen from Tajana's braid.

"This life is difficult, love. I dislike what it is doing to you—to us," said Tajana, leaning into the touch of Nyzaia's hand, who drew away quickly at the distant sound of knocking. The knocker waited a moment before the door opened, and in walked Farid a second later.

"Forgive the intrusion, my Queen," he said with a bow.

"There is no intrusion, Farid. You are welcome."

"The Queen of Vala and her procession have made their way through the Abis Forge and should arrive within the next two hours."

"Thank you, Farid. Please have the stable hands and guards meet them at the north of the castle at the edge of the caverns."

Farid bowed and left the room. The view at the northern side of the castle was partly obscured by the native red rock protruding from the sands.

"You do not wish for the Queen to be seen entering the city?" Tajana asked, confused.

"This visit will be quick, and we wish for as few members of the public to know of it as possible. We do not want questions raised as to the reasons for her visit." Nyzaia said. She spun from the view to enter her chambers and prepare for their arrival. They would stay for one night, allowing them time to look and discuss the clues left behind by their parents.

"You know what the ladies are like; it will be common gossip by morning," Tajana scoffed. She leaned against the stone pillar and watched Nyzaia undress, her skin glowing in the streams of sun cast into the chambers.

"But that is all it will be—gossip. The only people who will see Elisara are those attending the welcome ball, and the servants. It is still fewer than if we were to parade her through the streets. Some may remember her time training here and hold a grudge," Nyzaia explained, striding across the cool tiled floors in nothing but the dark lace of her undergarments like shadows on her skin. She felt Tajana's eyes watching her every move.

"What grudges would they hold? She was an eighteen-year-old princess undergoing training." Nyzaia looked back at Tajana, considering, before pulling items from her wardrobe. "What are you not telling me?" Tajana stalked forward, earning a sigh from Nyzaia.

"She killed Kazaar's second-in-command."

Tajana's eyes bulged.

"Izaiah?!" she exclaimed. "I cannot say many would be disappointed, but he was a large man. I'm surprised she managed it." Nyzaia had never liked the man. On too many occasions, she had removed him from the brothels after the Courtesans came to her with complaints.

"She should not have managed it, Tajana. She froze him and shattered him into pieces, and this was long before she was a Queen. Long before she inherited her family's power and the talisman. A girl who could pull a gentle breeze to listen to whispers—at a push, form frost. But when she was in Keres, her powers appeared to strengthen in response to her emotions. It only happened while she was in Keres." Nyzaia pulled a golden lehenga from the wardrobe while Tajana's brow furrowed.

"Why would her powers heighten in the fire realm when, by definition, she is the opposite?"

"Is she?" Nyzaia asked. "Fire requires air; lightning can create fire. Is she as opposite as we always assumed?'

"*From fire and ice, the King and Queen must hide; secrets from the past, the heirs must find.*" Tajana murmured. Nyzaia had been quick to tell her of the prophecy. If Kazaar could be trusted, then so could Tajana. "But I thought we concluded it must have been about your father and Elisara's mother."

"And that is most likely the link, but we should not completely dismiss the idea that fire and ice may reference Elisara and a connection to Keres' power. We cannot rule out any possibility with this prophecy." Nyzaia straightened the golden fabric against her figure while Tajana laid jewels against her neck, her hands grazing her back while she fastened the clasp. She shivered at the touch.

"I will watch her closely today. Then tomorrow, you can both attend your father's chambers. Something will come to light." Tajana kissed Nyzaia's shoulder from behind.

"Stop trying to be a distraction," Nyzaia scolded, slipping the bangles onto her arms to match the jewels on her neck and ears. Tajana continued her torturous kisses up her neck and moved her loose curls to the side.

"Tajana," Nyzaia said firmly. She stopped, meeting Nyzaia's eyes in the mirror. "We cannot." She regretted the words immediately as her love did not respond but left the room.

Nyzaia sighed while Israar's warning replayed in her mind.

Chapter Forty-Eight

Caellum

King Wren saw himself above the people, one of the many things straining the relationship with his son. As one of the least likely to take the throne, Caellum reached an age where he wanted to explore the towns and cities. To be among the people experiencing Garridon to its fullest. But when Caellum pulled Sadira back, hoping to stop her from helping his people, he realised how deep-seated his father's ways were. It had been instinctual to allow the guards to handle it, despite his heart wishing otherwise. Caellum often forgot he now had the power to reshape the monarch's relationship with the people, yet feared the realization came too late as his people witnessed the King refusing to intervene while their future Queen ran into the unknown.

Caellum ran after Sadira through the path created by the people. Vines climbed the buildings as she followed the cries emerging from the market square. Caellum did not intend to attract this much attention on their visit, yet that thought alone had him cursing again. Why did he care?

He caught up to Sadira as she reached the market. The square was empty this afternoon, aside from the small crowd having gathered by the fountain.

"Make way for the Princess!" The guards shouted, eager to help.

"What happened?" She asked, bending down to where a mother crouched beside an unconscious child, blood spilling from his head. He looked about five years old. Caellum bent down beside her as Sadira tied her hair back with a ribbon, and he matched her urgency, rolling up the sleeves of his tunic.

"Tell me what you need," he murmured to the princess. She gave him a slight nod of recognition before looking up at the woman he assumed was the child's mother. Her movements were panicked, and her eyes wide as she held her son.

"Tell the King what happened while I assess him," Sadira said gently. The woman's body trembled, but she did as the Princess asked, allowing Sadira to slide the child from the woman's arms. She positioned him on the floor and cupped his head in her lap.

"I was watching him throwing stones into the fountain until someone called my name. When I turned back, he was rushing atop the fountain after a cat," The woman choked with each word. "I told him to stop, but he slipped on the water and hit his head on the corner of the stone."

"Children hurt themselves playing all the time," Caellum said kindly. "I'm sure there is something we can do." He smiled at the woman and took her hand. "But to help your son, the princess will need space to work. Can you stand with my guard there?" He asked. The mother looked reluctant, but as Sadira rested a hand atop hers, it seemed to be the reassurance she needed.

As the woman rose to move aside, Sadira turned to one of the guards.

"I need you to bring me a pot of soil from that bed over there," she instructed, pointing to a flowerbed by a shop window. As the guard ran, she turned to Caellum.

"I need you to rip some of my dress." He looked at her, confused. What would the people think of a future Queen roaming the streets in torn attire? "Caellum!"

He grabbed the hem of Sadira's dress and ripped. She took it and began folding.

"I need you to place your knees under his head and keep him raised. Hold this onto the wound with pressure." Caellum did as she asked, trusting her implicitly as he followed her course of action.

When the guard returned with Sadira's pot of soil, she dug a small hole in the dirt then shielded it with her palms. She whispered so quietly Caellum was unable to trace the words. The crowd gasped as two flowers began to flourish, as seamless as if they had been there their entire lives.

"I need two cups of water," Sadira said to no one in particular. A guard quickly abided, grabbing a cup from a shocked spectator, and rushing to the fountain. In the meantime, Sadira inspected the plants, meticulous in which petals or leaves she plucked from it. While Sadira said her mother's line descended from the Wiccan, Caellum never expected she could enchant plants to create potions.

A healer, he realised. The healer on Doltas Island.

Caellum reached for her dress and tore another piece. Sadira did not question him but continued to work as he replaced the blood sodden fabric with a fresh strip. Picking up a rock from the ground, she crushed the petals and leaves on top of her dress until forming two separate piles.

Sadira briefly inspected the water before pouring nearly the entire contents out. Intently, the guard watched as she added the ground powder and mixed it with her finger, forming a pale green paste.

"Has the bleeding eased?" she asked Caellum. He removed the piece of fabric, significantly less bloodied than the last. She nodded then shuffled to Caellum, who tensed as their arms touched, yet it soon calmed him.

"What's his name?" Sadira asked the mother.

"Killian."

Sadira thanked her and pushed the boy's hair back.

"Hold here and here," She directed Caellum to hold the boy's dishevelled hair apart, exposing the depth of the wound. Gently, Sadira moved, applying a thick layer of paste onto the gash. The second it hit the boy's skin, the scent strengthened and reached Caellum's nostrils, one of mint, and another fragrance Caellum could not determine. Once the wound was covered, Sadira wiped her hands on her dress and added the remaining powder to another cup.

Placing the boy's lips to it, she spoke soothing words into his ear, encouraging him to awaken. The boy's mouth twitched and parted a fraction to allow the liquid to trickle into his mouth and down his throat, eyelids flickering until they groggily opened to peer at his mother, who sobbed with relief. Sadira offered a hand to the woman and pulled her down gently to swap places with Caellum.

"Mamma?"

Sadira blushed, as if suddenly returning from a trance. Glancing down, she suddenly realized the state of her dress and the King she had dragged onto the floor alongside her. Caellum pressed a palm to her cheek, his thumb wiping away any remainder of the paste smeared across her face. Sadira's eyes widened, and he stood, extending a hand to help her rise. Stumbling into him, she blushed when he caught her. Sadira's eyes glowed the purest green Caellum had ever seen as her gaze caught on their surroundings. He turned to find every building coated with ivy, where white flowers bloomed.

The crowd was torn between staring at the flowers or at their King and future Queen. The applause was a ripple at first, soon mounting to cheers. The crowd parted again as Caellum led Sadira away, while the guards carried the boy home, his mother trailing alongside them. With a protective arm around Sadira, she glanced nervously at him and the throngs of people bowing as they passed.

Caellum beamed. Auralia once said respect was the foundation for a strong marriage, and if his sister's words were true, then theirs would be as solid as the mountains of Vala.

***

Sadira was quiet as they journeyed back, and Caellum was desperate to know what she was thinking—feeling. Whenever Elisara was quiet, he mirrored her. There was no point in trying to get her to talk when she was trapped in her memories. As for Sadira, Caellum was unsure how to act, but wished to do the right thing.

"I am so sorry," said Sadira.

"Why would you be sorry?" he asked.

The sun was setting as Caellum pulled Sadira's horse to a stop beside him to marvel at the pink hues across the skies before crossing into the castle grounds.

"I suppose I am sorry because I drew focus from you," she whispered. "You are the King. I do not wish to undermine your position in front of your people."

The glow of sunset reflected off Sadira's pearlescent skin, and despite how much time she spent in the gardens, her complexion had not deepened more than one or two shades. Her long lashes cast shadows on her flushed cheeks. He was drawn to her lips as she chewed them, as if afraid of his response. Caellum's father would have never allowed a woman to act like Sadira had. To pull focus from his presence. But he was not his father, and with Sadira by his side, he could finally manage his role as King. As he leaned to grasp her hand, she turned to face him.

"*Our* people, Sadira. You are my equal in this." He swallowed, fearing his boldness. "From now until the day we die."

Sadira bit harder on her lips then, glancing back at the sunset.

"Hey," Caellum said gently, tracing circles on the back of her hand.

"I had a less than pleasant conversation with Soren upon our return to the castle this morning. She was unhappy with how I spoke to her in front of the other rulers," She admitted. "We have never had a good relationship, Soren and I. It has always been her aim—our lineage's aim—to retake the throne, and I fear that goal has clouded her judgement on what is best for the people." Sadira swallowed the lump in her throat.

After Soren's behaviour, her threat to Caellum's rule was clear.

"She has no care for what is best for me." Sadira wiped the tears from her eyes, and Caellum felt the pain like a stab to his own heart.

"Has she always spoken to you this way?" he asked. The princess nodded. "Sadira, you need not have her near if you do not wish it. My agreement was for Soren to be Captain of your Queen's guard once we marry, but until then, she does not need to be here."

"No, no. I could not take Garridon from her. She deserves to be here as much as I."

She appeared to be hiding something, evident by the stammer in her voice. Caellum sensed it, though did not wish to overstep. Sadira twisted her necklace.

"I had a partner on Doltas Island. If I do anything to displease her, she has implied harm will come to him." Guilt filled her eyes then.

"Sadira, my Queen." he said. "We both have love for others, and I do not hold that against you. You have witnessed my pain first-hand in Nerida, so if you need to mourn the loss of your love, you do so until your heart heals. The Gods know how shattered mine is." He paused. "What was his name?"

"Rodik," Sadira said sadly. "He is a Wiccan. He taught me the healing magic I use today."

"How a Wiccan came to be on Doltas is a conversation for another day," Caellum chuckled. Like the other rulers, Caellum knew little of the Wiccans. Yet, based on what Sadira displayed today, they connected with nature the same way the Garridon lineage did. Caellum pulled Oak up beside Sadira and wrapped an arm around her, where she nestled into the crook of his neck. "We are two broken pieces trying to be whole," he whispered.

"Here we find ourself, forced into a marriage of politics and control; that neither asked for. Tell me, Caellum, how are we to grow in such conditions?" She asked. He was struck by her candor and contemplated his response.

"I cannot promise you love, Princess," he responded with the same honesty. "But I can promise to plant roots with you and nurture them every day, so that some happiness may blossom in the weeds we are surrounded by."

Chapter Forty-Nine

Elisara

"How are you doing?" Kazaar trotted up beside Elisara as they journeyed through the winding paths of the red rocks, having passed the dreaded Abis Forge. A storm had festered at the memories the Forge ignited, and while Elisara had stopped it, it was as if the air was reluctant to obey her will.

"Have you ever had your power falter in listening to your command?" Elisara asked. She rested her hands in the mane of her stallion and turned to look at Kazaar. She squinted to keep the sun and sand from her face, while Kazaar wrapped a piece of black fabric around his own. He handed a similar fabric in white to Elisara, and she covered her face too.

"Once. Though I could not tell you why," he answered. The answer was of no help to her. "Why do you ask?"

The castle slowly came into view as their journey continued.

"Sometimes I wonder if the God Keres hates me. I can feel it—the *wrongness* of being here. I am born of ice and air, not fire and warmth. Maybe the earth knows that; it knows I should not be here," she mused. "It is like my power knows it too, thus refuses to follow my wishes."

Kazaar seemed deep in thought, and she appreciated him for not immediately dismissing the notion.

"These lands have long forgotten their ties to the Gods," Kazaar commented. Elisara gave him a doubtful look.

"I am not so certain, given the autonomy of the Unsanctioned Isle."

Elisara willed the horse into a canter, the dull sword from the

Isle moving against her thigh with the motion, providing her with a comforting reminder of her strength.

***

Arriving at the wall to the palace, Elisara was greeted by a new member of the Queen's Guard, having likely been a member of Nyzaia's syndicate in her life before Queen. Elisara nodded respectfully to him as he directed the pair to a more private courtyard where they dismounted.

Nyzaia emerged from the archway, a vision in her royal lehenga.

"I did not realise you employed assassins; I would have assumed you wished to be the most feared in the castle." Elisara pulled her friend into a hug, who laughed.

"You know I am the most skilled," she said, yet their smiles subsided at the look on Kazaar's face.

"She knows about you!" he hissed.

"You mean, I know she was the Queen of Assassins?" Elisara asked, smirking. "I would think so, given I was her first target."

Kazaar appeared even more outraged at that, dragging them both by an arm into the archway.

"You tried to murder a Princess of Vala? On whose order?"

"The King's," answered Nyzaia firmly.

Elisara remembered the moment well. She had been sitting reading by the fire when Nyzaia's attempt at a quiet landing on the balcony failed. "I can hear you breathe," Elisara had called to her, the sounds having passed in the wind.

"Calm down, Kazaar. She was merely sent to spy on me," Elisara laughed.

"She caught me on her balcony within seconds and fed me some measly information about the Lords, so I appeared successful in my task when I reported back to father." The tension in Kazaar's shoulders loosened at Nyzaia's words.

"Why did he send you?" he asked. The queen shrugged.

"No idea. He said it was an opportunity to test my skills." She smiled then; eyebrows raised. "You're being *oddly* over-protective." He narrowed his eyes at Nyzaia, who raised her brows at him. "Now, if you're done with your interrogation, I would like to steal Elisara and prepare her for the ball. You can meet us in the great hall at sunset." With that, Nyzaia steered Elisara away to her chambers.

Elisara had forgotten what it was like to have a friend to laugh with, who not only related to her but understood the intricacies of life as a Queen. While she had lived a vastly different life to Nyzaia, Elisara took comfort knowing their positions were similar now. The discomfort felt upon arriving in Keres was soon forgotten.

"Now, onto important matters," said Nyzaia, helping Elisara untie the laces of her corset to enter the baths. "What have you done to my old Commander?"

The queen smirked, despite a serious edge in her tone.

"I do not understand what you mean," Elisara shrugged off the question as she entered the pool, the water covering her modesty.

"I have used a different bath for the last few days to allow it to cool for you." Nyzaia said, taking a seat at the edge while dangling her legs into the water. Elisara appreciated the gesture, despite having found solace in the heat recently. "You are avoiding my question."

"I assure you, Nyzaia. I do not know what you mean." Elisara wiped the water from her eyes and took a bowl of soaps from her, raising each block to her nose. The majority held a scent too strong for her liking, except for one. It reminded her of Kazaar, a warm and spiced aroma. She favoured the least fragrant: a delicate trace of the palm trees in Keres.

"I have only ever seen Kazaar smile with a handful of people," Nyzaia twisted the talisman around her neck as she spoke, "and the last time you were in Keres, it was clear the two of you detested one another."

"I did detest him—"

"—You no longer do? Interesting."

"I have worked through a lot of things from my time in Keres, many of which I blamed Kazaar for. While he has taken ownership and apologised most of it, others he has pushed me to self-reflect on, and I have drawn conclusions that no longer warrant us being at odds." Elisara finished brushing the soaps through her hair and began washing it clean.

"If you were at odds with one another, you would be civil. What I have witnessed is—" Nyzaia stopped as Elisara met her eye.

"What?" She challenged, eyes brightening as her emotions shifted.

"There seems to be something more there, Elisara. Whether that be friendship, or perhaps he is simply warming your bed—"

"Enough," Elisara commanded. Frost appeared at the edge of the water, embarrassed by the accusation. Nyzaia did not seem fearful, however, as she assessed her with a smirk.

"It is not a bad judgement, Elisara. The two of you appear to be good for one another. You seem to have brought some light to the dark world he has kept himself in."

Elisara calmed her breathing, squeezing the water from her hair.

"Kazaar is an attractive man; there is no denying that. But there is no room for further heartbreak, given my current situation." Elisara asserted, ignoring the doubtful voice in her mind. She had been angry at seeing Caellum and Sadira together, for his betrayal. But she did not find herself wishing to be Sadira. She was adamant to all that she wanted to be alone, but as of late, alone included Kazaar.

"Fine, that's a no for Kazaar. But you need one night of fire and passion, and what better place to have that than Keres?" Nyzaia grinned and passed Elisara a towel, who rolled her eyes at the suggestion. She had no wish to be with another. "I assume Caellum was your last?"

Elisara's silence answered the question.

"Was he good?"

Elisara's silence answered that question, too.

"I have no measure. I have only ever been with Caellum," she said, wrapping the towel around herself. Nyzaia gasped.

"There was never anyone else?"

"We were betrothed from the age of five, Nyzaia. When was I to experiment with others?"

"And you believe he was loyal to that engagement?"

"Evidently he was *not*." She was silent for a moment, swallowing the anger at the reminder of his betrayal. Yet perhaps the betrayal would soon be forgotten in the arms of another. "But maybe it is time I experienced others." She smiled at Nyzaia, who eagerly dragged her by the arm and into her rooms.

"We must make you as enticing to the men of Keres as possible," Nyzaia said, beginning to pull countless gowns from her wardrobes.

"Something red," Elisara requested, a slight smile playing on her lips.

As Nyzaia readied Elisara for the ball, she was reminded of the moments with her mother. Upon selecting a gown, Nyzaia ushered in a tailor to make the appropriate adjustments, elements of Vala's fashion intertwined with the Keresian fabrics. She massaged oil into her skin to add a glow to her complexion while Nyzaia combed scented oil and sprays into her hair.

Very little jewellery was added as the dress spoke for itself.

"There is one more garment required," Nyzaia grinned, "One for underneath the gown to add to the element of seduction." She handed Elisara some folded cloth, and the gold glistened as she unraveled it.

Grinning, she allowed Nyzaia to finish helping her dress before the pair left for the hall, arm in arm.

***

She fidgeted while waiting by the closed doors to the corridor, which led to the staircase into the hall. Music played from inside, and laughter resounded. Nyzaia was in there, too, but was insistent Elisara wait at least three songs before making her appearance, adamant it would draw the eyes of all males. Elisara nodded to the guard at the door, who obeyed the signal, opening the ornate doors and the tiled floor came into view.

"Queen Elisara Sturmov of Vala," called the guard, silencing the revelers whose eyes turned upwards.

The music continued to play as Elisara padded gently down the corridor, a raised wall to her left hiding most of her body from view. Only her shoulder, head, and glistening crown were visible. There was no ceiling, inviting the waning evening heat to float in and ease Elisara's worry, while the curved archways offered unobtrusive locations for those of Keres seeking more than just a dance partner tonight. The intricately patterned tiled floor was barely visible from the many people dancing upon it, lit by the light of the flames flickering in the sconces on the walls.

From the corner of her eye, she spotted Kazaar below, standing with a Lord she recognised as the Lord of Khami. The Commander's hair was freshly washed and still damp, as if he had run overtime. While he wore some of his formal military attire, like his fitted leather trousers and polished black boots, a white tunic covered his upper half. A leather piece of clothing was fitted to his chest, housed with what Elisara knew to be small daggers.

Kazaar's conversation halted as the melody reached its crescendo and Elisara rounded the corner to appear at the top of the stairs. Lifting the front of her dress, she freed her bare feet as she descended, her thigh exposed from the deep slit crafted into the side of the gown. Blood red fabric covered the tops of her shoulders, melting into a deep V neckline exposing the curve of her breasts. Her loose curls rested to the side while no fabric covered her back, highlighting the base of her spine, and leaving her skin bare. Golden chains looped through the straps to hold the dress in place.

As Elisara reached the end of the staircase, her breath caught under the intensity with which Kazaar watched her, no longer taking notice of the Lord beside him. The amber glow of his gaze flickered with the flames in the sconces until his jaw clenched, and the darkness returned. He offered no smile or sign he would approach, something she had expected given his behaviour at their last ball.

She chastised herself for caring about his reaction. Nyzaia was right; he was her Commander. Why would he approach her at a ball? Straightening, she inclined her chin, holding his gaze as she strode to where he stood. His eyes were still dark, but she found an unknown emotion lying in their depths. She did not understand the change in his mood, nor why he tensed once she reached him. His hands tightened around the dagger strapped to his thigh as Elisara averted her gaze to the man beside him.

"My Lord, would you care to have this dance?" She smiled sweetly, sensing the pulse of Kazaar's power, a reminder of the intertwining essence they had experienced at the Unsanctioned Isle. She did not allow it to reach for her own.

"Of course, Queen Elisara. It would be my honour," said the Lord. He handed his wine to Kazaar and led her to the dance floor. As he spun her into her arms, she looked to where Kazaar stood, and to the wine glass now shattered on the floor.

"Lord Arnav of Khami," the Lord announced himself. "It has been many years since we last met, Queen Elisara." His hand pressed against her bare back; the other hand entwined with hers. He wore a red sherwani to match the turban on his head. The man's eyes seemed playful as he smiled.

"Of course, my Lord. It is a pleasure," She smiled while he led her around the dancefloor, the music more freeing than what she was used to. Elisara's lessons as a child often entailed the practice of dances native to the other realms, and in Keres, the dances were close and intimate. She struggled to loosen her limbs in his grip, and while handsome, she felt no draw to him.

"Is it the Commander in particular you wish to make jealous?" He asked, much to Elisara's surprise. "Please, your Majesty. The way you look tonight... it must be for someone in particular."

"Perhaps I simply aim to entice," she returned, "To make a statement that I, Queen Elisara, own my body and sexuality." His hand trailed up her back, his fingers twisting in the golden chains.

"I have no doubt, your Majesty. I am not offended, but if you *do* wish to make someone jealous, you may need to try harder." He smirked and pulled her closer. "I am happy to oblige. My tastes are not for women, though I do appreciate your beauty."

Lord Arnav continued leading Elisara across the ballroom floor as the pair spun to the sensual music; with each spin, his hand placement shifted, claiming every inch of visible skin on display. As the music reached its height, he dipped Elisara low, the slit of her dress widening to reveal the golden chains adorned with rubies strapped around her upper thigh, connecting to a garter belt of similar makings. Nyzaia's gift.

Lord Arnav pulled Elisara back into him then spun her again, but as he did, she collided with a wall of muscle—a distinct set of familiar hands gripping her waist and drawing her into his hold. Elisara breathed in Kazaar as he silently led their movements, relishing in his scent, the smoke and embers of Keres ash laced with the pine and snow of Vala. Over his shoulder, Lord Arnav winked before heading to the wine table.

Elisara ignored how her power reached for him and how she silently hoped his power would reach back. Glancing up through her lashes, he glanced down and straightened his hold, reminding Elisara again of how perfectly their bodies melded.

In such proximity to Kazaar, she took a moment to admire him—something she had never allowed until then. She was most enamored by his scent, and breathed it in. Glancing upwards again, the amber returned in his gaze. His firm jaw remained clenched and dotted with stubble. His hair had since dried, combed back in a way that highlighted the unique browns of his locks. Kazaar gripped tighter onto Elisara's hand.

"Are you finished devouring me with your eyes?" he jested. Elisara looked over his shoulder instead.

"I was simply trying to gauge why you are so tense," she said, gripping his shoulder as he spun her, lifting her body as he did.

"I dislike the way the guards are looking at you," he said stiffly. She glanced in their direction as their dance continued. A cluster stood against a wall, but only two seemed intent on watching them—or her.

"They were close to my second-in-command." Elisara stumbled at the admission, but Kazaar caught her and pulled her flush against him. "Exactly the reason I am tense."

He watched her closely, having sensed the change in her demeanor. The guards were drinking heavily tonight, and their eyes watched Elisara in ways she could not read. She thought back to that night in her room—at the vengeful eyes that leered upon her. Kazaar traced his fingers lightly down her spine, tethering her back into the room. With him.

"Is that the only reason? You did not seem to wish to engage with me prior, and now here we are." Elisara tried not to focus on the way his breath touched her face. He said nothing and continued the dance that neared its end. Lord Arnav had graced Elisara with his showmanship for dancing, while Kazaar's steps were imbued with intent; each movement of his hand drew her attention to him, and as the song came to its end, he dipped her low, only to pull her back up with excruciating slowness. While doing so, Kazaar drew her leg up to his waist, his hands sliding up her thigh to grip the golden chain that graced it.

"You're wearing red," he whispered, sending shivers through her body. The dancers moved again as the next song played, yet the pair remained frozen. Kazaar stroked his thumb over the chain, the darkness returning to his eyes. He lowered her leg as she cleared her throat, noticing the height of the flames gracing the wall—taller and brighter than before. Her eyes found Nyzaia on the throne who watched the flames too before looking to Elisara with a raised brow. The look conveyed every suspicion she had voiced earlier that day.

"Now is our chance," Kazaar whispered, his left-hand landing on her waist. Elisara's mind flitted to another scenario as her heartrate spiked. "If we leave now, no one will question us." She turned into him, his hand remaining on hers.

"Where?" she asked, her chest flushed. Kazaar swallowed.

"Everyone is preoccupied. This is our moment to search the palace and see if there is anything we can find without prying eyes."

"Of course," she said, embarrassed her mind had jumped to different conclusions.

"Follow me," he said, and as he grasped her hand, a part of Elisara wondered if there was anywhere, she would not follow him.

Chapter Fifty

Larelle

"Language!" Alvan scolded, glaring at the Lords busy arguing in the throne room. He gave a pointed look to the young Princess Zarya sitting in a smaller throne at Larelle's side: quiet and patient—regal. With her head raised, the tiara caught the light, and Larelle silently admired her daughter, who Olden and Lillian had spent many of their days preparing for this moment. Though Larelle doubted her decision to bring her daughter.

She thought having a child—a princess—present at this meeting would keep everyone's manners and words in check.

That was not the case.

Larelle's throne had been moved from atop the stairs to the head of the table, framed by the open wall behind them backing onto a view of the ocean. To the left sat all her Lords; to the right, the citizens of the realm elected by her staff: the new advisors. The staff were gathered, too. Larelle caught Lillian's eye, and the two shared an exasperated look.

The new advisors to the realm were a mismatch of people: an elderly woman from Seley, recommended by Alvan for her knowledge of the changing hands between Nerida and Garridon; a plump man from Amoro, who coordinated the workers on one of the largest vineyards, and a handsome man from Trosso, who had not stopped looking at Lillian. And from The Bay, a familiar face. Orlo. His son had agreed to take over the bread stall in his absence.

Meetings were to be held on a bi-weekly basis, and this was the first. The primary matter was to decide on what would be discussed in their meetings and how the Lords and new advisors would cooperate. Yet so far, the Lord's declared they wished to select their own advisors, having no reason to trust those who sat before them. The new advisors watched in silence, patiently waiting for the onslaught to stop. Larelle rolled her eyes. Only Alvan would initiate discussions on the most urgent topics to address, while the other Lords continued in complete ignorance of the elected townsmen and women.

Larelle observed, waiting to see if they would soon figure it out amongst themselves before she intervened. The doors to the throne room opened as a guard approached. He bent down to her ear.

"There is someone here to see you; they do not wish their presence to be known by others," he whispered. Larelle looked at him, confused, but rose all the same, curious as to who would arrive unannounced at the castle.

"Lord Alvan," Larelle called. "Please preside over the meeting in my absence." Alvan nodded proudly at the ask, while she sought Lillian's eye, tilting her head to Zarya. Lillian nodded, having understood the meaning.

As Larelle exited, she hurried to catch up with the guard.

"Did this person say what they wished to see me about?" she asked.

"Only that it was urgent he speak with you, your Majesty." The young guard blushed addressing her, and soon developed a keen interest in the door they approached as he held it open. She stepped into the small sitting room often reserved for visitors and noted a glass of water on the table between two velvet armchairs overlooking Mera.

Larelle circled the chair to greet her visitor. The shock must have been clear on her face.

"Do not tell me I look awful, Larelle. I already feel it, having travelled so far," said the raspy voice of the Historian with a wry smile.

"Of course not, sir." she smiled, lowering into the armchair beside him. "I am surprised, that is all. I have never seen you outside of the Neutral City."

He sighed and nodded, gazing across Mera. He appeared troubled as he fiddled with the belt on his tunic.

"That is true. I could not tell you the last time I left." Reaching for the water, he took a sip. "Mera is much changed. There are far more buildings, though beautifully carved as I expected." He smiled at Larelle. The capital city of Mera was indeed beautiful: pale sandstone buildings beautifully crafted with different sculptures of creatures and plants. Fountains filled with salt water from the sea dotted almost every street corner, and from where they sat, the spires of the church towered in the background, though Larelle rarely visited. Other than her daily morning prayer to the Goddess, she did not practice the religion of her people.

"I am thankful for your kind words, sir, as I am sure the people of Nerida are, too."

The Historian turned to look at her, yet Larelle felt like she was being analysed—*critiqued*, even—as she sat under his stare. He reached to clasp Larelle's hand.

"You always were polite, Larelle," he said with a wistful smile, "and calm and levelheaded. I was reminded of that during our last meeting at the Neutral City. You kept us on track."

"Someone has to keep the others from arguing," Larelle laughed, uncertain where the conversation was headed.

"It is for that reason I feel like I can trust you with some... *delicate,* and potentially dangerous information." His expression darkened as he leaned into Larelle.

"Of course, sir."

"I fear there is one among you who could call forth far more destruction than we have anticipated." He appeared to contemplate his next words. "There was a history book I read once regarding the past of Ithyion. Something was scrawled in the final pages that has always stuck with me." He began to recite it.

Only together can they defeat and restore,

Only together can they gain so much more.

The Gods may whisper and help them on
But only if all possess that from Ithyion.

Watch for the dark one that will bring suffering to all.
The rise of old power, the Kingdom will fall."

Larelle tried not to react at the two verses from the prophecy she recognized; they had not yet told the Historian.

"What does it mean?" she asked. She was not being dishonest, for the final phrases differed to the ones she knew. The Historian studied her curiously, as if searching for a lie in her expression.

"Do you know much of my history, Larelle?" She shook her head. "I descend from the Wiccan on Ithyion," he admitted, his lips down turning. This time, Larelle did not hide her surprise. "I have little magic, but I can easily detect one thing." He looked at her. "Power." Larelle frowned.

"During our last meeting, yourself and the other rulers accessed your power, but Kazaar could not. We concluded only the rulers could, given the extent of your powers as the last of each lineage." He paused, and Larelle nodded, remembering the absence of flames when Kazaar held out his hand.

"Kazaar was *lying*," he hissed. Larelle pulled back at the hatred clear on the man's face.

"Lying about what?"

"I could *feel* his power, Larelle. I could feel it in the air and around Elisara. It was *dark.* He was purposely not using it, yet I could feel the power humming." The Historian coughed, reaching again for his water.

"I do not understand," said Larelle. "Why would he lie? How could he have that much power?" She leaned forward in her seat. "What do you mean it felt *dark*?"

"It was as though it did not belong here, as if it was not from

Novisia or even Ithyion. It felt *other.*" Clearing his throat, he continued. "Do with the information as you wish, Larelle, but I needed to tell someone. Someone needed to know that he cannot be trusted." He gripped her hands so tight Larelle had to restrain from flinching as his nails dug into her skin. "You must watch him, Larelle. Watch for the dark one that will bring suffering to all: the rise of old power, the Kingdom will fall."

Chapter Fifty-One

Elisara

Heat rose in Elisara's cheeks as Kazaar dragged her down endless corridors, each narrower and darker than the last. Her breath quickened, though she did not know if it was from the thrill of secrecy or from being completely and utterly alone with her Commander.

"Where are we going?" she hissed, repressing a tang of laughter at the way he half jogged and dragged her behind him.

"Shhh! There will still be guards patrolling."

Right on cue, footsteps travelled towards them, and she looked at Kazaar wide-eyed before he jerked her into an alcove. Kazaar turned Elisara's body, so his back was to the corridor, keeping Elisara penned in the dark.

"I don't think th—"

"—I said shh," he whispered, pressing a finger to her lips. Her heart pounded harder against her chest as the guards drew closer. She restrained from anxiously licking her lips, Kazaar's finger still pressed close. Seeming to realise where his hand was, he removed it, though the amber in his eyes darkened with wisps of shadow as Elisara watched him in the dimmed lantern light. His mouth parted, and she felt his quickened breath against her face as he gazed down at her, their bodies flush to one another. His hand moved from her lips to her waist, tightening his grip. She squeaked as the guards passed their alcove. Their footsteps paused at the end of the hallway.

"Did you see what the Queen of Vala was wearing?" One asked.

"The garter? Gods, I wonder who is taking her to bed tonight."

The other laughed. Despite the darkness, Elisara knew Kazaar could see the blush flushing her cheeks as they listened. His hand travelled down her hip as he pushed her further into the alcove. Her bare back hit the wall and she tried not to gasp at the coolness of it, instead resting her head back, looking up at him as he leaned in.

"What were you thinking with that garter?" he whispered against the shell of her ear; his hand reached for the slit in her dress, caressing the chains of the undergarment. Her breathing hitched, spellbound by the rough skin of his fingers trailing against her thigh.

"Nyzaia told me I needed to forget I am queen and find a man for the night," she replied breathily. His hand paused, and she heard him swallow. Power hummed beneath her skin, calling to his, and Elisara moved to grip his forearm. In doing so, the same white essence from the Isle sparked at their contact. She gasped.

"Those are not the noises I wish to hear while you're clothed," he murmured. His jaw clenched and he closed his eyes, her nose softly grazing his as they leaned closer into one another, his breath on her lips. Her eyes fluttered closed. The guards slammed the door to the hallway and Kazaar stepped back suddenly.

"They're gone. Let's go."

Elisara could not ignore her disappointment at the cold air between their bodies as his stiff demeanor returned. She stood, breathless.

What was that?

Elisara raced to catch up to his hurried pace down the hallway.

"The King had a secret room in his private office that only I knew about. That will be the place to check." Elisara nodded, trying to clear her head as she followed him to the end of a dark corridor and into the late King's Office.

Large glass windows lined the wall—so clean it was like no barriers existed to the outside world, allowing a clear view across the Abis Forge and the Zivoi Mountains into Vala. Two faded armchairs were positioned before the window and a bookcase lined the wall behind, a reminder of Elisara's own.

"This looks like one of the studies in the Vala castle," she said as she strode through the room, trailing the spines with her hands.

"Mhmm," Kazaar mused. He made to move one of the bookshelves from the far wall, and with a flick of her hand, air blasted air along the edge and pushed it away. Kazaar stumbled, glaring once he regained his posture. "A little warning would be nice."

He ran his hand across the bricks behind, sensing for the perfect one; he pulled when he found it, a door swinging open to reveal a room inside. "After you," he mocked, waving his hand.

Elisara straightened and made a point of swaying her hips as she walked past him. They collided as she immediately stopped.

"Have you been in here before?" she asked.

"Obviously not," he said.

The two stood in silence.

The room was a near replication of the one found on the Unsanctioned Isles: a shrine to the Gods. The statues were scaled down in size, displayed on a large table in the centre of the room. Kazaar's hand grazed her waist as he stepped around to examine the mirror in the corner, etched in familiar gold and symbols. Writing marked its surface.

"This is the full prophecy," he said.

Elisara's attention was pulled to a small portrait perched on a desk. She picked it up, tracing her finger over the familiar woman with amber eyes staring back. Her stomach dropped as the weight of secrets fell upon her.

"Your mother," Kazaar breathed.

She nodded as the sense of betrayal returned, learning someone so close had hidden so much. Why would the King of Keres keep a painting of her mother? And why had he duplicated the room from the Unsanctioned Isles?

None of it made sense.

Was this where her mother had been while absent from home?

Here? Elisara glanced back through the door into King Razik's study. From the differing angle, she saw it as she did in the Azuria Castle.

"The study. It looks like my mother's," she said, the pieces coming together.

Light from outside fell across the armchairs, their faded blue nearly identical to the ones in her mother's office. The King of Razik cared enough to replicate her mother's most cherished room, the study where she spent most of her time gazing out over the balcony across the Zivoi mountains and the bordering Abis Forge. It all made sense now.

"My mother said she never loved my father but married him for duty. She never said for certain if there had been another," Elisara's voice trailed. Her mother and the King of Keres had been lovers. Turning back to the desk, she glanced down for other signs of her mother. A folded letter sat on the desk, the handwriting instantly recognizable to Elisara. She wondered if her father had known, if he knew of secret love notes and hidden affairs. Kazaar picked up the letter and read it aloud.

Iahabi,

The time has come. You must cease your attempts with the Isle. We cannot change the course of the prophecy. Ignite the flame, fulfil the prophecy, and I will be with you.

Fulfil the promise you made to me.

When we are gone, Kazaar must move to Vala. They will need one another in this time when his darkness meets her light. When the last of the heirs stand, the future rests in the children's hands.

I will love you until the air extinguishes the flame.

Your Flame, Vespera

"Iahabi?" Elisara peered questioningly at Kazaar.

"In translation it means *my love,*" he whispered.

Elisara stared, clueless as to what to say next. She turned the letter over in her mind. Her mother had been trying to protect her, and for reasons Elisara could not fathom, she played a part in Kazaar's relocation. *Ignite the flame, fulfill the prophecy.*

"She knew she was going to die," Elisara murmured.

"And it sounds like she and the King of Keres had some part in the explosion."

Elisara looked to him, searching for any signs of betrayal mirrored in her own expression. The man he saw as a father had kept this from him.

"They set the explosion," Elisara said plainly, her eyes meeting Kazaar's. "They had to." She took the letter from Kazaar's hand and scanned it again. "*Fulfill the prophecy,*" she choked. They had them all killed, Kazaar. All of them." She dropped the letter to the desk, covering her mouth to keep the cry from escaping. They had killed her father, her sisters, and set in motion all that transpired since.

"But why?" asked Kazaar. "What would they have to gain?"

Elisara had no answer, nor knew any explanations as to why her mother had been to the Unsanctioned Isles, and why they had remodeled elements of the chamber in Keres.

"She helped initiate the demands in the will too. Why would they think we need one another?"

"You must cease your attempts with the Isle," Elisara repeated. "Perhaps they were trying to get the sword to prevent the prophecy, and then when it failed, they knew we would all need to work together. Maybe that's why they paired us up." She suggested, rather unconvincingly

"There has to be something else in here," Kazaar turned to the rest of the room while Elisara did the same. They ignored the map of Novisia and peered again at the table in the room's centre, the four statues tall upon it. Black cloth swathed across the table and drooped to the ground. Elisara followed the fabric until her eyes fell on a wooden chest beneath. The wood was simple, with two faded circles carved on top. Elisara pulled out the chest and opened it, the hinges creaking as she did. She scanned the items: a wicker basket, a miniature wooden sword, a folded blanket, and a letter.

"Is this a baby blanket?" she asked, dangling the dark woven material in her hands. Kazaar crouched beside her to look inside the chest.

"These are mine," he said, rifling through the items. "I was abandoned at the doors of the castle in an open chest."

Elisara reached for the letter addressed to Kazaar in a messy script on the other side. Opening it, she read it twice before looking at him.

"It's the prophecy again," she said, confused. "Why would the prophecy have been in the chest you were abandoned in?"

Kazaar glanced away, refusing to meet Elisara's gaze. She could not take another betrayal. Power tugged inside Elisara then, but it was different to her air—it was the same pull she felt to Kazaar ever since returning from the Isle. She ignored it, instead focusing on pulling the air to her, preparing to cocoon her heart from the blow of another betrayal. He was hiding something. "Kazaar, why would it have been with you?" she demanded.

As Kazaar turned to face her, he sighed and grasped her hands. "I need you to understand I was never certain, and that is why I never told you. Only after seeing all this can I piece it together."

Elisara withdrew her hands, her eyes scanning his as the amber urged the darkness to retract. Did he, too, feel the power in his veins wrenching them together?

"Speak. Now." She commanded. Fear and pain glimmered in his eyes, remorse for whatever secret he kept hidden. Kazaar stepped back and rounded the table to create more distance between them, but the sudden absence of his presence felt wrong. Elisara shifted on her feet until they stood opposite one another. The Commander was rigid, arms kept by his side, while he gazed only at her, his eyes a burning amber, despite the flecks of white light and dark shadows growing more prominent.

Deep green vines spread across the table between them, and Elisara jumped as they snaked their way up the statues before reaching for the edge of the table and setting alight. The sweltering look in Kazaar's eyes remained locked to hers. She should be scared, she thought, but saw only loyal determination in his stare. The vines crawled, despite the flames encompassing them, and spanned the ceiling above. The last time Elisara was in Keres, she felt suffocated by the flames, yet they beckoned to her now, trying to tell her it was there for comfort. She swallowed, waiting to see what would happen next as her eyes met Kazaar's. Water pooled on the floor, spilling across the grey flagstone until coating the room in an even layer, and with a final—ever so slight movement—of Kazaar's fingers, the water froze. Elisara stared at her reflection in the glistening ice, her eyes glowing white and silver, like Kazaar once noticed.

"I am the one with all four," he said. He closed his fist, and the elements faded, leaving only the bitter truth behind. His entire time as Elisara's Commander, he hid his powers, veiling his knowledge of the prophecy they had found and read *together*.

He lied, too. A silly lie about 'the one with all four' perhaps referencing the Isle. How was it possible? How could an orphan dropped on the King of Keres' doorstep possess all four gifts? Whomever left him there must have known of the prophecy.

Elisara shook her head and began to pace, unwilling to accept what was so clear.

"No, no, no! It is not possible. It is not possible for you to wield all four elements so easily!"

"Elisara, please. Calm down!" Kazaar took a step forward to reach her.

"DO NOT TELL ME TO CALM DOWN!" she screamed and caught her appearance in the mirror as she did—the moment in which lightning flashed in her eyes before the same wisps of shadows she had seen in his, floated through her own. She blinked and felt her power manifest as ice surrounded the walls.

"I am not from here, Elisara. I was abandoned as a baby. We have no way of knowing where I am from or who my parents are. I have no answer because I do not know who I am." He pleaded, crossing to meet her.

"I do not believe you," she whispered.

"When we visited the Isle, who do you think parted the water?" Elisara thought back to her surprise as she believed the Isle protected them, remembering Kazaar's rigidity after the water chased them both. Today, when Elisara asked him whether his power had betrayed him, he answered, "Once." Elisara wondered if it was then. If the water refused to obey, the Isle having recognized him as an anomaly.

"When we were in Nerida, who do you think caused the waves to crash against the castle during our conversation?" Elisara had assumed it was her own power responding to her changing emotions. "I have tried to show you every step of the way; I hoped if you figured it out, we could avoid this." he pleaded.

"All this time, you have wielded all the elements. You have known you are a major player in the prophecy, yet you said *nothing*." Elisara's voice was ice cold. She wondered how much more he hid, if he in fact knew the King of Keres had been involved in the explosion. Yet confronting the notion would only invite more betrayal, and Elisara could not bear it. No mask concealed Kazaar's face. The man standing before her was not the Commander who once looked upon her with disdain, nor the man she was beginning to trust. She did not know who he was.

"What can I do?" He begged. "What can I do to prove my intentions are pure, that I wish only to serve you and our realm?" He paused and moved to step around the table. Elisara caught sight of her reflection in the mirror again. White essence glowed beneath her skin, trying to escape—to reach him, punish him, she hoped.

"Elisara," he growled, as if struggling with his own restraint. He was, Elisara realized. Veins protruded in his arms where he had rolled his tunic sleeves, his muscles tense; he braced his legs, as though he did not trust them not to run to Elisara's side. Where the open fabric fell open at his chest, a faint white glow seeped and threaded up his neck. The black of his tattoos was now a voluntary darkness against the purity of the essence.

"You do not get to call me that, Commander. My name is reserved for friends, and friends do not keep secrets."

Her power released.

White light exploded, forcing its way to Kazaar with a mind of its own—a wave of energy only felt once before on the Isle: the last time they had fought. It was eager, she realized, and not born from her fury. This was not ice nor air wishing to shatter Kazaar apart; it was a power caring of only one thing: reaching *him.* At the same time Elisara's power unleashed, Kazaar's did the same. The light under his skin faded and pulled towards her. The Queen of Vala's face was one of rage as the essence of her power did as it wished, and refused to harm Kazaar, his face a mix of shock and pain.

Instead of a collision of power like on the Isle, the power softened as it reunited. Tendrils of light danced around the pair as they locked eyes, the power in his faded as he was drawn to the white glow of hers, slowly being suffocated by darkness. A searing pain pierced Elisara's chest before ruthlessly clawing its way to her skin and across her collar bone, it was as though betrayal was carving its permanence into her skin as an eternal reminder that everyone had secrets. All those secrets might just be the breaking of her. The light from their bodies connected; Elisara soared.

And everything went dark.

Epilogue

"Elisara!" Kazaar called. He rushed from his slumped position against the wall, having been thrown back at the force of their power. Hair covered Elisara's face; her arms sprawled across the ground.

Fuck. Kazaar bent down to move the enchanting black locks from her eyes, and grasp her cheeks, willing life into her delicate complexion. He relived the shock in Elisara's gaze as their powers intertwined and sent them flying.

"Elisara, wake up," he urged, patting her cheek. Panic overcame him as he pressed his fingers against her wrist in search of a pulse. The steady beat eased some of his concern, and his voice cracked as he whispered, "My Queen, please wake up."

He shook her shoulders, but to no avail.

"Fuck!" he screamed. Kazaar punched the wall, ice cracking beneath his fist, and the shards bloodying his knuckles. He knew he would mess this up.

Since Elisara's departure from Keres, Kazaar spent years trying to forget her, trying to ignore the call of his soul to hers. He repelled whatever force tied her to him, and when he thought he had succeeded, he was thrown back into her world. Perhaps the universe offering him the opportunity to right his wrongs. Yet here he was, having done Gods knows what to her. When Elisara's essence merged with his, he felt an immense sense of peace, if only for a second. As if every missing part of his soul had returned to him. Yet as he beheld her now, the red dress spilling to the side, the torturous gold garter staring up at him, he felt nothing of that pain. Only deep-seated regrets.

Kazaar wished they had never come here—wished he had forgotten the mission as Elisara stood with her back pressed against the wall in the alcove. His soul yearned for her, yet it scared him to ache for someone who may not need him.

Kazaar lowered his head to listen to Elisara's heartbeat in her chest, and as he did, his stone talisman fell free from under his tunic, softly catching Elisara's skin. A soft hum resounded as it encountered her, and immediately, he pulled it back. When Kazaar first displayed his powers of flame, King Razik gave him the talisman, and admitted it was his only belonging as a baby when they found him. He had worn it ever since but did not trust it near Elisara. He trusted nothing anymore.

He moved the hair from her shoulders and traced a mark on her collarbone, where a perfectly shaped crescent moon appeared, like a scar forever engrained in her flesh. Yet it had not always been there. Kazaar spent enough time analysing the perfection of her skin to know every inch ever displayed. He ripped off his shirt, and reluctantly left Elisara's side to check his inkings in the mirror. There, on the opposite collar bone to Elisara's, was a sun.

When light meets dark in the rarest of times. Sun and moon. Light and dark. He wondered if, upon their powers merging, her brightness had forever marked him, and if his darkness had permanently tainted her.

Kazaar was no stranger to new markings appearing on his body; different scars appeared all the time and had done so for as long as he remembered. Immediately, he had begun inking over them. Kazaar kept a lot of himself hidden, but he no longer wished to hide from her. The only person who knew about his power. The only person he could trust.

Kazaar turned back to Elisara, pulling the hem of her dress over her bare legs, and gently lifting her. He cradled her into his body, her head slumped against his shoulder. Kazaar shivered as her breath tickled his neck. So many questions ran through his head—so many courses of action—but only one priority. Wake up his Queen.

Glossary and Pronunciation Guide

A

Aalto [Al-toe] - *Prince of Nerida, first in line to the throne*
Abis Forge [ah-biss] - *Working metal forge in Keres*
Adar [Ay-d-are] - *Lord of Port of Elvera*
Adrianus [Ay-dree-an-us] - *King of Nerida*
Albyn [Al-bin] - *settlement in Garridon*
Alvan [Al-ven] - *Lord of Seley*
Amir [Ah- mear] - *Prince of Keres*
Amoro [Ah -more - oh] - *Settlement in Nerida*
Antor [An - tore] - *Capital of Garridon*
Arion[Ah-ree-on] - *King of Vala*
Arnav [Are-nav] - *Lord of Khami*
Asdale [As -dale] - *Settlement in Garridon*
Ashun Desert [Ash - un] - *Desert in Keres*
Auralia [Or-ay-lee-ah] - *Princess of Garridon*
Azuria [Ah-zure -ee -ah] - *Capital of Vala*

B

C

Caellum [Cay-lum] - *Prince of Garridon*
Cain [Cay -n] - *Commander of Garridon*
Caligh Seruvian [Cal-ee-gh Sir -ooh -vee -an] - *Author*
Cormac [Core - mac] - *Lord of Asdale*

D

Daeva [Day-vah] - *Princess of Vala, first in line to the throne*
Dalton [Doll - ton] - *Prince of Garridon*
Doltas Island [Doll -tass] - *Island within Garridon's jurisdiction*

E

Edlen [Ed -len] - *Princess of Garridon*
Elharar [El - har - ah] - *Family name of rulers of Keres*
Elisara [El -ih - s - are - ah]- *Princess of Vala*
Ellowyn [El -oh -win] - *Princess of Garridon*
Elvera [El -veer -ah] - *Port of Vala*
Errard [Eh -r-are -d]- *Deceased King of Garridon [usurped]*
Eve [eeh -v] - *Princess of Garridon*

F

Farid [Far -eed] - *Member of the Queen's Guard in Keres*

G

Garridon [Gah -rih -don] - *Earth realm, named after the God of Earth*
Gregor Vernir [Greg-or V-ur-neer] - *High Priest of Azuria*
Gregor [Greg-or] - *Lord of Albyn*

H

Halston [Hol -ston] - *Prince of Garridon, first in line to the throne*
Helena [Hell -ain -ah] - *Bakery owner and friend of Princess Elisara*
Hestia [Hest -eeh -ah] - *Queen of Garridon*
Hybrooke [High-brook] - *Forest*
Hystone [High- stone] - *Forest*

I

Isaam [Is-am] - *Friend of Princess Nyzaia and member of the Red Stones*

Isha [Ee-sh -ah] - *Courtesan/alchemist apprentice of the Red Stones*

Ithyion [Ih-thee-on] - *Home Realm that was lost to darkness*

Izaiah [Ih-zie -ah] - *Deceased second in command to Commander Kazaar*

Izraar [Ih-zr-are] - *Lord of Port of Myara*

J

Jabir [Jab-eer] - *Friend of Princess Nyzaia and member of the Red Stones*

Jorah [J -or -ah] - *Caellum's grandfather [usurper]*

K

Kalon Hakim [Kay -lon H-ah-Keem] - *Merchant*

Katerina [Kat -erh-een-ah] - *Princess of Vala*

Kavean [Kay-vee-an] - *Prince of Keres*

Kazaar [Kah-z-are] - *Commander of Vala*

Keres [K-eh-res] - *Fire realm, named after the god of fire*

Kessem [K-eh-ss-em] - *Prince of Keres, first in line to the throne*

Khami [Kh-am -eeh] - *Settlement in Keres*

Kieren [K-ear-en] - *Prince of Garridon*

L

Larelle [L-are-elle] - *Banished Princess of Nerida*

Lillian [L-ill-ee-an] - *Friend to Princess Larelle*

Lyra [Lie-rah] - *Once queen of Garridon*

M

Marnovo [M-arn-oh-voh] *Settlement in Vala*

Mera [M-ee-rah] - *Capital of Nerida*

Meera [M-ee-rah] - *Consort to Prince Aalto*

N

Nefere Valley [N -eff-ear] - *Valley/canyon named after famed warrior on Ithyion*

Nerida [Neh-rid-ah] - *Water realm, named after the Goddess of water*

Nile [N-eye-l] - *Prince of Nerida*

Novisia [No-vis-ee-ah] - *Kingdom*

Nyzaia [N-zie-ah] - *Princess of Keres and Assassin Queen of the Red Stones*

O

Olden [Old -en] - *Grandfather to Zarya*

Oriana [Or-ee-an-ah] - *Queen of Nerida*

Orlo [Or-low]- *Baker and friend to banished Princess Larelle*

P

Petrov[Pet -r-oh-v] - *Lord of Vojta*

Port of Elvera [El-veer-ah] - *Settlement in Vala*

Q

R

Rafik [R-ah-feek] - *Friend of Princess Nyzaia and member of the Red Stones*

Rajan [R-ah-jan] - *Alchemist in the Red Stones*

Razik [R-ah-zeek] - *King of Keres*

Red Stones - *Rulers of the Kingdom's underworld/Assassins*

Riyas [Reey-us] - *Deceased father of Zarya and partner of Larelle*

Rodik [Rod-ick] - *Settler on Doltas Island*

Ryon [Reey-on] - *Lord of Stedon*

S

Sadira [Sad-eer-ah]

Seley [Seal-ee] - *Settlement that sits across Garridon and Nerida*

Sevia [See-vee-ah] - *Family name of rulers of Nerida*

Sitara [Sit-are-ah] - *Goddess of Dusk*

Stedon [Sted-on] - *Settlement in Garridon*

Sonos [S-on-os] - *God of Dawn*
Soren [S-oh-ren]
Sturmov [Stir-mov] - *Family name of rulers of Vala*

T
Tabheri [Tab-er-eye] - *Capital of Keres*
Tajana [Taj-arh-nah]- *Lover of Princess Nyzaia and member of the Red Stones*
Talia [Tal-ee-ah]- *Friend of Princess Elisara*
Thain [Th-ain]- *Captain of the Nerida royal fleet*
The Bay - *Location within jurisdiction of Mera*
Tisova [Tiss-oh-vah]- *Settlement in Vala*
Trosso [Tr-oh-ss-oh] - *Settlement in Nerida*

U
Unsanctioned Isle - *Land north of Novisia mainland, ruled by no family*

V
Vala [V-agh-lah] - *Air realm, named after the Goddess of air*
Vellius Sea [Vell-ee-us]
Vespera [Ves-peer-ah] - *Queen of Vala*
Vigor [Vee-gore] - *Physician and friend of Princess Elisara*
Vlad [V-lad] - *Personal Guard to Princess Elisara*
Vojta [V-oi–ta] - *Settlement in Vala*

W
Wren [Ren] - *King of Garridon [usurper]*

X
Y

Z
Zarya [Zah-rie-ya]

Playlist

Alternatively, search 'Secrets of the Dead' in playlists.

I see fire by Ed Sheeran *(prologue)*
Warrior by Alexa Ray & Randall Jermaine *(Chapter One)*
Slip Away by UNSECRETS & Ruelle *(Chapter Eight)*
Eyes Open by Taylor Swift *(Chapter Ten)*
Two ghosts by Harry Styles *(Chapter Eleven)*
Matilda by Harry Styles *(Chapter Twelve)*
Bloodline by Sam Thompson *(Chapter Thirteen)*
No Sanctuary by UNSECRET, Sam Tinnesz & Fleurie *(Chapter Fourteen)*
God is a Woman by Ariana Grande *(Chapter Fourteen)*
I want to see you smile by Aquilo *(Chapter Fifteen)*
Bring the Lion Out by Saint Mesa *(Chapter Sixteen)*
Calling Out by Bobbi Haanni *(Chapter Twenty)*
Her and the Sea by Clann *(Chapter Twenty-Four)*
Kids of the Night by Elley Duhe *(Chapter Twenty-Five)*
Chasing Shadows by Alex Warren *(Chapter Thirty-One)*
You should see me in a Crown by Billie EIlish *(Chapter Thirty-Three)*
Astronomical by SVRCINA *(Chapter Thirty-Six)*
Darkness of Light by Secession Studios *(Chapter Thirty-Six)*

Something in the Air by Steelfeather *(Chapter Thirty Seven)*

She gets the flowers(acoustic) by Beth McCarthy *(Chapter Thirty-Eight)*

The grudge by Olivia Rodrigo *(Chapter Thirty-Eight)*

Flight Risk by Tommy Lefroy *(Chapter Thirty-Nine)*

Favourite Crime by Olivia Rodrigo *(Chapter Forty)*

King by Florence and the Machine *(Chapter Forty-Two)*

Dynasty by MIIA *(Chapter Forty-Four)*

Say yes to Heaven by Lana Del Rey *(Chapter Forty-Four)*

Forever and Always (Piano Version) by Taylor Swift *(Chapter Forty-Seven)*

Half a man by Dean Lewis *(Chapter Forty-Eight)*

Middle of the Night by Elley Duhe *(Chapter Forty-Nine)*

Dress by Taylor Swift *(Chapter Fifty-one)*

No time to die by Billie Eilish *(Chapter Fifty-one)*

Love and War by Fleurie *(Chapter Fifty-one)*

Dancing after Death (stripped) by Matt Maeson *(Epilogue)*

Mad Woman by Taylor Swift *(Hardback bonus chapter)*

Acknowledgements

I always thought I knew who I wanted to dedicate my first book to, but then I realised there were too many people. So, instead, that original dedication has moved here. The first thank you goes to my mum and my nan for instilling my passion for reading, without that, I would not have become a writer. The second thanks are to my dad and grandad who taught me the value of hard work. That inherited determination is what made me actually stick to a new years resolution for once – writing this book. And finally, to my love, Jade. If I had not been listening to your own unending creativity and ideas, I would not have been prompted to return to my own dreams of being an author.

To you, the reader, (is anyone else singing Taylor Swift 'dear reader' at that), thank you for taking a chance on an indie book. This series only continues to exist as long as you and others continue to pick it up.

To my editor, Eden. Secrets of the Dead would not be what it is without you. I will forever be grateful for your dedication to developing this story, enhancing the characters, and perfecting it. You went above and beyond on so many occasions and have made this entire experience so much easier. You were the first person to read Secrets of the Dead, and I cannot wait for you to be the first person to read the following books in the series.

To Aly, for taking the mess that were my cover sketches and turning them into the beauty that is the paperback cover of this book.

To Jesamy, my brain twin. I will never completely understand how our brains are so in sync when it comes to how these characters look. I fall even more in love with Elisara every time I look at your portrait of her. Thank you for the beautiful art and for allowing me to use it for the hardcover. I cannot wait for your talent to grace all my covers. Thank you for not only being the most wonderfully creative artist but the sweetest friend.

To my Beta readers, Leah-Louise, Elisha, Kristin, Hannah A, Hannah B, Isobelle, Rachel, Amber. Thank you for your honesty and all round reassuring comments. Whenever I doubt myself, I sit and read all the comments on the original documents and smile.

To my ARC Readers, thank you for your excitment to read Secrets of the Dead (so many of you applied!) and thank you in advance for any reviews you leave.

To Elisha, I will forever be grateful that I met you. You came into, and stayed in, my life when I really needed it. I am honoured to share my dreams with you. I love you.

Finally, to all my online book besties and my unofficial Marketing and PR Team; Jordi, Mel, Chloe, Alexa, Monique, Cara. Thank you for inspiring me with everything you do and say. For being my biggest cheerleaders and making me realise I could still make new friends. You all came into my life at a time where I was conflicted by joy over my book and stress within my personal life. You will never understand the impact your beautiful souls have had on my life. I have never cried with laughter and happiness as much as I do with you all. I promise I will get book two to you as soon as possible. I love you all.

A Note from the Author

Reviews on Amazon, Good Reads, StoryGraph and other sites are one of the biggest ways to help indie authors. I would be eternally grateful if you could leave a review on your prefered platform as well as Amazon. Reviews have to exceed a set amount for Amazon to begin pushing indie books – so if you can, posting here will make a big difference.

I started this journey sharing this book through my socials, and I'm sure I've met many of you there. So, if you feel obliged, please share your thoughts and feelings around this book on your own socials so I can sit and cry tears of joy at this story reaching people.

Instagram: @author_lauracarter

Tik Tok: @authorlauracarter

So you've finished Secrets of the Dead, and you're (hopefully) eager to get your hands on book two in the Lost Kingdom Saga. Whilst I haven't released any details on book two yet, I share all my first looks and sneak peeks to my newsletter subscribers before my socials. If you want to be kept up to date, you can sign up through the links provided on my social channels.

About the Author

Laura grew up in rural Scotland before moving to London to study for her degree in English Literature, where she now lives with her boyfriend and Romanian rescue dog, Rez. She grew up constantly immersed in different worlds through reading and always dreamed of becoming an author. When her love of fantasy and romance was re-ignited after three years of only ever critically analysing work, her dream of creating her own worlds returned. She now balances working full time for a cancer charity with writing her debut series, The Lost Kingdom Saga.

Printed in Great Britain
by Amazon